All That Is Hidden

All That Is Hidden

Laura DeNooyer

All That Is Hidden

© **Laura DeNooyer 2012**

ISBN: 0-7596-7937-1 (e-book) ISBN: 0-7596-7938-X (Paperback)
Library of Congress Control Number: 2002091222 This book is printed on acid free paper. Printed in the United States of America Bloomington, IN
1st Books - rev. 06/20/02
Lighthouse Publishing - 2012

Book cover: Sherri Wilson Johnson
Photos of girl: DepositStock Photos, KsenJoyg
Silhouette of man: Photo by Ajmal Afghan from Pexels
Appalachian photos: Chris Ried from Unsplash, Micah Williams from Unsplash, Christine Jessel Grider from Pixabay

Published by
Lighthouse Christian Publishing
SAN 257-4330
5531 Dufferin Drive
Savage, Minnesota, 55378
United States of America

www.lighthousechristianpublishing.com

Praise for *All That Is Hidden*

"There's a touch of Laura Ingalls Wilder simplicity in the descriptions of home life, crafts, cooking and chores, a sprinkling of Stephen King in its authentic portrayal of small-town life and dialogue, and a dash of *To Kill a Mockingbird* in its deeper themes of truth, trust, love, betrayal and forgiveness. That's one heck of a mix."

--Ariane Jenkins, Epinions.com

"This novel captures a vivid sense of life in a family-bonded community in the Appalachian mountains, one in which many readers will see themselves growing up through Little League baseball and major league heroes at a time and place when children spent more time out ranging in the fields and woods than in front of electronic gadgets. The story gives such a strong sense of family interactions that you'll feel you've been invited to a reunion, rich in good food and conversation that often makes you laugh—but also presses on some deep wounds. Central is the clash of progress with a small tight-knit community in which people can be deeply concerned with the work and interests of their neighbors."

—Dr. Steve Eberly of Western Carolina University

"*All That Is Hidden* is a beautiful novel, the kind of book that sweeps you up in its story, makes you fall in love with its characters, and breaks your heart along with theirs when they go through suffering. The "secret," or, more accurately, secrets, of the first line of this book are artfully hidden throughout the novel, making their ultimate revelation both truly shocking and truly poignant. Tina is a very good narrator, but it is her father and his character who steals the novel--his life story is both original and compelling, and the pain and grace he experiences drew tears to this reader's eyes."

---*Writer's Digest*

"No reader can help but be drawn into the mesmerizing and absorbing world of Tina Hamilton, be transported back to 1968, to Currie Hill, to a world where family values and community held real meaning . . . This richly layered story is a most rewarding read . . . and heart-wrenching to realize the moment when a child sees the truth about a parent, and loses an idol, creating an emptiness that only forgiveness can heal. The gentle power of this book gains momentum until it reaches a dramatic and moving end."

--Ann Emanuel, *Commuter Week*

"My extended family is from the hills of Kentucky. I so enjoyed reading the Parts sections that preceded the chapters. . . It was like going home for a while. I consider those sections the strongest and most creative pieces of writing that I've reviewed for Writer's Edge in at least five years."

--The Writer's Edge

DEDICATION

To Sheri Dunham Haan, my second grade teacher,
who first inspired my love for writing

and

In memory of Dr. Gilbert Besselsen,
former Professor of Education at Calvin College
of Grand Rapids, Michigan, who first inspired my love for
southern Appalachia.

ALL THAT IS HIDDEN

PART I

Mom: Old Man Fuller. "He died with all those untold stories and unmade pictures still left up in his head."

——————————

I always knew my father had a secret. I must have known it by the time I was old enough to recognize the embarrassed hush that fell over a room of grown-ups the moment I stepped in. That's back when folks still talked about it. As I grew older, the subject was conveniently ignored, then all but forgotten. But after fourth grade, the secret returned without invitation, and made its home with me like an unwelcome guest.

In 1968, I was ten and oblivious to changes outside my world. The radio and TV raged. The Vietnam War, hippies, flower children, assassinations, civil riots, and the space race all aroused anxiety in Americans frantically searching for answers—ones that Peter, Paul, and Mary said were "Blowing in the Wind." But all of God's earth to my brother Nick and me were the streams for fishing, the fields for planting and harvesting, a world snugly enclosed by the blue-misted Smokies.

Other than the seasons, nothing ever changed. Until the summer referred to in major league baseball as "The Year of the Pitcher." In our town, some folks called it "The Year of the Suicide Squeeze," a high risk play at home plate. Currie Hill was never the same. Most blamed my father for that.

In my eyes back then, he was omnipotent and wise. So when I first saw him empty, I was afraid. But now, over thirty years later, I realize my father never tried to be a hero. Nor was he merely a victim of his silence. I guess I've grown up, for now I know wisdom and weakness sometimes walk hand in hand.

I started learning that with the tale of Old Man Fuller.

****

1968

"Mama, tell me a sad story."

My bed creaked. The worn mattress tilted as Mom sat next to me. I rolled to my side, propped on one elbow. Hearing a sad story proved as soothing for my melancholy as a spring tonic of sassafras tea was for Mom.

She stroked my hair. "'Bout time you hear this one, Tina." Lamplight outlined cracks in the walls. Her crow's feet came out of hiding, telltale signs of a ready smile that evaded her now. "Reckon your daddy can't tell it yet without weeping."

So I grew up with this story about my father, told in my mother's reverenced hush after dusk, a tone used when she didn't want her voice to rise and carry its load of cares into the vast, indifferent night sky.

"A mighty long time ago, when your daddy was just a knee-baby, Old Man Fuller lived in the mountain's spruce woods where it was dark as a pocket. Most folks would rather be a knot on a log in Hickory Notch than to live away back there. As fittin' a place for the likes of Old Man Fuller if ever there was one."

"Where is it?" I drew up the quilt to cover my shivers and glanced to the bedroom window, a black square of night pricked with stars.

"A whoop and a holler from our side of the mountain,

2

just beyond Strawberry Gap. Folks said he kept to himself, cared no more for people than a crow cares for a holiday."

"Was he mean?"

"No, he didn't contrary anyone, but folks will carry on with their slack talk. That mountain was your daddy's backyard, so he was bound to strike up with the man sooner or later."

"What was he like?"

"So thin you could see daylight through him, as butter-hearted as anyone. Once they chanced on each other, they stuck as close as a cocklebur on sheep's wool. Old Man Fuller told Daddy wild stories about bear hunts and Halloween pranks. Since Daddy liked carving toys and figures, Old Man Fuller took him to the shed behind his house. Step inside, and every which away you looked were machines, a whole slew of them, run by a generator, some bought and some custom-built by the man himself."

I fingered the ridge of stitches on the bear's claw pattern. "What kind of machines?"

"Better than a dozen drills, a jigsaw, and other saws and dumifutchets he'd concocted as simply as a cook throws together parts of a recipe, a dab of this, a smidgen of that. A right smart pile of hand tools to boot."

"Was he a carpenter like Mr. Hutchins?"

"Every bit and grain as good as him. A master hand at woodworking, called marquetry. He showed Daddy his work, different pictures so intricate, all kinds of wood cut and shaped into pieces that fit together like a puzzle. Landscapes, mountains, trees, birds, animals, all given out to be the best workmanship of its kind. Old Man Fuller told him, 'I have nary a soul to teach this craft to, and the use of these machines and tools. Reckon no one could figure these out without my help. When I go, they'll go, too.'"

Mom's ebony hair blended with shadows. "Daddy was plumb taken by it all and started learning, right then. It pleasured Old Man Fuller. They set to working, as busy as bees

3

in a tar tub. But Daddy was fixing to go to the Army for four years. The last day before leaving, he promised Old Man Fuller he'd be back directly after the war to learn it all. That was before the U.S. got into World War II.

"But instead of being gone four years, Daddy was gone a coon's age, a mighty long time." Her hand, always deft with needle and thread, pots and pans, or spades and hoes, couldn't rest even after dark, and she massaged my arm.

I plopped on my pillow, stomach tightening. "Why was he gone so long?"

"He went on to college, then worked as an architect, while Old Man Fuller kept busy in his shop, making beautiful wood pictures, waiting for Drew Hamilton. Then fifteen years later, out of the clear blue sky, Daddy came back. In 1956, during a blackberry winter, a cool spell plunked smack dab in the middle of May. Cold weather was hard enough . . ." She fingered the quilt's calico shapes. "That first day back he was fixing to see Old Man Fuller to finally keep his promise."

The knot in my stomach tightened.

"But his dad—your grandpa—said, ''Old Man Fuller's dead, son, buried most of two months now.'" Mom straightened her voice out from quivering. "Grandpa said, 'A passel of us traipsed up there so as to take care of his place. Had a severe fire in the machine shed. He never got out. We muscled up old machines and toted them down the mountain. Had to junk it all.'"

Mom's hand stopped on mine. I shoved my feet deeper into my sheets, wanting to feel only cool fabric against my skin instead of the twinge of distress.

"Grandpa handed Daddy a notebook filled with scrawled handwriting like pot hooks and hen scratches. They'd fetched it near Ole Man Fuller's bed. Daddy's name was in it. Well, he wept, all the man's beautiful pictures lost forever. The notebook said over and over, 'Drew'll be here any day now. I feel it in my bones.' Another page said, 'The war's over. He'll be here as he promised . . . He'll keep my work alive, he will.'"

Outside the window, night camouflaged a world of pain, of simple dreams gone up in smoke, yearning hearts that beat no more, bound to the dark earth. A chill crept under my quilt.

Mom blinked back a tear. "Your father couldn't abide the fact he didn't keep his promise, precious little he could do about it now. While Old Man Fuller depended on him, Daddy was tending to his so-called important work up in New York. Like dancing on the old man's grave."

Mom swiped a tear. "That man died with no heirs, every bit and grain of his work gone. He died with all those wonderful stories in his head, some not yet told. He died with his head and hands full of unmade pictures that no one'll ever see, a craft nobody but your daddy ever knew, and no hands to pass his work on to. This explains a lot about why your daddy is the way he is, Tina. And I'm powerful glad for that."

CHAPTER 1

My brother Nick and I raced home on our bikes, outdoing each other in our childish desire to be first as bearer of bad news. Gulping air, we dropped our bikes in the yard and stumbled over ourselves as we barreled through the kitchen door, Nick one step ahead of me. Unwilling to accept defeat, I shouted, "Marty's arm is broke!"

Mom, a streak of blue gingham whisking around the kitchen, stopped short and stared at us in dismay. "Marty Collier? How in the Sam Hill did that happen?"

"He was playing first base during scrimmage," Nick said in gasps. "He tried to catch an infield fly and crashed straight into the pitcher."

I filled in as he paused for breath. "Doc Kirby came and rushed him down to Asheville."

"That's awful!" Mom set plates on the table. "Is the pitcher okay?"

"Just a bruise. You shoulda seen it, Ma. Just like that." Nick smacked his hands like cymbals. "Soon as I heard the crack I knew it was gonna be bad."

"Hush now. Your father has company. Todd's here, too. Soon Marty'll be as strong as all-outdoors."

"Yeah, but our team's not," Nick said. "Marty's plumb out for the season, so we're one man short."

I sighed. "Those Grizzlies are jumping for joy already."

Hands on hips, Mom rolled her eyes. "If you two had even a lick of compassion, there'd be hope for the world."

"But we're both undefeated," Nick said. "We were fixing to face them for the league title till this happened."

Mom's dark hair contrasted her pale freckles that stood out prior to a reprimand. They darkened even as we stood there. "Spare me live martyrs."

Duly chastised, we slithered toward the front room. I tugged Nick's shirt. "Hey, I could take Marty's place."

Nick brushed my hand away. "You're a girl," he said as if pronouncing a sentence on me. "You can't even hit a barn."

"Not throwing, but with a bat I can hit the smallest tree in Hickory Notch. And I'm great at catching." Plus, I'd been their number one fan and scorekeeper. That should count for something.

In the front room, Dad stood with Phil Kepler and his son Todd. Dad's overalls, stained with field dirt, contrasted Mr. Kepler's pristine attire. Dad's brown eyes twinkled between weathered creases. With his face beard-covered, his eyes said everything.

Dapper Mr. Kepler held a briefcase and a tube of paper. His long-sleeved white shirt cast our walls to dingy gray. Crisp, pressed trousers defied all wrinkles. His broad cheeks were polished smooth and lustrous like Mom's copper teapot, no hint of a whisker.

Though Phil Kepler had visited town for four years and lived here for one, he was still a northerner. Rural folk with chameleon tendencies altered their speech to his, as with tourists. Phil and Dad were friends since their New York days, but after Phil bought a house and the Bear Wallow Inn, he rarely stopped by.

So I was surprised to see Phil Kepler here, practically luminous, the room getting drabber by the minute.

"Mr. Kepler's just back from New York City," Dad said, his usual southern drawl now seasoned with northern inflections.

"Did you go to a Yankees game?" Nick asked.

"Sure enough, and I got you a souvenir." Phil tossed him a set of baseball cards. Nick tore open the package. No Tigers, but power hitters, including Yastrzemski and Killebrew. Todd all but turned green. Nick would surely use them for bargaining power.

"Who needs the Yankees?" Dad ruffled Todd's hair. "I hope you're working on those curve balls, Todd. Nick's making predictions for the final Grizzlies-Wildcat game."

Mr. Kepler threw me a roll of Life Savers. I pocketed them to enjoy alone later.

Mom entered with a plate. "Homemade molasses cookies, straight from our cane patch." I was convinced she made molasses cookies more often than others because she loved the sound of the word molasses better than oatmeal or sugar. She was funny about words.

Our cocker spaniel, Paprika, a sprinkling of rust, scurried to Mom and waited in vain for a handout. Phil held up his hand. "This is a business call, Jennie."

Dad took a cookie. "No harm mixing pleasure with business. At least have a seat. It's just as cheap sitting as standing." He plopped on the sofa and stretched his legs, taking advantage of a rare afternoon break from working the fields.

Phil precariously settled into the threadbare chair, as if it would give way beneath him. "I'm full from lunch. Todd makes a mean tuna casserole." Todd's mother lived in New York, so he and his dad fended for themselves.

"Tuna casserole?" That didn't sound southern to me.

"Tu-na-cass-er-ole." Mom rolled the words on her tongue as if tasting them.

"A fancy northern dish with noodles, mushrooms, and cheese." Dad winked. "So fancy even hogs turn their noses up at it."

Sounded like a welcome change from fried pork, cornbread, collards, and grits.

Mom lured the boys into the kitchen with cookies. I stayed to listen, under guise of rummaging through the game shelf. What did Phil Kepler want? Was it news about the proposed theme park again?

Phil unclasped his briefcase and shuffled papers. "Drew, there's more we can alter to make this park agreeable to both of us. With the council meeting vote five weeks away, I could use your influence, not to mention your vote."

Dad laughed. "You just don't give up. How can I convince you? My side's on the integrity of this town."

"The changes will strengthen its integrity, not weaken it."

"You have a new angle? Will the park proceeds stave off starvation, wipe out big city street gangs, and provide cancer cures?" Dad munched his cookie.

"Come on, Drew. We had the time of our life on that project for Brown and Associates." Chuckling, they recalled how they'd talked stodgy Mr. Brown into taking a financial risk by using innovative yet over-budget building designs. "That was great teamwork," Phil said.

"Proving what a couple of desperadoes will do in a pinch. Our strategy trying to convince Brown was more ingenious than the designs."

The laughter left Phil's voice. "We could still be a great team, Drew."

"Phil, building a park, another inn, and more stores is like putting a heater in the desert. We've got enough sightseers. I'd rather they stay down in Asheville."

"This is less to stimulate tourist trade than for accommodating tourists we already have, and to provide jobs, especially for young people."

"One won't occur without the other. We've been through this." Dad flipped pages in a book. "If I can't persuade you, let the numbers do it." He found a page and quoted statistics. "More tourists will overwhelm us. Last year the Smokies and North Carolina had 6,500,000 of them. The Great Smoky National Park gets twice the number of visitors of any other park. Over a quarter of the people in the United States live within a day's drive from here. Also, last year, North Carolina took in 647 million dollars just in the tourist industry." Dad turned more pages. "And jobs? Last year in this state, 130 new industrial plants opened and 338 plants expanded facilities, creating 24,774 new jobs. Around 665,000 were employed in factories. We don't need to top that."

Was this how they talked in New York? I pulled out Yahtzee and Chinese Checkers, trying not to tip the tin box of marbles.

"I've done my homework, too, Drew, and the job problem hasn't been solved yet."

"Well, I don't care to have a repeat of the Blue Ridge Parkway project. That supplied jobs and necessary revamping but built so many new roads that life here changed forever, the biggest change being the tourist draw. We're not called the Good Roads State for nothing. And this park, to be successful, would warrant continued development."

"The Parkway project is an unfair comparison." Phil unrolled the tube of paper on the coffee table and pointed. "Besides, the theme park will complement, not destroy, the nature and heritage of these mountains, simultaneously improving the economy."

Dad dismissed the drawing with a wave. "We'll end up overcrowded with cheap souvenir shops and silly amusements. Investors will set up shop and exploit us. Fields and trees will be plowed over and we'll be run by clocks and schedules."

"Some things will be sacrificed, yes, but not without great reward. Think of all that land out there going to waste. We'll make it more available to everybody—"

"And reap money from their pockets." Dad leaned forward. "Is that how we measure the land's value, by how many use it? By how much money we make from it?"

"Drew, you're one of the finest members on this town council yet blind to the unemployment situation. Don't put a bigger price on preserving that land than you do on people's welfare."

Cringing at Phil's insinuations, I pulled out more games.

"That comment's out of line," Dad said.

"Look, when that whole rioting business blows over, both colored and whites alike can be served by this park. We could be a model town of progress, in both county and state. Your vehement opposition is unfair to those who are easily influenced by you."

I lined up Parcheesi pawns to make sure they were all accounted for.

My father took a deep breath as if to compose himself, the way he did with me on the verge of rebuke. His pace slowed, his tone reasonable. "Phil, I don't appreciate your inference. The list of cons outweighs the pros and I'm happy to pass that list along to any interested party. Not to mention, this is the south. Let's face it. A park that serves both colored and whites alike isn't going to be welcome." Couch springs squeaked as he popped up and paced. "Even with all your Economics Research Associates feasibilities studies, you've no guarantee of the park's success."

Not wanting to miss a thing, I pretended to debate between Scrabble and Dominoes.

Phil rustled more papers. "The same numbers you quoted earlier to prove that the tourist industry is alive and well are the same numbers that guarantee the park's success."

"But you can't operate on idealism. Every attempt to mimic Disneyland's success failed, a sure waste of resources. We don't need a Disneyland duplicate."

Disneyland? In January, one of the rare occasions Dad let us watch TV on Sunday, I saw an episode on *Walt Disney's Wonderful World of Color* about the new Pirates of the Caribbean ride at Disneyland. It looked like fun. After Walt Disney presented a scale model of New Orleans Square, sculptors were shown creating Audio-Animatronic pirates, the brain child of Disney's Imagineers. At the grand opening, pirates staged a victory at sea in the lagoon, then park guests took the ride accompanied by lifelike buccaneers singing "Yo Ho, A Pirate's Life for Me."

In the revitalized Tomorrowland, a man in an air suit somehow flew into the air and safely landed. Folks rode a sky highway through a tunnel that simulated shrinking to snowflake-size. During a film of a genuine rocket launch, men on the moon demonstrated effects of the moon's lesser gravity by jumping around in slow motion. That last part was fake, of course. Nobody had ever been on the moon.

Disneyland seemed amazing--full of bands, rides, parades, fireworks, Mickey Mouse and his friends, and Tinker Bell's flight. I hoped to go there sometime. But California might as well be in China. My family never traveled beyond Asheville.

And since Dad disapproved of a park in our town, it must be a bad thing.

Dad paused at the mantel where his carved wooden figures stood beside Mom's dulcimer. "I've seen what happened to the Cherokee tradition around here, adulterating real Indian crafts and customs. Something is lost when things go on display like museum pieces that tourists can walk by, point to, and remark how quaint it all is."

I stacked the games in order of priority.

Phil spoke as if delivering a diagnosis for terminal illness. "I'm sorry you've grown so opposed to progress."

"Progress?" Dad flung out his arms. "You mean marketing ourselves in order to be worthy? Is it progress to link our town to highways and big cities, the rat race, and rushing around? When kids wake up wondering who's going to beat them to the big job or the big salary? When they count money and positions instead of old-fashioned values and—"

"Baseball cards, Drew. Baseball cards and home runs. Kids can't stay sheltered. They've got to learn there's more to life than just a sandlot game. Besides, we're not cashing in small town values. We're introducing big town ideas for everyone's benefit. Now that's progress."

Maybe Phil had a good point. I re-stacked the games with Yahtzee on top.

"You may see the park as a ticket for that," Dad said. "But I see it as a one-way ticket from tranquility and plenty of things I never want my children to see."

Phil's voice sharpened, an arrow headed for its target. "Like what you did in New York?"

What happened in New York? I dropped the Chinese checkers box. An avalanche of marbles rolled, making as much ruckus--Uncle Ross would say--as skeletons wrestling on a tin roof.

Frowning, Dad glanced at me.

"It's a shame we can't work together anymore," Phil said. "I hoped there'd be a speck of the old you left."

Todd poked his head through the doorway. Nick followed him into the room. Both men exchanged looks as if realizing something had profoundly changed, then pulled themselves together as adults usually do when protecting children.

"I gotta get to baseball practice, Dad," Todd said.

"You sure do if you want to keep up with us Wildcats," Nick added. "We're counting on you-uns to make it to the final game."

"That'll be a game worth seeing," Phil said.

Dad chuckled. "Yes, but we all know there's more to life than a sandlot game."

Phil lifted his chin. "I'm sorry we can't count on your support."

When Phil stepped out the door, so did any hopes or worries about the park. Whatever this park was, it didn't stand a chance. Dad would see to that. He had the annoying habit of always getting his way. But his wrinkled brow unsettled me.

Mom appeared. I thought she'd ask him about New York, but she said, "Why do you let him rile you so?" No answer. "Especially with such a longstanding friendship."

Though Mom was Dad's best audience, he hustled outside, his expression clearly stating that whatever lay buried inside him about his past, he intended to leave there, for now.

Later, I saw that moment as another chance he lost to tell us about those years, possibly circumventing the trouble to come.

CHAPTER 2

The next day, Nick and I biked to the sandlot.

"I brought the new player," Nick told Coach Hudson.

"Tina?" Hud raised an eyebrow, but slotted me as pinch hitter during the practice game.

I winged that ball, a double on the first pitch. Hud welcomed me to the team.

After that, I had difficulty feeling sorry for Marty and his broken arm.

Since every ball I threw fell like a wounded duck, Hud assigned me to first base. Being a lefty helped. Hud was happy, and so was Wally, the leather smith, whose shop sponsored our team. On being dubbed a member, I received the official team shirt, yellow with bold blue words: Wally's Shoes.

The novelty of being on the team soon wore off. But the teasing didn't. One day at practice, kids from Todd Kepler's team, the Bear Wallow Inn Grizzlies, dropped by and warmed up, waiting to take the field.

"Look, a girl!" Stan Randall, the restaurant owner's son, was forever shaking his head, lifting his chin, and looking down his nose in order to see past greasy bangs. "Is that all the better you-uns can do?"

"Leave her alone. She's good," said Byron Simpson, my teammate. His dad owned Simpson's Ice Cream Parlor. Byron was one half of a pair we called Cue Ball and Eight Ball. Byron was Cue Ball because his bleached-out butch grew like a tight cap. His brother Rex's Eight Ball butch was jet black.

"Yeah, if your dad can cook, she can play baseball." Nick swung two bats at once.

"Reckon we'll win easy." Stan shook his head, his bangs like windshield wipers.

The bats in Nick's hands whirled faster. Nick, who avoided battles of any kind, was easily ruffled by Stan who boasted a history of such provocations.

Todd, their pitcher, moseyed over. "Hey, Hamilton, leave my players alone." Unable to land on the same team, he and Nick pretended to outdo each other. Actually, Todd hurled his curve balls to Nick, and Nick offered Todd his best pitching secrets.

Todd held a baseball with both divine devotion and a secure grasp of flesh. While Nick was all arms and legs, Todd's performance on the mound resembled ballet. In contrast, with no grown-ups around, he usually had a tobacco leaf hanging between his teeth. He thought nothing of raiding Grandpa Hamilton's tobacco patch or paying Old Lady Balch five cents for a twist of his own. Nick, under pretense of preferring the manufactured stuff, refused to partake. That's because he feared getting sick or caught.

Todd displayed a handful of Topps baseball cards. "My dad brought these from New York."

Nick stared into the faces of Detroit Tigers, including Mickey Lolich, Bill Freehan, and Al Kaline. We followed the Tigers, a preference acquired from Dad. "Any Denny McLain?"

Bargaining ensued. Nick made a valiant effort at hiding his envy, though their ploy at cool-headed business deals proved for naught. Both ended up with whatever they wanted. Todd preferred power hitters and Yankees, while Nick collected pitchers and Tigers. Eight Ball joined them, his cards wrinkled from riding in his back pocket, spattered with chocolate drips from the ice cream parlor.

"Let's see that McLain one," Nick said.

Eight Ball flipped through them. "Got something to trade me for it even to boot?"

"My '62 World Series cards." Nick inherited our

cousin Scott's collection before he left for Vietnam.

"What's the big deal about McLain?" Eight Ball asked.

I spoke up. "Have you been sleeping? He's already twelve and two. It ain't even July yet."

"He's gonna get thirty wins this year," Nick said.

"Now look who's sleeping." Todd chewed a blade of grass. "Dreaming, too. Nobody ever does that."

They slugged pitcher stats around like baseballs, from Dizzy Dean to Sandy Koufax to Don Drysdale's numerous scoreless innings.

"McLain was a twenty-game winner in '66," Nick said, undaunted.

"But last year he lost as many as he won." Todd kicked the dirt. "If he does it, I'll treat you to anything you want at Simpson's." Todd got more allowance for breathing than we did for a month's chores. He could buy a sundae every day.

"The bet's on," Nick said. "Pay up this fall when Detroit wins the World Series."

"Now you're really dreaming," Todd said. "I'll bet double or nothing on that."

Bored with their claims and predictions, I wandered to first base with my mitt. Their constant bantering drove me crazy. Though I loved the game, I was forever being told what a girl my age should like. Last year, Uncle Sid in New York sent Nick an autographed baseball he'd caught at Yankee Stadium. He sent me a bottle of perfume, a pink plastic dove adorning its cap. I took one whiff and promptly stuffed it into the back of my underwear drawer. I preferred the smell of a new baseball glove.

I scooped up an imaginary ball, tagged second base, and threw to first for a double play. No sooner had I turned to catch another imaginary infield hit when I heard a shrill "Tina, heads up!"

Stan Randall at home plate pointed skyward at a pop-up. I situated myself under the ball on the baseline. It dropped neatly into my glove. I threw it back.

Darrell Culver, Stan's buddy, swung and cracked another ball my way. "Think fast!" The ball took one hop before settling into my mitt.

"Watch out!" Stan smacked a ferocious grounder to my left. Dropping the other ball, I dove to put my gloved right hand in its path. The ball rolled in as if home for dinner and the evening.

It was luck. As much as Dad hated that word as opposed to God's providence, it was pure, homespun luck that I snagged three in a row.

Prostrate with a mouthful of dirt, I prepared to be pelted by more baseballs, the target of male disdain. But Stan slung his bat on his shoulder and gave Nick a scowl. "She'll do," he huffed.

CHAPTER 3

We never knew what we'd find on the other side of the MacNeills' front door.

Carrying a basket of leftover dinner, Mom gave a hearty rap. Overloaded with my basket of canned goods, bread, and spring tonic, I wound my way through the maze in their front yard: an old tire, rusty tools, apple cores, tin cans—all begging to be toted off to their final resting place.

The door slowly opened as if by itself. A pair of gray eyes peered from behind. The face brightened and Susan MacNeill, second of seven children, stepped forward to greet us. Thin and pale, she looked older than twelve. "Mama, Miz Jennie and Tina's here. Mama's resting, tuckered out from mopping, I reckon. She'll be so glad to see you-uns."

You'd think she hadn't seen us in months, but we visited weekly.

Inside, the worst smells assaulted: moldy bread crumbs, rotting chicken bones, and putrid fruit, mingled with the ammonia of a freshly-mopped floor. Dust gathered thicker than last time, dirty dishes piled higher and greener—was it mold? A potato plant rooted in the rug. I couldn't wait to tell Nick and gross him out.

Lucy MacNeill sat on a kitchen chair, glassy-eyed, her meager frame nearly transparent. High cheekbones suggested her former beauty.

Susan followed Mom around the room like a wart on a foot. "Watch out for that there pail, Miz Jennie. Mama's been so busy we ain't had supper." She relayed an interminable tale about her own disastrous experience fixing lunch.

Mother handed Susan the dish soap. "Let's fill up that sink and you start on dishes."

"Yes, ma'am. Why, that's a pretty color soap if I ever did see one. Ain't it, Tina? Does it make good bubbles? Let's see now—"

Mom faced Miz Lucy. "You don't look like you should be mopping floors, dear."

"I was feeling right perky this morning, Jennie. Had to get work done."

"You got yourself two able-bodied daughters to do mopping and such. Where's Melissa?"

"Out yonder with her brothers. Checking on the cows, I reckon."

Mom withdrew the bottle of spring tonic. "This'll cure what ails you. Sassafras, spicebush, sweet birch, and morel." Everything Mom made had sassafras. She loved that word.

"Thank you kindly, Jennie."

Grandma Dorothy always said Mom "did her proud" because Mom learned everything Grandma taught her about herbs and embraced their medicinal value.

Mom washed a cup. "Drew says he's sorry he can't come tonight for repairs. He'll drop by tomorrow for certain."

"Don't bother, Jennie. I don't need nothing done now."

"What about those broken chairs, and that table wanting some paint?"

Lucy patted the table and pointed to the chairs. "See?"

"Well, that beats all." Mom scanned the furniture. "Like brand new. Did Barry do it?"

"Barry wouldn't work in a pie factory if he had a tasting job," Lucy said. "I got me another helper."

Barry MacNeill was a man more skilled in drinking than in caring for his farm. Lucy was often ill, with little energy to keep house or rein in kids who had the run of the place like spring goats, doing everything but work. If their property had any pride at all, it was brought by others' helping

20

hands.

"Miz Jennie, these bubbles sure are pretty." Susan cupped bubbles in her hand. "See all the rainbows? Look here. I never seen so many rainbows in one place, have you?"

Mom placed dishes in the water, popping several rainbows without even an apology. Susan gaped. "Tina," Mom said, "please take that garbage out back."

"Yes'm." Why did I get the nastiest jobs? I shuffled to the corner, holding my breath, and lugged the hefty bag outside where more rotten, rancid food remains awaited. I gagged.

I slung the bag onto the garbage heap and bolted across the yard for fear of losing my supper. I panted, stomach heaving, then stumbled and fell forward. Face in hands, I tried to control the lurch in my stomach.

Soon I lifted my head. A foot-high white cross blurred in a clump of bushes. I crept closer. It was freshly painted, no name or date. To my knowledge, none of Lucy's children had died.

I rose and held my breath as I returned to the house. Susan was still doing dishes. The dirty stack looked no shorter. Lucy slurped Mom's stew. Her two youngest children, ages one and two, whined at her feet, one climbing onto her lap.

Mom swept the little guy up and set him in front of a bowl. He slapped the stew, grabbing a hunk of meat. Mom pulled it away and cut it up. The little girl on the floor whimpered.

That's how I feel. I wanted to go home.

"Miz Lucy," I asked, "what's that cross out there for?" Mom frowned, so I added, "Did you have a dog that died?"

Lucy stared at her stew.

"We don't have no pet," Susan said. "Unless you wanna call them brothers of mine pets, I wouldn't mind a bit. They're just as much of a nuisance. Why, the other day—"

"Susan." Lucy rubbed her temples. "Reckon you all have no way of knowing, but that's in memory of my first baby. I miscarried."

"I'm sorry." Mom touched Lucy's shoulder.

Ten-year-old Jason barged in. He wore a permanent scowl, emphasized by grease and dirt. The screen door slammed behind him, nearly hitting two younger brothers in the nose.

Lucy spoke in her calm voice that never changed decibels. "Jason, be a nice boy now and run that blue chair out to the barn."

"I'm busy." Jason bumped my mother's arm and cussed. She nearly spilled the stew.

If that was me talking, Mom would have doused my mouth with that dish soap Susan admired, rainbows and all.

"I reckon you're not too busy for dinner," Mom said. "When you get back from taking that chair to the barn, I'll have a bowl ready for you, piping hot."

Jason sniffed the stew. Within two minutes, he'd taken the chair out and returned.

"Lucy," Mom said, "Drew will come by tomorrow to mend that chair."

"No need. I have a helper."

Susan told animated stories all through supper as if she'd just come out of hibernation. Afterward, Mom settled Lucy on the front room couch with the toddler and baby. She sent the older kids outside for chores, including Susan. When the door slammed behind them, my mother sighed, her voice lowered. "That girl's tongue moves like a clapper in a cowbell."

Mom and I finished dishes, then joined Lucy. Mom mended while I sewed buttons. Lucy rested on the threadbare couch, springs popping through cushions. I sat facing the open window, anticipating the inevitable woman-talk. Outside, the kids romped. Crickets chorused.

Lucy clasped her teacup. "You remember your first love, Jennie?"

Mom eased into a smile. "Truth be told, Lucy, my first love was a curly-headed boy in second grade. Even when he lost his two front teeth, I couldn't take my eyes off him."

"Was there anyone before Drew?"

"I was plumb took in by Drew, like nobody else. He's my first and only true love."

"You're very lucky, Jennie." Lucy seemed to gaze into the distant past. I tugged thread through my button. "I'll never forget my first love. I was fifteen. He walked by our place daily and called to me. He was right friendly, he was, but had to hurry along. Odd jobs here and there."

"What's his name?"

"Robert. You wouldn't know him. He went the roundabout way to work so as he could come by my house. For three years."

"That's a long time. What became of him?"

"After three years we were madly in love, but . . . it weren't the kind of situation pleasing to my daddy. He had other plans for me."

"He didn't like Robert?"

"He never knew about Robert. Robert only stopped by when daddy wasn't home, a while after mama died."

"He didn't ask to court you?"

Lucy took a sip and looked toward the window, though the gathering dusk didn't afford much of a view. "He wasn't one of us."

Mom's needle threaded in and out while I pushed mine through another button.

"But he and I were one in spirit, one in heart. I went to the woods and other places to meet up with him. But if my daddy ever found out, he'd kill me. Meanwhile, along comes a couple of fellows, including Barry, a-wanting to court me. Barry didn't drink back then, though we knew what kind of stock he was from, drunkards from way back. So Daddy was fixing to set me up with one nice fellow, but something happened."

I paused, not sure if I should be listening.

Lucy wrapped fingers around her cup, an intimate,

graceful gesture. "I was with child. Robert's child."

Mom looked my way "Lucy—"

"Jennie, I have to tell somebody before my time comes."

"Don't talk that way. You've been improving all along."

Lucy leaned back, a delicate line creasing her forehead. "We'd done wrong, and we were sorry. But my daddy would never forgive me. I didn't know what to do, where to go. Robert wanted to help, but what could he do?"

"Couldn't he marry you?"

Lucy whispered. "Robert was the wrong color."

Mom's shoulders stiffened.

Lucy wiped her eyes. "The world was over for me. I wanted to hide out till the baby was born, then come back and start over, but I had nowhere to go."

"What'd you do?" Mom asked, voice full of compassion.

"Around five months I was still at home, showing but hiding it well. Then I was took down sick, with terrible pains. I went into labor, midday, at home by myself. It was awful. I prayed Daddy wouldn't come home till everything was done."

Lucy went from a trickle to full stream, no stopping her now. "He came in early from the fields. He was furious, and so ashamed, he didn't call anyone to help. When that baby finally came out, he only lived a minute. Daddy saw that tiny, precious baby, as black as it could be . . . and Daddy . . ." Lucy clutched her throat.

Mom stroked Lucy's arm.

"He slapped me, hit me, called me horrible names. He kept asking who done it, but I wouldn't say. He didn't want nothing to do with me anymore, how could I shame our family like that? No decent white man would want anything to do with me now, so he called it off with the one nice fellow, and said if Barry MacNeill was the only one interested after that, I'd best count myself lucky. I didn't deserve better."

"I'm so sorry, Lucy." Mom shed tears with her. "Nobody ever knew?"

"Not even Barry. He thinks I put that cross in the yard for a miscarriage during our first year of marriage. But I never had one."

The screen door slammed. "Lucy!" Barry yelled. "Where in tarnation is that saw I keep in the barn?" His words slurred together. "I keep tripping on one dumifutchet after another. Keep those kids out of there." Boots tromped across the clean kitchen floor.

"I don't know where your saw is." To Mom, Lucy added, "Fact is, the barn's in good order now. All spruced up. That's why he can't find nothing."

"Who fixed it up?" Mom asked.

"What was all that racket last night?" Barry poked his head around the doorway, then stepped through with mud-covered boots. "Hey ya, Jennie. Did you hear that racket in our barn? I'm going to bed. I'm beat." He yawned the size of Snake Hollow.

"I mopped the kitchen floor, Barry."

He looked at Lucy, dazed. "Well, it needed it." His sentence sounded like one word.

"Will you please take Jasper and Shannon up with you and put them in bed?"

"I can't lift another thing. I'm plumb wore out." Probably from lifting the bottle too many times. He disappeared into the kitchen. Cupboard doors squeaked open. "What's to eat?"

"I'll tuck the little ones in." Mom carried them upstairs. She and I stayed to mop the floor.

CHAPTER 4

Hey batter, batter, batter, swing!

Stan Randall's annoying chant still echoed three days later. I rarely swung at bad balls, but with his whiny voice dribbling, I couldn't even hit good pitches.

Today I finished chores in record time. Seeking respite from Stan's anthem ringing in my ears, I pedaled my bike down the dusty snake of a road, past farmhouses and green pyramids of tobacco plants. The shoulders sloped into fields of green flowing capes trimmed with chicory. Cornstalks reached better than knee-high. Soon they'd offer up leafy stalks of corncobs and yellow silk for dresses and hair of Grandma Hamilton's dried apple dolls. In the distance loomed Blue Ridge Mountain foothills, glens, knolls, and hollows, a land formed by celestial hands. God in His gardening had dropped scoopfuls of dirt in sporadic piles, each sprouting oaks and maples, brush and wildflowers.

Near the woods, I left my bike. The path took me through dense velvet shadows of a spruce, balsam, and pine forest that juggled torches of sunlight from branch to branch. In the clearing by my favorite red oak, I lay on my back watching squirrels.

Among a flourish of coneflowers, jack-in-the-pulpits, and brown-eyed susans near cushions of phlox and white violets, I felt miles away from my troubles. I convinced myself that Dad's and Phil Kepler's argument was no more substantial than floating dust flecks. So I dismissed Phil's sarcasm, his accusations, my Dad's defensiveness, and the cool tone with which they parted after a warm friendship of years.

Dad would keep the park out, getting his way as with everything else. I knew about that firsthand, starting with Sundays. Other kids played baseball on the Lord's Day, but not us. Dad once explained that the face cut into the full moon was the man who burnt his brush pile on Sunday. He said that with the earnestness of a starving man bargaining for a five-dollar dinner with only a quarter.

My last time at home plate streamed through my mind. Wally's boys hoped I'd bat in Cue Ball to tie the score. Already oh-for-three that game, I merely hoped to leave the batter's box with my self-respect intact. Stan talked loudly enough to bother batters and quietly enough to elude the umpire, no doubt a feat he was mighty proud of. His droning continued long after we went home and hung up our baseball caps.

Stan provoked Nick, too, but Nick remained the conscientious objector with regard to fighting. Nick kept his irritations to himself, most generously saving some for me.

With myrtle and mountain laurel hovering, the voice dissipated. Soon the perfumes, cool shade, and tickling grasses lulled me to sleep.

Hey batter, batter, batter, swing!

I jolted awake. Muscles tightened as the scene replayed. Stan's home plate shenanigans had made me strike out. Plain and simple. Not with any fancy curve ball either. I swung so hard I was dizzy. Stan's raucous laughter followed. Every piece of self-control I ever possessed poured into that moment. I wanted to whack him over the head with my bat.

Time for practice. I biked to town. On Currie Hill's Main Street, I passed Randall's Diner (specializing in twenty-four cent hamburgers), Wally's Shoes and Leather Goods, Neal Collier's Bakery, Griffin's Barber Shop, Sam Simpson's Ice Cream Parlor, Duncan's Hardware (above which was Uncle Eddie's apartment), Mr. Hutchins's wood shop, the Currie Hill Daily News (issued weekly), and Mr. Kepler's Bear Wallow Inn, a newer building attempting to look old.

Most Little Leaguer pitchers were happy with a decent

fastball in their repertoire, but not Nick. He worked to perfect pitching the way Mr. Drummond, the blacksmith, made a horseshoe. Sandy Koufax retired two years earlier due to an inflamed arthritic elbow. Hud predicted the same end for Nick by age twelve. Nick tried to duplicate Koufax's sidearm curve, but instead acquired the screwball by accident.

Nick spent hours helping Todd master the screwball. Together they coddled their self-assumed glorified status as pitchers and informed me of their right to do so. "Good pitchers stop good hitters, not vice versa," Nick claimed as though he'd coined the phrase and not heard it on television. "The Dodgers of '63, '65, and '66 won pennants with nothing but good pitching."

Jay Griffin, the barber's son, greeted me when I arrived at the sandlot. He was always the last one in line for his uniform and ended up with hole-y knees or pants three sizes too big. Emulating the Detroit Tigers second baseman Dick McAuliffe, Jay stood at home plate poised to bat with his right elbow in the clouds, left toe to the pitcher. Stan Randall laughed. But Jay's contortions served him well. He hit a single past the shortstop. On first base and pleased with himself, he beamed a smile, shamelessly revealing buck teeth that I could see from the bench.

Toby Hutchins, our catcher, was a fan of Tiger catcher Bill Freehan. Toby's face exhibited intense concentration, as if he'd been told by some grown-up his face would eventually freeze that way. Either the prediction came true or he was trying to challenge it.

Todd's team and ours decided to scrimmage. Hud wasn't there yet, so I was elected umpire for one reason: I had a good eye, despite being a girl.

"Batter, batter, batter, swing!"

I wasn't sure if it was an echo or the real thing.

Wally's Shoes Wildcats took the field. Nick was pitching. Stan Randall sauntered to home plate. Like the Pirates' Willie Stargell warming up, Stan swung the bat 360 degrees from the wrists above his head several times. His six-foot ego matched Stargell's size. He either got a strikeout or a home run each time up.

In the batter's box, Stan shook his head till he found an open spot in his greasy bangs through which to see the pitcher. I wanted him to strike out.

"They had enough of a girl on their team?" Her voice reminded me of someone drooling.

Wanting him to miss the ball, I talked. "I hear tell you struck out against Larry last week."

"The ball was out and the ump was blind. Was that you umping?"

"You went down swinging."

Nick pitched. Low and outside. Ball one, I called it. I was about to signal to Nick for a brushback pitch, but remembered to be neutral.

"Good eye, ump." Stan sneered.

"Shut up, Stan," said Toby, the catcher.

"I'll shut up after I'm long gone on a home run."

"That means he'll be around for a long time." I smirked.

"You'll think I'm still here," Stan said, "'cause I'll run those bases so fast and be back again, you'll never miss me."

"You're right about not missing you," I said.

Nick was taking forever. He concentrated so hard that Mount Mitchell could drop in front of him and he wouldn't blink an eye.

The next pitch came, high and tight, sending Stan reeling to the ground. Ball two.

Undaunted, Stan got up, dusted off his seat, and knocked the bat on his heels. He took another practice swing over his head. His eyes poked at me from behind greasy blond strands. "Toby, you-uns ain't got a chance at the league title, not with a girl on your team. She went a measly oh-for-four last time we played."

Due to his chirping behind the plate. I clenched my

fists. We needed a strike on Stan now.

The ball zipped right down the middle. Stan swung and fouled it off. His bangs swished back and forth with the force of the swing.

"Sterrrr-ike!" I gestured emphatically like umpires on television. It brought great satisfaction.

"Hey, that was good," Stan said as if he had fouled on purpose. "You practice that at home in front of the mirror?"

"If you spent more time in front of the mirror, we wouldn't have to look at you here."

"You contrary me one more time and I'll tell everyone you're heckling me."

I'll tell them you're nauseating me.

The next two pitches arrived. A ball, then another foul-off. The count was 3-2.

"He's throwing spitballs!" Stan looked down his nose at me through mop-like hair. "Go check that out, ump."

I stomped out to Nick and examined the ball. "You throwing spitballs?" He said no. "Now's as fittin' a time as any to start." He laughed. I jogged back to home plate.

Nick wound up. A curve ball sailed in just outside the strike zone. It was so close that only Toby, Stan, and me would know the difference, so fast that only I could be sure. Stan threw his bat and started walking to first.

But I called it a strike.

****

Gratified, I left the sandlot with my chin higher than when I'd arrived. I rode to Mr. Hutchins's carpentry shop in town on an errand for Dad.

I peered through the screen door. Mr. Hutchins's furry white head bobbed as he spoke. "Was took down sick with a touch of the fever plus the sore throat. Got so thin, Patsy said she saw daylight through me."

Mr. Collier, the baker, patted his own stout bulk, round

as a dumpling. "That won't ever happen to me, no, sir."

"That's from living like a crab, Neal. All stomach and no head."

"It's my Linda. She won't stop feeding me."

"She's done right by you." Mr. Hutchins leaned over the counter, lowering his voice. "Them biscuit-bread and gravy of hers are heavenly. I've a hankering for 'em right now. Maybe she can learn Patsy to make 'em." He nodded toward the back door. "I ain't skin and bones for no reason. Forty years of overcooked asparagus and hominy grits is enough to—"

Mr. Collier's snigger drowned him out. "Fault yourself then. Beauty never made the kettle boil. I'd rather have the kettle boiling any day. Did you take any doctor-medicine?"

"Granny sakes alive, no! Don't trust that stuff any more than I can throw a cow by the tail." Mr. Hutchins vigorously shook his furry head. "The only thing that sets well with me is onion."

"I'd rather have the illness." Mr. Collier's hands plunged into mailbag-size pockets of baggy pants.

"Onions baked in sugar, a sure cure for the sore throat. One spoonful at a time. If the medicine don't cure you, the odor will." Mr. Hutchins held up a scrawny arm, highlighting his biceps. "I'm every bit and grain as good as I need to be. There'll be sleeping enough in the grave. Now I gotta traipse out for a right smart stack of timber to cure, and them chairs in the back are hurting for another coat of varnish. I'm as busy as a one-armed paper hanger with the seven-year itch."

Patsy Hutchins's voice meandered from the back room. "He'll wear out before he rusts out. He still ought to be on the puny list."

"I'm right tolerable now. Why, Tina, is that you? Come on in! Powerful glad to see you."

I resembled an eavesdropper rather than a waiting customer, surely a telltale screen imprint across my face. He waved me in. A sprinkling of dust had settled comfortably in his bushy hair.

"Hey, Mr. Hutchins. Hey, Mr. Collier, how's Marty doing these days?" I attempted genuine sympathy. After all, his son Marty's mishap landed me on the ball team.

"Well, he ain't throwing no baseballs yet," Mr. Collier replied. "But Doc Kirby says his arm should be good as new in six weeks."

Whew. I could play till August.

Mr. Hutchins led us to a sawdust-free room in back where he varnished furniture. He stood beside a walnut rocker. Dad had taught me how to discern different woods, so I recognized the narrow grains. "Your ma's birthday, July first. It'll be ready." He beamed at the chair. "Ain't she a beauty? Here, let me show you how I make it."

He explained how he enjoyed walnut, a hard wood that split easily. Seasoned, it was great for furniture, particularly liked for its aesthetic quality. Unseasoned it was usually split for paneling and fence rails, but he quickly interjected, "It really disgusts me that they don't make walnut fences now, like they used to."

In another room, he let me hold scrap pieces as he demonstrated machinery.

"Mr. Hutchins, how long does it take you to make one chair?"

He chuckled, a raspy sound as though sawdust had found his throat, too. "I couldn't rightly tell you, Tina."

"Hours? Days?"

"Can't even make a guess. Reckon if I kept track, I wouldn't enjoy making 'em. But two or three days a week I make chairs. The rest of the time I prepare the wood, same way we done it the last four generations in my family. Don't buy the timber. I fetch it myself, traipsing through Strawberry Gap. A right smart of good timber there."

He picked up a rectangular piece of wood, three inches square and a yard long. "You ever see how a bat gets made?" He attached the wood to the lathe. It buzzed and whirred so fast

I was dizzy. His hand glided the tool over rotating wood, spinning my head into a blur until I averted my gaze to look for wood chips. Dad said you could know a carpenter by the wood chips: the fewer, the better.

The bell on the front door jingled. We returned to the front room to find Phil Kepler. Mr. Collier and Mr. Hutchins shifted to more correct grammar as they did with northerners.

"How was New York?" Mr. Hutchins asked.

Phil shared a humorous anecdote without hinting at any business. "How's that desk order coming?"

"I been flat on my back for a week, Phil. It'll be done soon."

"Have you considered making the cabinets for the park offices? Pending the outcome of the vote."

Mr. Hutchins shuffled his feet. "Well, I studied on it—"

"Assuming Ross Hamilton and his sawmill prepares the wood, your workload will only be the construction."

"I know, but—"

"Is the pay too low? We can negotiate that."

"No." Mr. Hutchins shook his furry head. "I don't care for the money, see. I got enough work as it is. Besides, chairs are my specialty."

"Don't care for the money, eh?" Phil Kepler stroked his chin. "How's this for incentive—what if I lower the pay?" He let loose a hearty laugh. The other men exchanged amused looks before joining in.

"I don't care if you let me do it for nothing," Mr. Hutchins said. "I'm not interested." This drew more laughter. "But Gordy Matheson in Fenville may be your man." Fenville, four miles away, was so tiny that one sign announced your arrival both ways. The town name was printed on either side. "He does good work. Our grandfathers worked together during the first big war."

"Mr. Hutchins don't even know how long it takes him to make a chair," I blurted.

All eyes looked my way. Phil dug into his shirt pocket and threw me a package of Life Savers. "The red ones are especially good. Todd loves them."

"Thank you, sir." I tucked my new prize safely into my pocket.

"It's true," Mr. Hutchins said. "If I work for you, you'll be laying down deadlines. I can't work that way. I won't be able to take chair orders."

"I'd rather employ area businesses than bring in outsiders," said Mr. Kepler, the outsider.

"Yes, sir, it's a mite far to tote wood from New York." Mr. Collier grinned. Phil was known for his numerous business trips there.

"I once hopped a freight headed north." Mr. Hutchins shared one of his well-known stories. Less than sixty seconds into the tale, Phil's vivid green eyes paled to the hue of tolerant indifference. He checked his watch and cleared his throat. "Excuse me, gentlemen, I must go. I'm meeting Brent at three."

After he left, I asked, "How far is New York?"

The mountain dialect returned as quickly as it left. "A right smart distance from here." Mr. Collier's hands were lost in his pockets, fingers thumping against his thighs like giant spiders. "A body's gotta be plumb addlepated to wanna go there."

"Strenuous train trip, too. Don't recommend it to anybody under eighty-five." Mr. Hutchins tapped the countertop. "I can't much confidence that park idea of Phil Kepler's. There won't be no need for those cabinets he's a-wanting. Not with your daddy as town council chairman. As good a man as God ever blowed breath in, your daddy."

"Dad says nobody's good. He says the closer you are to God, the bigger a sinner you realize you are."

Mr. Collier chortled. "No wonder folks would rather keep their distance from the Almighty."

"It wonders me how he does it, but your daddy's got

the ups on Phil," Mr. Hutchins said. "I'm pleased as a dog with two tails to wag that he's got influence here. We're depending on him to turn that council vote against the park."

"It's the beard, sir." Weary of the praises, I hoped to end them.

"How's that?"

"Miz Doris says a beard's a sign of wisdom. So all a body's gotta do is grow a beard."

"Honey, if beard were all, the goat might preach." Mr. Collier guffawed, his spidery pockets jiggling.

Mr. Hutchins rattled on. "Phil's knowledgeable but he's journey-proud. I don't confidence that much. Reckon he's the getting-aroundest man I ever did know. He's everywhere talking to everybody." His bushy hair jounced with his voice. "He's expecting a passel of folks to go along with this park notion but your daddy's given out to be the best one for getting his way. He studies on the situation and folks'll go along with whatever he says. Phil—I hate to say it—it'll be like a bug arguing with a chicken."

I spent half my life shrugging off talk like that about my father. Only four more weeks until the vote, thank goodness.

CHAPTER 5

Stabbing a forlorn hushpuppy on my plate, I brought the matter up. "Stan Randall's a big, fat creep."

"Is that so?" Dad said as though I'd forecasted rain.

"He's a bully, always insulting me 'cause I'm a girl. He hates all girls."

"Then why do you get special favors?" Dad asked in the same tone.

"I'm serious, Dad. The other day he purposely distracted me at the plate. I struck out and everyone was mad at me. No one knew it was his fault."

"You do nothing to prompt this?" With her love for the word hushpuppy, Mom indulged herself in three of them. Nick snickered.

I wriggled up to a straight, self-righteous posture and divulged tales of awe and terror that would surely bring them to my side with breathless sympathy.

Mom dribbled gravy on her meat. "The only good martyr is a dead one."

Dad reached toward me. "May I shake your hand, Miss High-and-mighty?" I pouted.

"Sometimes the ones you despise the most are the ones you favor later," Mom said. "Someday you'll be bragging to all the world how much mind Stan Randall paid you. You gonna eat up your food while it's hot or later when it's cold?"

"I'd rather complain than eat right now."

Dad eyed his steaming plateful. "Girl's gotta warped sense of priority." He delved in.

I crossed my arms and kicked the table leg.

"Tina." Dad's eyes pierced mine. I stiffened into a shield awaiting the blow of his reprimand. He leaned over his plate, fork in one hand, knife in the other, as if about to carve a great beast and I was the beast. "So this fellow may be hurting for some manners. Now there's plenty of ways to fix such a problem, but one thing I won't abide is you proposing marriage to Stan Randall."

Mom's face didn't flinch. Nick smirked.

"Sometimes a girl borrows trouble by taking everything into her own hands." Dad resumed eating hushpuppies in the most casual manner. "Like your mother here. We had our upscuddles, too. But she fixed that. She asked me to marry her."

A clatter of silverware turned our heads to Mom. We'd heard this argument before, but enjoyed it each time. "I most certainly did not."

Dad faced Nick and me. "She's shy about it now, but she did the proposing."

"I'll not abide you telling our children I'd stoop to such improper behavior."

"I've got witnesses. Grandma Dorothy heard the whole thing."

"Did Mom get on her knees to you?" Nick asked.

"No, I wish she had, but I reckon she wasn't used to proposing."

"Why, Andrew Hamilton!" Mom popped from her chair like toast from a toaster.

"I had to say yes. Marrying her was the only way to get revenge for the frog incident."

"What frog incident?" I giggled. That one we hadn't heard.

"I don't regret that frog deal," Mom said. "I've half a mind to repeat it here and now."

Dad finally broke from his poker face into laughter. He went behind Mom and wrapped his arms around her waist.

Rigid, Mom crossed her arms. "You're feeding our children tall tales."

Dad nuzzled her ear. "I'm sorry, my Cotton Jennie." He looked at Nick with a straight face. "Remember this, Nick, when it comes time for you to marry. Don't contrary your girl. Just plan on being wrong, outright admit it, apologize on your knees, and promise never to do it again. It's the only way you're bound to get along with a woman when you got to live with her."

****

We didn't wait long to hear about the frog incident and Mom's side of the proposal story. The next night she took Nick and me camping. Dad never had time or money to take trips, so we occasionally headed for the foothills behind our fields with tents and sleeping bags. There bulged a balsam-spruce woods laced with the stream where Dad used to stand pulling out floating wild ducks he'd shot upstream. After building a fire, our parents told stories, some true, some legends, and some of which nobody knew where truth ended and legend began.

Dad couldn't join us this time, but Mom relished the chance to tell a story without his interjections. She poked a stick in the fire. "Your pa already got his revenge for that frog incident, before we married."

Embers glowed. Nick's and Mom's faces stood out from the darkness.

"Can't remember a time I didn't know your daddy. He's a distant cousin so he'd always be around for family reunions. He was ten years older, one of those big boys who horsed around and teased us young-uns. As long as those big ones paid us any mind, we'd latch onto them like a cocklebur in sheep's wool.

"When he was seventeen, he up and worked with my pa—your Grandpa Ross—and my grandpa and uncles in the woods, logging and such. They lit out for Sugar Cove or Linnet to chop trees and send logs down the river, some to your Grandpa Hamilton's sawmill. When Drew spent the spring of 1940 logging, Ma was chief cook and bottle washer at the logging camp.

"We five kids, all under twelve, tagged along. Uncle Garrett, Aunt Elaine, and I were getting old enough to help with washing dishes and serving food. Got to know those loggers well. Your daddy, he always had a twinkle in his brown eyes, and a ready laugh. Liking him was as easy as falling off a log. Folks said Drew was as goodhearted and hardworking as all-outdoors."

Mom traced a heart in the dirt. "Sometimes Garrett and I got to feeling mischievous. We'd play pranks on the loggers, 'specially ones who teased us. That's when I pulled that frog incident.

"What'd you do?" Nick asked.

"One morning when he was fixing to light out for the woods, Daddy joked with my ma and ordered frog legs for dinner that night. I chanced to overhear him and decided that frog legs was exactly what he was gonna get, a lavish of it, right on his dinner plate. Elaine would've tattled, so Garrett and I hunted for the best frog with the best pair of legs. Somehow we got it on his plate, right alongside his biscuit and beans.

"I never will forget the look on your daddy's face when he saw a big bullfrog a-staring back at him, right atop his 'taters, too. Boy, was he furious! After a long, hard day of work, and famished, he had to wait in line again for another plate. Garrett made sure I got the blame and Ma walloped me. 'We've 120 mouths to feed,' she said, 'and you up and spoil perfectly good food. How dare you task me like that.' And Daddy promised revenge to boot."

"How'd he do that?" I leaned against a tree stump.

"You'll see. First, after high school, he joined the Army and went as far as Paris, France to fight in World War II. But he didn't come back afterward. He went to college in

Michigan, then worked in New York. With such distrust of big
cities, folks here speculated the worst. Some said he failed
school, others said he was leading a life of crime. Truth be told,
he was an architect. His family didn't hear much from him."
She paused, as if lured into her own reverie. "He married a
New York gal, but didn't write home about her till after the
fact. Then she took ill and died before he could ever bring her
back here."
    We'd heard about Dad's first wife. Grandma
Hamilton's opinion on the matter stifled any questions.
However, Nick seized the moment. "How'd she die?"
    "She took ill, son."
    "Did you see a picture of her?"
    "She was a pretty thing. I don't know why he didn't
come back here all that time, why he never brought her here."
    "Why don't you ask him?" I spouted.
    "I don't ask about such matters." She blinked and
continued in her former rhythm. "Anyhow, his brother Sid
moved away, too. Fifteen years after Daddy left, he returned,
1956. Said he was here to stay. He was all broke up after
hearing about Old Man Fuller dying, then took to working odd
jobs, logging and running the sawmill with Uncle Ross.
    "Meanwhile, I'd grown up, graduated from high school
and went to Durham two years for college, wanting to be a
teacher. I was home in Rindlewood for the summer, working at
a drugstore. In June, a month after your daddy returned, I was
closing shop. A face peered through the window, a mighty
thirsty one. I opened the door and the man stepped in, quite
pleased I'd succumbed. 'Let it be to your credit that you're
saving a life right now, miss,' he said as he gave me money for
a fountain drink."
    "Was it Dad?" I shifted to wake up my numb legs.
    "It was for certain. I recognized him and said, 'Why
it's you, Drew Hamilton! Welcome back.' He was puzzled that
I knew him and seemed embarrassed he couldn't place me, but
I was seven when he last saw me. So I prompted him. 'I didn't

ever want to call this to mind, but remember that frog . . .' He broke into a wide grin. 'No, I'll never forget that,' he said. 'That's on your permanent record, Jennie Ross.' I handed him his soda pop and said, 'Let's hope my credit in saving your life today remains clearer in your memory than the other incident.'"

Mom leaned forward as if telling a secret. "Now something was different about the way he talked, sounded more northern than southern. But he had that same schoolboy face, with a lot more wisdom. And handsome as ever. Your daddy says, 'I'm sorry I didn't recognize you, but you come back and the mountains and trees, excusing the chestnuts, look the same, the streams, the hills. So timeless, I'm surprised folks are older, children have grown up.'

"I recollect we sat at the counter, talking quite pleasant-like while he drank. He was working a job down the lane apiece, and came by the next night, too, at closing. I let him in and we drank and talked. After three evenings, he said, 'Sorry I can't get here earlier. I'd like to do this right proper, though, and drop by your house next Sunday and ask your parents for permission to court you.' I was flabbergasted. He was so much older and smarter, and more educated. I consented and he left. For all his worldly-wise ways, his concern with tradition by asking permission impressed me."

"Did it bother you that he talked funny?" I asked.

"No, but when I told my folks, Pa rocked back and forth in his rocker without a word. Ma said, 'You beware of any man that's a-gone and left his family for the big city for such a spell and that's a-come back and won't breathe a word about his work nor that wife of his, God rest her soul. It sounds chancy to me. He's surely street-wise, city-wise, and woman-wise and wants nothing better than to take advantage of an innocent like you. As fickle as the wind, taking up city ways and coming back here. I don't like it one bit.' Pa said, 'I don't put much stock in it, Jennie, but we'll let him come by. He's always been a hard worker and good at motivating the others.

That ain't no crime.'"

"Did they think he was a bad guy?" Nick threw a napkin in the fire and it blazed.

"No telling what a body might be up to, when he won't talk about where he's been. 'Specially one that's been in the city for so long. They figured he couldn't be one of us anymore. Ma said, 'He'd better do you right. You'd best find out more about him, where was he all them years.' I said, 'Maybe that's nobody's business,' but she wouldn't abide that notion.

"Sunday evening Drew came. We sat on the porch and talked. I was attentive, but he only offered vague comments about his Army years, schooling, architect work, and his marriage. He flew back to New York once for a couple days in August, but that was the last of it. Said something about his last commitment on the job, and he visited his brother Sid. But he assured me he was a Tar Heel now, wanted nothing more than to be a farmer on his daddy's property, and rear a family someday. What else mattered?"

Plenty of things mattered. "Did he have money?"

Mom laughed. "What he had, he set aside for your college education. Some said he should have a right smart of money on account of working in the big city so long. But it made no difference to me. Over the summer we saw each other twice weekly, fishing, sitting on the porch, going for ice cream. We didn't court as if he had big-time money. Ma kept saying, 'Nothing good's gonna come of this. You've got stars in your eyes, girl!' Pa said, "I don't see no grounds for objection yet,' but I sensed his discontent, too."

Mom stoked the fire again. Flames highlighted her eyes. The stars Grandma Dorothy spoke of still sparkled, and always would.

"Late August, I prepared to return to Durham for school. Drew and I walked through the woods, the week before I planned to leave. He asked me all about schooling, my plans and goals. I wanted to come back to this area and teach third grade. He sensed my excitement. We were sitting on a log, and he says, 'I don't know if I can match all of that but I'm gonna try.' He drew a deep breath, and says, 'I want you to be my wife, Jennie. I can't offer you a teaching certificate or job satisfaction but I can offer you my land and my house and all the love I've got. If you wanna continue schooling, I'll wait for you, but selfishly I want to marry you now. There's no other woman I want for my kids' mother.' I was shocked. He kept talking. 'I love you, Jennie Ross. If you need time to think it over, you can tell me before you leave for Durham.'"

"We know the ending to that story," Nick said. "'Cause here we are."

"This story's not over," Mom said. "First you gotta hear your daddy's retaliation for the frog episode. I studied on the situation. I loved my schooling. But the bottom line was, I'd rather devote my whole life to a few children than touch the surface of many, that's where my heart truly was. If I married Drew Hamilton now, I may not finish school, but I could still learn and read, teach my own kids, and garden to my heart's content."

"What did Grandma and Grandpa say?" Nick asked.

"I didn't tell them yet, considering their concerns. Was I being too hasty? Too taken up with the man at face value? I waited to decide till the last day before returning to Durham."

"Do you ever wish you'd finished your schooling?" I asked.

"Sometimes, but I don't regret it. Your daddy knows how to treat a woman like she's queen. You'd still want to give your heart to him, even after the rush of the moment. Not a ladies' man or a romancer, but loyal and hardworking, honest and true, single-minded. Those silent years never bothered me, 'cause whatever happened then made him into the man I admire and love now. I could trust him and always will.

"Daddy came by a week later, the day before he knew I'd be leaving for school. I'd pondered what to say, wanting it all to be so romantic. We went for a walk. I was wearing a pretty white frock. We laughed and chatted, and I got more nervous about my planned speech so I kept putting it off and prolonging our walk. When we turned a corner I slipped in the mud and toppled into the creek, white dress and all."

Nick and I stifled our laughter.

"He scrambled in after me and took me home. My evening was ruined. We were muddy and wet. My answer would have to be rushed and matter-of-fact. The whole mood was gone. I told him Pa had dry clothes he could wear, but to my dismay he said he should leave and let me pack. Ma offered Pa's clothes, too, but Drew said he had to go, and I should get packing.

"Besides being wet and muddy, I was downright scared he'd leave and I'd never see him again, so with a burst of vigor and a complete lack of good manners, I yelled, 'I'm not going anywhere tomorrow, and I'm not packing anything tonight, or tomorrow, or the next day, or ever again, because I'm not doing anything but marrying you, Drew Hamilton, whether you like it or not!' Well, that stopped him dead in his tracks. He stared at me as the screen door slammed shut behind him. Just then Ma walks in, appalled. She says, 'Why, Jennie, you gone about it all wrong. The man's supposed to do the asking.'

"Daddy's face lit up and he laughed with joy. He says to Ma in all seriousness, 'I accept your daughter's proposal of marriage.' Ma rolls her eyes and for once in my life I wanted to smack Drew Hamilton. But he walked over and said, 'I thought you'd never ask.' He hugged me, mud and all. I melted right then and there in his arms.

"Ma and Pa gave consent for us to get married at Christmastime. Ma said it gave me time to back out. But we married, and you came along ten months later, Nick. And to this day your daddy tells everybody that I did the proposing."

"Did Dad know you were gonna say yes all along?" I asked.

"Later he admitted he was afraid I wouldn't reply for another hour or more, so by trying to leave earlier he'd get an answer out of me. You see, he finally did get his revenge for the frog. He may be loyal, but he's as mischievous as a boy let loose on the last day of school."

CHAPTER 6

Saturday evening began in the typical manner. In some respects, it ended that way. But somewhere in the middle, when the uncles came over, things went awry. Most likely, I didn't start us out on the right foot at suppertime when I asked Mom about having tuna casserole.

If she liked the sound of those words, she'd say yes-- my time-tested theory. Words sent her into joyful delirium. She adored puns and tongue twisters, the worse the better. The more ear-tickling the word, the more pleasurable the food. She'd choose huckleberries over blueberries, in spite of seeds. Green peppers appealed more than beans. Her preference for scuppernong wine ranked high above peach. Corn couldn't compete with dandelion greens. Flapjacks won hands down over eggs.

She read us everything from Dr. Seuss to fairy tales to Tom Sawyer. We had to ponder beautiful, rhythmical arrangements of words. The only time she took my side over the teacher's was when I had to write a dictionary page for talking out of turn. She called the teacher: "You give children words for punishment? You want your students to grow up hating words?"

"Todd and his dad eat tuna casserole," I said as if they were one up on us.

"It's so fancy you don't even have to go to the ocean for it," Dad said. "Reckon they sell it in a can up at Burly Corners." A bite of stew disappeared somewhere behind the beard.

"How 'bout macaroni and cheese?" I asked.

"I survived on it for better than two years of my bachelorhood," Dad replied.

"Must be good, then."

Dad smirked. "I've heard it described in terms that would make a hog blush."

Despite the insult against it, a surge of pride swelled through me. My dad had fought in World War II, lived in New York City, was town council chairman, and was well-acquainted with foreign dishes. Mr. Kepler certainly had no edge over my father.

"Will you fix tuna casserole, Mom? I've a hankering for it." I dropped a scrap of meat for Paprika. She scuttled across the floor and pounced on the pork.

Mom's freckles darkened. I prepared for her rebuke. "That dog's as spoiled as all-outdoors. What's wrong with the food you got?"

"Nothing. But we always eat the same food."

"Thank your daddy for that." Mom made what Dad liked and Dad never changed. That meant plenty of stew, fried pork, fried chicken, fried potatoes, hushpuppies and hominy, cornbread and biscuits. "I trust this isn't your roundabout way of complaining about dinner." She nodded toward the wooden plaque, hung for the benefit of Nick's and my ungrateful souls: He who complains does not eat here.

"All the more food for the rest of us." Dad drowned his cornbread in honey.

"I'm not complaining." I stabbed a potato.

"That's a relief," Dad said. "Because the best cook in the county lives under this roof. Can't do better elsewhere."

"Especially at the Hutchins," I said. "Miz Patsy ain't such a good cook. Mr. Hutchins says it's how he stays so lean."

Mom's freckles darkened again. "Since when does Mr. Hutchins confidence you about his wife's cooking skills?"

Dad tucked his napkin into his shirt, speaking with nonchalance. "Reckon he told Tina this about the same time he mentioned current stock market reports, his great-grandmother's three husbands, and the color of underwear he put on this morning."

Nick rescued me from further humiliation by discussing our team's prospects, particularly Jay's base stealing and Byron's fielding. He neglected my excellent hitting.

"Nick's gonna be owing Todd a sundae at Simpson's come autumn," I said.

"What are you betting on now?" Mom rolled her eyes.

"Whether Denny McLain will get thirty wins this season," Nick said.

"He's off to a good start," Dad said. "But I'm staying out of this bet. I'm still paying on the last one." He and Nick had bet three hours of manual labor on how many piglets Henrietta our sow would give birth to last month.

That evening we stayed home—no visit to the MacNeills, thank goodness. After a bath, I picked up *Ivanhoe*. Dad and Mom had a way of reading that swept us from this century and continent and placed us firmly in others, far and away. They told us Jack tales and family anecdotes going back five generations. The stories we shared wove in and out of us like a needle in fabric, piercing us in such a way that we were forever changed by each one—however slightly—bound together by our memories.

Nick and I strung beans, called leather breeches when hung to dry. In winter, Mom dropped them into pork stew. She made coffee from dandelion or chicory, preferring the sound of those words. Dandelion roots substituted for coffee. We'd dig them up. Mom washed and peeled them, then roasted and ground them. Sassafras tea was made from the blossoms, twigs, roots, or root bark. We scrubbed bark till it was pink and clean, peeled it off, boiled it, then sweetened it with sugar. Tonight she chose chicory.

Smelling Mom's coffee put me miles away from the MacNeill household with its stench of garbage and shame. My neck prickled from Lucy's story, not only from her confession, but from the hatred of a father who bequeathed her his anger and unforgiving spirit. His resentment sentenced her to a lifetime of public shame at the hands of the town drunkard, the man she had to call husband.

With forgiveness and a good man, Lucy would've blossomed. I hated her father, though I'd never met him. He disappeared years earlier, died according to some, but the filth of the MacNeill household was no match for the stink of that old man's rotting bones.

The security of my parents' love undergirded my life and inspired me to avoid actions that displeased them, in as much as I was able. Would I ever do something so terrible they wouldn't forgive me? At least such shameful things happened only in other people's families.

Sitting on a stool, Dad whittled a chunk of wood, his feet wading in shavings. He carved movable wooden toys-- animals, wagons, lumberjacks, and fiddlers--in the tradition of his father. He usually gave them away. He worked like a thirty-year-old in the field, but at night seemed much older than forty-five. Mom often teased him about turning fifty any day now.

Dad set down his handiwork, claimed his favorite chair, lit his corncob pipe, and waved me over. He insisted on reading Mark Twain. "One cannot indulge in *Ivanhoe* while in a cynical mood."

Mom picked up her appliqué. She'd recently joined a society that featured a return to the traditional quilt-making to preserve the old ways. The women made quilts to donate to various fairs to sell. She also joined the Southern Highland Handicrafts Guild out of Asheville. Mrs. George Vanderbilt set it up in 1901 to continue the hand-weaving traditions of the area.

After a chapter of *The Prince and the Pauper*, I said, "I'd rather be a princess than a pauper." I was far from adopting Mr. Hutchins's philosophy about money and no need for it.

Dad puffed on his pipe. "There's a heap more advantages to being poor. Not everyone can handle riches. If

I'd been filthy rich, your mother wouldn't have married me."

"What'd she marry you for then?" Nick asked without shame.

"She couldn't resist a man who smokes a good corncob pipe." Dad inhaled. Mom rolled her eyes.

"If I had my druthers," Nick said, "I'd rather be lucky than rich."

"Hush now," Dad said. "I want no talk of luck, good or bad. There's no such thing in a God-centered universe." The word luck was equivalent to a swear word in our house.

"Speaking of riches and royalty," Mom said, "there's a movie I'd like to see, with Richard Harris. It's been out since last year. *Camelot.*"

"Don't take her to *Camelot*," Nick said. "She'll come home and bawl her eyes out. We won't have no supper for a week." Dad raised his eyebrows at Mom.

"It's true, Dad," I said. "Every time she plays that record you got her—"

"You never shoulda taken her to the play in Asheville," Nick said. "That's when it all started."

"When what all started?" Dad's eyes twinkled in amusement.

"When she's down about something she plays that record," Nick said.

"Real loud, too," I added. "It sets her to crying more. Only when you're not around."

"She used a whole box of tissues once," Nick said.

"Now you all hush," Mom said. "That bit about the whole tissue box isn't true."

"The rest is?" Dad asked.

"The kids have imagination, they do. So I cry a little. It's such a sad story. King Arthur, Queen Guinevere. Just one moment of forsaking to do right and the whole kingdom was ruined."

"Yes, but why do you play it all the time?" he asked.

"Drew, think of it! The whole thing is God's

magnificent dilemma, with Arthur as God, and Guinevere—the lost people." Mom's tone took on the theatrical. "What are you going to do, Arthur? Kill Guinevere and your life will be over. Don't kill her and you've killed the law, the kingdom. It's God's dilemma all the way through. He can't kill the law, yet He loves the people who broke it."

"She plays the record when she's sad already," Nick said. "I came home from ball practice one day and she's sitting at the kitchen table sobbing."

"So I get my sadness out all at once and don't spread it out over a long time, like others do. But, Drew, don't you worry, these children have up and fixed the problem. They hid my record. I searched this whole house but can't find it. Next it'll be my scrapbook of newspaper clippings."

Dad chuckled. "Don't fret, Jennie. You'll get your record back." His gaze settled on Nick and me. Nick trudged upstairs and got the record. Dad made him put it on the record player and turn up the volume. "It's about time I hear the cause of all this commotion."

"I'm not in a *Camelot* mood," Mom said.

"You will be by the time it's over," Nick said. "I'll get the tissues."

Dad handed her his handkerchief.

"Stop it! I don't cry on demand." Mom was saved from further teasing by a hearty knock on the door. I answered it, Paprika yapping beside me.

"Did you bring your cards?" Dad asked his brothers as Ross and Eddie stepped inside. Uncle Eddie scooped me up to his shoulder. I ran fingers through his bushy, reddish-gold hair, like rows of earth at plow time.

"No cards tonight, Drew," Ross replied. "Pa bet me I can't go a week without playing cards and I gotta last three more days."

Mom shook her head. "I declare this is the bettingest family I ever did see. Well, how about some blackberry brandy? Or did you bet that privilege away, too?"

"I'm not fool enough to do that, Jennie," Ross said. She scooted from the room.

In recent times, being Presbyterian allowed us the frivolity of cards, movies, alcohol, and smoking without guilt, unlike the Baptists who, in Dad's mind, add their own laws to the ten commandments the way our government adds amendments to the Constitution.

Uncle Ross was a broader and beardless version of my dad, with a thicker, raspier voice. Eddie's boyish face belied his mischievous nature. If my dad was a Huckleberry Finn, Ross was a Mark Twain, and Eddie was a prankish Tom Sawyer.

Ross and Aunt Abby lived across the stream in front of Grandma and Grandpa Hamilton's clapboard house and walked over often. Eddie was a regular here, too. His apartment above the hardware store could barely contain him and his love for the outdoors. He did painting and construction, sometimes helping Dad and Ross in the fields.

Under my dad's tutelage, Mom—who severed ties with her Baptist upbringing—made scuppernong wine and blackberry brandy in the springhouse cellar. Since ours was a dry county, many folks made their own liquor to the disdain of those who wouldn't partake. According to Ross, some folks around these parts were so dry, they had to prime themselves to spit.

Mom returned with brandy for the grown-ups, lemonade for Nick and me.

When I settled on Uncle Eddie's lap, Ross said, "Those MacNeill cows are so thin I could hang my hat on their hips."

Eddie piped up. "Those kids are so spindly they gotta stand up twice to cast a shadow."

Mom pulled a thread. "The man can't raise enough corn or beef to bread and meat his family.

"But for the grace of God, that would be us," Dad said.

"You should have seen Ross last night along about sundown," Eddie said. "So mad he couldn't spit straight."

Ross jerked his pipe in a wild gesture. "Those MacNeill young-uns were making more ruckus than two skeletons wrestling on a tin roof. And that older boy—a-swearing like a preacher's son."

Inspired by righteous indignation over Lucy's plight, I felt inclined to enlighten everyone with idle gossip I'd heard. "Barry MacNeill's so no-count he can't keep himself in sassafras tea and rabbit tobacco."

I seemed to have stifled the conversation. They must have realized their contribution to my indiscretion and dropped the topic.

"Have you heard from Ted or Scott lately, Ross?" Eddie asked. Ted and Scott were Ross's sons in the Army, headed for Vietnam after basic training. They'd been gone a month.

"Yes, and some things ain't changed a bit since Drew and I was in the Army," Ross said. "Folks take you for a fool just because of where you're from, or the way you talk."

"Abby was telling me about some pranksters," Mom said. "Drew, did you ever hear tell of such?"

Dad leaned over, elbows on knees, staring at the floor.

"What pranksters?" Eddie asked. "Same incident or a new one?"

"New one," Ross said. "Same victims. And pranksters, that's too kind. They're vandals and worse. They threatened to get after those hillbillies but good."

Dad's knuckles turned white from pressing his hands together.

"Boot camp instructors are the worst, especially to rural southerners. They try to intimidate, call 'em stupid hicks, among other things." He shared an anecdote.

Dad still faced the floor.

Ross rambled on. "You'd like to think the enemy was Vietnam, not your own barracks mates. Why, back in '38 when I arrived at camp, this one fellow—"

"Ross." Dad looked up, face red. "That's enough

now."

Ross stopped, mouth open, as if suddenly aware he was treading on sensitive ground.

Eddie cleared his throat. "Whatcha been hearing about this new park? Seems Phil Kepler's got as many followers as a dog has fleas."

Dad straightened. "They probably haven't heard but one side."

"You should call a council meeting to get this all talked out," Eddie said. "Folks ain't knowing what to believe."

"Phil may be as slick as an onion but that park ain't so bad as you think," Ross said. "Sakes alive, he's gone through every red tape in the country but our town council. It's state and county approved, pending our response."

Mom jabbed a needle into her cloth. "That's jumping the gun. He wants the world with a fence around it and a slice of the moon. I'd be beholden to him if he took his wild ideas elsewhere. He wants to make a tourist trap out of us, but he disguises his intentions."

"Exactly," Eddie said. "He's as smooth as maple syrup."

"And twice as sticky," Mom added. "Last year he talked me into ignoring the signs and planting my beans on the new of the moon, not even when the signs were in the arms, mind you. I regretted it ever since. The few beans that did grow plumb rotted and specked. Did you ever hear tell of such? I should've known better." The men laughed.

Dad didn't prefer to depend on the location of constellations for determining when to plant and harvest. But Grandpa Hamilton would take him to task if he didn't, so he conceded when planting potatoes and corn. Mom, however, was devoted to the signs.

"How'd he convince you, Jennie?" Dad asked. "I'll have to learn a thing or two from him next time I want you to do something for me."

"You always get your way." Mom threw a spool of

thread at him. But he was used to that kind of play. He caught the spool and slid it into his pocket with a "come and get it" look.

I had a brilliant idea. "Maybe if this were more like a city place, Uncle Sid would come back."

Seems I had a gift for stopping conversations. Eddie readjusted me on his lap. "Uncle Sid'll never come back here. He don't belong to these mountains no more."

Nick asked what the big deal was with the park anyhow.

Todd tried to explain it once. At Simpson's, he'd set his soggy tobacco leaf on the table while we drank root beers. "This isn't just any amusement park. It's a theme park," he said as if it made any difference to us. "Haven't you been to Cedar Point in Ohio, Six Flags over Texas, or Disneyland?" I depended on Nick to come up with an important-sounding place. He proudly announced, "We've been to Asheville!" Todd laughed.

Dad explained the theme park would be bigger than five farms and ten sandlots put together. Rides included roller coasters, carousels, and ferris wheels. Activities encompassed performances, museum-like displays, games, historical figures, refreshments, and more. The theme part referred to the South, its history and culture.

"Sounds like a great place," Nick said.

"Maybe for a day," Eddie added.

"Most people consider the park as welcome as the itch." Dad puffed on his pipe. "It's such a chancy thing. Comes with too much commotion."

"Yet somehow Phil's talking folks into it," Eddie said. "He's been among us long enough, five years now. Folks are trusting him."

"You can tame a grapevine but you can't take the twist out," Mom said.

Dad threw the spool of thread back at her. She caught it with a prim smile.

"There's bound to be an upscuddle soon," Ross said.
"I know plenty who'll feather up to Phil Kepler,"
Eddie said. "What do you think, Drew?"
    "I'm in favor of that park as much as I'd be in favor of
riding sidesaddle on a sow. But getting our town council to
vote it in would be like tying the wind in a sack."
    "A right smart wind too, coming from Phil," Mom
said. "He wants to get rich off us all."
    Ross gestured, nearly spilling his brandy. "Rich
nothing! Phil cares for money no more than a hog cares for the
New Testament. He's genuinely interested in folks and has
good solutions to disturbing problems. You can't fault a man
for being a civil, hat-holding citizen. You have to give Phil a
heap of credit, not only for all he does in the community but for
single-handedly raising that young-un of his. No easy task, let
alone without a mother."
    "I'll grant you that, Ross," Mom said. "Todd's a fine
boy. Well-mannered. Very friendly."
    "And a good pitcher," Nick added.
    "He hurls a mighty fine curve ball," Eddie said.
    Nick straightened. "I've been teaching him."
    "Teaching what?" I said. "How to spit and tie his
shoelaces for good luck?"
    Nick scowled at me. He worried that Dad, with his
disdain for the notion of luck, might discover his superstitious
habits.
    "If he is lucky," Eddie said, "it ain't from no spitting
and shoe tying. You ever see that face he makes just before he
pitches the ball? Like a twitch, but it stays there till the ball's
plumb out of his hand. Almost a grimace."
    "That's determination," Ross said. "That's a face you
used to pull, Drew. Nobody wanted to be anywhere near the
batter's box when you looked like that."
    "That's because they feared wild pitches." Dad
chortled. "But Todd's a strong player. And luck has nothing to
do with it." He sent Nick and me a stern look. "Ross, what are

these problems and their solutions for which our town is so indispensable?"

"Too many folks, not enough jobs. Across the state and beyond. This park will provide plenty of jobs, year 'round and summer. Think of Gordy Matheson, Hank Bailey, Isaac Burnett, Olly MacKitterick. This park would suit them fine." Ross leaned forward. "I've got four college-age kids I don't have a nickel to give to, and they be hurting for a college education. Uncle Sam'll see to Ted and Scott's schooling. But Maggie's scholarship'll be wore off soon. Rick don't wanna do mindless labor all his life. They and other youngsters could work at this park for decent money and save for college. Colored kids, too." Ross poured another glass of brandy. "The Blue Ridge Parkway's already built, but this would be permanent. Maybe President Johnson'll see part of his Great Society after all."

"Most folks ain't obliged to be giving colored folks jobs, least not in our town," Eddie said. "If the park's a draw for colored, it won't be a draw for whites. Civil rights or no civil rights, that's just how it is."

"Well, it ain't just jobs for college kids that interests me." Ross fingered his brandy glass. "Phil offered *me* a job." Everyone seemed stunned into silence. "He'll need a right smart of timber cut up if it goes through, and offered a pretty penny for use of the sawmill. He wants local business. It'd be in conjunction with Bob Hutchins, enough to send Rick and Maggie to school for two years for only a year's worth of work."

After a long pause and a sip of brandy, Dad replied, "Why, that's a fine opportunity."

"But it's depending. If there's no park, there's no job, no money, no college, no nothing for my kids. But I could only run that sawmill with your help, Drew. We could go into full-time business again. With your tinkering ability, that mill would be in tiptop shape. You'd be salaried, too, with enough to send Nick and Tina to college."

Dad and Mom exchanged glances. Mom pointed us in the direction of the stairs. Bedtime, too early as usual, right when things were getting good and sticky.

I tromped upstairs. Through my bedroom window, the outdoors was a manageable slice of the world. With my shade, I could pull it all in or squeeze it all out. In daytime, I imagined the world beyond the neighbors' cornfields and believed it all belonged to me. At night I'd bask in the moon's glow, allowing myself to belong to it.

My gaze landed on the MacNeills' house. I'd never be able to see their property as just another garbage heap. All I could see was Lucy, Lucy, Lucy.

Moonlight silhouetted their house and barn. In the stillness, a silver sheen covered all. I squinted at a dark blob crossing the MacNeill yard. The blob sharpened into a man's silhouette. Was it Barry? No, it wasn't his posture or gait. This man was tall and broad, with a tool—or a gun—over his shoulder. He went right inside the barn.

Maybe it was an apparition. If not, no concerns. Many people gave that family a helping hand. I climbed into bed accompanied by the buzz and staccato of voices winding up through the stairway and floorboards, talk about parks and jobs and unemployment and opportunities and economy.

Shadows shifted near the doorway. Something swished into my room. I screamed. Uncle Eddie popped up, throwing a blanket off his back. Nick joined us for Eddie's story of "The Hairy Toe." Though we anticipated the part where he'd grab us, we still shrieked.

After the uncles left, Mom and Dad went to bed. A crack of light from their room pushed its way into mine. After a bit, I heard Dad go downstairs, followed by the usual late night sounds: the squeaky pantry door, the cereal box lining rustling, corn flakes dropping into the bowl, milk slurping. I crept downstairs and around the corner to catch him in the act, a ritual too sacred to warrant teasing. I sat cross-legged, chin in my hands. He stood at the counter eating, a nightly routine.

He read the *Asheville Citizen* article Mom had posted on the refrigerator. When he turned and saw me, he stopped short. "When one is reading Leviticus, one needs a diversion."

He led me back upstairs. We laid down together and faced the moon, talking quietly of the man who lived up there. When I grew sleepy, he went to his room. I knew he was still reading and the lamp would stay on for twenty more minutes.

Nothing ever changed at our house.

CHAPTER 7

I woke up to a piece of toast dangling in my face from the end of a fishing line that Dad cast over my bed from the doorway. The sun was barely up. The smell of Mom's fresh-brewed coffee, hominy grits, and fried eggs did little to inspire me, but since I didn't want to be annoyed by the toast, I got up, dressed, ate, and took off with Dad through our backyard forests and foothills.

One remaining chestnut tree trunk stood beyond our farm, the rest having disappeared, killed by the 1940s chestnut blight. The tree had reached higher than the surrounding red oaks and Virginia pines, now nothing but a white spindle poking through. I knew what to expect when we reached that old chestnut at the stream's bend. It never failed. Dad stopped, grasped my shoulder, and asked, "Tina, did you ever hear tell about the time your uncle and I cleared up a log jam here?"

"No." Which was true, guaranteed to be a different version of the classic story. This time, I removed my shoes along with my skepticism, the way Moses removed his shoes on sacred ground at the burning bush. I stood in a hushed awe.

The first time I heard the story, the whole episode was a mild afternoon adventure. By the fifth telling, Uncle Ross had not only fallen off the log but been knocked unconscious. By the tenth telling, Ross and Dad both experienced near brushes with death.

He began the story with stream water from thirty years ago sparkling in his eyes. I couldn't help but laugh—no more at the story itself than by the earnest way he told it, despite changes.

"How many stitches did Uncle Ross need?" I asked near the end.

"Fifty-seven. Right here." He drew a finger across his forehead. "Nearly bled to death."

"You sure he didn't die and get raised back to life?" I asked after we'd stepped off holy ground. If Uncle Ross ever told it his way, he'd probably be the heroic rescuer of them both.

"You're too skeptical for your own good."

We walked another two minutes to our regular fishing spot, next to a five-foot-diameter chestnut stump. Last summer I caught an eighteen-inch rainbow trout there, so we deemed it our lucky—or rather providential—spot, despite often walking away empty-handed.

On these days our world was the stream in dazzling sun, a silvery sequined snake that wound and swished its way around rocks with gurgling hisses. Above us ruled a sky of many blues, depending on its mood: cornflower, steel, azure, melancholy, pastel, or a mixed palette of violet and white wisps that gradually distilled into diamond stars and a pearl moon at dusk. That day it was periwinkle.

When we settled down, Dad pointed to the mountainside. "That's where we raced hogs to the mast before breakfast every autumn morning." Mast was the chestnuts and acorns that had fallen from the trees. "If we beat them there, we could get enough to sell in town." He proceeded with a tale about one particular incident, then tugged on his pole. "Those confounded fish ought to be used to our voices by now." I giggled. We sacrificed many a fish dinner due to Dad's long-windedness.

I tried to situate my pole between two rocky protrusions so it wouldn't flip off the bank.

"It's a bit strenuous holding a fishing pole for all of thirty minutes."

"My hands hurt from yesterday's batting practice."

Dad asked how baseball season was going, prompting

my complaint about getting teased for being a girl.

He laughed as rich as the smell of Mom's coffee. "There's always a trade-off, Tina." One of the invaluable quotes from his mental filing cabinet with lines for every occasion.

I grumbled about Stan Randall driving me crazy with smart aleck remarks and insults regarding my throwing ability. Nick was so embarrassed about my bad aim that he forced me to play catch with him after chores. As if pulling another quote from a drawer, Dad said, "It takes a sense of humor to survive in this world. Otherwise, you might as well curl up and hibernate."

We exhausted that topic, having condensed it to a "grin and bear it" lesson. I leaned against a rock. "Dad, why didn't you want Uncle Ross to talk about boot camp?" I wondered if he'd dismiss my question the way one might shoo a fly.

"Boot camp wasn't such a good time for me, Tina."

"What happened?"

"Nothing your little ears are ever gonna hear from me."

He cast his line. As I watched it fly, I felt part of my father go with it, into deeper waters where I wasn't invited.

"How can you and Mr. Kepler be good friends even though you disagree about the park?"

"How come Nick and Todd are good friends even though they don't agree about Denny McLain and the World Series? See, years ago Phil helped me land my first job in New York, sorta took me under his wing. My gratitude to him runs deeper than differences of opinion, even if we have to duke it out in town council."

"Duke it out?" A picture of a ring and boxing gloves popped into my head.

"Discuss. Pass words."

"Fight. Yell. Scream."

He smiled. "I think we'll discuss things peaceably enough."

"Did Mr. Kepler know your first wife?"

Dad squinted toward the water. "Yes."

"Was she like Mom?" I'd always wondered.

He fidgeted and gazed beyond the river. "In some ways. Sonia was a good cook, like your mom. She was compassionate, too, like Mom. But your mother's more . . . independent. With a great sense of humor."

"Do you miss . . . Sonia . . . sometimes?" There, I'd said that word. A word to which I could attach no image or feeling because I never wanted to picture Dad with anyone but Mom, no matter how long ago.

Dad fiddled with his fishing lures, probably hating my efforts to pry open a closed book of fifteen years that he'd never re-opened. "Tina, there's always gonna be a part of you that misses people you've lost. That's how our hearts are made. Holes don't get patched up, but new parts are added on, like pockets, filled as full as they can be."

He faced me. "Missing someone else doesn't take away my love for your mother, you, or Nick. Your mother means the world to me. I love her, more every day. Are you concerned about that, Tina?"

"No, I just wondered . . . about her." If she were still alive, Dad wouldn't be married to Mom and I would never have been born.

Suddenly I wanted to be whisked away from everything, from what ifs, from Dad's sadness about his memories, from Stan, Nick, and other boys who knew how to turn the wonderful game of baseball into a miserable chore equal to carrying out the garbage. I shut them out, imagining myself in a flowing gown at a grand ballroom dance on the floor of the mountain meadow across the stream. I asked Dad to escort me there. No fish were biting anyhow.

We left our fishing gear and crossed on stones at a narrow part of the stream. Hand in hand, we walked into a ballroom decorated with Catawba rhododendrons in purplish-rose hues. The weeping cherry became a southern belle in a sweeping hoop skirt, perfumed with violet. Sweet birches and red spruces bowed and swayed to a symphony of mockingbirds, breezes, and a gurgling stream.

Nature seemed to have her hold on us, as usual, yet inspired such affinity with her that to this day, I don't know whether she determined our moods, or we determined hers.

CHAPTER 8

Our three hogs fretfully tried to out-grunt each other. Seems they could sense when Mom was fixing pork stew.

Their distress gave me an excuse to abandon the garden where Mom had left me weeding and picking beans. At the hog pen, I offered my best smooth talking to calm them down, squelching images of pork chops and mashed potatoes. I loved naming the animals--such as our sow Henrietta--but when Dad beat me to it and named them Ham, Bacon, and Sausage, I knew not to get too attached.

Next I fed the chickens, a dozen Plymouth Rocks, Rhode Island Reds, and leghorns. I only named a few dependable egg layers that I trusted wouldn't end up on my dinner plate. The leghorns Florence, Matilda, and Bertha waddled over, squawking. The rest followed with their appetites and pecked at chicken scratch like kids bobbing for apples.

I surveyed the garden and yard--the corncrib, potato hole, springhouse, and smokehouse. Everything screamed chores at me.

Beyond were fields of wheat, corn, sweet potatoes, cane for cane syrup, a potato patch, and apple trees. A thicket of berry bushes bordered the woods. Dad had long ago moved his tobacco patch to Uncle Ross's to keep it from us kids. We risked our lives if we went near Ross's tobacco leaves or the rafters where they hung to dry.

One little bridge over the river took us to Uncle Ross's near Grandma and Grandpa Hamilton's house. I went there often. When Grandma was pickling, I'd help. "If the signs are in the bowels, pickles'll be slimy and soft," she explained as emphatically as if quoting Scripture. "The new moon is for making kraut, and pickling beans, corn, or green tomatoes. Of course, it's ideal for any activity if the day falls on both an ideal sign and a good phase of the moon."

Grandpa sprinkled his conversation with unsolicited tidbits, advice he considered fact though many folks instructed to the contrary. "Don't plant till the moon gets full," he warned. "Don't plant on the new moon 'cause it'll grow high and won't make as much."

Grandma and Grandpa were appalled at the space race and the government's goal to put a man on the moon. For years they scoffed, but as reality closed in, disapproval and fear overtook. "Men can't go meddling with the moon," Grandpa said. "They'll offset the cycles, throw off the natural order of things."

Grandma once shook her finger at me as if I were the one launching rockets. "Some folks dismiss the cycles altogether. They plant beans and peppers when they please, and get away with it. But nobody gets away with meddling with the moon. That's borrowing trouble for certain. Nothing will ever be the same."

"Tina!" Mom called from the back porch, pointing at a slew of hanging rugs. "Those rugs needs beating."

I hadn't finished the bean picking. "I'm tuckered out from working all morning."

She waved me to the porch. I sauntered over, in no hurry.

"Sit in the shade a spell. It's high time you try your hand at sewing again."

I cringed as she handed me a needle, thread, and thimble.

"Don't Grandma's quilts inspire you to learn?"

Grandma's handiwork inspired me to nobler causes: the appreciation of fine art, not to the sweat of my own brow and the frustration of doing a task my fingers weren't shaped to do.

Ornery, I refused the thimble and poked myself several times. "Ouch!" I shook my finger, blood trickling.

Mom held out the thimble. "Put it on."

Wanting to avoid Mom's famous martyr lines, I plunged material to the porch floor, announced my resolution to never touch needles again, and flew down the front porch steps, across the yard past waiting chores. I fled for protection across the bridge at Uncle Ross's.

He was at the sawmill. When I dashed in, his eyes lit up. "Hey, Tina. Help me muscle up this here timber."

I gathered a few pieces and followed him to a wood pile.

"I'm expecting to get to this timber today. The last of the winter logging, some leftover stands of pine and hickory."

I helped in silence till he took note. "Now what in the Sam Hill's the matter? You's a-pouting so big I could perch a rooster on that lip."

"Got so much work to do. Feed the chickens, pick beans, beat the rugs, mend clothes. And that's just the start."

"Child labor laws in this here region ain't as strict as they should be, eh?"

"Then Dad tells me to move wood piles across the barn. Can you muscle 'em up with me, Uncle Ross?"

Ross blasted a laugh to Mount Mitchell. He paused with logs in midair and looked at me as if I'd just asked him to pick up the state of North Carolina. "No, siree. Why, I do more work by accident than you ever do on purpose."

I was indignant. "That ain't true. Why, the other day I spent half the afternoon painting that old table in the barn. And Dad wasn't pleased."

"What was wrong with it?"

I followed him to the corner. "He says I didn't finish the job, that I never looked behind it to see if the rest needed paint."

Ross set down the logs. "Well, you tell your daddy that a brave soldier never looks behind."

We went down the rocky bank from the mill door to the river's edge. After he inquired about baseball season, I asked, "Why'd you stop going to church?"

He cocked his head. "That question warrants a serious answer. Let's sit a spell." We sat on rocks. "What happens is that folks meet God, then start making their own rules, things not taught in the Bible. If you don't do everything their way, they're ready to whisk you off to hell."

"But ain't it wrong not to go? Grandma seems mighty upset about your being unchurched."

"Folks can't save their souls by going to church, Tina. Only the grace of God does that. Maybe someday I'll step foot back into church again. Your daddy will be right pleased about that." He winked. "But right now, I get along better with folks that don't go to church than those that do. Church people like to play judge, and care more appearances."

I drank in what he said, like the sawmill drinking in water for power, then surveyed the wood. "All this gonna be for that park of Mr. Kepler's?"

"Maybe. He wants some, but can't do nothing yet till they decide to build the park."

"I don't confidence him much. He ain't honest," I said, repeating gossip.

"Now listen here. No niece of mine gets by saying something as sassy as that. You can't judge a man without proof. Even with proof you have to be mighty careful." He gestured to the sky. "Only God can be trusted with full knowledge of a human being and still love him. He don't give us full knowledge, and without it we can't rightly judge anyone at all. Understand?"

I shook my head.

"Let's put it this way. In grade school, I had a teacher I didn't favor much. She didn't know how to handle us. We was always playing pranks, making her feel foolish. She had good

68

teaching skills, from what the townsfolk said, but she didn't never have a chance to prove it with us. Downright interfered with my learning."

"Mrs. Reynolds?" She was older than the hills.

He nodded. "The one with the Olyve Oil legs and the Fred Flintstone face, to put it in terms you can see for yourself."

One time at dinner, Dad told the story of Mrs. Reynolds writing on the chalkboard. Every time she faced the board, the boys with their desks inched to the front in barely noticeable increments until by the end of the lesson they'd nearly pinned her to the wall. Dad told the story with visual aids. He'd use salt and pepper shakers and cups to show the finesse of their movement.

Ross continued. "Though I'm proud of thinking up the ideas, I ain't proud of what we did. She was with us two years. That second year I was fixing to go into sixth grade. I'd made me a resolution I wasn't gonna partake in foolish notions no more. I was gonna study and listen and mind the teacher. I'd plumb outgrew that addlepated hogwash, and wanted to start over. Well, the first day of school, Rich Macy let a snake loose during class. He put the snake box on my desk. When the teacher saw it—knowing me from the year before, mind you—she lit into scolding me and sent me to the corner. She told my folks and I got a flogging to the moon and back."

"No one believed you didn't do it?"

"Nope. Nobody. They knew what I was like before. It's enough to make a fellow wanna give up the straight and narrow life altogether. If I's gonna get punished for pranks, I might as well be doing them myself and enjoying it to boot."

"So did you go back to pulling pranks?"

"No, but that weren't the last one I was accused of. And it downright hurt. I changed but nobody owned up to it. So even when we think we know someone, we really don't."

"But aren't you judging church folks the same way you don't like them judging others?"

"I reckon none of us can completely avoid judging. But over the years I've seen a passel of church folk act that way. I don't like what I see."

"You think Mom and Dad are those kind of church folk?" Dad was a deacon.

"Your daddy don't fit into any man's mold." Ross snickered, sounding like Dad. "Your daddy couldn't be a hypocrite if he tried."

"Maybe church is a bad influence and I should quit." I hoped for support and someone to blame for my pending abstinence.

"You do and I'll tan your hide, because your dad'll tan mine for telling you all this. I can't keep my mouth shut like he can. Believe me, Tina, your daddy's a wise man. It wonders me how he stays in the church, but he don't make you do nothing that's not good for you."

I wasn't convinced. "So if working for Mr. Kepler ain't a bad thing, why haven't you told Grandma and Grandpa Hamilton about it?" Surely I had him cornered.

"'Cause your grammy would take to whooping me and I'm too old to lay across her knee. God bless her unenlightened soul, but you could talk the legs off a black iron pot before you could convince her there's a mite of good in Phil Kepler, or in change."

"Dad's trying to get folks to vote against the park and you're for it. You're even gonna work for Mr. Kepler. I thought you and Dad were friends."

Ross set a hand on my shoulder. "Your daddy and I are two peas in a pod, always will be. That don't mean we always see eye to eye. And whatever I owe to anybody, I owe to God, my wife, and my children."

"What do you mean?"

"I mean, when I make a decision, it's them what better benefit the most. All's the townsfolk do is argue over that park and the principle of it. But I don't care about all that as long as I can make money to send my young-uns to college for book-learning."

Ross seemed to study the river. "For farmers, there ain't a whole lot left over once you bread and meat your family. Ain't nary a man happy in this world if he gets all he wants but can't live to see his children happy. They got dreams. And ain't nary a way to help them, unless I get this job with the park."

Another question plagued me. "Dad was upset hearing your talk about Army days. What all did happen back then?"

"I surely ran off at the mouth. Plumb forgot about your dad. He don't like no reminders of his Army time. He had mean tricks pulled on him. Pure deviltry. Some folks just don't like us southerners. And you won't get more out of me, 'cause it ain't fittin' for the likes of you."

"Did you have a bad time of it, too?"

"That was a few years before Drew went in. But I was bigger and mouthier. I fought back. Your pa was too peace-loving and quiet. If you ain't gonna stand up to folks, you get it worse."

I couldn't picture it. Dad was still peace-loving, but definitely not a wallflower.

"Men who were supposed to be comrades acted like the enemy. Your daddy was a short, skinny kid who talked different, barely out of high school, and didn't know the ways of the world. It was more than he could take."

"Why didn't he just up and quit?"

Ross looked over the fields. "The Army don't let anyone just up and quit, Tina. Even so, he's no quitter. He was quiet, but stubborn. Man, is he stubborn. No one's gonna get the better of him. All's I know is he didn't want to call this place home anymore. He grew ashamed of who he was, his home and culture. That's gotta be part of why he didn't come back here for such a long time. A powerful long time."

No more could be said, for now we treaded on sacred ground.

PART II

Uncle Eddie: Giants and Moonshine. "You can believe what you wanna believe. You can ignore what you wanna ignore. But it don't change the facts one bit."

———————————

Dad and the uncles rivaled each other's stories: Great-uncle Charles with his mastery of regional folklore, Jack tales, and Grandfather tales; Uncle Parker's yarns of logging with horses in a camp of 140 men in the early 1950s and logging with helicopters in the '60s; Dad's bear hunting escapades; and Uncle Ross's barnstorming adventures in the late '30s. He'd learned to fly in the service, courtesy of the United States Government.

Grandma Hamilton wrung her hands at them all. "I'd like to believe you were lying about those adventures. Defying bears and gravity like that. I should have worried more about you-uns back then."

"Well, Ma, it's half lies, to be sure." Dad nodded toward Ross. "He's so full of canal water that tugboats come out of his ears at night when he's sleeping."

Aunt Abby laughed. "You'll never know whether he's lying or not. Every time he tells that story it's different."

"Well, I ain't never lied," Uncle Eddie said. "Never lied excusing once in my whole life, and nobody here knows when."

"Oh, sure, Ed," Uncle Ken said.

"Believe it," Ross said. "I'll vouch for him. This boy don't have a rebellious bone in his body. I can't understand that one bit."

Eddie straightened. "You can believe what you wanna believe. You can ignore what you wanna ignore. But that don't change the facts one bit, so what the Sam Hill good does it do to lie? Like my buddy Red and his ideas about giants."

"Reckon I'd rather not hear this story." Grandma Hamilton's fingers repeatedly locked and unlocked, as if making up for all those times she didn't worry enough.

"When did you lie, Uncle Eddie?" my cousin Brian asked.

"It's high time I tell you all and get it off my chest. But Ma'll have to pick up her jaw when I'm done. I was ten. My best buddy and cohort was Red Forbes. That's his nickname. Earned it when he was caught red-handed stealing watermelons from Gilmore Duncan's field. Red never did tell the truth, but one person believed him anyhow. That was me. That's why we stuck as close as a cocklebur on sheep's wool."

"I never did trust that boy," Grandma said.

"This man, Old Man Abbot, lived yonder in the field behind town. Some folks called him wicked, but everyone agreed he was lazy. His wife toiled away in the garden, and carded wool almost straight from the sheep. While the floorboards were a-rotting and the field grass a-growing, he'd set and rock on the front porch all the livelong day, nursing a jug of corn whiskey.

"He never lifted a finger but to lift that jug to his lips. He and the devil drank out of the same jug, they said, and he weren't ashamed of it. Why, he weren't even ashamed of not being ashamed. Reckon that's about as low as a man can go. His wife let half the county in on her woes. He was so lazy, if he even got up and considered working that day, he rewarded himself with a half pint of homegrown corn whiskey and promptly went to napping on the front porch. The tables were reversed in that family. She wore the britches, and he'd dispose of with a spoon faster than what she brought in with a shovel."

Eddie leaned forward as if getting to the heart of the story. "Well, one day, me and Red was stalking the woods looking for giants. We heard so many of them Jack tales that Red thought he himself was Jack. He was gonna whoop a giant like Jack did. We'd take off, hunting for giant tracks and signs, like a body looks for bear signs in hunting season. We'd listen to the ground for heavy footsteps, and investigated every beanstalk in the county. Red was for certain we'd find a giant there.

"One night we lit out, it was as dark as the inside of a cow's belly back in those woods. We heard strange noises. 'Shhh!' Red warns when we hear a noise what sounds like steam a-rising from a kettle. 'That's the giant's temper rising,' Red explains. 'Steam's spouting out of his big ears.'

"I didn't wanna chance on striking up with no giant, so I turned back, but he grabs my arm and says, 'You wanna make him madder?' so I stay put. Then we hear a loud tinkling sound like a cowbell echoing in a cavern. 'That's the dinner bell. The giant's wife is calling him in for dinner,' says Red."

Eddie's eyes widened and his face reddened, rivaling his hair and freckles. "I gulped, 'cause I knew what giants liked for dinner and I weren't prepared to be skinned alive. Then there was a chug-chugging, like a train coming 'round a bend. 'That's the giant's stomach growling. He ain't had a good human meal in a long time,' Red reckoned. I panicked. Then came a gurgling sound, like stream water. 'Either his wife's pouring his drink or he's washing his hands for dinner,' said Red. I didn't think a big, mean giant was gonna bother about washing his hands for dinner, but I said, 'Let's get out of here.' 'Are you kidding?' Red says. 'This is my chance of a lifetime. We gotta sneak up on him and lick him good.'

"So we crouched in the bushes and made our way toward the steaming and the tinkling and the chugging and the gurgling, and when we heard a popping sound, Red explained it was the giant burping after his first course. We came closer, and it got noisier but we couldn't see nothing. The woods was so full of dark it filled our eyes plumb full."

Eddie's voice boomed and several of us jumped. "'What're you doing on my property?' someone yelled. We must have shot three feet in the air. As it was so dark, all we could make out hovering over us was a bulky shape of a man, with a long, thin rod sticking out of his shoulder blade— figured it to be a rifle-gun.

"This time Red was a-quaking as well. The giant was larger than the tallest man we knew. We couldn't see his face but I sensed it was ugly as sin and not half as pleasant. 'What're you all doing on my property?' came the voice again, as fittin' a voice for a giant if I ever heard one. That gun bounced up and down on his shoulder, like nothing would pleasure that giant more than using it to make dinner out of us.

"Those same noises started up, the steaming and the tinkling and the chugging and the gurgling, and it wasn't that old giant 'cause he was standing right there. Then this pungent smell of corn whiskey wafted over, no mistaking that. In the starlight I saw fear leap out of Red's eyes in a moment of weakness. He pulls himself together and says, 'You ain't no giant. You're Old Man Abbot and that's a still you got running!'

"Well, now we were borrowing trouble for certain. I squeezed my eyes shut, waiting for that man to light into us. Instead he asked if we wanna see a still with our own eyes. Of course we said yes.

"So he takes us back into this cave-like place where he made old time double still corn liquor out of corn, malt, and dry rye. Makes twelve gallons of good moonshine. He kindly offers us a taste of his fresh batch of brew, and we jump at the chance. He gives us a tablespoon of that corn liquor straight from the vat, then tells us to skedaddle out of there and if we ever tell a soul, he'll haunt us."

Eddie puckered his lips and crossed his eyes. "We hardly made it home. That whiskey turned our eyes green and our insides out. We were taken down sick with fever for two days, so as we couldn't breathe a word even if we wanted to. That suited Old Man Abbot just fine, 'cause in two days he had his whole moonshining operation moved. I was so scared and sick I never woulda told a soul even if he hadn't moved it. I figured I'd been drunk on just one tablespoon of corn whiskey."

He glanced at his mother who sat spellbound.

"So when Ma asks how's come I got so took down, did I eat or drink something bad? I didn't have the heart to say that her son got drunk, though by accident. It would have broke her Bible-believing heart to think her ten-year-old son was a drunkard. So I told her I ate some green apples and she coddled me till I was plumb vigorous and it all worked out."

"Did Old Man Abbot get caught?" cousin Tommy asked.

"No, he kept many a man in the county supplied for years, surely raking in hundreds of dollars from night hours of brewing. Would it have been worth breaking my ma's heart in order to put him out of business? You decide that for yourself. But it didn't wonder us anymore why he never lifted a finger to work, though he didn't spend money fixing up his place. Red reckoned that after he licked his giant someday, he'd operate a still of his own."

Grandma wrung her hands again. "I should have worried more about you back then."

"Ma, all your worrying is enough to cover five families and ten generations," Ross said.

"I couldn't tell you-uns what happened," Eddie said, "'cause I remembered how Daddy plumb wore Drew out when he came home drunk once in high school."

"That was the last time that happened," Dad said.

"What—a flogging or getting drunk?" Mom asked.

"Both."

"All moonshiners ain't crooks like that," Grandpa explained to us kids. "Now, in fact, they're more commercial, but back then they were just trying to bread and meat their families. Sometimes that corn liquor was quality stuff, not that junk of Old Man Abbot's. Though it's all a mite strong for young-uns."

"Just like the truth was a mite strong for Ma at the time," Eddie said.

"So you give it to me in a later dose," Grandma said. "You were just saving your own skin. Break my Bible-believing heart, nothing. More than likely it saved the palm of my hand from the calluses I would have got from tanning your hide."

CHAPTER 9

Old Lady Balch took the nickel Todd entrusted to me. Nick and I needed a good excuse to visit her so we asked Todd if we could get him a sprig of tobacco. The old lady grew her own. Nick still claimed to chew nothing but the manufactured stuff.

She closed bony fingers over the nickel, her gesture stuck in midair as if in a film that suddenly quit. She dropped the nickel into a coin jar.

She was forever giving us advice and cures. When I had warts, she told me to rub a grain over them and feed that grain to a chicken. Another cure involved greasing warts with stolen bacon, then hiding it. She also had me tie up as many stones as I had warts in a rag and leave them in the road. When someone picked them up, the warts would go away. Well, no one picked up the bag of stones for two weeks, and Mom was confounded about the disappearance of her dishcloths and bacon. The warts went away each time though, so I deemed the remedies valid.

Nick was convinced she was a witch. Mom and Dad said she was a harmless, lonely woman, but we never told them things she said that might make them think otherwise. Nick carried a red pepper in his pocket to prevent her conjuring and slept with a silver dollar under his pillow on nights after visiting her.

"Sit for a spell." Her spindly arm directed us to stools, her motion barely coinciding with her words, like out-of-sync speech in a foreign movie. She picked up her mop, a burlap sack tied to a pole, and poised awkwardly as if waiting for someone to press a button for her to move again. When she did, she pushed the mop and rearranged the dirt. Satisfied, she set the mop back and sat across from us.

She shared an eerie tale that took place in the mountains behind her cabin. "I wouldn't advise going back by way of Coulder Pass, not tonight. Too close to the full moon."

Though her tone chilled me, I made considerable effort to mask my alarm. After all, it was barely dusk and the full moon was five days away.

"What happens on the pass at full moon?" Nick asked. Surely he planned to walk back that way, feeling safe with the red pepper in his pocket.

"You ain't never seen him?" Her eyes widened.

"Who?" we chorused, mirroring her eyes.

Her voice fell to a hoarse whisper. "The Negro. With the rifle-gun."

"Does he hurt folks?" Nick asked.

"I'd rather meet a bear what ain't eaten in months." She went to the window, studied the view as if she could see through the brush, then closed the shutters. "He don't tolerate nobody cavorting around these parts. He reckons them his. Why, one time a white man come up from town to go bear hunting and the townsfolk never saw the man again. It weren't because of no bear, I promise you. I seen the Negro many a time, a ways off, but he don't never see me. Bewitching powers, you know. But you two ain't got no bewitching powers. I don't recommend you to go down the pass."

"The pass is his property?" I shuddered thinking of how many times we'd gone that way.

"Don't matter whether it's rightly his or not. Under the full moon he stalks about the pass because that's where he lost his dog. A white man shot the Old Negro's dog. Since then the Negro don't hesitate to shoot white men. The whiter the better."

I suddenly resented my parents for passing their genes on to me. Nick was as white as I was, and we were both the paler from hearing that story.

Nick fidgeted. "Reckon we should get going. Dad expects us before dark."

Old Lady Balch moved toward the window, hesitated, then went forward. "You'd best go by way of Sandy Gulch. Out of your way, perhaps, but better coward than corpse, they say."

Nick and I exchanged frantic glances. He grabbed my arm and we charged out. Surely he was scared out of his britches.

We wound down the path toward Sandy Gulch. "All slack talk, you think?" I asked, heart hammering.

"It ain't the first time I heard about the Negro with the rifle-gun. They jaw about it in town."

"Yeah, but I ain't believing it."

He sneered. "Okay, Lady Jane, you wanna go down the pass?"

"Maybe after next full moon." I'd feel a whole lot better dying after baseball season.

"Come on, you're too poky."

"Then help carry these rocks." My pockets bulged with rocks we'd gathered before arriving at Old Lady Balch's. Cue Ball had promised to buy Nick's rock collection so Nick would have enough for a new glove.

Why Cue Ball preferred to buy from Nick rather than traipse up there for free rocks was a mystery. Unless he was frightened off by tales about the Negro. On second thought, maybe Cue Ball was smarter than we were.

A snarling noise in the brush stopped us short. A small snout and forelegs poked from the thicket—a hog.

Nick's protective instincts rose to the fore. His arm slung into my chest to shield me. Little good that would do with a wild boar.

But this looked like a domestic pig turned loose. "He won't hurt us, Nick."

"But he ain't got no sign, no tag or anything. They ain't supposed to let hogs run wild."

"He's young. And tame. Somebody feeds him by hand every week." I walked around Nick's arm barricade, still stuck straight out. "Don't worry. I know how to gentle him." I dug past rocks in my pocket, found Life Savers, and held one out. "It's okay, piggy. We're friends."

The pig stepped forward. His snout nuzzled my hand and ate the candy. Running pigs loose was illegal, but some folks did and lured them back in the fall with sweets. "Now who do you belong to?" I asked the hog as if he'd reply. I checked his ears for a tag or clip. Leaves rustled behind me, probably Nick looking for nuts to feed the pig. "We should take him down the mountain. Probably escaped from the MacNeills." Barry MacNeill would likely have a pig he never got around to clipping and didn't notice was gone.

A deep, coarse voice blasted behind me. "What's your plans with my hog, missy?"

Still on my knees, I swiveled. Through the veil of dusk came a big white shirt, a big black face, and a big long rifle. I couldn't breathe. Manners escaped me, replaced by suffocating fear and the desire for flight.

"I asked you a question, missy. Where you be toting my hog off to?" He prodded the butt of the gun into my shoulder blade.

I found my straggly voice. "I . . . I thought it escaped from down the mountain."

"Anyone can see there ain't no sign on it."

The gun's warm wood pressed harder.

"We ain't allowed to let our hogs run anywhere but on our own land—"

"This *is* my land," he boomed. "I let things run free as I see fit."

"Yes, sir."

"That your brother?" He nodded toward Nick without taking his eyes off me.

Nick stood as stiff as the General Burns statue in Burnsville's Town Square.

"Yes, sir."

"You all come with me," he grunted. I got off my
knees with a boost from the gun and it led me up a narrow path,
Nick beside me.

So much for baseball season.

We soon found ourselves inside a cabin no bigger than
my bedroom. He made us sit on two stools. The only other
furniture was a cot, table, and cupboard. As he rummaged
through the cupboard, I surveyed the room. On the wall, tins
and jars were stacked on shelves. A battered towel, a flannel
shirt, and overalls hung over a horizontal poplar pole by the
wood stove. A sardine can nailed to the wall served as a soap
dish. Canned tomatoes and beans lined up under the cot. One
corner housed an onion pile, ax, walking stick, kerosene lamp,
and bucket and dipper. The door pull was the crook of a laurel
branch and a spool of thread. One window was blocked by the
big black Negro who seemed to be growing bigger and blacker
by the second as dusk slowly gave way to night, just like Old
Lady Balch warned.

"Now what y'all be doing on my parts?" His glare
fastened on Nick, then me. He held the gun like a cane.

For once, my mouth was incapable of forming words.

"We didn't know it was your parts, sir," Nick said.
"We swear we'll never trespass again."

The man chuckled, the gun barrel twitching with each
breath. Then his teeth disappeared into a black hole. "Anyone
that trespasses on my property makes it up to me."

"We got rocks of yours," I said. We stood to empty our
pockets, Nick apologizing profusely. Pockets empty, rocks and
Life Savers piled on the floor, we waited for absolution.

He frowned upon our rocks as if we'd dumped a barrel
of dirt. "Sit down!"

We were seated before the words left his mouth.

"See that there leaf on the branch?" He opened the
screen-less window, leaves barely visible in the dusk. He lifted
his gun and hit a leaf in one well-aimed shot. The blast rippled

through the air and thudded my chest like a gong.

Nick dripped with sweat. "We'll make it up to you, sir. We'll bring you more rocks. We'll bring you Life Savers. We'll bring anything you want."

"Hush," he said. "There ain't nothing I need. Everything I want is right here."

I scanned the cabin interior again in case I'd missed something.

Nick babbled, suffering from my own malady. "Sir, I'll give you anything you want to make up for taking your rocks. Anything if you let me and my sister go home safely now."

"Anything?"

"Anything."

The Negro fiddled with the door latch, locking us in. I went numb. He lit the lantern and sat across from us on the cot. "Now, now." His teeth formed the shape of a crescent moon as he gave what one might technically term a smile. "Don't be so hasty making deals you'll be regretting to keep for the rest of your lives. Y'all are too young to be selling your souls to me for such a small price. Then you're no better than the jaybird, see."

We nodded.

"When the bait's worth more than the fish, 'tis time to stop fishing, they say."

I'd no clue what he meant.

"Y'all know about the jaybird, don'tcha?" We sat frozen. "Don't ring a bell, eh? There's good reason you never see a jaybird on Friday, see. Long ago the jaybirds sold theirselves to the devil for nothing but an ear of corn. Imagine that! And they pay for it now. They're obliged to take sticks and sand to the devil every Friday to make his fire hot. You never see a jaybird on Friday 'cause they're so busy toting wood to hell and telling about all the meanness and bad deeds on earth that week. And that ole devil, he stokes the fire hotter and hotter."

That fire couldn't be too far away since sweat was

dampening my shirt and dripping off my nose.

"So it never needs to wonder you why them jaybirds are so sassy. They got good reason. Does it remind you of someone else?"

Absolutely not.

"Esau. Ah, yes, he sold his birthright for nothing but a bowl of stew, and regretted it ever since. A big bowl of stew, that's a-tempting, I tell you. Don't get much stew up here. I ain't the best cook in the world, but I make do, that's for certain. When there's a bad spell, scraping the bottom of the meal bin is mighty poor music." He pointed out the wooden bin on the tabletop. "Now don't your ma and pa be wondering where y'all are right now, trespassing all over the mountainside?"

My parents had no idea, but that was better left unsaid.

"What are your names?" He fidgeted with his gun.

"N-Nick, sir. This here is Tina."

"What's the rest of it?"

"Nicholas Calvin Knox Hamilton and Christina Ross Hamilton." Nick let out a huge breath, like a collapsing balloon.

The Negro looked up. His eyes changed—a glint, a light. Perhaps a twinkle masquerading as a twitch. He tinkered with the gun again. "Hamilton, eh? There's a mighty heap of that clan in these parts. Which one are you?"

"Our dad's Andrew Hamilton, sir," Nick replied.

"Andrew Hamilton. Uh-huh. Ummm."

Nick drew another breath and risked a question. "Who are you?"

I cringed, fearing Nick had stepped over the edge, but the Negro clasped Nick's hand. "I'm Joseph Ethan Abraham Arthur Clemons. Had four uncles, they couldn't decide which one to name me after, so all four won out. But those what know me just call me Joe. Ole Joe."

He shook my hand, too. It disappeared in his warm grasp. Surely a man his size was equal to such a lengthy, distinguished name.

"Well, now, I recollect there's one man who has more than me." He revealed his crescent of a smile. "Barry MacNeill."

"You know him?" Nick asked.

"No, and don't plan to. But I seen his zucchini and yellow squash. He got hisself a right pretty patch, he does."

Only because neighbors tended it for him. Again, better left unsaid.

"The dinner bell's always in tune for me, 'specially with zucchini and squash." Joe scrutinized us. "Now then, I been studying what to do with you two."

Keeping my arms and legs from shaking was as futile as keeping chimes quiet in a tornado-infested wind.

"Now here's the deal. Y'all bring me one of those zucchini and yellow squash every week till autumn comes. Once a week, you hear? You'll be safe—" he leaned forward, tobacco wafting over— "long as you don't go telling nobody." As if we needed more incentive, he caressed the gun barrel with a cloth until it shined in the lantern light. "This here baby aimed straight and true for many a year. Stacked up eighty-four bears, thirty-seven foxes, a hundred and ninety-two possum . . . well, I don't need to go on, do I?"

We shook our heads fervently.

"I want something that's not been rooted more than a few hours, whole, straight from the MacNeill garden. The biggest, ripest one every week, nothing store-boughten. I'll know the difference. The kind I want can only be dug up in the dead of night, whole in the wheelbarrow. You harvest them in the same manner watermelon's supposed to be planted. Ideally in the dark of the moon, if it falls on that week, before sunrise. You crawl backward to the patch in your night clothes. Dig it out before you eat or speak, so insects won't destroy the food. And don't be telling nobody."

We agreed.

"Next Sunday night I want my first delivery. Leave it

at the chestnut stump on the south end of Coulder Pass. We got a secret, now, you-uns and me."

He picked up the rocks, tied them up in a piece of soiled cloth, and handed them to Nick. "You all remember that jaybird, you hear?" He undid the latch and we hightailed it home. We ran through Coulder Pass, Sandy Gulch, Strawberry Gap, and Hickory Notch so fast that my legs pounded the breath out of me.

CHAPTER 10

Small towns like Currie Hill don't exist without disadvantages. Especially if you're a kid growing up in the home of Drew Hamilton.

I sat on the porch swing, the radio beside me playing Glen Campbell, Johnny Cash, even newfangled Beatles' tunes. The purple martin gourd swayed from its front yard post over a lawn of crusted eggshell tidbits ignored by the birds. The porch railing leaned lazily near Mom's fruit trays drying under the sun.

Suddenly the radio music stopped. Dad appeared in the doorway holding the cord's plug. "Tina, did you hear me calling you?"

"No, sir."

"Did you hear me ask you to take out the garbage earlier?"

I glanced at him. "No, sir."

"Do you hear me now?"

I slid off the swing and took out the garbage.

When I returned, so did he. "Tina, I'm concerned about your hearing lately. Seems
you're missing out on a slew of opportunities."

"My hearing's fine, sir. Can you plug the radio back in?"

"Where'd you go after practice?"

"To the creek."

"What'd I tell you this morning before I left?"

I fidgeted with the volume knob, to no avail. "I don't know, sir."

"I asked you to help your ma with lunch fixings."
I groped feebly for an excuse. "I . . . um . . ."
"On top of disobeying, you're slower than molasses in January these days getting home for chores."
"I didn't hear you this morning."
Dad called into the kitchen. "Jennie, Tina and I will be back shortly. Hold lunch for us."
He grasped my small hand in his rugged farmer hand, pulled me up, and walked down the porch steps to his 1959 Chevy Apache truck. Mom looked helplessly out the window as I stared helplessly out the windshield, not an clue where we were going.
Soon, we stepped into Dr. Kirby's office. The tall doctor, sporting a kind smile, approached with a sprightly step and extended hand. "Good day, Drew. How can I help you?"
"My daughter has a hearing problem, Doc. I thought it would've mended by now, but she's constantly telling me she hasn't heard a thing I've asked her to do lately."
My face warmed, but I didn't flinch.
"Well, that is a predicament." The doctor produced a metal tool from his pocket and brushed hair from my ears. "What's your favorite ice cream at Simpson's?" he whispered as he fiddled with the tool.
"Peppermint."
Another whisper. "What's your favorite sundae?"
"Butterscotch."
The cold metal probed about my ear and perked my skin. Humming, he examined the other ear. His whisper lowered. "I hear tell you hit a home run this season."
"No, four, sir."
"Nice job." Barely audible, he asked, "Was that you they caught in Ross Hamilton's tobacco patch last week?"
"No, sir!"
Dr. Kirby removed the instrument and smoothed my hair down. "She's got excellent hearing. In fact, extremely sensitive ears. You shouldn't have any problem now."

"Thanks, Doc," Dad said. "Saves me a mighty heap of worry when it comes time to be marrying her off in a few years. What husband wants a wife that doesn't hear him?"

"Glad to put your mind at ease, Drew. My pleasure. No charge either."

We hopped in the truck and puttered down Main Street. At the intersection, Patsy Hutchins waved from the sidewalk. "Say, Tina, I hope you don't have the croup, like my grandson. Seems to be going around."

How many others saw me leaving the doctor's office? Face flaming, I managed a strained smile and prayed Dad wouldn't state the true nature of our trip to Doc Kirby's.

"No croup, Patsy," Dad said. "But Doc's nothing short of a miracle worker, yes siree."

We jerked forward and continued down the street toward home. Dad shook his head. "This town's got all the privacy of a goldfish in a bowl."

****

In midsummer I was destined to help Mom gather herbs and spices to dry, grind, and steep in teas. Besides strawberries for jam, we canned pailfuls of mulberries and huckleberries since she loved the sound of those two words.

Many kids in our town weren't forced into such hard labor, but Mom and Dad wanted us to learn the old ways. It led to painstaking, sweaty days on hands and knees in the garden, woods, or field, trying to gain appreciation for what our grandparents suffered through for a rejuvenating cup of sassafras tea.

Dad and Grandpa Hamilton showed us how to notch logs for building a cabin, and how to make a fiddle and banjo. I cooked ashcakes, baked pies, and crafted dried apple and cornhusk dolls with Grandma Hamilton, hooked and braided rugs with Grandma Dorothy.

For every skill our family couldn't teach, an expert in

town taught us.

Though Wally Abernathy, our team's sponsor, didn't make as many shoes anymore for customers outside his family, Dad struck a deal so Nick and I could each have a handmade pair, in exchange for a custom-made woodcarving. Wally demonstrated how to stretch and tan hides, cut patterns, and tie the parts together. Dad said he had one pair a year as a kid. If he wore it out, he went barefoot.

One evening Dad took us to Jim Drummond's blacksmith forge. Though the trade had vanished in many areas, Jim Drummond would never allow blacksmithing to die in Currie Hill. Nobody else did either. Word of mouth alone kept him in business, some from passing tourists. For the townspeople he repaired tools, made tractor parts, hinges, and latches. For tourists, he formed ornamental railings for their homes up north.

The smell of fire, coal smoke, and hot iron greeted us. Jim threw more wood on the fire, then showed us the miniature electric train. He and Dad owned it together. Dad designed it and Jim built most of it in the forge.

Alex Drummond, Jim's son and our teammate, joined us. The train chugged along the track. Watching it wind through the miniature landscape, I imagined God peering from behind the clouds, viewing His earth, proclaiming it good.

Like the train, the landscape and buildings had been designed to the smallest detail: a depot, general store, tunnel, plenty of trees, hills, and valleys, and a railroad bridge over a creek. The engine glistened, even whistled, manipulated by hand controls. As Jim and Dad ran it, I debated who looked like more of a child.

When Dad wearied from his bout with relived childhood, we entered the forge.

"What can I make for you-uns today?" Jim held a metal rod as if drawing his lifeblood from it. It guided restless fingers, flushed his cheeks, brightened vivid blue eyes.

"Ask for a leaf," Alex said. "He made a fancy leaf for

decoration for someone's house."

Nick and I agreed.

Jim held a rod to the fire while he and Dad chatted. We kids talked baseball until Alex asked me, "Is it true about you and Stan Randall?"

"Is what true?"

Nick piped in. "You mean about her hating his guts? That's for certain."

"It is?" Alex asked. "That's not what I heard."

I panicked. "What did you hear?" Last week, Ray Kamp threatened to tell Stan Randall I liked him unless I let him borrow my glove at practice, so I did. As far as I knew, Ray kept his end of the bargain.

Alex leaned in. "I hear tell Ray Kamp is informing everybody you like Stan Randall."

Fuming, I jolted to attention. "What in the Sam Hill?" What did Ray have against me? My feud was with Stan. "That's a big fat lie."

Alex was taken aback. "I wasn't aiming to upset you, Tina. I shouldn't have said anything."

"It's better you did. I don't want anyone thinking I like that big fat creep."

His dad called us over, the metal rod glistening red. Jim set it on the anvil and pounded away. He handed the hammer to his oldest son Joel, the apprentice. They stood on opposite sides while the elder communicated to the younger where to pound the rod by hitting the anvil from different directions and on different sides, like playing percussion in a jazz band I'd seen on television.

"The apprentice works on that side four years," Jim said. "Then four years on the other side, and two years in a specialty. Hear those tones? They come out different depending where on the anvil I'm drumming."

When they finished, Jim set the leaf aside to cool. "I'll give you this leaf after I give you all a sermon you ain't gonna hear in church." He lifted another iron rod. "Revelation says,

'He will rule with a rod of iron.' There's a mighty heap of similarity between Christ and iron, so it shouldn't wonder you why that rod for ruling the eternal kingdom is made from iron. For one thing, iron don't mingle with any other metal, it don't break down. It's always in its pure form, like Christ." His fingers glided across the rod. "The atoms run in a straight line, never crooked, like Christ's rule is without blemish and corruption. Perfect, in fact. Another thing, other metals are attracted to it, but iron isn't drawn to other metals. If one has enough iron in the body, it builds resistance to disease. Like having Jesus in the soul. We need Him in order to be free from the disease of sin, to have peace with God."

Jim handed Nick the leaf. Nick let me touch it, still warm from the fire, perfectly formed. It symbolized the dedication of every craftsman to his work. Every blacksmith, every leathersmith, every carpenter, sculptor, quilter, or weaver. Whether their hands formed leaves from rods of iron, shoes from hunks of leather, chairs from branches, quilts from fabric scraps—whoever held their creations held a part of the artist who fashioned them.

On our way out, Jim reminded Dad, "We're all counting on you for the upcoming vote."

Alex pulled me aside. "Don't you worry, Tina. I'll see those rumors get put to rest."

Outside Nick said, "We got our sermon for the week. Can we can stay home Sunday morning?"

Dad chuckled. "Only if the hogs whistle Dixie."

92

CHAPTER 11

I killed those rumors myself next time I saw Stan Randall at the sandlot. I casually mentioned that, in case he'd heard the rumor, it was nothing but a big, fat lie.

"Thank goodness," he said. "I'll quit bothering you for good if you bring me one of your Uncle Ross's boots for a peace offering."

"You should give *me* a peace offering. What do you want his boot for?"

"None of your business. Just bring it and I won't bug you no more. But if you tell him or any other grown-up, you'll never hear the end of me."

How was I going to steal one of Ross's boots without him knowing?

Providence was on my side. Two nights later, the uncles came to play cards. After tag and Capture the Flag with cousins, I paraded around the table, absently looking at everyone's hand.

"Don't you be peeping at our cards unless you're on my side." Uncle Eddie pulled me to his lap. "We're trying to figure out how your daddy and Uncle Ross cheat. It's high time we put an end to this bafflement."

"That's half the fun," Uncle Parker, Mom's brother, said. "Once we figure it out, there won't be no point in playing." Parker's scraggly beard topped his tall, gangly body.

Dad was as honest as the day was long. The only thing he'd cheat on was cards. It would have been dishonest not to cheat, since everyone expected it.

Soon I scrambled down and played with Paprika.

Across the room, Mom, Aunt Elaine, Aunt Abby, and Aunt Sheila chatted over their needlework.

When Dad dropped a card to the floor, I expected him to bend over to retrieve it, but he didn't. I ducked under the table to get it. But the card rested under his foot—curiously enough, his shoeless foot.

He pushed the card toward the only other shoeless foot—Uncle Ross. Ross expertly picked it up between two toes, lifted it to his opposite knee, and snatched it with his hand. So this was how they'd won all these years! While the others scrutinized for the sleight of hand, Dad and Uncle Ross got away with the blatant.

I refrained from giggling. Another card dropped, from Ross now, but I nabbed it before Dad's foot claimed it. I also seized Ross's lone boot.

I awaited the right moment to exit. Kids moseyed inside, accompanied by laughter, chatter, and barking. While tussling with Paprika, I discreetly took Ross's boot and hid it outdoors in the chicken coop. Fear of consequences escaped me, now that I'd survived the worst under the threat of a gun barrel.

Dad and Ross lost that game, deemed a misdeal due to the missing card. After hooting and hollering about Dad's and Ross's cheating getting them nowhere, they embarked on another game with a new deck.

While playing with the kids, I noted more dropped cards, and kept the secret with pride.

Next game, Dad and Ross won. Parker popped up. "I've got it!" He gave a long explanation of subtle trickery involving eye and facial movement that hinted at the contents of each other's hands, like baseball signals. I wanted to blurt out the secret but bravely held onto it.

Later, when everyone but Eddie and Ross left, Ross complained about his missing boot, blaming the dog. Dad recruited Nick and me to find the boot. We searched the house before retiring to bed, while Eddie and Ross lingered downstairs. The stolen boot would be safe tonight, neatly delivered in a bag to Stan Randall tomorrow.

Eddie sneaked up to our rooms, playing "ghost" again. My head was so full of wild pigs and guns, he nearly scared me to tears. But we couldn't tell him why we were so jumpy. We had to plan our first zucchini and squash escapade, which we started doing when they left, barefooted Ross carrying a boot.

An hour later, still wide awake, I inhaled the night air so as to hypnotize myself to sleep. Two more nights would find Nick and me in the MacNeills' garden rousting up vegetables, praying not to get caught. The dilemma of stealing weighed less on me than concern for my own life at the mercy of Joe and his gun.

As I stood at the window, movement caught my eye. A man's silhouette plodded toward the MacNeills' barn, the same tall, broad shape as before, a gun or tool resting on his shoulder. This time the motion seemed vaguely familiar, like out of a dream.

But it was no dream. It was from Coulder Pass, four nights ago. Ole Joe.

****

Dad was an enigma to me, never more evident than one afternoon running errands in Asheville.

We stopped for gas. Dad hopped out of the truck. He never sat while attendants filled the tank. Nick and I went to the candy counter, hoping Dad would notice our plight and offer a quarter or two. He did, so Nick and I agreed to share a Snickers bar. Nick split it and I got first choice.

Back outside, another car pulled up with an Illinois license. Its slickness dazzled compared to our dull, dirt-streaked 1959 Chevy Apache truck. Out of the car hopped a middle-aged couple—a man with a camera growing from his belly and a woman with a velvet smooth purse, apple red lips, and spidery lashes.

"Excuse me, sir." The woman approached my father. "Can you please tell me where to find some hillbillies?"

Dad stared at her, then developed a glint in his eye that worried me. In an exaggerated southern drawl, Dad asked, "Just why do you all wanna see hillbillies?"

"We're taking pictures to show our grandchildren, so they can see how other people live."

"Hmmm." Dad stroked his beard. "It's a crying shame your grandkids can't come see for themselves."

"So where can we find them?" the lady asked.

"Hillbillies, ma'am? You're looking at one. No, three."

The woman's eyebrows raised, then her face brightened. "No, a real hillbilly."

Dad looked insulted. He rotated clockwise as if part of a Miss America pageant, then slipped hands in his pockets. "Ma'am, it don't get no better than this."

The man interjected. "You don't talk much like a genuine hillbilly."

"Well, just how does a hillbilly talk, sir?"

"With more of an accent, and, uh, different ways of saying things, like Jed Clampett. Oh--you probably don't know him."

"Ah, the Beverly Hillbillies, of course."

"You have a TV?" The man's expression registered surprise.

"Me? Of course not. But I seen 'em on my cousin's telly-vision set from the east. A right tolerable show. Say, I know exactly what you're a-wanting." He pointed to himself in various gestures. "Overalls, mud on shoes. I never clean 'em, you know, except once a year whether they need it or not." He produced an object from his pocket. "A corncob pipe. Now don't that beat all. I'm plumb jiggered I left my moonshine jug on the porch, but I can do better. Come here, Jethro. Say hi to the nice man and lady from Illinois, wherever that is."

Nick walked to Dad, half confused but thoroughly enjoying the game. "Hallo, sir. Hallo, ma'am. Powerful glad to meet you."

"That's it," the woman said. "He talks just like one."

"This is genuine, ma'am, as sure as you were born. Real hill talk. Now this one has her grammar down pat." Dad squeezed my shoulder. "Greet our tourists, honey child. You all listen closely. Language directly descended from Shakespearean England. You've heard tell of Queen Elizabeth I, Sir Walter Raleigh, and the like? And Shakespeare himself for certain. It's all the same. Reckon you all weren't knowing to that." He quoted some Shakespeare, and added, "Now she might seem a mite shy to you all. She gets so embarrassed with strangers she turns as red as a bear's behind at pokeberry time."

"Howdy, ma'am," I said. "Howdy, sir."

"Of course, howdy ain't Shakespeare." Dad looked sheepish.

"Isn't she cute?" the woman said. "Honey, are you enjoying your candy bar?"

Dad grabbed my Snickers. "This? She never eats this stuff. Liza May, where in the Sam Hill did you get this?" He tossed it into the truck. "Strict diet of 'coon and 'possum and corn pone and chicken dumplings. Grits, too. Granny sakes alive, I don't know where she got the notion to eat a candy bar. It just ain't fittin.'" He winked at me. "What will the tourists think? They drive all this way—"

"May I take your picture?" The man lifted his camera.

Dad covered the lens with his hand. "Tsk, tsk. You didn't do your homework. Hillbillies have this superstition about having their pictures taken. You don't wanna bring bad luck on us, do you?"

"Where can we find more hillbillies?" the woman asked. "I want to see their houses, too."

Dad signaled Nick and me into the truck. He climbed in and started the engine. "In Mayberry, ma'am. Just a whoop and a holler from here. Take that road yonder into them mountains. Keep heading west past the sycamores apiece, then turn south. You're bound to see signs for Mayberry.

Incidentally, this ain't my truck. We walk everywhere. Average twenty miles a day if the mule's not broke down. This is my cousin's truck from Mayberry. Listen—" he turned up the car radio— "bluegrass. The only station we get. Remember the Darlings? Genuine hillbilly."

"The hillbillies—how far down the road before the turnoff?" the man asked as we rolled away. "Where are they all?"

"You all just happen to be here at the right season for hillbillies. Last winter you wouldn't have been able to find them any better than you can throw a cow by the tail. They're only here in the summer, you know. The rest of the year they're getting their degrees at the universities. Chapel Hill, Raleigh, Chicago, Boston, New York and the like."

On the road, Nick burst with laughter. "Why'd you do that?"

"Didn't wanna let those tourists down." Dad smirked. "I reckon keeping that park out of our town will help a heap in avoiding folks like that, bless their ignorant little souls."

"Are you angry?" I asked.

"Used to be. But if folks as simple-minded as that can live with themselves all their lives, I can surely tolerate them for all of five minutes."

CHAPTER 12

Five evenings after meeting Ole Joe, Nick and I reviewed his instructions for retrieving our first zucchini and yellow squash: before sunrise, in night clothes, crawl backward to the field, dig before eating or speaking, deliver it whole in a wheelbarrow. We concocted hand signals and determined the hows and wherefores to prevent slip-ups. After dark, we took Dad's wheelbarrow and shovel to Barry's garden because we had foresight to realize we couldn't crawl backward and push a wheelbarrow at the same time. We put Paprika in the laundry room, hoping she wouldn't yap.

At four-thirty in the morning, Nick opened my door. I slipped into a robe. We tiptoed outside. In the field, we spotted the garden and wheelbarrow, starkly lit under the full moon's domain. We plopped on all fours and headed out tail first.

With all the hushed reverence of the Lord's Supper, we scouted out the biggest zucchini. I picked it while Nick chose the squash. I was so nervous, twice I dropped the zucchini and twice it almost hit my toe. Twice I nearly broke the spell by yelling, but Nick's scowl and finger over his mouth reprimanded me. Surely Joe would hear the slightest utterance and our doom would be sealed.

The whole operation--as Uncle Eddie would say--was as awkward as putting socks on a chicken. After setting vegetables in the wheelbarrow, we spouted off a gazillion words simultaneously to make up for our frustrated silence.

"I'll push first," Nick said.

Sweating, we headed toward the mountain. During a break, he withdrew a bulgy napkin from his pocket. In his grubby hands were two corn cakes that we devoured, dirt and all.

The lumpy ground made pushing difficult, but in our trepidation, we'd never cooperated so well. We knew the stakes. I strategized how to get dirt off my robe and pajamas before Mom saw them in the wash. Nick calculated how much earlier we'd have to leave next time to reach home before sun-up, Dad's rising time.

Panting, we reached the chestnut stump a short way up the mountain. We set the food on the stump. The trees rustled. Bears?

"Just in time," a voice bellowed. It might as well have been a gunshot the way we popped up. Ole Joe stepped out. "I'll carry the food. Y'all tag along."

Surely my worst fear had come true. We'd missed part of the instructions and Joe knew it. Under strict inspection, the vegetables would tell all.

Inside Joe's cabin, the lantern shed light without warmth. Joe set the squashes aside. As we sat on the cot, he dug through a box on the table. We awaited our fate with thumping hearts, thick heads, and pajama-clad bodies.

He faced us. Light gleamed on the slick metallic surface of a knife. I closed my eyes as if shutting out a nightmare. Nick grabbed my hand, surely to be his last chivalrous move.

Joe was talking when I finally comprehended. "This kind of knife is for bigger work, when you're starting out with a piece of wood and wanna hone it down to size. See this blade? It's like a saw. Now look here, Miss Christina, you ain't gonna see it that way. Open those eyes."

I did. Joe was on a three-legged stool holding a knife. Nick slid his fingers over the blade.

"You too, missy," Joe said.

I touched it. Slick, cold. Sharp.

Joe picked a piece of wood from a box of scraps and crude-looking tools. "Now these here tools you have to take good care of, 'cause they do special work. Don't use 'em for whittling or cutting melons and rope and such. Only use 'em for carving. Y'all ever try this?"

"I whittle," Nick said. "My dad taught me. But I don't have a knife like this."

"Of course you don't. This here is homemade by a friend of mine. He took parts of old tools and put them together in new ways." Joe showed us how to peel the wood, then gave the knife to Nick, whose hands shook. "Steady now, Nick. Gotta be calm and steady-handed. Gotta be in charge. This is just practice. Always stroke away from yourself."

Nick peeled shavings and passed it to me. I froze, knife in one hand, wood in the other.

"Go ahead," Joe said.

"I ain't never done this."

"Just give it a try."

"I'd feel a heap better if you'd move out of my way, sir." Nick scooted back. I brought the knife to the wood. Joe put his hand over mine to reposition my fingers, then retreated. I caught the blade on the wood's edge and applied pressure. The blade took off, sliding off the wood. It swooped into the air, full circle, my hand still attached to the handle.

"Golly!" was all I could say. Perhaps it wasn't Joe's intention to hurt us at all. He figured we could do a right proper job of that ourselves.

Joe caught my hand and brought it down. "Try again," he said, kind amusement tempering his voice. "You done right working the blade away from yourself." He was probably groping to find something praiseworthy in my clumsy movements.

I tried several times. With a meager pile of shavings at my feet, I handed the knife to Nick.

Joe showed us another tool. "This here's an awl, straight from the Sears Roebuck catalog, about 1908. But just as reliable now. It's for cutting little pieces out of the front surface. You can cut letters or pictures, any kind of decorations. It makes a tiny round mark like this." He demonstrated, then showed how to change tools by screwing them in and out of the handle. Some ends had points, some had forks or flat edges. "Like carving mud with the end of a stick."

We tried it with more ease. "Do you have pictures you've done?" Nick asked.

"Sure, but they ain't fittin' to behold." Joe laughed. "I keep them yonder in a box on the shelf." He nodded toward the far wall.

Hints of dawn meandered through the window. Nick seemed antsy. "We have to go. Dad'll be up soon. If he finds us gone—"

"Say no more. Next week we'll meet at the same place, but earlier. I'll show you more tools. Call me Joe now, you hear?"

We ran down the pass and across our field, taking turns dragging the wheelbarrow. Dad's bedroom light was on so he wasn't outside yet. Mom usually rose at seven.

We waited behind the barn till Dad entered the shed, hoping he didn't need the wheelbarrow. We ran to the house and tiptoed upstairs, shoes in hand. I stuffed our pajamas into the closet to be rinsed out later when Mom was in the garden.

We went to bed, but I couldn't sleep. My head was too full of a secret we'd never be able to tell. Even if Joe hadn't cared, it was too delicious to share. Even with Todd.

CHAPTER 13

Our family tree was complicated with so many kin connections in our town that I didn't know where our family ended and the rest of the townsfolk began. Within my family, I wasn't sure where Dad's side ended and Mom's began, since two of my great-great-grandfathers were brothers.

The Hamiltons, Rosses, and others peppered the Blue Ridge hollows of Yancey, Buncombe, and Madison Counties in the mid-1700s. Scots-Irish in background, they were drawn to the mountains by the similarity to the Scottish highlands. The awkward hills and hollows invited only the hardiest of pioneers. Nonetheless, new towns sprouted.

In 1927, Currie Hill was officially incorporated with a population of 1,248, which hadn't altered much since. It grew only in births. Growth evened out by folks moving after each war. Those who left for the city rarely returned. Folks said those who succeeded in the city didn't belong to us anymore, such as Dad's brother Sidney. Those who failed didn't belong to either us or them.

****

Any occasion provided an excuse for a family gathering. Mom turned thirty-five on July 1st so Dad invited the whole clan, both sides of the family.

Mom was thrilled by the rocking chair my father special-ordered from Mr. Hutchins. It greeted her in the living room that morning.

Exhausted from our escapade at Joe's the night before,

I struggled to get out of slow motion. While cousins ran around outdoors, I wandered inside. The aunts were setting up food.

"If I told you once, I've told you a thousand times, don't you go picking at my cream pies." Grandma Hamilton shook a long, slender finger as if it were a big stick. Her hair was as white as goose feathers, smooth as down.

Caught red-handed, Uncle Eddie blushed. Pity the man who found himself the object of Grandma's disapproval and pointy finger.

Grandma never let an issue rest and had the last word on family matters. "From the day you was born you snitched things that wasn't yours. I slave twelve hours making a gooseberry pie what's disappeared in five minutes at the table, but Edward here sets a record for thirty seconds."

Grandpa Hamilton appeared in the doorway, a dollop of whipping cream dotting his mischievous grin. He was an older, grayer version of my dad. Many a night found us eating popcorn grown in his patch as I sat snugly on his lap listening to stories.

Everyone burst into laughter. Grandma did a double take on Grandpa and wasted no time lighting into him--until Grandpa intervened. "Now listen here, Sweets, you ought to be grateful we're pleasured by your cooking. Can't say that about all the womenfolk in our family, their burnt grits and biscuits stinking clear 'cross the county for weeks."

Grandma Dorothy herded us to the table. Paprika and Grandpa's dog Mercy moseyed over, too. Great-uncle Charles asked a blessing on the meal. His rich voice engulfed me in its enchantment. He loved telling us kids stories, particularly Jack tales and Grandfather tales originating in southern Appalachia. White hair flowed over his shoulders, beard hiding his neck, his eyes the color of blue jays. Fuzzy white eyebrows had lives of their own.

We ate in the shade of the large oak, plates laden with crispy golden-fried chicken, zucchini, bell peppers, cucumbers, molasses sweet bread, bran bread with apple butter and blackberry jam, cone pone, watermelon, fruit salad, peach cobbler, and strawberry pie. Some folks returned for seconds before the rest of us were halfway through firsts.

"Like one hog waits for another," Dad said.

After eating, with stomachs comfortably stretched, Grandpa Hamilton told us about Great-uncle Finlay's notorious hunting dog. On the edge of the oak's shade, I engaged in a sock-pulling game with Paprika and Mercy, who'd just swiped my watermelon. Tug-of-war kept me awake.

Mom opened gifts. "All this fuss about turning thirty-five. You'd think I was as old as Ross there." Mom was often teased for being so much younger than Dad and Ross. She in turn heckled them about their advancement in years.

"Watch out," Ross said. "You might have the Geritol bottle in one of those boxes."

Geritol was a long-standing joke between the two Grandmas. One year, after seeing a television commercial for Geritol, Grandma Hamilton had Uncle Sid send her some from New York. As a joke, she gave it to Grandma Dorothy as a birthday present. They'd both laughed. The audacity of taking anything from a bottle versus a home-brewed remedy!

Since then, the two women contrived more creative ways of exchanging the bottle from one household to the other. At first it was wrapped in a gift box. Then Grandma Dorothy frosted the unopened bottle between two cake layers for Grandma Hamilton's birthday. The following year it was wrapped inside the sleeves of a knit sweater for Christmas, and after that it was hand-delivered with a basket of flowers by a local delivery boy.

Mom received two books, an embroidered handkerchief, and a wooden seamstress at a sewing machine, hand-carved by Grandpa. The arms and machine parts moved. After compliments subsided, Grandma Hamilton said, "Looks like a new toy. Once an old man, twice a child."

I admired its intricacy and tugged on Dad's shirt. "Can you make me something like that for my birthday?" It was a three weeks away. He tousled my hair but made no promises.

After the last gift, Mom said, "Hmm, no Geritol? Maybe it's being saved for Ross's birthday."

Grandpa handed Dad the family Bible. "You get the honors. Choose a Psalm, any you want."

"Mercy me," Grandma Hamilton said, and the dog trotted over. "Lord knows we don't sing 'em enough in church now that we're singing them manmade hymns. It'll be the doom of us all, singing some man's words and not the Lord's."

Grandma Dorothy clicked her tongue. "If you-uns were Baptist like me instead of Presbyterian you'd never know what you were missing."

"I wouldn't be Baptist for all the psalm-readings in the world," Grandma Hamilton quipped good-naturedly.

"You all hush now and let Drew read," Grandpa said.

Dad held the Bible as if it were delicate crystal about to break, yet with the confidence of a sword thrower. This was no mere formality. The words held sway over his life.

He read from Psalm 139: "'O Lord, thou hast searched me, and known me. Thou knowest my downsitting and mine uprising, thou understandest my thoughts afar off.'" He paused as if to relish the words, as if gleaning comfort. Breezes brushed the trees, and birds twittered as if waiting for him to continue.

"'Thou compassest my path and my lying down, and art acquainted with all my ways. For there is not a word in my tongue, but, lo, O Lord, thou knowest it altogether. . . . Search me, O God, and know my heart; try me, and know my thoughts: And see if there be any wicked way in me, and lead me in the way everlasting.'"

"You read just like a preacher, Drew," Grandma Dorothy said. "How come you ain't never been a preacher?"

Dad chortled. "I may have the Scripture reading voice down but I'd have to work on my funeral and wedding voices."

Grandma Dorothy Ross hooked rugs during the Depression, before she became chief cook and bottle washer at the logging camp. Together we carded wool. Her delicate hair was woven with strands of gray, from smooth silver to deep metallic. Her deft fingers and straightforward, common sense business manner belied her superstitious nature. Grandma never threw away egg shells before the cake was baked, for fear of bad luck.

"What do you think about them new hymns in your church, Drew?" Grandma Dorothy often asked her son-in-law's opinions, especially since he'd turned her daughter from Baptist to Presbyterian.

"The so-called new hymns are over a decade old and so is this argument."

"I don't understand that debate. We been singing manmade hymns for decades and it hasn't hurt us any. There's a heap more trouble in churches than what they sing at the service."

This comment only deepened Grandma Hamilton's stand in the trenches, which led to a doctrinal discussion usually dominated by the males. The grandmas flung definitions of worship, the total depravity of man, and common grace, until the verse-slinging rose to such a pitch that all a man could do was what Uncle Charles did next: lean back, stroke his beard, and say, "Ah, the marvel and mystery of the onion."

"What in the Sam Hill are you talking about?" Grandma Dorothy asked.

"Women, they're like onions. You peel off layer by layer and still you got layers to go before you get to the heart of things. Onions are deep."

Uncle Charles was a master at comments like this, squashing arguments faster than anything else did.

"Emma." Grandpa Hamilton patted his wife's arm. "You'll get used to the new songs. You're just a mite old-fashioned."

"Old-fashioned!" Ross said. "Look who's calling the kettle black." The aunts and uncles laughed. Grandpa was notorious for sticking to the old ways at any expense.

"There ain't no danger in doing something new in church," Grandpa said. "We still sing the Psalms so what have we lost? Some folks act like we're going to hell in a hand basket."

"That ain't far from the truth." Grandma Hamilton shook her head. "The woes of modern life. With everything young folks have nowadays, they've no appreciation for their elders and all we did. Ingratitude sows the seeds of greed and discontentment."

Uncle Ross cocked his head. "You'd rather grow up with a scrub board and butter churn than a washing machine and the corner store?"

"Maybe a blend is good," Mom said. "My kitchen has modern conveniences, a pantry, and an antique pie safe. Modernity and antiquity rolled up into one."

Grandma Hamilton shook her finger. "I'm saying, Ross, with all the modern conveniences today, kids get spoiled. They don't have to work and there's plenty of time to get into trouble. They'd be bored to tears with a taffy pull or an ice cream social, and we used to mark our calendars by them." Her face brightened. "Why, I'll never forget how my heart a-fluttered the day Jimmie Beasley asked me to pull taffy with him. Or when Nicholas was the red-ear winner at a corn shucking." She blew a kiss to Grandpa. "Now that was a grand time. But nowadays a kid ain't happy without television or an automobile. They don't need ingenuity anymore."

Grandpa scooted forward. "Fact is, families may be getting smaller these days but they's less together than ever."

"Conveniences free up time," Ross said. "That's a good thing, if a body's headed in the right direction."

"Values are a-changing," Grandma Hamilton said. "Folks killing other folks, Robert Kennedy and that Martin Luther King, Junior. All this rabble-rousing. And young folks are wanting jobs so they can get themselves a car, never mind their ailing neighbors."

"There's always been folks who put things above

people," Ross said. "And it's no sin to own a car."

"Unless greed makes you buy it." Grandma Hamilton's arm flew up like a preacher's. "It's love of money and material gain."

"And education," Grandpa Hamilton added. "Nowadays folks put too much emphasis on a lavish of it. Kids get learned but not in the proper subjects. They grow up too far from the soil, no use of heart and hands. It's just head that matters. Kids don't know how to build a fire in a wood stove or survive in the woods, but they can drive a car. They don't confidence the moon and stars when they finally do set to planting and harvesting."

"Pa," Ross said, "the signs are valid but not necessary. Plenty of folks don't plant by the signs, even back when you was farming."

"Your argument ain't with me, son. It's right there in Genesis One, verse fourteen. Plain and simple for all to see. Signs to mark seasons and days and years. Created into the very order of things."

"You're right, Pa, I ain't in any position to argue with the Good Book. But at least allow that folks need book-learning, especially in history and science and all, to take care of new problems as they arise."

Grandpa snorted. "Who cares if we can send a man to the moon if we can't properly tend our soil?"

"The moon!" Grandma Hamilton crossed her heart. "Granny sakes alive, they'll never put a man on the moon. That's just a bunch of fancy talk."

"Honey, get your head out of the sand," Grandma Dorothy said. "They're preparing to send a rocket up shortly. With a man."

"The moon is God's country. He won't allow no human being up there. It would offset the cycles. Besides, why in tarnation do we need a man on the moon? It's an almighty waste of money with mouths down here to feed. If Kennedy hadn't been elected president this wouldn't be happening."

Gangly Uncle Parker wiped crumbs off his scraggly beard and attempted to explain the value of moon exploration, new discoveries, and improving one's quality of life. He then broached the subject of the new park's possible assets.

"We don't need that park any more than a cat needs two tails," Grandpa said. "It wonders me why Phil Kepler goes all around Robin Hood's barn to talk folks into this idea by saying it's all for jobs, while he just wants to make a buck off us all."

"Can't a man kill two birds with one stone?" Ross asked.

Grandpa raised an eyebrow. "Efficiency is one thing, double-mindedness is another. He cares no more for folks' jobs than a crow cares for the New Testament. But I think Phil Kepler's gonna be mighty letdown."

"Meanwhile, he's got folks a-bumbling like bees in a tar tub," Uncle Parker said.

"I don't know if I can take two more weeks of all this commotion till voting time," Aunt Elaine, Mom's sister, said.

Dad faced Grandpa. "I don't favor the park either but you gotta give Phil the benefit of the doubt. He means no harm and he's got a good head on his shoulders."

"Well, so has a pin," Grandpa said. "But why pour water on a drowned rat? I can't get all broke up about some park that won't come to pass. Folks won't abide his nonsense."

Uncle Charles stroked his white silky beard. "For every discerning soul there's ten suckers."

If Ross mentioned his job offer from Phil, it would surely cause an uproar.

Grandma Hamilton crossed her arms. "The man wants to bring the city to us."

"It's not so much the city as the tourists," Grandma Dorothy said.

"Same thing. By the time the first passel of tourists comes we'll have ourselves a city. Then so-called progress with a northern corporation running it. When we're too big for a corporation, a machine'll be in charge. Yes, sir, a machine will run this town if we let that park in. Mark my words."

"You mean a computer?" Ross asked. "The old ways will be preserved, but it's modern times now. Technology can serve us well. We can't maintain the old ways at the expense of economic stability."

Grandma was undaunted. She cited evidence to support her stand on computers: eighty-year-old Marla Ebsen recently received a hospital bill from Asheville charging her for labor and delivery services, thanks to computers. Parker pointed out that computers made fewer mistakes than humans did, and were less violent, too, which prompted Grandma's tirade on all that rabble-rousing at the universities.

"That has nothing to do with education," Uncle Ken said. "Some colored and white folks hate each other no matter how much book-learning they have. Currie Hill ain't exactly a model town as far as desegregation goes, or we'd have more upscuddles ourselves."

Like a toy that had just been wound up, Grandma Hamilton spouted opinions on President Johnson, peace talks in Paris, the Battle of Saigon, and the TET offensive.

Grandma Dorothy turned the tide by asking Ross and Abby if they'd heard from Ted or Scott recently. Ross began to relay his sons' boot camp horror stories, but glanced at my dad and halted.

Grandma Hamilton jumped in again, lest anyone be unclear about her stance. "Mercy me." The dog's ears perked up. "Why should them city-trained doctors get so much credit? They ought to come to the mountains for their training. I ain't yet seen a sick one not respond to sassafras and spring tonic."

"It ain't the city that's bad," Grandpa said. "It's the attitudes. Sidney writes about it all the time. Folks fighting for jobs, folks competing, folks putting jobs above wives and families. I daresay that's why Sid ain't ever married. But we got folks here walking in a bad way, too. And they ain't never been to the big city." Like the MacNeills.

"You're right," Grandma Hamilton said. "I got two sons that don't go to church no more and one's right here in this town." That was Uncle Ross. "But when you got one son still off in New York City who ain't been home for five years, and another son who's been to who-knows-where after the war and gets married but won't let on—" She eyed my dad. Rarely did anyone mention my father's mysterious, silent years and his first wife.

A hush of secrets is different from any other kind. It's not like the thin silence after the wind combs and tickles the leaves of the sassafras tree, nor is it like the sweet quiet of the morning sky after it echoes and swallows the chatter of the purple martins. No, it's more like the pregnant hush of thick storm air right before it inhales and gulps the countryside, and reluctantly lets it go again.

Grandpa put an arm around his wife. "You got four healthy, happy sons, three of them right under your nose, with grandchildren to boot."

She stared at him as if he were putting a bandage on a hemorrhage, or handing her a clock to control changing times.

Breaking the awkward silence, Eddie brought out his jew's-harp. Dad got his fiddle, Mom her dulcimer, and Parker and Ken their mandolins. The two uncles sang an original humorous ballad about our family. The others joined in traditional songs. Aunt Abby led the dancing while Aunt Elaine and Aunt Sheila prodded us kids to join them, a welcome change. Grandma Dorothy must have thought so, too. Her toe tapped underneath her chair.

An hour later, dusk chased us indoors. To top off the evening, Uncle Charles rocked in Mom's new chair and told the Grandfather tale "Soap." I lay on the floor, chin propped up on my hands, easy prey lured into his story. His voice became a chorus of sound effects. His animated eyebrows and eyes, silvery blue in the dusk, were full of bewitching. The rocker went back and forth, hypnotizing, as predictable as the moon's cycles.

During the third story, I fell victim to its enchantment, now sound asleep, not to be wakened until the purple martins sang in the morning.

Later in the month, Grandma Dorothy gave me a handmade quilt, a gift she gave each of her granddaughters on their tenth birthday. It was stuffed with three pounds of homegrown wool and had twelve patterns, including a Dutch windmill, a sunflower, and a bear paw.

"If a young girl sleeps under a new quilt," Grandma said, "she'll dream of the boy she's going to marry." I was afraid to go to sleep that night for fear of dreaming.

My father presented me with a woodcarving of a miniature baseball player. The figure had two braids, like mine, and was poised with a bat at home plate. The upper torso and arms pivoted as if hitting a ball. He'd started it when I joined the ball team weeks prior, and worked on it late hours after my bedtime. I gave it the place of honor on my bedside table, my gaze often lingering over each intricate feature.

Snug under my new quilt, viewing the silhouette of the baseball player, I reveled in the birthday glow and the regular patterns of my life, as warm as the quilt, as dependable as the rhythm of seasons. My father, who'd spared many hours to create my gift, never missed a beat in his schedule. I heard him rustle the cereal box liner, click the spoon on the bowl, and shuffle back upstairs, pausing at my doorway. Then his bed creaked, the pages turned. His light went off after twenty minutes.

Nothing ever changed at our house.

PART III

Grandpa Hamilton: Vittles and Courting. "All that worry and fuss for nothing, when the real problem steps right inside the door while we ain't looking."

———————————

Everyone in the Hamilton clan from the last three generations was immortalized in one of Grandpa's tales. Nick, my cousins, and I were his best audience.

"My Aunt Ruby Clare never did marry till she was thirty-five and it's no secret why. She couldn't get a man to partake of her fixings if she paid him. She had a reputation. The whole county knew she wasn't worth her weight in pine cones so far as good cooking goes. What man wants to commit himself to a lifetime of that?

"I'm talking about burnt grouse, and batterbread what's more batter than bread, and vegetables that fall to smithereens so as you're obliged to eat 'em with a gravy ladle. Anyhow, my ma took to worrying about Ruby never getting a husband, so she was bound to remedy the problem once and for all. She invited a young gentleman for dinner. He was new to the area and had been spared from Ruby's tarnished reputation as a cook. Ma planned for Ruby to fix the meal, and Ma would guide her step by step so as she couldn't spoil it. Well, the day came and Ma told Aunt Ruby everything from how to mix up flour and sugar for biscuits to putting the right spices on the pork. Ruby did it herself, every last bit.

"The gentleman, Barney, comes that evening and we

all sit down to eat, us five kids with Ma, Pa, and Ruby, 'cause Ruby lived with us. I was seven. The vittles were better than delicious! We ate till we was plumb full. Barney says, 'I declare that was the most wondrous meal I ever had,' and Ma says, 'Ruby cooked it.' Barney's eyes grew wide and the sparks of love were there. It was plain to all."

Grandma piped in. "You hear tell the way to a man's heart is through his stomach. I reckon some gals don't stand a chance of getting married otherwise."

Cousin Tommy snickered. "'Specially the ugly ones." I punched his arm.

"Now wedding without courting is like vittles without salt," Grandpa said. "But Ma was more intent on getting Ruby married off than in courting, before Barney found out she couldn't cook. But they courted a while. The townsfolk hardly believed Barney ate Ruby's cooking and survived, let alone found it right tolerable. Then Ruby had a hankering to invite him for dinner again. She asks Ma to help, and would we all please vacate the house so as Barney could call on her in private. Of course, Ma wanted Ruby married off, so she was obliged to do it.

"That night, Pa and us young-uns went to the Turners up the road apiece, aiming to be gone a spell. Ma stays and barks orders to Ruby to get this and get that and grind this and mix this and churn that. Ruby's running around all a-flutter, and Barney shows up an hour earlier than expected. So Ruby shoos Ma up to the loft so as Barney doesn't know she's there. Barney sits at the table and talks to Ruby all friendly-like.

"But Ruby's distraught. She runs upstairs to the loft and asks Ma what to do next. Ma says, 'Mix milk into the biscuit flour.' So Ruby goes downstairs and mixes up biscuit batter, and tries to talk with Barney. Then she runs upstairs and asks what to do next. Ma says, 'Scoop the batter into piles on the pan and put it in the oven. Take grease from the pork frying and add flour and milk for gravy.'

"So Ruby goes back downstairs and scoops spoonfuls

of batter onto the pan, and pours grease into a bowl. Barney says, 'What do you keep going upstairs for?' and Ruby says, 'I keep valuables up there that I need for dinner.' It was surely a true statement.

"Next time Ruby trotted upstairs, Ma said, 'I'm coming down with you. I can't stay up here all evening.' Ruby pleaded with her not to. Ma studies out the window looking for an escape, but no luck. So Ruby says, 'He won't stay long, I promise.' She went down and they ate. Dinner was good and Barney said it was powerful good. Ruby took some up to the loft to Ma, but Ma was so mad she couldn't spit straight. Just when Ma thought Barney should be taking his leave, he stayed on and on. Ruby forgot all about Ma up in the loft. She and Barney talked and laughed till the rest of us came home."

"Didn't you all wonder what became of your ma?" Nick asked.

"Pa figured Ruby talked her into staying. He reckoned it right proper for Ruby to have a chaperon. Even though she's thirty-five."

"Did they get married?" I asked.

"They surely did, my ma saw to that. Says that's the only way it was worth it, being stuck in the loft all evening."

"How'd Aunt Ruby's cooking go after the wedding?" Cousin Melanie wondered.

Grandpa chortled. "Ruby begged my ma to help her cook the first month of her marriage, but Ma said, 'I got you a husband but it's up to you to keep him.' Ruby was afraid she'd spoil a meal and Barney would be downright furious.

"Well, a month after their wedding, Ruby had us over for dinner. We didn't expect much so we crammed ourselves with fruit and bread before we went. And it was the worst meal ever. Whatever could be burned was, whatever could be raw was, and whatever should be soft crunched, whatever should be crunchy was soggy. The spices for applesauce were on the vegetables and vice versa. But nobody dared say anything and we all choked it down.

"After supper, Barney wipes his chin and we watch with bated breath. He grins and says, 'Honey, that was the best meal you ever fixed. They keep getting better and better from the first day we met.' We young-uns had to cover our mouths to keep from laughing."

Tommy wrinkled his nose. "How could Barney like it so much?"

"Turns out Barney's taste buds were out of whack. Had some illness and lost all sense of taste and smell. He'd been known to eat worse things than Ruby's biscuits, though nobody knew why till later. We figured he had an iron stomach or was more tolerant than the rest of us put together."

"Or a liar," Nick said.

"Regardless, Ma got all worked up for nothing. The real trouble in that marriage weren't cooking at all. Barney was the bettingest man you ever laid eyes on. He lost half his income to bad gambles. All that worry and fuss about vittles for nothing, when the real problem steps right inside the door while we ain't looking."

CHAPTER 14

"Christina Ross Hamilton! You get the Sam Hill down here this instant!"

Uncle Ross's yells from the living room jolted me from an early Saturday morning sleep. I charged out of bed and downstairs as if on fire.

"What's the meaning of this?" Ross held his stolen boot, missing four days.

Throughout the ragged course of the next two minutes, I learned that Ross found the boot on his doorstep that morning with a note supposedly signed by me. When Ross put the boot on, his foot and ankle got covered in toothpaste that had been generously spread inside.

Dad frowned, already sweating from an hour's work. Mom shook her head, hands on hips. All three stood on one side of the room and I on the other, the room tipping, as if justice was being weighed on the living room floor and found in their favor.

"What kind of pathetic joke is this?" Mom asked.

"Let's hear Tina's side first," Dad said, as if it would do any good.

"I didn't do it. Stan Randall did. He hates my guts."

"How did Stan Randall get my boot?" Ross asked.

"I . . . well, he . . ." I swallowed hard. "He promised he wouldn't never bother me again if I gave him your boot as a peace offering." Stan had kept his word. He hadn't said one word since I delivered that boot. I'd been relishing the peace and quiet, little dreaming he was contriving this scheme. He'd certainly mastered the art of retaliation.

"Leave the boot here, Ross, and be on your way." Dad looked chagrinned at having to deal with juvenile delinquency in his own daughter.

"Not till I give this child a piece of my mind," Ross said. "You're crazy to think that boy's gonna stop bothering you. Use your head instead of my boots to get yourself out of trouble from now on." He stomped out. I prepared to get walloped into the next decade.

Without a word, my father handed me the boot, rags, and soap. I scrubbed that boot for two hours in silence.

****

That evening, laying on the porch swing, I predicted which stars would wink next out of a velvety backdrop.

Dad disrupted my game when he lifted my feet and sat beside me. "This Stan Randall saga is way out of hand."

"I know. I'm sorry. I never should have listened to Stan. Or taken Uncle Ross's boot."

Dad slid his arm around me. "I called Mr. Randall. Maybe some of this nonsense will be curbed, if he holds Stan in tow."

"And if he don't?"

"We'll take one day at a time. Tina, folks that vex others are usually covering up bad feelings they have inside."

"What?"

"Meaning, Stan's probably like a hurt puppy dog. He's gotta act tough on the outside so as nobody sees it. You can't trust appearances."

"Then why ain't he nice even when I'm nice to him?" I shared several efforts, including the time I'd offered Stan my baseball glove since his was wrecked. He'd spit on it.

"It's best to stay out of his way for now."

"Don't be nice to him?" Fine with me.

"Be kind, but generosity might be like casting pearls to the swine."

A picture grew in my head of Stan with a big snout and curly tail.

"Tina, it's not what you do to love a person, it's why you do it. When I was in grade school, a lad named Arty was so poor he came to school without pencil or paper and nothing but stale cornbread for lunch. Another boy, Mitch, gave Arty pencils from his ample supply or a chicken leg from his lunch. They sat in the front row and every time Mitch gave something to Arty, Mitch made sure plenty of us kids were watching. Arty was embarrassed. Even if he didn't accept the pencil or chicken, Mitch made a big scene.

One day I got the notion to help Arty a different way. It was autumn, so I invited him over the next morning before breakfast. Ross and I took him with us, and we ran to the mountain behind our house to gather mast before the hogs got to it. We filled flour bags plumb full of chestnuts and acorns that had fallen from the trees overnight. We hid 'em in the barn. After school, we went into town to sell 'em. Arty made enough money to buy twenty pencils, if he wanted. He went with us weekly after that. Now which arrangement was better?"

I squinted, observing stars changing position in the sky as I covered first one eye, then the other. "I reckon you and Uncle Ross showed a heap more respect for Arty than Mitch did. Does that mean you should never give folks things without getting something in return?"

"No, Tina, consider why you're giving. Is it to make yourself look better? Because you want recognition or thanks? Does it embarrass the receiver? The best thing to give somebody is their dignity, their independence. It's better to teach a man how to fish than to bring him a fish every day and keep him dependent on you."

Swine like Stan didn't eat fish anyhow. "What about all that stuff you do for Barry MacNeill? Isn't he dependent on you now?" Maybe I'd back Dad into a corner, a rare feat.

"If Barry was left to his own means, his family would be dead and buried by now." Dad sprung out of that trap like a bear who merely lifted the lid and crawled out.

"What does this have to do with Stan?"

"Just think twice before you give him anything. If you gave him a whole new catcher's uniform it's not worth more than the respect you should treat him with. Kindness reaps other dividends. That's walking in the light, God's light." He gestured to the sky. "Like the stars and moon. We're supposed to reflect the light of God the way the moon reflects the sun. Then darkness won't cover us up."

This conversation was too much for me. I wasn't ready to treat Stan with mercy. Just thwarting his blows took all my efforts. Besides, problems with Stan seemed eons away as I rocked on the swing with my father. I felt so little, incapable of doing right. Yet Dad was strong and knew how to walk in the light. His words held me steady.

"Tina, you need to forgive Stan."

"Forgive?" I'd be less shocked if he told me to dive off Mount Mitchell.

"Anyone can forgive a friend, or get along with someone they like. But Jesus calls us to higher ground, to forgive enemies. That's part of walking in the light."

"I don't know how."

Dad dug ten pennies from his pocket and gave me five. "Let's say I'm Stan."

You don't have a big enough snout.

"Let's say I call you a bad name. That's like stealing from you. Stealing respect and dignity." He took a penny from my hand. "You're angry, so you call me bad names and wish bad things on me." I took a penny from him. He cleared his throat. "That's worth two. It gets worse each time." I took another one. "Now I'm really out of sorts. It's time for action. I distract you at home plate so you miss the ball. In front of everybody."

Dad took three pennies. "Now you're losing patience and you hit me." I took two pennies from his hand. His hand remained outstretched so I took one more. He nudged me and I took another one, for a total of four. "Now I'm so mad I can't see straight and I'm not letting you get the better of me. So I smack you and swear at you and throw your baseball glove in the mud." He scooped all seven pennies out of my hand.

I piped up. "Now I go home and plan my revenge."

"No, now you forgive me."

"What? How? After you did all that? First I get even, then I forgive."

"Forgiveness means you settle the score without getting back at someone. Look." He pointed to his hand. "How many pennies?"

"Ten."

He closed his hand. "Forgiveness means you don't take away any more from me. The wrongdoer doesn't owe you anything." He pointed to my hand. "How many?"

"Zero." I stared at my empty palm.

He gently curled my fingers and closed my fist. "Forgiveness means you bear the consequences of his wrongdoing. You've settled the score—in your heart. You treat him as if you're even. See, when your hands are closed, you can't see who has more and who has less."

"So you're saying folks should never be punished or make amends?"

"No, not at all. Whether or not they get punished by the proper authorities and make amends, we still have to forgive. Otherwise, you're just plain miserable."

A whack over Stan's big, ugly snout sounded much more gratifying.

Dad slipped the ten pennies back into my hand. He shook it until they jiggled onto the porch floor. "Any treasure we hold in our own hands we can lose. It can slip through our fingers. But earthly treasure we don't claim becomes treasure in God's hands, if we let it go."

I sighed. I needed him so. He was as stable as the red oak by the creek, the oak whose roots tangled and wedged into the ground with such power, making the tree an immovable force.

Back then I couldn't put those feelings into words. Instead, I rested my head on his shoulder, then lay down, his lap my pillow.

We were in the middle of a night sky that seemed to absorb everything but us. My feet grabbed and poked at stars as if tapping out a code. Dad may have been like one of those stars, ever faithful, never covered up by the dark. But I wasn't ready to take his words to heart. The applications to my own life eluded me, much as the shooting stars escaped the sky as they glided down a giant black slide of lights and fizzled into oblivion.

That's the kind of light *I* was.

CHAPTER 15

Eleven more days remained until the vote that would decide Currie Hill's fate. But that was far from my thoughts during the town's annual Fourth of July celebration.

A huge pig was barbecued, basted until the fat was crispy. We ate with zest from plates full of breads, fruit, cakes, pies, and ice cream. Games beckoned young and old alike. At dusk we gathered in the park where the barbershop quartet entertained, and finished the evening with fiddling, clogging, and square dancing in Gerald Duncan's barn.

In our town, with Dr. Kirby's prodding, a barbershop quartet craze recently took hold, reminiscent of an era that bypassed our town. While the rest of the country was strolling through the park in May, sipping afternoon tea and singing Stephen Foster songs around the parlor piano, plinking ragtime tunes or kicking up their feet with the Charleston, our people tapped their toes to the fiddle and mountain dulcimer after bear hunts, house raisings, or corn shuckings.

During the picnic, the barbershoppers captivated us with "When Irish Eyes are Smiling," "Shine on Harvest Moon," "Sweet Adeline," and "Carolina in the Morning."

At the barn, we danced to Roger Griffin's banjo, Patsy Hutchins's dulcimer, and Dad's fiddle. I wore myself out with "Skip to my Lou," "Turkey in the Straw," and "Old Mountain Dew." Mom and I were part of a clogging presentation. Mom's peppy jig-like movements contradicted her Baptist background with its condemnation of dance. Uncle Parker's knees jerked to his waist with each step, as if manipulated by an energetic marionette puppeteer.

When Dad put his fiddle away, Mom grabbed him for "Grapevine Twist." She talked Nick into being my square dance partner. He tolerated me for all of two songs.

Catching my breath, I stood by Dad. Man after man approached, probing for his opinions about the park and our town's future. After all, time was running out.

"Don't let town council buy into Phil Kepler's schemes," Jim Drummond said.

"If you can't persuade 'em, no one can," Bob Hutchins added.

Doc Kirby chimed in. "This town's depending on you."

Roger Griffin nodded. "You're the only one who can stand against Phil Kepler."

Dad snickered. "Sounds like this town's going to the hogs when I'm gone."

****

After so many accolades that elevated my father to the status of Currie Hill's patron saint, I was shocked three days later at church. Rev. Perkins announced Dad's decision to step out of active service as deacon—one year before his term was up. Murmurs of surprise rumbled through the congregation. Mom sat in wide-eyed shock.

In our church, men were elders and deacons for life, alternating three-year terms of service. Rarely did anyone withdraw early, except for dire circumstances or serious sin.

That same hour, Dad also passed up the bread and the wine.

Our church had communion quarterly. Dad believed four times wasn't nearly enough for such a holy privilege and reminder of grace. He'd say the Lord's supper was not to be taken lightly, and never while engaged in intentional sin.

How many folks noticed the plate as it passed by Dad untouched? On the heels of his resignation, I couldn't shrug it off. Maybe he wasn't as close to God as I thought.

We plowed through awkward dialogs on our way out of church, surely leaving behind a bewildered bunch of shaking heads and clucking tongues.

"Why, Drew?" Mom asked on the way home. "Why'd you quit? You had a year to go."

He stared straight ahead. "I don't feel right about staying on."

"Why didn't you wait till after the park vote? Folks'll be bothered by this."

Dad looked at her with sad, distant eyes. "Jennie, one should never postpone acting on a conviction." Nobody dared ask more questions.

All day I was plagued by his refusal of the Lord's Supper and his withdrawal from active service in the diaconate. Mom's alarm distressed me more. In a community where church commitments were esteemed above all others, surely his decision would impact his influence on the town council.

Ross dropped by that evening. "It would be easier if you'd stepped down from town council instead." He sniggered. "Then we wouldn't be butting heads so much about this park."

"If it weren't the park, it'd be something else," Dad said. "You always find a way to contrary me."

"Look who's calling the kettle black. Are you coming around to my way of thinking, about church and all?"

"Don't get your hopes up, Ross. Let's just say . . . I'm more effective on town council than in church leadership right now. Just speak your piece at the town meeting and don't mind me."

CHAPTER 16

It was the night of the Major League All-Star game on television.

And the night of the tuna casserole. Mom conceded to my request, but I predicted she wouldn't like tuna. It had a dull ring next to words like snapper and lobster, macaroni and spaghetti, though we'd never had those either.

While I set the table, Mom said, "Drew, you won't need to miss any of the game after all. Lucy said the chair's all mended."

"Well, that beats all. Who fixed it?"

"I'm not knowing to that."

"Maybe Bob Hutchins, when Patsy dropped by to clean."

"They haven't been to the MacNeills lately. But it was fine work, as good as new."

"Reckon I'm not needed anymore." Dad feigned a pout.

"Reckon now you can put a hand to mending our fence." Mom kissed his cheek.

At the refrigerator, I read the column Mom clipped from *Sports Illustrated*. It mentioned a letter from a boy who'd written to Harmon Killebrew of the Minnesota Twins. The boy asked if he had to eat tuna, as his mother insisted, in order to hit the ball. Mr. Killebrew said if he ever wanted to play at all, he'd better obey his mother, even if it meant eating tuna.

What was wrong with tuna? I approached suppertime with great anticipation. Mom carried a hot dish trailed by steam. Nick sniffed.

We held hands as Dad murmured a prayer. At the end he tagged on, "And bless this tuna casserole, and us after we eat it."

Mom rolled her eyes. "Now what's that supposed to mean?"

"No telling what's inside a casserole." Dad tucked his napkin in his shirt.

Mom pushed the dish my way. I lifted the lid.

"Don't keep that cover off long," Dad said in earnest. "Half of it may crawl away."

"Nonsense." Mom plopped a basket of cornbread on his plate.

"Thanks." Ignoring her exasperation, he took one and buttered it.

I scooped casserole on my plate. It looked like a blob of reeds washed up on the riverbank.

Nick lifted a spoonful and scrutinized it an inch from his eyeballs. "Just looking for critters."

I winced. "What's in it, Mom?"

"Been to Old Lady Balch's?" Dad asked.

Nick and I were startled frozen, eyes wide. Did he know about our visits to her?

"She specializes in bat wings, toad stools, and gnats." Dad pointed to the casserole. "Had a special running last week, a dozen for thirty-nine cents. Your ma here took advantage of it."

"Granny sakes alive, Drew, quit your fibbing. And don't talk that way about her."

Dad raised his hands and backed away. "If I'm lying I'll eat that whole thing."

It wasn't fishy tasting as I expected, just mushy with the noodles. And cheesy. One serving was sufficient—and one casserole sufficient for my childhood.

After finishing our portions, Dad asked if we wanted more. We didn't. He dumped the rest of the casserole onto his plate, and devoured it. It disappeared bit by bit behind the beard. He patted his stomach and sat back. "I fibbed. Always loved this stuff."

Two days prior, on July 7, Denny McLain won his sixteenth game, with half the season left to achieve thirty wins. Nick was optimistic. Todd still teased it was all a fluke.

Four Tigers were voted in for the All-Star game: McAuliffe, Horton, Freehan, and McLain. Denny McLain flew in and pitched two scoreless innings, another feather in the cap for Nick. But the National League won 1-0.

Afterward, Nick asked, "Can we go to a Tiger game sometime?"

Dad lit his pipe. "When hogs learn to Do Si Do and Promenade."

"How about New York?" I asked. "We could visit Uncle Sid and see the Yankees."

"You wouldn't like it," Dad said. "Multiply Asheville by a thousand and stretch buildings to the clouds. Put fifty honking cars on each block and you've got yourself a New York City."

"Didn't you have fun there?" Nick asked.

"The food was great, whatever I had a hankering for. Fettuccine and spaghetti in Little Italy, then head to Chinatown for egg rolls, dim sum pork, and moo goo gai pan."

I wrinkled my nose. "Dim dum pork?"

"Moo goo gai pan . . . " Mom tasted the words.

"Only to be eaten with chopsticks. The first time I used 'em was at a hole-in-the-wall restaurant in Chinatown. Phil Kepler bet I couldn't last the whole meal without a fork."

"Did you?" Mom picked up her crochet.

"I lasted half the meal, until he went to the restroom. Then I ate as much rice and chicken sub gum as possible with my fork until he returned. He never knew the difference." Dad chuckled. "I won ten dollars off that bet."

"He should have known better than to trust you." Mom narrowed her eyes.

"Then there's this Italian bistro, Antonio's. The best

pasta ever. And the best octopus."

"I grimaced. "Octopus! You're joking."

"If I'm lying I'll eat another dish of tuna casserole."

"How'd it taste?" Nick asked.

"Bland, actually. Folks must eat that stuff for the texture."

"Ugh!" Nick and I chorused.

"It's those little suckers—"

"Drew, that's enough." Mom hooked a stitch.

"Yes sir, only the Italians know how to do octopus right."

"Why can't we go to more restaurants?" I asked. "There's plenty in Asheville."

"Who needs restaurants with a cook as great as your mother?"

"Yeah, but she always cooks the same stuff."

"Now that sounds like a martyr if I ever heard one," Mom said. "Spare me live—"

"Spare me your martyr quotes, please!" I said.

"Then spare me your complaints." Mom waved her crochet needle.

"I'll ask about importing octopus for you two next time at the diner." Dad winked.

"Sounds like you had fun in New York," I said. "Uncle Sid likes it."

"Uncle Sid has an expert sense of direction and an iron stomach, the only way to survive there."

"Is that why you had to leave?" I asked.

Mom dropped her crochet and looked up, wide-eyed. Nick perked up, all ears. An invitation. Would my father reveal something about his mysterious past?

Dad's brow furrowed. "Yes, Tina, New York sapped the life out of me. Reckon I just couldn't take all the bagels and spaghetti."

****

Three nights before the vote, Dad went to a town council meeting. He left in a chipper mood, but returned looking as tired as a mule at plow time. Town council was the only thing standing in the way of the new park, both state- and county-approved.

After lying awake in bed, I started downstairs for a drink, but stopped and sat halfway down the steps to listen to Mom and Dad.

"Jennie, that's the worst meeting I've ever been to," Dad said. "No telling what direction this park is headed now. The council appears to be evenly split, but a few will stick with us."

"Who?"

"Roger, of course. Doc Kirby and Bob are staunchly against it, and influential with the other council members. And Wally, I think. We can count on Parker, but can't say the same for Sam and Jim, who are swaying like treetops in the wind. Not to mention the others wrapped around Phil's little finger so tightly they're ready to burst."

"How does Phil do that?" Mom said. "Those men grew up right here in Currie Hill."

"Phil had the men off their chairs, either rooting for him or trying to upstage him. Like bulls in the arena, pawing at the dirt. All in the name of employment opportunities and progress."

"I thought Phil didn't have much of a chance at first."

"So did I, but he's making the whole idea look like apple pie after a week of collards. That's why Sam Simpson, Jim Drummond, and Neal Collier are sitting on the fence and all three were originally dead set against it. Expanded business will help put their kids through college. Chandler wants greater newspaper circulation, Randall wants to expand his restaurant, and Culver says the town layout is ideal for new buildings and streets to accommodate more tourists. Not to mention Phil's push for supplying jobs. But they're not measuring what we'd lose in this great humanitarian effort."

"He sounds like Johnson and his Great Society speech," Mom said. "He's picking up where the president left off when he turned his attention to Vietnam. Creating jobs."

"But folks don't see the trade-off. What we gain in jobs, we lose in commercialism and greed. Folks are as complacent as a hog at butchering time."

"Why in the Sam Hill doesn't Phil take this park somewhere else? There's plenty of places wanting his ideas, without protests to boot."

"This is where the Economics Research Associates did their feasibility studies." My father sighed. I held my breath, straining to listen. "There's something in it for him, Jennie."

"Oh, sure, big bucks and big business. Recognition and glory. But why here?"

The couch creaked. Dad must have stood up. "There's more in it for him than that."

"Like what?" Receiving silence for an answer, Mom asked, "What is it with Phil anyhow? I know you don't see eye to eye, but you used to be such good friends. You've been acting strange for over a year now, since he moved here."

"He's got a different agenda for this town than I do. I can't abide all that."

"You wish the park wasn't coming between you?"

"That's part of it." Footsteps headed toward the stairway.

I scooted up the steps and directly into bed. He passed my door.

I reached for the wooden baseball player on my bedside table and fingered the girl's hair and baseball cap, the uniform, the bat. I needed my father like a shapeless hunk of wood needs an expert carver to give it life. My father could shape things however he wanted, so perhaps there was hope for me yet, as he guided me down the straight and narrow path toward the light.

His mind was full of designs. His strong, capable hands

crafted them into beautiful works of art. He was equally adept at shaping circumstances his way. Surely he agonized for nothing.

Nevertheless, I couldn't sleep. Why'd he step down from the diaconate? Why'd he skip communion? I went to the window to find solace in the moon and look for the man up there. Instead, I saw the man walking into the MacNeills' barn again. My mind's eye filled in the dark silhouette, fitting perfectly with the outline of Ole Joe.

On Saturday, Dad took Nick and me fishing, but I sensed Dad's tension even as he told stories and made jokes about the fish.

The night before the council vote, my father sat in his chair by the mantel for a long time without even a book or a woodcarving in his hand.

CHAPTER 17

People filed in, one by one, two by two. We were as crowded as Noah's ark and waiting for the storm. Tonight was the final vote on the park.

The meeting was open to anyone. Mom consented to let us go with her. Outside, the hot air stifled, even at dusk. Our fresh clothes soaked with sweat, peeled away from clammy skin a dozen times before the meeting started. Inside was stuffier.

Seems everybody was present: friends, relatives, locals, northerners, plus church folks who had criticized Dad's relinquishment of deacon duties. We were all at the mercy of sixteen men who'd decide the course of Currie Hill that night.

Dad, the chairman, opened the meeting with reminders and preliminaries, then introduced the issue at hand. He explained that prior to the vote, both sides of the park proposal, its entailments and ramifications, pros and cons, would be presented, with time for questions, answers, and discussion. This vote would either sanction or reject the park.

He called up Phil Kepler. Phil, accompanied by enthusiastic applause, stepped to the front. He pulled a sheet off an easel, revealing an artist's full color rendering of the park--his vision captured in one drawing that would surely entice many to share his dream.

The applause didn't lessen until Phil raised an arm. Somewhere in that commanding gesture and winsome smile was the secret that brought many from total opposition to open-armed acclamation. Despite the heat, he wore his usual long-sleeved white shirt.

Nick's brows furrowed, jaw set. Mom's eyes hinted at the buzzing tension, her forehead glistening with July's humidity. She smelled faintly of lavender.

Phil began, his face animated. "If I ask, 'Where did the Wright Brothers make their first flight?' I'll bet every one of you could tell me—Kitty Hawk, North Carolina. Common knowledge, you say. That's what I thought, too. So perhaps you'll be appalled to hear that in polls conducted last year, thirty-five percent of those surveyed thought Kitty Hawk was in Connecticut. Twenty-one percent chose upstate New York. Nineteen percent couldn't even name Kitty Hawk as the site. I find that astounding, and here—" he pointed to the drawing—"through this park, is a sterling chance to educate the country about our fine North Carolina history."

He checked his notes, but seemed like a walking encyclopedia on theme parks, spouting their history and why this one was a guaranteed success. Enthusiasm pulled his voice up and down the full range of tones, with a tranquilizing effect.

He described the only three successful theme parks: Disneyland since 1955, Six Flags over Texas since 1961, and Cedar Point in Ohio, existing for decades but recently evolving into a theme park. "Attempts to open others have failed for many reasons, one of which is that it's sure failure to copy Disneyland, the model park. A park must be innovative in its own right, and I assure you, folks, this park is." His palm smacked the podium for effect.

Disneyland's Audio-Animatronic singing pirates and the "people mover" zooming along the sky highway came to mind. Was that why Dad figured this park couldn't compete?

"I'm thrilled to show you drawings that demonstrate the ingenuity behind this park, but first understand that the ERA, the Economics Research Associates, considers all factors when determining a site. One of their clients, The Walt Disney Company, has benefited from the ERA's expertise, with plans underway for developing a second theme park, this time in Florida."

Would that park have a pirate ride, too? Will they show it on *Walt Disney's Wonderful World of Color*?

"As feasibility studies pointed out, we have myriad reasons why our own Currie Hill is the perfect location. First, the site is determined by freeway access and water, sewage, power, trees, rivers, elevation, and change. The amount of land needed is 200 to 250 acres, one third for parking, one third for the park, and one third for future expansion, administration, and physical requirements. Obviously, land and good freeways are something we have plenty of."

He turned over the drawing to reveal a map. "Concurrent with ERA studies, Brent Culver and I worked out the most favorable plan for park placement and new buildings for handling the business this will bring in. This map shows that our town is conducive to expansion without destroying existing structures. Current buildings will receive a face lift, to maintain architectural consistency with nostalgic appeal. We'd like to preserve both facades and interiors."

He discussed location. The park would be four miles north of Currie Hill, far enough from downtown, residential areas, and farms so as not to intrude, but near freeways for easy access. It would be close enough to enjoy its advantages and interact with park guests--he avoided saying tourists. Nor did he mention the sandlot.

Phil revealed another drawing, an idyllic scene of a river, footbridge, ferryboat, and greenery along the riverbank. "A theme park is distinguished from a mere amusement park that features centrifugal force rides, arcades, games, funhouses, and bawdy entertainment. This park will have none of that, mind you. Great care has been exercised to ensure a natural fit into its surroundings of the Smokies. The plan consolidates and capsulizes all of North Carolina's geography, its European history, and its mountain culture into one park."

No pirates, then.

"In fact, the entire south is represented through cultural and historical exhibits. Themed areas will prove entertaining and educational, offering a variety of activities with universal appeal, something for all ages. This is truly exciting, folks. Multiple factors guarantee the park's financial success. The tourist trade, because of the Smokies and Blue Ridge Parkway, is already thriving here. The park will complement and enhance the visitors' experience. They'll enjoy the convenience of paying one price for all day, the most efficient way to handle money exchange. The cost per person is seven dollars for an average eight-hour stay."

He set a graph of numbers on the easel. "Multiply that by the daily, weekly, monthly, and yearly number of visitors. It's absolutely fascinating how these details have been determined. To make a profit, the park must be able to handle 25,000 people a day and 1.25 million people annually, which, again, due to the tourist trade, is no problem. How does it accommodate so many people at once? Through the right amount of entertainment units. That includes eating and sitting places, rides, and shows—enough for everyone to be occupied simultaneously. Our plans include well over the minimum number of necessary units.

"According to the ERA, predicting an accurate number of guests determines the physical dimensions, facilities, and budget." Mr. Kepler's arm swooped up as he stepped forward. His voice matched enthusiastic gestures. "These numbers are why the cost of this park is nothing to be alarmed by. Yes, it's five million dollars for land and services and twenty million dollars when all is said and done, but the tourists are already here." He cited figures that my father quoted to him weeks earlier, in our front room, then concluded, "These facts coupled with the ERA research on location confirm the wisdom of placing the park here in Currie Hill."

Next, Phil turned to a diagram showing the park layout. He explained how sections were arranged in a loop allowing easy access either way, with eight themed areas. "First, The

Old World features European architecture of countries where most North Carolinians originated, including Germany, home of the Moravians. The Irish section is called Kilkenny. Medieval and Renaissance England capitalizes on the rich literary heritage of Shakespeare, Dickens, Chaucer, and the legendary Arthur. Of course the Scottish Highlands are represented: Strathie, Balmoral Castle, Sir Walter Scott's *Ivanhoe*, and Robert Louis Stevenson's *Treasure Island.*"

Ah, ha! Pirates, after all.

"Folk music, folk dancers, old world bakeries, bistros, and import shops supplement that section. A ferry or footbridge will take people to the next section, The New World, just as many of your forefathers immigrated over the water."

Another opportunity for buccaneers.

He referred to the river picture again. "The focus will be pioneers who made their way here in the seventeenth through nineteenth centuries, including the likes of Daniel Boone. A wildlife preserve includes hiking trails, log cabin guesthouses, camping, rivers and fishing, petting farms, and a chair lift ride for a bird's eye view." He turned pages on the easel, pointing out highlights. "Next will be the entire state of North Carolina and other southern states in miniature, a topographical, geographical view, stretching from the ocean to the Appalachian Mountains."

Again, he sought aide from the drawings. Each colorful image lured the viewer to enter its domain. "A Turn-of-the-Century Village has a train and original, restored log cabins, a large screen film of turn-of-the-century lifestyles, and a re-enactment with costumed characters who churn butter, card wool, build cabins, sew shoes, and so on, plus a roller coaster ride simulating an old mine and a flume, and a mill ride called a 'Log Jammer.' Craft demonstrations include quilting, pottery, spinning, woodcarving, soap making, blacksmithing, weaving, basket weaving, and chair making."

He grinned. "The snack bar here is called The Moonshiner. The general store has a cider press and taffy pulls.

138

A sawmill will give log rolling demonstrations. Three theaters feature hourly entertainment, such as folk music with dulcimers, mandolins, fiddles, and banjos, plus storytelling, cloggers, bluegrass, country, jazz, rhythm and blues, gospel and Negro spirituals--music from all over the South."

Sweat frosted my forehead. Someone sneezed, feet shuffled. Behind me a boy tapped fingers on the bench like a galloping horse.

"Next, Our Literary Heritage gives tribute to literary traditions. Mother Goose Land, from our English roots, will be a miniature village of nursery rhymes for children, populated by wandering trolls, elves, fairies, minstrels, nursery rhyme characters, and puppets. Another village features storytellers, shows, and monuments commemorating Jack tales and Grandfather tales, Uncle Remus and Brer Rabbit, African folk tales, European folklore and fairytales brought by our ancestors, and North Carolina authors such as Carl Sandburg and Thomas Wolfe.

"'The Melting Pot—the Deep South' will highlight New Orleans, Cajun Country, and pay tribute to great men and women who have heralded from our deep southern states, with music, cooking, storytelling, and more gift shops, restaurants, and snack bars."

He flipped through more drawings. "The last section, The Roaring 20s, has barnstorming with original old planes and a model of the Wright Brothers Bicycle Shop. There will be air shows, hang gliding, parachuting, chopper rides, an old auto track ride, gondolas, a carousel and ferris wheel, in the tradition of the grand old parks, with workers in 1920s costume." He patted his forehead with a handkerchief. "For families who can't afford to travel to all these locations firsthand, they can capture the southern flavor and experience, past and present, even if this park is the only place they visit."

Phil clapped twice as if calling us to attention. "Another exciting thing is how soon the park can be ready. Opening date is usually three years from purchase of the land, but I have the necessary contacts for speeding the development and installment of many entertainment units. The park will open within three years, the entire park completed in ten."

A baby cried and a mother whisked her out the door. The boy behind me tapped his feet as if keeping beat in a marching band.

"The fast track method is the way to go, which entails designing and building simultaneously, saving time and money on loans. Though many designs are completed, some are undergoing modification. Despite reservations you might have about this venture, there's little risk. Though the fast track method sometimes results in unforeseen delays and problems that don't appear until later, we've pored over the master plan in anticipation of potential problems. I'm positive we've ironed out wrinkles, leaving no cause for concern."

Someone sneezed, another coughed, and a baby whined, expressing exactly how I felt with the same voice trickling like a leaky roof.

"When bids are in we'll hire a construction manager. It takes a year for fiberglass molds of carousel horses and other rides to be built. In the final design stage, personnel is hired. This is where the unemployment problem in our county can be alleviated. We'll need thousands of employees for running this park on a yearly basis, from monitoring rides to ticket-selling, from food service to sanitation, and other positions.

"The initial work should be done locally, as much as possible. I stand behind this community one hundred percent. Using local workers not only saves money in the initial investment but boosts the morale and fosters economy here. I'm involved in selecting planning groups, such as architects, artists, and engineers for visual design led by a project architect coordinator. Ross Hamilton's sawmill will cut wood for cupolas and cabinets needed for offices and shops. A machine shop will be set up to aid in installing rides and keeping them running. An operations manager will be hired, too."

Had Ross told Grandma and Grandpa about his job

offer, or were they hearing it for the first time? Dozens of folks appeared mesmerized, drawn into the park's magic spell as Phil explained the necessary personnel, including merchandisers and employee relation coordinators. Food specialists would oversee the twenty-two restaurants and snack shops. Intamin Corporation and Arrow would create flume and train rides and an observation tower at 330 feet for 1200 people. Each required eight months fabrication time.

Phil shuffled papers. He set another chart of figures on the easel, showing financial and employment benefits to the community. Then he flipped back to the first park rendering. He escalated his sales pitch as his captive audience shifted and zeroed in for the finale.

"The advantages of this park are hundredfold. First, it will create a thriving economy, supplying jobs across the state, to college students and the unemployed. Workers can take pride in preserving a heritage that might otherwise get lost in modern times. The park will foster appreciation for this culture and its traditions, and the beauty of its mountains.

"Concern has been expressed over the possible consequences of bringing in such a park. Drew Hamilton will discuss those shortly. But perhaps I can dispel some of the myths that crop up with such a venture. One objection is the growth itself: overcrowding, a hurried pace, irreversible changes. One thing that offsets these problems is the careful planning of the layout of streets and buildings that can efficiently handle many people at once. In this way, the small town atmosphere is enhanced, not destroyed. In that lies part of the park's charm.

"Others fear the threat of technology, which no doubt will be utilized. But the purpose of technology is to meet our needs, not vice versa. As technology captures the rest of the world, let us not protect our children from it and prevent them from functioning elsewhere.

"Your forefathers didn't have it easy carving out a living in these mountains, but they made you what you are today. Your children are rich in spirit because of it. Don't they deserve all you have to offer them now? This park will give your children the best of two worlds. One world consists of your small town values and a priceless heritage to carry wherever they go. The other world is one of progress, a booming economy, the utilization of talents and limitless opportunities, using their heads and hands for growth, achievement, and service to mankind."

CHAPTER 18

Applause welled up. Phil Kepler swaggered off the platform, his eloquence having greatly benefited him, surely leaving in his wake dozens of new converts. Roger Griffin, the vice-chairman, introduced my father with a reminder that questions would be taken afterward. Dad walked forward accompanied by just as much clapping. Mom squeezed my hand.

Dad made no pretensions. He wore old slacks, a blue shirt with sleeves rolled to his elbows, and an open collar. A wisp of bangs strapped across his wet forehead. He seemed to relish the quiet moment following the applause.

"Gentlemen of the Council, my fellow citizens of Currie Hill, I have no long speech to convince you of the invalidity of the one preceding mine, for much that Phil Kepler told you was valid. I think we can all understand his reasons for wishing to bring about the changes he outlines, particularly the positive effect it would have on unemployment, an increasing problem in our country. But I'd like to put to you all some questions that I trust, before you're swayed one way or the other, you shall thoughtfully consider while deciding the future and possibly irreversible course of this town."

Mom's eyes were riveted to him, settling me. She loved him fiercely.

"First, is our own Bob Hutchins any less rich a man because he can't tell you how long it takes him to make one chair? Can his enjoyment in his work be traded for an assembly line production of five hundred chairs a day or a thousand dollars a week? Does a goal of service to people rank lower than the goal of getting our money's worth? Does discovering our potential and talents mean using them in a thing-centered society, in a me-centered way, with only economic concerns?

"The park can do great things, as Mr. Kepler explained, but if we adopt it, we also adopt permanent change in the structure of our community. I've seen cities where mobility, technology, and free enterprise are idolized at the expense of relationships and community. Following naturally are greed, more monetary gain and power, commercialism, and an individualistic society. The park itself, if installed, may be beautiful, but as a result, shops and enterprises will be popping up like warts beyond control, defacing our town like graffiti on a wall. We'll wake up one morning and look out the window to find billboards in our cornfields and neon signs blinking by our mailboxes.

"I've been in the city where folks don't even know their neighbors, much less know when they're ill, needing help. It's rare in our day and age to see such advancements in the hands of men without taking its greedy toll and sacrificing all we've tried to rear our children to be. As long as there's evil in the heart of man, cities and big business can only be base and depraved, despite good intentions. Will the ramifications of this park eventually take its toll on all we have, especially on our children's values?

"Does the concrete of buildings and sidewalks have more to do with reality than the wildflowers of the field? Does our heritage need to be capsulized and molded to a plastic and concrete substitute in order to be valued and preserved?" His voice cracked. "Is this not prostitution of culture?" He scanned the audience. "Is the quality of life measured in numbers and economic success alone? If so, then perhaps our fathers, grandfathers, and great-grandfathers were all failures. They tilled the soil all their lives, choosing to remain in the mountains rather than increase the urban population. Were their trials, illnesses, obstacles, and dreams less important than those of a man who makes his living in the city? Did they pave our way in the wilderness only so we can live in concrete?

"Many other towns would welcome the park's installation. It's not a matter of right and wrong. But do we want to change the nature of *this* town? We must ask ourselves why we live here in the first place. We've made that choice, consciously or unconsciously, and we've chosen to rear our kids here." He paused again. "But aren't we richer for it? And won't our children be?"

Cheers erupted as he took a seat on the platform. Some folks clapping were the same ones who'd passed judgment on my father for abandoning the diaconate.

Roger Griffin went to the podium to ask for questions. Several people asked about details in Phil's maps and drawings. A few questions were addressed to Dad.

Wally Abernathy, the shoe store owner, stood. "I have a question for Phil." His thumbs poked into his pockets, his feet rocked back and forth. "Why'd you leave New York City to come to Currie Hill? It don't seem quite right that a polished, citified, and educated man like yourself can come to our little town and be properly content."

"Wally, that's a good question," Phil said. "I came down here to work with the ERA feasibilities studies five years ago, and a while before that as well. I've always been interested in problem solving, economic progress, and easing the unemployment problem. When we hit upon the park idea, it seemed like a realistic solution for multiple challenges. The ERA has proven this to be the ideal location. I finally made my home here. If I pilot this project, I need to know this place as home. I need to know firsthand the people and traditions of this area."

Bob Hutchins popped up, his white furry hair bobbing with every word. "So you're saying that when you started coming here five years ago, you planned to bring this park into our town? Even though we just learned about it the last few months? That's as crooked as a barrel of fish hooks."

Phil jumped in before the crowd could. "No, it's not. I consider myself a citizen here. This is my home now, for my son Todd, too. I own the Bear Wallow Inn. But I haven't kept it any secret that I still have affiliations up north. The companies I've worked for are responsible for engineering this project, and put me in charge. The idea hasn't been broached until recently because there's much to do prior to such a move. Red tape, public relations, designs. Little good it would have done to bring this up five years ago, before research was complete, before the county and state approved it. Without the feasibility studies, talk about this park would have been a waste of time. I wanted to be prepared with every detail and leave no question unanswered. The fact that it's been approved at higher levels speaks to the wisdom of it."

Dr. Kirby rose. "In other words, you've befriended us in order to fashion this town according to your whims."

A hum of voices affirmed the doctor. Phil, never at a loss for composure, smiled. "My words and intentions are being twisted—"

Matt Bridges, one of Phil's avid supporters, stood, but Jim Drummond, the blacksmith, cut in. "This sounds like exploitation to me. Your northern corporation's gonna get rich off this." Jim, supposedly straddled between both sides, sounded like he'd made his choice.

"The goal," Phil said, "is the economic improvement of this area and beyond."

"Mr. Kepler," Doc said, "using us as a means to this end can only be right if we're on board with it. If the ERA did further studies, they might find areas that suit them better."

Brent Culver swiveled out of his seat. "Dr. Kirby, ladies, gentlemen. First of all, the ERA studies did extensive research before narrowing it down to this location. Secondly, I can attest to Phil's sincerity. He means no harm. I've worked with Phil many years. He's a man of deep conviction and seeks to serve the community."

"Aren't you from New York, too?" Bob Hutchins asked.

"I was an urban planner outside Detroit originally. I

met Phil in New York. He recommended moving here. I brought my family here four years ago."

"So you also came with the intention of changing our town?" Gerald Duncan, the hardware store owner, sneezed and wiped his nose with a handkerchief. "I suppose the other northerners came for the same reason? The likes of Russ Chandler and Matt Bridges."

Tall, lanky Uncle Parker jumped up, marionette-like. "And Cliff Randall and Peter Kamp, too. There's something in it for all of you, right?"

"Gentlemen," Phil said, unruffled, "everybody here has something to gain."

"And nothing to lose?" Parker said. "What if the crowds aren't drawn? What if the whole thing flops? How much would we stand to lose then?"

The chirping crowd echoed him.

Phil was undaunted. "The chances of that happening are very slim. The ERA has already studied diligently to discern reasons for successful versus failed theme parks in the past decade."

"How long has the ERA been around?" Jim Drummond asked. "Did it prevent failures before?"

"The ERA was founded in 1958," Phil said. "Due to its meticulous attention to examination of every detail, it has met tremendous success in many endeavors, besides theme parks."

Wally stood again. "Maybe we're not fond of hundreds of strange folks wandering about. Maybe we like yonder hills and trees the way they are. So do tourists that already come to see the mountains. They don't need no park. Besides, we got too many tourists."

"That's exactly why the park will work," Phil said above crowing voices. "View it this way. You'll shatter in their minds any mountain stereotypes they carry with them. They can delight with you in your clogging and fiddle-playing. Isn't your culture worth sharing?"

"Mr. Kepler." Dr. Kirby spoke over the drizzle of

objections that drained in at the end of every speech. "You're saying it's not worthwhile to pass on our culture only to our children. We need large quantities of people appreciating it. Then again, numbers are everything."

"Can't we even have the wilds without a profit?" Uncle Eddie spouted. "Do we reckon land a waste unless thousands are looking at it?"

Bob Hutchins piped up. "Maybe we don't want our culture on display like a stage show. Maybe it's a deeper part of us than that, one that'll be lost if it merely becomes a performance."

Phil wiped his brow. "People, I'm not asking you to change your values, your priorities of family or community. I'm just trying to stress that as our world grows and changes— and we have no control over that—we must adapt. This isn't a compromise of values. There's a lot out there for the taking, but we also have much to give, and a responsibility to do our part in solving problems, those of unemployment, conservation, education, job skills, and so on." His eyes baited us, seeking out unbelieving souls, daring us to be enlightened, preparing to reel us in. "Why should we stop short of the best for this town? That's like being satisfied with a finger painting when we could have the Mona Lisa."

"Phil." Gerald Duncan sniffled. "You talk so much about family and children and small town values. But what do you know about those? Where's the rest of your family?"

Murmurs rippled across the room. Most people knew Phil was divorced, that his wife left him and Todd years ago.

Uncle Ross charged from his seat, face cherry red. "That question is completely out of line. Phil should be commended for raising his kid single-handedly, no easy task. The issue here is our town and our jobs, not Phil's personal life. Wake up, folks—jobs! We can send our kids to college. If not college, they can make a living. We can give them choices they've never had, that we never had."

Ross's blustering did little to blow away my anxiety.

Phil tried to speak, but Wally interrupted. "I think Drew Hamilton has the right idea about our town. Who knows better than him? He grew up right here among us. He's truly one of us. His wife and kids have been here since they was born. He's a farmer and has been on our council for twelve years, chairman for four. If he thought a park was fittin' for this town, he'd have said so. I think Drew speaks for most of us who grew up here. The heart of the town is in the folks here and in the soil of them hills. It ain't in no concrete buildings. Or park."

Cheers and applause arose. Mom squeezed my hand again. Surely we would win this vote.   Mr. Kepler embraced the podium. All eyes and ears awaited his rebuttal. "Fellow townsmen, you've raised worthwhile yet difficult questions tonight, and I've tried my best to answer them truthfully. You're an intelligent people. I respect your pride in your town and your right to make your own decisions. I know you'll vote in all objectivity, but this last comment by Wally makes me think that perhaps you're more dependent on Drew Hamilton than you realize. It has been stated many times that what's good enough for Drew Hamilton is good enough for everyone. This man is highly regarded here. He speaks with wisdom and sensitivity. But consider this: are you making up your mind on the basis of one man's influence instead of the facts? Are you putting too much stock in his sentiments about this town?

"There's a reason for my grave concern. You're so sure that Drew has nothing but the best of intentions and the purest motivation for his statements. You say his word is good because he's one of you. But I challenge that. Is he one of you? You claim he was born and reared here, and rears his family here. But I ask you: where was he in between those times?"

Seated behind Phil, Dad's eyes widened as if he'd seen a bear step in the doorway. He squared his shoulders.

Phil continued. "I didn't want to bring this up, but I fear you're being led blindly. The facts must be shared, here and now, so we can see the issue clearly."

Dad stood, but Phil waved him away. Phil's voice went

from drizzle to downpour. "You claim he's one of you, but
have any of you left for so many unaccounted-for years? Dr.
Kirby, didn't you attend medical school within the state and
return immediately to begin your practice here? Parker, didn't
you go away to major in journalism, then return to use your
abilities and knowledge in this community?" He addressed
others as well. "But what did Drew do with his education?
Wasn't it enough for him to live here and take over his father's
sawmill and farm? Your town council chairman stands before
you an educated man, with a master's degree in architecture,
and a minor in business administration, very specialized. Was
that so he could come back and work the fields and fix
machinery?

"I'll tell you this much. After four years in the service,
he completed five years of schooling, then landed a job for six
years at a major corporation in New York City, working his
way up to head architect. Is this the type of drive that
epitomizes your non-competitive atmosphere here?"

Dad moved toward Phil with fire in his eyes. Roger
and Dr. Kirby called out, but Phil silenced them. "You'll get
your chance at rebuttal." Dad froze.

My hand went numb from Mom's squeezes.

Phil continued. "When he finally returned here, what
was his reason? I know it's not mentioned in this town except
in speculation behind closed doors, all but forgotten. Perhaps
he made it up to you by serving on your town council. And
tilling the soil like many of you do, but with degrees in
architecture and business. Even his southern inflections have
been softened by northern influence, though nobody seems to
notice the difference anymore, all testimony to the subtlety of
the deceit."

Facing awestruck stares, Mr. Kepler went full steam
ahead. "You claim that if a man leaves and is successful in
adopting the big city American value system, he was never one
of us. But if he fails there and returns, he belongs to neither
them nor us. Ask yourselves—did this man fail? Is this man

protesting the park installment and progress of this town because he couldn't achieve his own dreams? Why else would he never choose to talk about his past? What else but failure silences a man? If he'd succeeded, would he be here with us now?"

As if sitting on hot seats, Ross, Eddie, Parker, Dr. Kirby, Roger, Bob, Jim, Wally, and others jumped up to protest, a dissonant chorus of shouts.

"This is outrageous!" Jim Drummond barked.

"Get out of here!" Bob Hutchins roared.

"You've gone far enough!" Ross bellowed above the bedlam.

Dad gestured to them to sit down. He stepped over to Phil. Sweat drenched his face as if he'd just stepped out of the river. Phil had trounced my father's character with a deluge of well-chosen twisted words, flowing from him as easily as a summer rain, oppressing us with a cloud heavier than July's heat. Yet surely my father would easily clear his name even after the lowest of accusations. Phil would be left standing in the rain, alone and bedraggled.

Dad drew a deep breath, as if to measure every forthcoming word before it fell out and permanently made its mark on our lives. "Folks, what you're all hearing right now from Phil is what I would term a kind lie. Yes, part of what he's saying is true. I went to college, I majored in architecture. Because of my professional relationship with Phil back then, I found an excellent position immediately after graduation. I worked hard, like many of you do.

"But the lie is this. I didn't fail there. Phil was being kind in that lie because I did much worse. I succeeded."

People gawked, as if preparing to forever cement or change their loyalties at the drop of a convicting word.

"It's a kind lie, folks, because Phil knows I have great shame in my success there. During that time, I exchanged everything I inherited from my culture, values, and upbringing for the false satisfaction of approval by those in higher places.

And I didn't do it for the purpose of bettering anyone else, but for the sheer delight in perfecting my art and receiving the praise of men. My crowning achievement at that time, the one I wasted all my time on and feel the most shame for, is this theme park. I designed it myself."

The crowd gasped. Mom's face paled. My heart quickened, stomach tightening.

Dad continued. "That's why I can tell you today that no matter what the benefits of this park, it's not worth the cost of what you'd have to give up."

Dozens of objections tangled with Phil's retorts, but Phil prevailed. "People, can't you see? Of course he doesn't want you to vote it in. It would be like running him out of town, a continual reminder of someone he once was when he wasn't one of you." He stepped forward. "In New York, he got people sold on a great idea. They backed him up with money and crew for three years while he worked on it. The only reason he originally returned here was to look over the area as a potential park site, on the sly, you might say, back in the summer of '56."

People glanced around, as if to determine who knew.

Doc yelled over the clamor. "Drew, is all this true? Let's hear from you."

Dad rolled his sleeves up farther. He grasped the podium anchoring him to the platform. "As was mentioned earlier, I believe this park is a prostitution of culture." He winced. "I didn't realize that while working on it. But by the end of three years on the project, I ascertained the harm it would bring to Currie Hill. When I returned here in '56, I'd already quit my job, and I came back here for good."

"That's not true," Phil said. "He made one more trip back to New York."

"That trip was in order to destroy all the plans I could find." Dad ran fingers through his hair. "Phil, this is enough. We've covered the issue."

Voice full of fervor and desperation, Phil faced the

muttering audience. "You still might not have seen him again if his first wife hadn't died in New York. Not much time elapsed between burying Sonia and marrying Jennie Ross."

His stabbing words penetrated the din, surely having clinched his victory the way a hook pierces a fish. The storm of protests flared again. Mom paled another shade. I shrunk.

Dad, red-faced, turned to Phil. "You have no business bringing up these things, especially with my family here."

Roger Griffin hopped up. He touched my Dad's arm, then stepped between the two men, obviously uncomfortable with his referee role. "Let's stick to park business."

"Folks," Dad said, "for years I wanted nobody here to know about my part in the theme park. I knew it would cause you to look at me differently. Now I only tell you about my role in it so you can trust that I know where it's coming from and where it'll take us. Perhaps your understanding my previous foolishness will prevent its acceptance here.

"Yes, I knew city ways for those years and I'm not proud of it. I stand before you a changed man, convicted by my upbringing. I don't want to see any part of my past again, but more than that, for our children's sake, I don't want to see the ways of the city, what we call the American way, adopted here in our town, in our own families. This park will bring all of that in."

Phil cut in for his final blows. "This park reminds Drew of a past he'd like to forget. The changes this park will bring offer him no escape. He has ulterior motives for dismissing its growth and progress. Because of the extremes Drew experienced in this trade-off of values, he can't see a moderate balance between the two, and would have you suffer and remain ignorant of a wealth of opportunities."

Phil's torrent of accusations flooded us with shock and dismay, leaving us flailing, sinking, no way to bail out. Only Mom's hand kept me afloat.

My father grasped Phil's arm—for fear of what Phil might reveal next? "This has gone too far."

Phil was shaky. "It hasn't gone far enough."

Voices bubbled up. Dozens of men stood. Roger silenced the crowd. He asked my father, "Drew, do you have final words for us?"

Dad stood stock-still, fists clenched. "I've told you the truth because I don't want any of you caught in the trap I was once stuck in."

Amid a flourish of exclamations, Roger mustered more volume. "The council has heard both sides now. Gentlemen of the Council, I ask you to consider this vote on the merits of the issue alone."

Dad and Phil retreated. My mother pulled Nick and me out, burrowing through the drone of whispers, mumblings, and gasps.

They were going to vote now.

CHAPTER 19

Mom whisked Nick and me home before the vote, put on her *Camelot* record, and wept.

My father came home a broken man. He sat silently by the mantel as Mom cried in the bedroom.

The last exchange of words between Dad and Phil Kepler made their final impact not only on town council—whose votes sent our town reeling head over heels into a new way of life—but on our family as well.

The following day he resigned from town council.

That evening, Mom asked Dad why he created a theme park of southern culture.

He swallowed hard. "After my army experience, I had to convince myself of the value of my roots, and at the same time find approval from others outside of my roots and tradition. I was trapped serving two masters, trying to find out who I really was, and what was important to me. After three years on the project, I discovered the answers."

"Did you know five years ago that Phil came down for instigating the park?"

Dad nodded. "When he first arrived, we passed words, more than I'd like to bring to mind. Even then he had state and county support, not to mention half of New York City. It was like a bug arguing with a chicken."

Mom started another question but he held up his hand.

An hour later, someone knocked. My father reddened when he opened the door to Phil Kepler.

Phil stepped in of his own accord. "Drew, I know you feel I've betrayed you, but it would have been a shame for the council to vote down the park—"

"No need for explanations." Dad's jaw tightened.

"Please, let me finish. I couldn't neglect my duty in pursuing the potential of Currie Hill and helping to remedy the socio-economic problems. But I never intended to sacrifice you to that end. I'm sorry, Drew. I got nervous the whole thing would fall through, not just the park, but my job, my career, everything I'd worked for the last ten years."

Dad cocked his head. "How's Todd doing? How's he going to fit in with all the park demands?" I deemed it a strange question.

Phil balked. "What? You needn't concern yourself with that. He's excited about this park."

"I see."

"Look, Drew, I apologize. I never should have brought up Sonia. I was out of line."

"Yes, you were. But whatever your tactics, you've got what you want now."

"No, I don't have everything I want."

"Well, what are you missing? A pat on the back from me and hearty congratulations?"

"I'll miss our friendship. I regret it won't be the same now. But I also consider the good of many people as more important than the good of one."

Dad's mouth dropped open. "Just who is that one, Phil? Is it me? Is it just my good you're forfeiting? Or is it going to be Todd's?"

Phil's eyes blazed. "Good day, Drew." He left.

****

A smattering of people stopped by the next few days: Ross and Abby, Eddie and Grandpa; Uncle Parker, Aunt Elaine, and Grandma Dorothy; Dr. Kirby and Roger Griffin. Grandma Hamilton was too angry to step foot in our house. No one dared come alone. And no one knew what to say.

We had Sunday dinner at Grandma and Grandpa's, like usual. But it was as torturous as pushing a tractor uphill.

"How in the Sam Hill could you make a park like that?" Grandma Hamilton shook her finger at Dad over a plateful of pot roast. "How could you let Phil Kepler contrary you?"

"The man has his reasons," Grandpa Hamilton said. "He already explained everything."

"Ain't no reason good enough for me. We all thought he could have kept that park out of here. Come to find out he made that dad-blasted thing! What in blazes drove him to New York anyhow?" she asked Grandpa as if Dad wasn't sitting there. People were passing dishes of fried chicken, mashed potatoes, gravy, and green beans, but not eating much.

"He's a grown man, Emma," Grandpa said. "He don't have to answer to nobody but God. And his wife."

"Wife? That's another thing. Was he so ashamed of us he couldn't bring his first wife here to meet us? Couldn't invite us to his wedding? And didn't even tell us about her till after the fact? The city's a devil's place. I wish Sidney would hightail it out of there. It's gotta grip on him—"

"Now calm down, Emma. The food'll get cold."

"If only that were the worst of my problems! We're suffering a worse fate than cold food right now."

"Would you say grace, Edward?" Grandpa asked.

"We already said grace, Pa," Eddie replied with a mouthful of bread.

"Well, say it again. We need some peace and quiet."

Eddie bowed, swallowed, and prayed a litany that blessed the missionaries, sick people, and food at least twice more.

Grandma piped right back in. "It ain't right when a man keeps secrets. That's borrowing trouble for certain. A right heap of good that did! All those men up and vote in the park. It'll be the end of us all. Lord, have mercy. Drew, would you still be in New York if you hadn't seen the error of your ways?

And Sidney! Lord, bring him to ruin, if only he'd—"

"Mother." Ross stood, his voice sucking the breath from us all. "Leave Drew alone or I'm leaving this table and you won't be seeing me for a powerful long time. He's a bigger man than most and has a right to privacy."

It became the quietest meal on record since Grandpa Ross died years earlier.

PART IV

Grandpa Hamilton: Bear Dogs and Mercy. "See, you can't make a silk purse out of a sow's ear. Who needs silk anyway? Sometimes all a body needs to get by in life is a little mercy."

On Grandpa's lap I was comfortably crowded in the crook of his arm. My head rested against his bumpy chest pocket. I fingered the hard shape. "What's in your pocket?"

"I'm carrying a dream too big for my heart."

I reached in and withdrew a tin of chewing tobacco. He snickered.

Grandma handed us a bowl of popcorn, made from his popcorn patch. The dog Mercy trailed her, then sniffed the bowl on my lap. I tossed him a few kernels. He snatched them.

"Mercy me, stop spoiling that dog," Grandma said. The dogs ears perked up.

"How'd Mercy get his name?" I asked.

"He comes from a long line of Mercies." Grandpa rocked back and forth. "They earned the name by being so undeserving of anything else. This dog's line should've been snuffed out long ago."

"God miraculously preserved them." Grandma sorted corn silk and husks for her handmade dolls.

Grandpa smirked. "He preserved them all right, with help from my brother Finlay. It's all Finlay's fault, no doubt."

"What happened?"

"Finlay had himself eight young-uns. It ain't no piece

of cake to raise a passel like that, let alone Finlay who's so strict. Why, if one of his kids so much as batted an eyelash after he told him to stay put he'd have him tote around ten bushels of field hay. After a day of farming and running that family, he was fit to be tied, and that's all he was fit for. So he was plumb out of gumption for everything else. That's why he couldn't do nothing with a new dog." Grandpa scooped a handful of popcorn. "He loved hunting, but couldn't train a hunting dog if his life depended on it. My brother Roderick trained dogs for him.

"There was one dog Finlay got suckered into buying. Was told he was a real champion and pick of the litter, a bear dog. Finlay took him to Rod to train, and Rod was a good trainer. But turns out the dog was half-brindle-to-buck."

"Half what?" I asked.

"Of uncertain pedigree. The dog could've been half Tasmanian devil for all I know. Rod couldn't do one thing with that dog. He wouldn't learn a trick but the next day he'd forget it. When they hunted for bears, which is what Rod trained him for, he'd think we was hunting squirrels or rabbit. So then Rod reckoned he'd be a better squirrel or rabbit dog than a bear dog, and trained him to hunt rabbits. Well, darned if that dog only chased grouse and pheasant after that. There weren't no learning that dog nothing."

"Ain't no different from some men I know." Grandma narrowed her eyes at him.

"Rod finally recommended Finlay get shet of that dog. He weren't worth keeping and they couldn't afford it. But Finlay, he fell in love with the dog and couldn't bear the thought of parting ways. Fact is, he still took him on bear hunts because he was convinced the dog was just a late bloomer. Rod swore up and down it weren't true. The only way you keep a bear dog from taking off after rabbits and such is by beating it, and not even that worked with this dog. While the other dogs were treeing a bear he'd run off and distract everybody with something else. And he was the fightingest dog I ever did see.

Dumber than a box of rocks."

I giggled and dug for more popcorn.

"Rod thought about taking the dog out and shooting it. He couldn't get no money for it, and it gobbled up so much game, he was a bad influence on the other dogs. Fact is, one time he met headlong with a skunk and went about stinking for the better part of a week. No amount of washing him in tomato juice or lemon juice worked on him."

"Ooh, pee-you." I plugged my nose.

Grandpa chewed a mouthful of popcorn. "Try living with that smell for a week. But even that wouldn't make Finlay part with him. Anyhow, Rod wanted to put that dog out of our misery. He planned a hunting accident so as the dog would meet its end, but only after it sired a pup we called Mercy. 'Cause mercy was the only thing that pup ever had going for it.

"I named that dog myself. See, you can't make a silk purse out of a sow's ear. Who needs silk anyway? Sometimes all a body needs to get by in life is a little mercy."

CHAPTER 20

The next four weeks after the vote, we had numerous baseball practices and play-off games. Jay was so tense, every time he tried to steal second base he tripped. Eight Ball dropped more flies and Cue Ball barked more orders, rivaling Hud who kept yelling at us all to calm down, for heaven's sake, did we think we were playing the World Series?

No, but the championship game would be the last one ever played on our sandlot before it got swallowed by the park.

I couldn't decipher which scowls came from pre-game tension and which were from the certainty of this park squashing and overtaking this town. Worse, my father turned out to be someone other than the hometown boy folks grew up with. That contaminated me as well. Eyes stared my way then averted. Whispers increased as backs turned.

Folks buzzed about the final game, anticipating the climax between the Bear Wallow Inn Grizzlies and Wally's Shoes Wildcats. Nick practiced something fierce, wearing his arm out between practices. I asked if he was still working with Todd on his screwball.

Nick frowned. "He mastered it. He don't need my help anymore."

Nick's superstitious tendencies rose to the fore as insurance. Before each at bat, he spit on the ground and rubbed his foot in it. He never changed bats during a game and never took one handed to him by someone else. He laced and tied one shoe completely before putting the other one on. It wasn't pitching he was worried about. It was hitting.

My three RBI double won our final play-off game against Duncan's Hardware. Phil Kepler's Grizzlies had cheered us on. Next week they'd be the enemy.

But for now, victory called for celebration at Sam Simpson's Ice Cream Parlor. Mom once renamed it "Sam Simpson's Stupendous Sundae Specialties." She'd repeat it, faster and faster without tripping, then laugh. But such lightheartedness evaded us tonight.

Dad and Mom remained somber from the last council meeting. Besides experiencing estrangement from townsfolk, we felt like strangers with each other. At the restaurant, at least the noise could fill up the silent spaces between us. And going there was a stride toward normality.

Typical visits meant being greeted by chocolate smells, juke box tunes, and half a dozen families—handshakes and laughter all around with plenty to spare. If Nick or I played an exceptional ballgame, Sam Simpson served out treats on the house, no matter how loudly Dad protested.

But tonight was different. The shop buzzed and hummed, busy as usual. Familiar faces abounded. But Bob Hutchins's eyebrows knit into a frown. Cue Ball and Eight Ball nearly collided in their haste to turn away. Alex waved but Mr. Drummond stopped him with a firm hand. Neal Collier, the baker, said hello without his usual buoyancy.

I doubt anyone meant to be rude. Dad's confession as the park's creator stunned us all. Seems everyone was tongue-tied.

We sat and Sam dawdled his way over. Though he'd been in favor of the park, his face was rigid, as if wary of this venture to the Hamilton table.

Sam cleared his throat. "Evening, Drew, Jennie. What'll it be?" he said in monotone.

"The usual, Sam." Dad made a lively effort to pretend nothing was wrong. "We're celebrating good pitching and hitting."

"Rex and Byron sure did you proud," Mom said. "I declare, it was a sight to behold when Rex got that throw into home plate right on time."

Sam spoke without inflection. "Exciting game." He scribbled on his pad. "The usual, eh? Let's see." His writing endeavor looked painstaking, his voice dragging like a needle on a scratched record. "Hmmm, Nick, for you that's a root beer float. Tina, a butterscotch sundae. We're busy tonight so it'll take a while."

He turned to leave, but Dad stopped him. "Jennie here will have a dish of peppermint, two scoops."

Flustered, Sam jotted down the order. He wrinkled his face as if concentrating. "Peppermint in a dish, two scoops." Again he turned away.

"And," Dad said as Sam spun back around, "if you don't mind the extra business, I'll have a dish of rocky road. Only if it's no trouble."

Sam scribbled more. Odd for a man who usually took our orders from memory. He peered at us over his tablet. "How many scoops?"

"Reckon two will be plenty."

When Sam left, I fought tears. Dad hugged me. "Honey, that's the best he can do right now." His voice cracked. "It'll take time for folks to get used to me all over again."

Sam's awkwardness was painful, but so was the knot in my stomach from my own anger at Dad. Confusion and resentment replaced trust. Aloofness from townsfolk confirmed my fears.

By the time our ice cream arrived, I'd lost my appetite. I took two bites then swirled my sundae into golden mush. Blinking through stray tears, I looked up to see Roger Griffin sliding into our booth next to Nick. "Hey, sweets," he said to me. "That double of yours was a gem. Nick, great pitching job."

Nick insisted he was having a good season because of Denny McLain, and was confident of winning the thirty-win season bet.

Roger chatted with Dad. His wife Gail and their two

boys, Jay and Ryan, joined us, too. The men talked baseball, the women discussed quilting, and Jay babbled about our game. Apparently, the Griffins weren't infected by everyone else's malady.

My appetite returned but my ice cream had melted. I used a straw. Several Bear Wallow Inn boys huddled at a nearby table, spouting a barrage of predictions about next week's game. Nick would have to do a lot more spitting and lace-tying to beat them.

In surveying the room, I realized that Phil's team consisted of boys whose families had moved from up north, while our boys were born and bred in Currie Hill. The teams had been thrown together by chance, but I wondered if they were destined that way for a reason.

****

Dinner the next evening was painfully subdued. Dad and Mom attempted small talk, then fell silent. I asked Nick to pass the corn chowder, then the biscuits and honey, just to break the stillness.

Afterward I went to Nick's room. He was organizing his baseball card box, the McLain cards spread over the bed. I examined his autographed Yankees baseball from Uncle Sid.

"Put that down. You'll smudge it."

"What's wrong with you? You haven't spoken in days."

"I just wanna win this game."

"You trying for thirty wins, too?"

"I just wanna win. For Dad."

Did he think winning the game would make up for losses at the town council meeting? "Dad doesn't care who wins."

"I know."

Bewildered, I left.

****

The next day, Dad took Nick and me fishing. In a grim voice, he said, "If I had my druthers, I'd cancel that game tomorrow."

Nick frowned. "How come?"

"I reckon there's gonna be hard feelings over this game. Folks are bumbling like bees in a tar tub. You need to be prepared."

"Prepared for what?" I asked.

"For folks to be upset, regardless of the game's outcome. It'll be the last game played on that sandlot . . . before groundbreaking for the park."

After supper, I rode my bike to the empty sandlot and sat on the home team bench. I scooped a handful of sand. Grains slipped through my fingers as thought fragments sifted through my mind.

What was happening to Nick? He wouldn't talk about the meeting, the vote, or any encounters with folks since then. His vocabulary had shrunk to grunts and growls. I hardly knew him anymore.

I walked to the pitcher's mound and pitched to an imaginary batter.

How long would Dad's dreariness dominate the house? What kept him from communion and prompted his retreat from deaconry? It couldn't be whatever transpired in New York. That was ages ago. And surely the current park issues weren't sins that rendered him inadequate for receiving the bread and wine.

How long would it take folks to trust him again? How long would it take me?

I gazed over the outfield and cornfields beyond. How many fields would they plow over to build this park? How many stands of pine, hickory, and oak trees would be demolished?

Nick's distressed face, Phil Kepler's unyielding stance, and Dad's sullen posture imprinted my brain. I picked up another handful of sand and dropped it into my pocket for comfort.

Our team needed to secure the victory at the sandlot. I would win the game for Nick. And Dad.

CHAPTER 21

The day of the championship game, I rode my bike to the sandlot. The stands bowed and bent with the weight of dozens of parents. A strange atmosphere permeated pre-game activities, like a mental tug of war between the two stands. Like bulls pawing at the dirt, the way Dad described a council meeting.

Tension thickened during the first five of our seven innings, even with no score. A close call at home plate in the Grizzlies' favor provoked our parents to vigorous protest. The next inning, controversy rose over a potential two-base hit gone foul.

The game evolved into a pitchers' duel, probably due to batter nerves rather than pitcher expertise. Like the major leagues, our game climaxed into the Year of the Pitcher. A Kepler-Hamilton duel prefaced the World Series confrontation between Gibson and McLain.

At the top of the sixth inning, the Bear Wallow Inn Grizzlies were up. Nick was still on the mound. I could tell his arm hurt because his fastballs dropped sooner. I urged him to have Hud take him out. No game was worth killing your arm for. But Hud refused.

Ray, the banker's son, was at the plate. Boys on first and second, no outs, the count 3-0. Nick had trouble throwing strikes.

Shouts from the stands. "Come on, Ray, smack that ball! Wing that ball over their heads!"

Nick pitched and Ray fouled it off.

Shouts. "Come on, Ray! Down their throats!"

The pitch--a hard liner to second base. Jay tagged the runner out and threw to me at first for a double play. The runner was out but I fumbled the ball and it rolled toward the stands. Stan Randall on third headed home.

I charged to the ball, the heat of the Grizzly stands breathing down my neck. The high school boys, older brothers of Ray, Stan, and Dempsey, chanted.

"What do you gotta girl for? Where are your men?"

I couldn't tell if it was Stan's brother or his dad.

I threw the ball home. Fortunately, all my throwing practice paid off. The ball arrived as Stan scored. But the umpire declared him safe. Stan stuck out his tongue at me.

The Grizzly fans hooted and cheered. "Way to go, team!"

Some of our parents argued with the umpire, to no avail.

"Get back, you farmers!" the other parents yelled as if farmers were the worst insult they could think of.

Looking pensive, Mom and Dad waved in reassurance.

I trotted to Nick on the mound. "Arm hurting bad?"

"Feels like snakes under my skin, shooting venom. But Hud won't let me leave."

The parents' shouts must have infected Hud. He hadn't sat down since the second inning, his barking more ferocious. It wasn't like him to ignore Nick's complaints. Then again, it wasn't like Nick to quit.

"Go, Barton! Slug that ball," Mr. Randall yelled. "Let 'em have it!"

"Aim for first base," Ray's brother added. "They'll miss it for sure!"

And on and on and on.

Nick finally got his slider in and Bart Chandler struck out. We were up and I was first at bat, in my usual left-handed stance. Comments about the inferiority of the female gender trickled over. Nick sat on the bench, rubbing his arm.

Todd tried to fool me by alternating his curve ball and

fastball. He didn't try his slider or screwball. He would have considered that a betrayal of Nick who'd labored teaching him those.

I hit a triple off Todd Kepler. Our fans cheered. Leo Abernathy got on base and Alex Drummond batted me in. The score was tied at 1-1. Roy flew out to centerfield and Rex hit into a double play. Our side retired. My triple made up for my first base error. But if we lost by one run, I was doomed to take the blame.

With all the screaming and quarreling, an extra inning game would be worse than a loss.

The Grizzlies hit a lot of foul balls, forcing Nick to throw more pitches. He walked a guy. Two outs and three boys later, the runner was batted in. We watched the line drive chased by Byron in left field. Nick's shoulders dropped in resignation. He turned to Hud with pleading eyes. Hud walked out to the mound. I joined them.

"My arm's throbbing," Nick said.

"Well, who do you think can do better?" Hud said. "We gotta win this game. Hang in there for one last out. You'll be fine."

I glared at Hud as he walked away. Dad went to Hud, probably interceding for Nick.

The batter bunted to me and I tagged him out.

It was our last ups now. Without another run we'd lose.

Toby Hutchins, the carpenter's grandson, was up. Grizzly fans started up again. "Go nail your bat to a two-by-four, carpenter boy!" Stan's brother yelled.

Our side piped up, mostly older brothers of my teammates. "Hey, third baseman, why don't you have your dad just buy you the trophy?" To the editor's son: "Right-fielder—wait till you read this write-up in tomorrow's paper!"

My head pounded.

Toby struck out. Jay hit a double, and Byron flew out to right field so Jay advanced to third base. If Jay got batted in, we'd have a tie game and a chance to win. But we already had two outs.

Nick was up. Yes, my brother Nick was facing Todd Kepler in the final pitches.

I fumed at Hud. Let the Grizzlies have the game. Why should we win at Nick's expense? In my anxiety, I found myself carrying out Nick's superstitious habits and spit all over the place.

Nick took the first pitch as a ball, a fastball high and tight.

The second mimicked the first. The third pitch was a strike, fouled off. So was the fourth. Both curve balls. The count was 2-2. The determination on Todd's face equalled Nick's. Neither was going to let up.

Next pitch. Nick fouled to the right. Again and again he fouled off each pitch. Todd would throw a change-up, then a fastball, then a curve in predictable order, as if trying to give Nick a chance to outguess him.

I wiped my sweaty face with my cap. People in the stands blurred together, voices blending into dissonance.

Todd was poised for the pitch. Nick stood steady in the batter's box. Todd wound up. This pitch had a different delivery.

The ball arrived right on target over the plate, but Nick didn't swing. He didn't even flinch but took it, a called third strike.

The game was over. Nick had made the last out, a victim of the screwball pitch he'd taught Todd. In the end, Todd used it against him.

After obnoxious Grizzly cheering, the kids dispersed. Mom and Dad would wait for Nick. I brushed past bodies and started home on my bike, hardly able to see straight.

Soon, Todd overtook me on his bike. We both stopped. He set his bike down and blocked my path.

I squinted at him in afternoon sunlight that haloed his hair. "What do you want?"

"I know you're mad, Tina. But I gave Nick chance

after chance. The game had to end."

My face heated. "You should be happy then, now that you've paid Nick back for all his help." I wanted to hit him, because he was too much of a gentleman to hit me back.

So I smacked him. As hard as I could.

Tears streaming, I hopped on my bike and bolted down the road, as fast as I could pedal.

CHAPTER 22

Miss Prinz's smile looked fake, as if she were holding an invisible coin between her teeth. With that smile she announced, "The final pair in our group project will be Christina Hamilton and Todd Kepler."

My worst fear came true. I knew it before she said it. Why'd she put us together? Perhaps she got a morbid thrill by pairing the son and daughter of the two park opponents.

My cheeks burned. I felt Todd's eyes penetrate me. We hadn't spoken for three weeks, not since I hit him. Then school started in a flurry of activity. Though we were in the same classroom--he in the sixth grade, I in fifth--we'd managed to avoid that awkward first encounter that invariably occurs after such a foible as mine. Fortunately, he'd visited his mom for two weeks in New York between the last game and school starting.

Nick got matched with Jay. Todd, a year older than Nick, should have been in seventh grade, in another classroom, but he'd started first grade late, during the turbulent time when his mother left.

Three weeks had not diffused my anger over the pitch that sailed past my brother. For Todd to use the screwball or slider against Nick was a slap in his face. Thus it warranted at least one belt from my clenched fist.

But maybe Todd did the only humane thing possible by ending the game and everyone's misery. Either way, I hoped Todd wouldn't tattle. Dad would be furious with me.

Whether or not Todd deserved my punching him, I'd never be able to look him in the eye.

Nick's arm recovered from the game, but his pride hadn't. Barely two words a day passed between us. His aloofness hurt, but I couldn't press him. I'd wait out his silence.

The teacher's whiny voice drew me out of my rumination. She explained the adventure upon which we were to embark with Napoleonic grandeur. Her wonderfully creative and educational idea stipulated our pseudo-role as park planners, for designing sections of the upcoming theme park. She assigned Todd and me a concession stand and stage for the Turn-of- the-Century section.

Todd pulled a chair over and sat. "Hi, Tina."

Did he hate me? Had he forgiven me for hitting him? He sounded normal.

"Hi, Todd." Hoping it smoothed out my quaking voice, I added, "I don't understand this project."

"Good thing you got with me then." He grinned. Fake? He must hate me, hate Nick. His dad probably told him to. "How's Nick doing?"

"Ask him yourself."

An awkward pause followed. He fingered his pencil as I fingered my braid. "Got any ideas? I'll write them down."

Agitation edged my voice. "I don't know what it's supposed to look like. I've only seen a pirate ride and that was on TV in January."

"I've seen lots of neat concession booths." He babbled as he produced a set of crude drawings, reeling out a string of phrases reminiscent of his father's speech at the council meeting. Fortunately, Todd had visited enough theme parks to carry us through.

Did he side with his dad's public denouncement of my father? Phil's eloquent speech had been translated as "Drew Hamilton is a two-faced liar and a coward."

Our townsfolk are loyal, but easily feel betrayal. My

father's role in the park's creation and his initial silence shattered their trust.

The bell rang for three o'clock dismissal. I scooped up my books with the sketches and headed outside. September sunshine, hot and stuffy indoors, turned warm and inviting. I hopped down the steps into its embrace. Kids jostled by in giggles and yelps.

A hand touched my arm. Todd, again. "Tell Nick to come over sometime."

"Tell him yourself."

I looked for Nick among the jumping bodies and books.

"Better hurry home, Tina Hamilton," Stan Randall jeered. "And take your brother before he gets beat up."

In the middle of the schoolyard, inside a circle of onlookers, Nick stood face to face with Darrell Culver.

"Your dad wants to put my dad out of business!" Darrell shouted.

Nick scowled. "Does not!"

"Then why didn't he wanna give my dad construction rights?"

"My dad don't wanna put anyone out of business."

Darrell stepped closer. Nick's fists tightened.

"Answer me!" Darrell yelled. "Can't you admit the truth? Or are you a coward like your old man?"

Stan sniggered behind me. "That's why he choked and couldn't hit that ball. Thanks for making the championship easy for us, Hamilton!"

"Shut up, Stan," I muttered.

Poor Nick. I knew he didn't want to fight. And now the entire schoolyard watched. I wanted to rescue him without further humiliating him as his sister.

Stan bellowed to Nick, practically in my ear. "Defend yourself! Or don't cowards like you Hamiltons do that?"

Before I knew what happened, Stan Randall was sprawled on the ground, and my fist stung from the impact with his chin. My books had dropped, the crowd had silenced, and nobody was watching Nick and Darrell anymore.

It wasn't the rescue tactic I had in mind.

All eyes were on me. A few *oohs* and stifled *wows* waffled over.

Stan staggered to his feet. I grabbed my books and darted away. Nick followed. I ran into a barricade of boys. Stan caught up, winded. "I don't usually hit girls, but you've changed my mind."

He jumped at me and wrestled me down. The books dropped again. I shrieked, then rassled with all my might. Nick tried to pull me out. Three teachers pried us apart, shook their fingers, and wagged their tongues. They sentenced us to a week of chores in our respective classrooms, assigned an essay on the perils of fighting, and promised to call our parents.

But it was worth it. I'd made a fool of that swine Stan Randall, a higher priority than turning the other cheek. I rescued Nick and stood up for my dad, all in one punch. I was proud.

Hitting Stan was far less regrettable than hitting Todd.

Fortunately, I had no obvious scrapes, but dreaded the phone ringing that evening. I debated giving Mom and Dad my side of the story before they heard the teacher's. Nick couldn't tell on me without making himself look foolish.

At the tail end of another quiet supper of chicken and dumplings, Dad asked, "How come we haven't seen much of Todd here lately?" No reply. "Nick, don't you spend time with Todd anymore?"

"Todd was in New York at his mom's for a while," I said.

"He's been back a week now." Dad faced Nick. "After being together all summer, a week's a long time to go without seeing him."

"Should we have Todd over Friday night?" Mom said. "After the fall festival."

"No, ma'am," Nick said.

"Why not?" Dad asked.

Nick shook his head. "We ain't been talking much lately."

"Are you still sore about losing that game?" Mom said. "It's been almost a month."

Nick looked at his plate.

"Are you angry at Todd for striking you out?" Dad asked.

I feared another lecture on forgiveness.

Tears rolled down Nick's cheeks.

"Why are you and Todd not getting along?" Dad asked.

"Drew." Mom touched Dad's arm. "Maybe he'll talk about it later."

"Jennie, this is important. They've got a good friendship. Nick can't let it go by the wayside."

"I'm sure he won't," Mom said. "Why do you care about Nick and Todd so much? After all, you and Phil won't be speaking for a powerful long time."

Dad seemed taken aback. The phone rang.

My hands turned clammy and my neck heated.

Dad answered. "Good evening, Mr. Richards. How can I help you?"

Mr. Richards was one of the teachers who stopped the fight.

I stared at fork prints on my potatoes. Chicken and dumplings no longer enticed me. They grew colder as my face burned warmer.

A series of one-syllable words ensued, "Oh" and "I see" and "Hmmm," prophetically intoned like a dirge. I slunk in my chair.

"Thank you, Mr. Richards. Do what you have to do and I'll take care of things on my end. Goodbye."

Dad rejoined us at the table and resumed eating as if the caller had been a salesman.

"They need someone to run the school paper drive this

year?" Mom asked.

"Reckon so, but that seemed to have slipped his mind," Dad replied nonchalantly.

My father sure had a way of prolonging tension. I hated that.

"Seems the kids didn't tell us about all the excitement after school today. Recollect anything, Tina?"

I should've told my version before he heard from the teacher.

Nick jumped to my rescue. "Dad, don't get mad at Tina. That Stan Randall—no one can keep from belting him when he yells nasty things right in your ear. Tina was just . . . defending . . ."

"Herself?" Mom said. "Stan hit her first?"

"No, ma'am," I said.

"Defending Nick then?" Mom said. "Let Nick fight his own battles."

Telling them I was trying to take attention from Nick's plight probably wouldn't help.

"Who were you defending?" Dad asked. How do you tell your father that your peers insulted him? But he was too smart for this game. "Was it me?"

I blinked at my plate. A tear squeezed out. "Why do they call you names? Liar . . . two-faced . . . coward . . ."

Mom wiped my eyes. "Your father is none of those things, sweetheart. Some men don't understand why he doesn't agree with them about the park and such. They don't understand about his time away. It'll pass, child. It'll pass."

I sniffed. "Everyone thinks he's some kinda bad person, excusing Jay and Alex."

Mom patted my hand. "The important thing is you don't believe them."

I needed answers first. But Dad seemed in no hurry to give them.

After supper, he went to the living room, probably contemplating my punishment and planning to leave me in suspense all evening. He paused at my homework and Todd's park sketches on the couch, then sat in Mom's rocker with the newspaper.

When Mom went to the MacNeills, I sat on the floor next to Dad and leaned against his knees. "Why do they call you . . . two-faced?"

The paper rustled near my ear. He set it aside, pulled me to his lap, and rocked. "They say I'm afraid of what they call progress. They say I was once in favor of it, back when I designed the park, but now I've changed my mind. Some folks don't understand those changes."

"That's it? That's the only problem? You just changed your mind?" I was relieved. It seemed so simple.

"There's more. The problem is . . . I never told anybody. I kept it secret."

"Why did you?"

"Because in this town, folks don't understand others who don't live the way they do. I reckon it's like cats and dogs. If a cat wakes up one morning and decides to leave the cats and his cat-ways, and goes to live with the dogs to take up dog-ways, the cats ain't gonna be too pleased when that cat leaves, then comes back to be a cat again."

"So you were a dog in New York."

"For the sake of analogy . . . yes."

"What about Sonia? Was she a dog, too, so you couldn't bring her back here?"

The soothing pattern of rocking stopped. Dad's jaw at my forehead shifted. He sighed.

"Well?"

"Tina, I never planned on coming back here. I was busy with my job, and it led to foolish decisions. I had my own life there, and . . . I didn't fit in here anymore." He paused. "I don't care to talk about those times, not even with your mother."

Unsettled, I was certain of more beneath the surface. I twisted out of his arms.

He caught my wrist. "I love you, Tina."

After Mom returned from the MacNeills, she washed dishes. I joined her. "Why won't Dad tell you more about his New York time?"

Mom gazed out the window. "It's a painful memory for him."

"Don't you ask him about it?"

"When your father and I started courting, he'd just returned from New York. He said he'd gone to school after the war, and worked as an architect. He got married but his wife died. After we got engaged, he made me vow one thing only. I could spend money we didn't have, burn meals three times daily, even wreck the car, but I couldn't ask him about his time in the Army or New York. I promised I wouldn't. I plan to keep that promise."

I crossed my arms. "I wouldn't have married him unless he told me."

She faced me, hands on my shoulders. "Tina, when you love someone deeply, and he loves you, you don't have to make him prove it to you by forcing him do something he doesn't wanna do. That doesn't prove love anyway."

Near bedtime, Dad cautioned me about future fighting. "I know you were defending me. You don't need to prove your loyalty by fighting. There's better ways of defending honor. Fighting only steals it."

Before I could ask about other ways, he delivered my sentence: no bijou for a month. Rather light, but I didn't protest.

Normally, Dad would've called Mr. Randall about Stan. But because of their differences on the park issue, he didn't.

****

I was fed up with silent walks home, weary of Nick's one-word replies and grunts. The only difference with our parents was that he punctuated his grunts with "sir" and "ma'am."

One night I swept into Nick's room and plopped on his bed, without pretension of diplomacy. "Nick, I'm tired of this. Let's have it out."

He was sprawled across the bed reading a comic book. His baseball cards spotted the floor. His sullen expression wreaked havoc with my frustration, nearly bringing me to my knees in an apology.

But I held firm. "Why won't you talk to me anymore? What's going on?"

Nick burst into tears, an outburst I hadn't expected.

I started apologizing, the response I hadn't expected. "I'm sorry, Nick. I'm sorry." I picked up another comic book and lay beside him, pretending to read.

He finally spoke. "We could've won that game."

The game still, for heaven's sake.

I told him what Todd said that first day of school, and asked why he wouldn't go see him. He mumbled some glib excuse, squeezing his Yankees ball so tightly that his knuckles turned white. "When I was facing Todd in the last pitch, I could've swung and winged that ball out of there. I was ready to sock it. But the screaming . . ."

The autographs on his ball smeared. Such an act, when my fault, was worthy of murder.

"Mr. Kepler yelling, the parents screaming, the kids upset . . . I couldn't even think. I could've hit that ball but we might've tied and kept playing. If I let Todd strike me out, the game would stop and so would the screaming."

His voice trembled. "I saw the ball coming. I knew the pitch 'cause that's how he winds up for it. It was that screwball I taught him for right-handed batters. I knew how to hit it, too. He'd pitched plenty to me this summer for practice."

He stared out the window as if watching a replay, and chiding himself. "But I didn't swing. I knew the ump would call it, but I just stood there. I wanted the screaming to stop more than I wanted to win."

I was glad I'd hit Todd.

"I don't think Todd threw my pitch to be mean." Nick sniffed. "He was pitching so predictable. If I hadn't kept fouling them off, he wouldn't have used the screwball. But I think he wanted to catch me off guard, 'cause he wanted the game to be over just as much as I did. He gave me plenty of chances before that."

Nick wiped his eyes. "Mr. Kepler calls Dad a coward for not telling folks about the park earlier. But Dad's no coward, Tina. I'm the coward."

CHAPTER 23

On September 14th, Nick and I were riveted to the television set. Denny McLain faced the Oakland A's in an attempt at his thirtieth win of the year, upon which Nick still had riding an ice cream sundae. This was the first time Nick smiled in days.

That night's game was nationally televised. Mom popped a huge bowl of popcorn, made lemonade and molasses cookies, and created a score card and pitching chart for Nick.

By eight and a half innings, Reggie Jackson had homered twice off McLain and the A's were ahead 4-3 in the bottom of the ninth.

"Any other pitcher would have been long gone out of this game." Dad smirked and puffed on his pipe. "They're milking this one for all it's worth."

"I wanna be a pitcher like him someday," Nick said.

Dad chuckled as Al Kaline got up to bat, pinch-hitting for McLain and leading off the bottom of the ninth inning. "You want to do the Las Vegas circuit and rile the fans as well? Watch out or they'll be calling you Mighty Mouth, too."

Through a series of incidents, the Tigers managed to win on Willie Horton's last hit. McLain ran out of the dugout and waved at fans. Cheering, Nick jumped around the room.

"Can't say it was one of McLain's classic games," Dad said. "It's a fluke, a weak year for the league. McLain's got no long-standing record behind him."

"How can thirty wins be a fluke?" Nick asked.

"The highest batting average all year is barely reaching

.300. And that's Yaz."

"The year of the pitcher," Nick pronounced, undaunted.

"I hope it's the last year," I mumbled.

"You should've bet more than a sundae," Mom said. "When does Todd pay up?"

Joy drained from Nick's face as real life prevailed, his vicarious victory no longer sufficient. "Someday."

****

By our eighth night visit to Ole Joe's, our fear of him had been replaced by a strange combination of security and mystique. He was always ready with a folktale, a Bible story, or a tale of his great-grandparents' life in the antebellum south.

As dead leaves crackled underfoot, we headed to Joe's cabin. That night he showed us how to shave the wood's surface with a chisel. "Soon y'all will be ready to make a picture with these here tools. You learned how to cut shapes, straight or curvy, and how to mark the surface. Next week we'll start something big."

"Did your dad teach you how to carve wood?" Nick asked.

"My papa was good with his hands. He carved pipes and taught me how to whittle. These fancier things I picked up along the way."

I cleared my throat. "Why do live up here all alone?" Nick kicked my foot.

"Better to ask questions than make assumptions," Joe said. "My papa grew up in North Carolina, Piedmont area, and moved to these mountains before I was born, to escape poor treatment by the white man. He carved out a homestead nearby, and lived proud knowing he could bread and meat our family, living off the land. Mama had twelve children. Three died as young-uns, not very hardy. I was the oldest. Mama, she worked hard to bring us up right, read us Bible stories and prayed over us."

Joe steadily scraped his chunk of wood. "Some folks came to this region to escape the colored man in the cities out east. But something about these hills and hard times make many a man forget their prejudice, and we was friends with families here. Till one year a disease killed some folks off, including three of my siblings. Papa got accused of bringing the disease to these parts. Folks grew afraid of us. Thought the sickness in our family was judgment from God."

Joe turned the wood around. "But Papa and Mama taught us not to be bitter. The devil closes folks' eyes, Mama always said. 'Folks only rule your life if you let them root in your heart.' I went off and sought my fortune and came back empty-handed. I reckoned it was easier to live in peace in the hills alone than in town with everyone else. Some folks have peace in the middle of the storm. But I like to come in out of the rain myself. I'm here because I like it. It's where I grew up."

"Then you're not one of those colored folks everyone's scared of?" I asked.

Joe raised his eyebrows.

Nick gave me another kick, along with the evil eye. He took over. "There's lots of rabble-rousing in the cities 'cause of black folks who don't get fair treatment."

Chuckling, Joe took a few jabs at his wood. "I'm about as much threat to their society as a mouse is to a council of cats." He shook his head. "But be careful you don't suffer from that deadly malady that puts a different value on folks who be different than you."

"Do you ever go into town?" Nick asked.

"Now and then for coffee or sugar."

"Where do you get the money?" I shifted my leg so Nick couldn't kick it again.

"Odd jobs here and there. I manage." Joe set down his chisel. "Y'all got school now and need sleep. Harvest is mostly over, but I be much obliged to see your faces here by daylight.

It's still our secret, see. I got plenty more wood, and things to teach you. When you stop for your sprig of tobacco, you can stop here, too." A request, not a command.

I'd never considered that his world and Old Lady Balch's might overlap, or that he knew about our tobacco runs. Had she purposely set us up to run into Ole Joe that first time?

****

Miss Prinz pointed at my park planning project. "How much work did you do yourself, Tina?" Her voice chilled me.

"About half, ma'am," I lied. "But Todd did the final copying." That was true.

She asked which parts I'd worked on. Though Todd and I met twice weekly to devise plans, creating park sketches felt disloyal to Dad. Todd did all the work. I rattled off a list of ideas and explained our unique collaboration.

"That's as clear as mud. I wouldn't doubt if your father told you not to do any of it."

"He always makes me do my work."

"Humph," she said like so many leaves snapping off a branch. "Show him this when you get home." She handed me an assessment sheet, a large, red F gracing the top.

I showed Dad that night, expecting a painful form of punishment after he talked to the teacher. But he said nothing.

Surely winter was on its way.

****

"Ladies and Gentlemen, we've gathered for a very worthy and exciting occasion . . ."

Strains over the loudspeaker vibrated as I approached the large gathering at the sandlot, amid dozens of newsmen. Now late September, this was ground-breaking day for five of the park's themed areas. I shuffled toward the crowd.

Only two months had passed since the council voted in

the park. Dad said Mr. Kepler surely had connections to get work rolling, long before it was voted in.

"To grace us with our ground-breaking day speech, please welcome Mr. Phil Kepler."

The crowd broke into happy applause as Phil strutted to the platform. I'd come out of curiosity. Nick, Mom, and Dad were home. But I didn't hear a word Phil said. I was too busy fretting about the F on my park planning project, and the looming punishment.

At least Todd got the A he deserved.

Mr. Kepler's droning voice added to my melancholy. I felt so distant from Nick and Todd, from everyone. Dad wasn't the Dad I knew. Mom was as down as I was, weekly listening to *Camelot* beside a box of tissues.

As *Camelot* helped her, a sad story helped me. So I'd asked Mom for one last night. Once again she told me the tale of Old Man Fuller, his marvelous pictures, and my father's broken promise, all the more poignant now, knowing what replaced that promise.

"This park constitutes the betterment of our community. We've encompassed all that makes up North Carolina and the spirit of the Appalachian people, the hardiness of our forefathers who first cleared this land. In this park is a legacy to leave to our own sons and daughters . . ."

Some legacy. Faces turning away. Silent dinners. Nick crying on his bed.

Someone tugged at my sleeve. A piece of paper waved before my face. The letter A came into focus. Nick held it.

"What's this?" I whispered.

"Your park planning assignment. Miss Prinz gave this to Todd this morning."

"Then why do you have it?"

"Todd told me to give it to you."

"It can't be mine. There's an A on it."

"Look." He moved it closer.

My name, with an A in the teacher's handwriting.

"This is a joke."

"I was by school this morning, turning my assignment in late. I heard her and Todd talking. Todd insisted you'd done as much as he had, even listed things. He lied so you wouldn't get an F."

A shiver rippled up my spine. Why wouldn't he want the credit himself? In the fog of my confusion sparked a shred of light, of hope. Todd was the far bigger person all along—not for lying, but for reaching across what I'd erected between us.

Nick shuffled. "After hearing him stick up for you, I reckon he's not like his dad."

That afternoon, Todd made good his bet and bought Nick a huge sundae at Simpson's.

CHAPTER 24

Though I appreciated Todd's gesture of repairing the breach, I couldn't live with the lie. I confessed my negligence to Miss Prinz and took the F.

Nick made up with Todd none too soon. The following Wednesday, October 2nd, the World Series began. The major league season had been a real yawner except for folks who favored pitchers. Detroit and St. Louis easily slid into the League championship and the meeting of baseball's two best pitchers: Gibson with his 22-9 record, McLain with his incredible 31-6 record, and both with their fastballs.

Nick invited Todd for the first game. "I gotta prove to my dad that Denny McLain's gonna pull through, that thirty-one games was no fluke."

"Fluke?" Todd said. "So what? He still did it. Flukes ain't all bad. I was one."

"What do you mean?" I asked.

"My dad calls me a gift, a fluke of nature. He and Mom tried for years to have kids, but doctors said they couldn't. Something wrong with my dad, I think. Then boom! There I was. Like God opened up the sky, dropped me out, and closed it back up again. My mom and dad were happiest the night I was born."

"Then why'd your mom leave?" I never dared pose the question before.

Todd shook his head. "She just wasn't happy anymore."

"Don't you wish you saw your mom more often?"

"Sometimes. But I'm fine here. She's got her own life.

She's married again, has two other kids." He said this the way one might quote baseball statistics.

Maybe it was the only way he could say it without feeling the sting.

In the first game, McLain was replaced in the sixth inning and lost to Gibson 4-0. Nick shrunk into limp sadness.

The next day at Todd's, Detroit's Mickey Lolich pitched and secured the game. On Saturday, St. Louis had another victory, but Nick was confident Denny would have his stuff the next day to tie the series.

Sunday morning brought communion, fourth time that year. Again, my father didn't partake. What sin kept him from the bread and wine? If it was his betrayal of the town, that was over and done with.

Fortunately, Dad allowed television that Sunday. But for Nick it was no blessing. McLain faced Gibson again. The progress of the game could be charted on Nick's face and posture by his dejected countenance and drooping shoulders. By the third inning, McLain was replaced. After going through six pitchers, Detroit lost 10-1. McLain got the loss.

On Monday, Lolich clinched the game for Detroit. The series score was 3-2. St. Louis needed one more to win four out of seven.

On Wednesday, Detroit bats hopped and Denny reversed his previous game, winning 13-1, while St. Louis went through seven pitchers. Nick was ecstatic but wished McLain had been saved for the climactic seventh game against Gibson.

Mickey Lolich and Gibson faced each other in the seventh game. Detroit won a 4-3 series. Lolich was the first southpaw to win three World Series games. The papers sported Lolich, Lolich, Lolich, and folks shook their heads over Denny McLain.

Even so, McLain was awarded Most Valuable Player and the Cy Young Award for 1968. Thus ended the Year of the Pitcher, both in Currie Hill Little League and the major leagues. Shining moments glittered for each hero, but at the end was nothing but a dim light.

****

Meanwhile, Indian summer waned. All that comprised autumn made up our days. Dad repaired the cider press and we made apple cider by the gallon for neighbors and church families. Though many farm families didn't have old-fashioned hog slaughters anymore, Dad did, with the ripest of our hogs. The uncles assisted. We fed the hogs on mast--chestnuts and acorns--several weeks, which put on weight and made the meat less fatty. Uncle Eddie asked if I'd been pulling their tails since the hogs looked leaner that year.

Dad finished the harvest. Earlier we'd given fodder—corn stalks, shucks, and leaves—to the animals, reserving shucks for Grandma Hamilton's mats, hats, scrub brushes, and dolls. I helped Mom gather, dry, and can fruit and vegetables. We buried potatoes and cabbage to keep them from freezing, since Mom preferred an old-fashioned potato hole.

During harvest moon in early October, we built our traditional campfire from hickory, which popped when burning. Later, Dad and his brothers were in the forest the first day of both turkey and deer hunting seasons.

Ole Joe granted Nick and me respite from our weekly produce run, but we visited him and Old Lady Balch on weekends. Her tales of black cats, witches, and goblins filled us with horror, while Joe's stories of slavery in the south and the children of Israel in the wilderness moved us to tears.

Shifts in color and temperature were the least of the changes. Seven families, including ours, still kept the corn shucking tradition. This year's gathering was smaller and not as pleasant. Several men engaged in a heated debate over the park's future impact, making remarks that smarted like autumn wind. Ross's presence didn't help. Many didn't appreciate his cutting up lumber for park office cabinets.

"We might as well take on their business," Jim

Drummond said. "If we turn down their offers, they're gonna bring in foreigners to make a profit off our land."

Some folks didn't go beyond small talk with Dad. And it was the smallest of talk. Others remained aloof.

I knew why. I used to think the world could rise and fall, people could love or hate me, and I'd be fine as long as I could go home and feel safe with Mom and Dad. But now Dad was a stranger, as if withholding something vital.

I used to love climbing into his lap, tucked in by his warm arms, and be filled with the smell of dirt and field hay on his shirt. But now it only emptied me, a good excuse to abandon lap-sitting altogether.

After the corn shucking, Ross and Dad talked in the front room where Nick and I played checkers.

"You didn't say much tonight, Drew," Ross said. "It wonders me what you've been thinking about the park now, with me working for Phil."

"What difference does it make what I think?"

"'Cause I can't deal with your silence. If I had my druthers, I'd take your hollering at me. But when you say nothing, we ain't no further than two bears rolling in tar."

"You're afraid I think you're betraying me, after Phil's condemning me at the council meeting?"

"Yes, that concerns me, but I'm working for one reason only, to send my kids to college."

"I know."

"I don't expect your help when my machinery needs fixing."

Tongue in cheek, Dad replied, "That's powerful kind of you, Ross."

"We gotta separate business and kinship. I don't want nothing to change between us."

"It shouldn't."

"How's Jennie doing? How's it between you two?"

"Fine."

"No, I mean how's she holding up in the backlash of

all this—"

"She's a strong woman."

"That's not what I'm asking."

"Look, I'm not prepared to talk about this, Ross. As much as you hate silence, you're gonna have to live with it. You're not gonna get all your questions answered."

"Don't tell me it's none of my business. We're family. I can respect your privacy if you can respect my questions. There's a heap more unasked."

"Just don't ask the wrong ones."

****

Winter passed, longer than ever, though I welcomed some snow--the old woman shaking out her feather bed, according to Grandma Dorothy. Uncles Garrett and Graham and their families came for Christmas, joining the rest of our clan. But it was safer discussing politics and religion than to reference Dad, Ross's job, the park, or changes in town.

The park fiasco had been Grandma Dorothy's fear all along—her son-in-law had a questionable past. Even so, she conceded to her philosophy: "Before marriage keep both eyes open. After, shut one." She told Mom, "Whatever he did don't matter now. He's a changed man, the most devoted husband I've ever seen. Just keep doing him proud."

Grandma Hamilton was another story. After all, her own flesh and blood committed this regrettable deed. She took it as a personal affront. Through criticism or stiff-lipped silence, her manner evoked the equivalent of a constantly wagging finger. Grandpa often had to hush her. The tension even drained the pleasure from eating peach cobbler or pecan pie.

With all the family strain, I wondered how my dad's past affected my grandmothers' friendship, and if they still passed the Geritol bottle back and forth.

Aunt Elaine, Mom's sister, came often but handled us

like glass. Eddie and Ross still dropped by for card games, but avoided controversial topics.

Sometimes Mom was her usual self--easygoing, energetic, and cheerful. Other times her eyes hollowed out from less sleep. She listened to *Camelot* while cleaning house.

At least there was plenty to discuss in politics. In January, Richard Nixon became president, the first time since Herbert Hoover in 1928 that North Carolina voted Republican. We were still unofficially engaged in the Vietnam War. My cousins Ted and Scott sent home horror stories worse than boot camp.

In 1968, the major leagues had 150 shutouts in 810 games. The powers-that-be wanted to ensure the Year of the Pitcher would never recur. They shortened pitcher's mound from eighteen to twelve inches, juiced up the ball, and shrank the strike zone. To prevent one team from dominating the league, they made east-west divisions in each league and play-offs to qualify teams before entering the World Series.

In spring, ours was a world of earth. Soil stained our fingernails. Our scraped hands were callused from digging and planting peppermint, parsley, red clover, tomatoes, and collards. Grandpa gave Dad a copy of the farmer's calendar with the moon's phases, though Dad planted whenever he felt like it.

On Vine Day, May 10, we planted squash, cucumber, and melon. Tradition dictated planting corn when poplar leaves grew as big as squirrel ears, when dogwoods bloomed and the whippoorwill called, usually early June. We were never short on hominy grits, cornbread, or popcorn.

Paprika gladly welcomed spring. She bounded from the house into everything we did. She followed me as I weeded Mom's garden, then romped through laurel thickets, cushions of phlox, rhododendron in glossy coats and party colors.

Strangers had crowded our town all winter: tourists, builders, engineers, businessmen, and reporters. New buildings went up near the main streets. Others were face-lifted. At least there'd be no more impromptu doctor visits. Doc Kirby was too busy for walk-ins. One had to make an appointment.

We couldn't see the park's daily progress. Fences, a huge wall, and rows of transplanted trees blocked the view, leaving the park one big mystery. So when the park's first installment opened only eight months after groundbreaking, I was shocked. Dad said Mr. Kepler's backup must have gone back years for him to erect things so quickly. Had he commissioned workers even before receiving state and county approval? Newsmen from within a 300-mile radius attended opening day ceremonies, pushing and shoving their way in with the rest. Phil was quite the public relations man.

I thought Dad would never step foot inside the park, but he must have been curious. He took Mom, Nick, and me on opening day and acted like a schoolboy let out for summer. After a solemn winter, perhaps he decided to live by his own axiom: if you lose your sense of humor you might as well roll over and hibernate.

At the park, I tried to decipher expressions when folks glanced our way. They ranged from pity to distrust. Though Dad spoke to old friends, small talk seemed to expand the discomfort.

The park resembled sketches we'd seen at Todd's house and at the town meeting. Phil Kepler never let us into his office, but he'd bring out pictures and diagrams to show us. Even packed with crowds, the park exuded serenity, with plenty of greenery and running water. Dad walked with an invigorated step and held Mom's hand, commenting on layout and designs. Despite his regrets, his brain child in the flesh surely intrigued him.

We stayed until flashing colors lit the darkness and our legs wore out. On the drive home, I turned around to watch the park shrink. Above us, lights followed. Stars deserted us.

When Dad tucked me in bed, I asked if he liked the park.

"Yes, though not in our town. But no sense boycotting

it anymore." He went downstairs to eat his corn flakes.

CHAPTER 25

On the first day of summer, Mom took me downtown for new sneakers. The main road was crammed with people. Folks who'd been at the park the day before and stayed in the new cabins or campground overnight browsed in remodeled shops. I used to cross the street without seeing a single automobile. Now we walked at our own risk, dozens of cars ready to plow us down. I couldn't see storefronts. Mom pulled me along.

Inside Wally's Shoes, we were fourth in line. When it was finally our turn, Wally didn't have time to be his usual talkative self. He was merely polite. At the bakery, jovial Mr. Collier usually gave the sales pitch for his special of the day, joking around while I surveyed the display counter. I always ordered a Bavarian cream doughnut. But he couldn't joke today. A dozen people stood in line. More followed us in. I couldn't see the counter's delicacies anyhow.

Outside, Mom and I dodged people left and right before arriving at Griffin's Barbershop, at my request. I wanted to see Jay. Roger greeted us warmly. Jay gave a happy shout.

"Looks different in here." I scanned the brighter walls and mirrors.

Five men waited for haircuts, all strangers but one, Bob Hutchins. I distracted him from his magazine with a friendly hello.

"Oh, uh, hello, Tina," he said flatly. "Hey, Jennie."

Roger saved me from figuring out what to say next. "It's different-looking all right, sweets. I done fixed it up.

Look—new chairs. And the walls—fresh paint. And mirrors—newfangled and just arrived from Raleigh to boot. Like it?"

"It's nice." Which was the most vague and least insulting word I could think of. Untouchable, like Todd's newer so-called ranch house.

Mom surveyed the room. "Very . . . light and bright."

A man in the chair grunted. "I don't have all day, you know." Obviously, he wasn't from Currie Hill.

"I'm mighty proud of it." Roger tended to the man beneath his scissors. "I can keep pace with styles like anyone else. Got me some hired help, too."

Two women passed on the sidewalk and peered in the screen door. "Look, an old-fashioned barber shop," one said. "How quaint."

No matter what Roger did, the shop was terminally old-fashioned.

I asked Jay if he still wanted to play baseball this summer. Fenville, four miles down the road, was opening up their leagues to Currie Hill kids. Jay wanted to, if Nick and I did.

That evening Roger, his wife Gail, Jay, and his younger brother Ryan dropped by. After dinner, the grownups sat on the front porch. The purple martins warded off mosquitoes. We kids caught fireflies and played Capture the Flag. Later inside, Dad played his fiddle while we clapped and sang. When Uncle Charles arrived, he captivated us with "Jack and the Giant Killer." Somewhere during my favorite, "Jack and the Northwest Wind," I dozed on the living room floor.

Inadvertently waking me, Dad carried me upstairs, then shuffled back down the steps. The pantry door creaked open, the cereal box wrapping rustled, the flakes dropped into the bowl, the spoon clicked. Slippered feet padded back upstairs, then Dad was in bed reading. My eyes were closed, but I knew his light would stay on for twenty minutes. He'd kiss Mom and go to sleep.

Our town had undergone changes aplenty, apparent

whenever we ventured from the house. But they couldn't knock us off balance for long.

Yet some changes pricked like a cocklebur. My father hadn't taken the Lord's supper for a year. The minister said only those who deliberately lived in sin or held a grudge couldn't take communion. I didn't dare ask Dad about it.

Another change was Nick's ability to play baseball. He couldn't relax, even at practice. He threw beanballs by accident. His arm ached. The new coach was pro-park and knew of Dad's fall from grace. He made snide remarks to Nick and me. After one week, Nick quit and spent time with Todd instead. Todd didn't go out for ball since he was occupied helping his dad.

Denny McLain was off to another good start. Nick pretended he didn't miss playing and pitching, but I knew better. He spent more daytime hours with Dad in the fields. Evenings, he helped at the MacNeills with repairs.

Summer also brought its joys. We resumed our weekly vegetable-swiping for Joe.

Paprika reckoned herself important enough to forsake the end of the bed and moved near my pillow. She was as sprightly as ever as we romped through woods and fields.

One day, Paprika and I roamed through the woods on the edge of our field. She disappeared. Despite my calling and whistling, she didn't return. I thought she was playing hide-and-seek until she whimpered. I found her behind a tree--and found myself facing Stan Randall. His hand gripped Paprika's collar and snout.

My heart thunked. "What are you doing here?"

"I could ask you the same thing. Unless, of course, these are *your* woods." His voice had the usual sneer. He threw back his head to toss bangs out of his eyes.

"Let go of my dog."

"I ain't got hold of your dog. I'm holding his collar."

"Why are you such a smart aleck?"

"It's my favorite pastime."

"Come here, Paprika." I clapped. The dog tried to pull away but couldn't. Her big eyes drooped.

"Paprika—what a stupid name. You might as well call him Oregano or Dill Weed or Parsley."

"Shut up. Give me my dog." I stepped forward. The schoolyard scene from last fall flashed through my mind. I needed to avoid a fight without anybody around to keep him from pounding me. He was highly motivated.

"You wanna fight me for him?"

I marveled that he hadn't clobbered me already. I'd been waiting for his revenge all winter. "She's a her, not a him. And I don't wanna fight. Just give her back." Speaking softly to Paprika, I bent down to take her collar.

Stan tightened his grip. "I wouldn't mind keeping this mutt, even if she does have a stupid name. I'll change it."

"She's not for sale. Besides, no dog would ever like you."

"Well, dogs are the *only* thing that like you!" He blasted a laugh that shook the hills.

I fumed. In a flash, I punched him in the mouth. He released the dog and slugged my arm. Paprika jumped, yapping her head off. Stan wrestled me to the ground. That's when Paprika bit him on the seat of his britches. Stan jumped up and yelped, holding his rear end.

He cursed at the dog so loudly, shopkeepers surely heard him downtown. "I hate you, Tina Hamilton. Always have. And now this." He pointed to the dog. "So you win this round 'cause your dog's on your side. Next time you ain't gonna be so lucky." Panting, he leered at me, spit on Paprika, and charged into the woods.

I ran home with Paprika.

CHAPTER 26

Sundays were dreadful, every week the same: 8:30 wake-up call, 8:35 second wake-up call, 8:40 wake-up warning "get up or else," 9:30 all freshened up in blue gingham, white ribbon, and patent leather shoes, Nick in a bow tie, and walk to church, 9:50 settle into a hard flat pew, 10:00 Rev. Perkins welcoming all in his Sunday-best monotone, an octave lower than his weekday monotone. Nothing ever changed.

The special music selection was the only variation. Sometimes a pious male quartet sang a Psalm, the choir bellowed "A Mighty Fortress is our God," or Miz Doris crooned "Amazing Grace," an amusing diversion.

Miz Doris Eugenia Lydell, the church organist, dressed in various shades of purple ruffles resembling a giant iris. When she sang or played the organ, music reverberated through her like a windblown flower. The only time the congregation increased volume was in joining Miz Doris's refrains to drown her out. Rev. Perkins smiled as if pleased to inspire a more joyful noise out of his flock.

But aside from special music, nothing veered from the dull routine. The only yearnings we had for midmorning naps were thwarted. Mom nudged us awake if we showed the slightest hint of drowsiness. She expected us to look angelically receptive. If church did nothing else, it inspired ingenuity, for Nick and I had to dream up new ways to communicate without looking as though we were aware of each other's presence.

Operation camouflage. We sent messages to each other by pointing to words or letters in an open Bible or hymnbook, often spelling out afternoon plans. Today Nick wanted to leave Uncle Ross's early. He had an idea.

The Presbyterian church stood on the doctrines of John Calvin and John Knox of the 16th century Reformation. But somewhere between Knox's Scotland and 19th century North Carolina, that was lost until a Presbyterian revival came along in the late 1800s. Great-grandfather Hamilton had been a Baptist, like most folks here, until the revival. No doubt where my father stood. One look at Nick's entire given name told all: he was baptized Nicholas Calvin Knox Hamilton. Dad broke a long-standing tradition of family names by insisting on it.

The worst thing in the Presbyterian tradition was the way everyone kept Sunday, the Lord's day, in which no work was allowed. Although one might argue semantics, work included play. We kids couldn't fish, ride bikes, or play baseball or checkers. After church we'd go to Uncle Ross's for a fried chicken dinner and visit all afternoon until the evening service.

The women didn't sew or embroider. The men did nothing but sit around debating and pontificating. Dad did the bare minimum on the farm to keep the animals fed. Potatoes for Grandma's dinner soaked in a pot of water since Saturday night because they had to be peeled before the Sabbath. Grandpa would sooner go without potatoes than test God's patience. Sunday's table was set Saturday night, the corn shucked, the wood brought in. In the old days, spring water for Sunday and Monday morning had to be drawn Saturday night.

If we asked to do the impossible, Dad retorted with, "You want your face carved into the moon, too?" like the man who burned his brush pile on Sunday. This was the paradox of the Presbyterian church: every other day, work was sacred and glorified God, but on Sunday, work became anathema. Even eating and drinking glory unto God was questionable. Television, too, especially during the day. But sometimes Dad let us watch *Walt Disney's Wonderful World of Color* after the evening service.

Though the Scots-Irish were in the majority in our region, Presbyterians were one of the minorities. I could see why more people were Baptist. They sang rousing hymns and eliminated folks' chances of falling asleep, as did their hellfire and brimstone sermons.

Baptists weren't as picky about Sunday, but they condemned the smoking, drinking, dancing, theatergoing, and card-playing that our church members were allowed. Perhaps the best arrangement was to grow up Baptist as a kid, and do what he wanted on Sundays, then as a teenager switch to Presbyterian in order to dance, attend movies, and play cards. By the time Sunday rolled around, he'd be ready to rest up from it all.

I asked Dad if going to the movies was a sin, as the Baptists claimed. He said, "Going to the grocer's is a sin if it leads to gluttony."

On the way home Nick asked if we could stay home from Uncle Ross's. With his propensity for understanding childhood, Dad agreed. Mom made us sandwiches. The minute they left, Nick revealed his plan. He wanted to see how many drops of brandy it took for a chicken to get drunk.

It wasn't breaking the letter of the law, so I went along with it. At least he didn't suggest an egg-pitching fight like last year. That was trouble.

Nick climbed onto the countertop to reach Mom's homemade peach brandy on the highest shelf while I found a medicine dropper and small bowl. We went outside.

The first chicken, a black and white spotted Plymouth Rock, turned up her beak after the first taste. "You get a hold of her, Tina," Nick said. "I'll get her head and pinch her beak to get this stuff down her." He poured brandy in the bowl.

Though it was like grasping Jell-O, I managed to get a firm hold. She snapped at me but in my usual way with animals, I took charge. Nick dipped the dropper into the brandy and squeezed it into her beak. She protested but I held tight and Nick gave her another dropperful. We set her down. She shook her head vigorously, wings flapping.

Nick wanted to observe her before trying the others. In minutes, that chicken was swaying and fidgeting, staggering like a drunk pirate dragging a bottle of rum. She appeared dazed, then took off into a terrific fit of flailing and fussing, nearly knocking over three hens.

The others were just as disagreeable about swallowing the stuff. Despite spilling brandy on our hands, we persisted. We got through three Plymouth Rocks and three Rhode Island Reds with six leghorns to go when we ran out of brandy. We sat on the fence and roared with laughter as the chickens squawked, fluttered, and collided.

Nick asked me to fetch another bottle so I ran into the kitchen. The high shelf held no more bottles with the same label. I looked through other cupboards and finally found an identical bottle in the laundry room. I grabbed it and ran back.

Nick was doubled over laughing. "Look! That one looks like Barry MacNeill after he's had too much liquor. See the way she squats and her legs look like rubber bands?"

I pointed. "That red one looks like Betty MacDougall when she *isn't* drunk." She was an older girl at school.

Inside the coop, we administered the potion to the other six, with three instead of two droppers, for a comparison study. Nick took on a professor-like stance in a style reminiscent of science class. "We're here to calculate the effects of peach brandy on the system of a chicken. The first six are our control group." He continued until my cackling caused him to break a straight face.

We followed the last six into the yard. Two roosters on the fence watched as if spectators.

"Look at this one," Nick said. "You ever notice Ole Man Tyler on Sunday mornings? She struts like he does."

Two others resembled baseball players with unusual stances at the plate. I picked up a white leghorn. "Who was the first person in our house New Year's Day?" Tradition dictated that a man's chickens would be like the first person who entered the house the first day of the year.

"The chickens are kinda chunky this year. Maybe it was Miz Doris."

I put the hen down. She couldn't move as fast on her spindly legs. Imitating Miz Doris's shrill voice, I belted out a few bars of "Amazing Grace." I envisioned the woman swirled with purple ruffles and perched at the organ like a nesting hen.

"Why, Old Man Krueger, how nice to see you." Nick bent over to greet a Rhode Island Red. "See the eyes, Tina? It's just how he looks at you when you're too restless in Sunday School and expects you to be naughty."

A spotted hen waddled our way, swaying back and forth. "It's gotta be Libbie Macon putting on her make-up and trying on her wardrobe in front of the mirror."

"And this one . . ." Nick turned to see a white hen sprawled on her side as if she'd passed out. He picked her up. "This one's Mr. Bruce, always falling asleep during the sermon." He shook the hen. "Why, this one's really out." He shook her again. No response. "She's dead!" Nick's eyes bulged.

Another white hen arched her neck, stretched out her wings in a spastic flutter, and collapsed, rigid as a breadboard.

I nudged her with my foot. She didn't budge. "She's dead, too."

A third chicken mimicked the same convulsions and fell over, then another, and another. Within ten minutes all six leghorns were dead.

"Guess our experimental group overdosed," I said solemnly.

"Overdose nothing. They couldn't have died on three teaspoons of brandy, not so quickly. What did you bring me when you got that second bottle?"

We went into the coop to find it, half full of liquid the color of Mom's homemade peach brandy. Nick pointed to a piece of masking tape I hadn't noticed in my haste. "Ant poison," he read with disgust. "Tina, where'd you get this?"

"The laundry room."

"How can you be so addle-brained? You better get used to the notion of living on another planet because that's where Dad's gonna kick us."

"We'll be lucky if we have any breath left after he kicks us."

"You should've known better." Nick went off on a tirade over my stupidity until he felt better about his own negligence in the matter. But we had to use our time wisely to plan the right cover-up.

Volunteering to feed the chickens permanently was no guarantee Dad would never make the discovery. Replacing hens wouldn't work either. We had no money or time, nor a neighbor who wouldn't tell on us. Blaming an eagle wasn't believable. They didn't come around like they used to. Neither did chicken hawks. We settled on foxes.

We plucked feathers to spread haphazardly around the coop. Nick cut a chicken open for blood to spurt about. We filled a flour sack with dead chickens, wheelbarrowed it across the field, and buried them. Upon returning, we dug a hole under the fence, big enough for a fox to get through, and plugged it with a rock.

I wiped my brow. "I don't care about six dead chickens. Dad deserves this."

Nick agreed and went to the house for the shotgun. He wasn't supposed to touch the gun rack without permission, but this was an emergency. The rack housed Dad's prized possessions, including a Bean rifle and a Kentucky long rifle.

On the back stoop, Nick fired five shots in the direction of the coop. "They'll be home in a flash."

We went inside. He put the gun back. Mom and Dad arrived minutes later.

"Any trouble here?" Dad's eyes darted around the room.

"Foxes." Nick straightened in his chair, looking frazzled from an imagined bout with the furry beasts.

I felt sick.

"Are you all right?" Mom stroked my hair.

"Yeah, but they got away with six chickens."

Dad shook his head. "If God doesn't want us to work on His day, then why'd He send foxes?" He headed outside to assess the damage.

"You must've had quite a scare," Mom said. "Go get changed for church."

Several minutes later we were ready. No *Walt Disney's Wonderful World of Color* for us tonight. Or ever. No TV in outer space.

Dad stepped in with a bag. He set it on the table. It clunked. "I don't understand. It's a downright puzzle." He looked at us, as intent as a dog set on licking every last crumb from his dish. "We must have got ourselves some downright smart foxes."

Nick's eyebrows raised. "Sir?"

From the bag, Dad withdrew empty bottles of brandy and ant poison. "How in the Sam Hill did a fox smuggle this into the coop? Unless I'm dreaming, that coop was tidy last night, but somebody left bottles under a shelf. And mighty perplexing, those foxes went only for the white hens, no red or black ones. The others weren't touched one bit. Not a feather. And I thought only human beings favored white folks."

Even if we hadn't forgotten to pick up the bottles, Dad would have known.

Nick confessed all, face full of remorse.

"Do you have anything to add, Tina?" Dad asked.

I cried. My stomach hurt from the lie. Plus, Dad worked hard to run this farm. Six dead chickens was money lost due to my stupidity. "No, sir." My voice quivered. "I'm sorry, Dad."

"Come here, both of you."

It was all over now. Nick looked at me as if to say, "See you on Mars." The moon was already inhabited by one man. Nick would get whooped first, then Dad would wear out the switch on me.

Dad flipped through the Bible and read aloud two verses. First, Colossians 1:13,14: "Who hath delivered us from the dominion of darkness, and hath translated us into the kingdom of his dear Son; In whom we have redemption through his blood, even the forgiveness of sins." Then Ephesians 4:1: "I therefore . . . beseech you that ye walk worthy of the vocation wherewith ye are called."

Yes, Dad was from the old school of doing things. Many activities he wouldn't do on Sundays, but spanking wasn't one of them. A sin committed on Sunday reaped a double portion.

We also had to earn money to buy six new chickens.

CHAPTER 27

Last summer was full of baseball. This summer was empty even with baseball. Last summer I received the ball player carving, my father's gift. This summer I lived with all he'd taken from us. One of those losses was Nick.

Our town continued its own festivals apart from park involvement. But due to tourists, the annual Fourth of July festival was the most crowded one ever, more reminiscent of crammed downtown streets than celebrations of mountain life.

At home afterward, exhausted from clogging, I sprawled on the living room floor. Paprika curled at my side. Dad's face beamed from the joy of fiddle playing. Mom mixed a batch of lemonade. Nick and Todd rolled up their shirt sleeves at the dining room table.

"What do you think of this, Nick?" Todd leaned over, his nose twelve inches from strewn papers oddly resembling a school project. Lately, Todd was in the habit of pretending he was solving the park's problems. He used Xeroxed copies of his dad's diagrams and piqued Nick's interest. Maybe Nick's working on the park was retaliation against Dad.

"Mr. Culver's an urban planner," Nick said. "He shoulda figured out that problem."

"I guess he didn't count on all this congestion," Todd said. "But my dad's knowing how to fix it. He's an architect."

"So's mine," Nick said. "Hey, Dad, can you look at this?"

Dad looked up from the *National Geographic*, then strolled to the table.

The boys explained the problem, far beyond my

comprehension or interest. Dad ruffled Nick's hair, responding with glances at the papers. He examined a diagram, then set a hand on Todd's shoulder. "Your father's quite capable of working out a problem like this, and he's got a paid crew. I suggest asking for his advice."

Nick looked crestfallen. Dad ambled toward the kitchen.

I asked the boys if they were coming to my game tomorrow, but they had plans volunteering at the park. One time they picked up litter, another time worked in a booth. This would be the first time Nick missed my game.

I stomped to the kitchen. "I don't know why he's so taken up with that park," I snapped.

Dad only sighed.

****

"Search your hearts, as the Psalmist says, and see if there be any wicked way within you. Do you come to His table with a clear conscience? Have you made amends with all men? Have you received forgiveness? Any man who partakes of the bread and the wine but has not forgiven his brother eats and drinks reproach upon himself."

The minister admonished us in his usual Sunday monotone, making every bare, hard surface in the sanctuary even more bare and hard. The room's only color was a stained glass window above the pulpit. Sunlight spilled red, gold, and violet hues onto the front row pews. Usually, the light-play was beautiful and warm, but today it looked fake, gaudy, and cold. Just one cloud could diffuse the light and rob the room of life. Nothing was permanent but these stiff, brown pews.

Dad's gaze fastened to the front, his dark eyes like stained glass without light—cold, transparent. His jaw twitched under the beard. Would he finally take communion today?

In the narthex before the service, an older deacon in a gray suit had commented on Dad double-crossing the town by living a double life. Another man in a brown suit faulted Dad for the park's intrusion since his former role not only destroyed his credibility but counteracted his influence and pleas to vote against it. Dad's avoidance of communion hadn't escaped their attention either, and further confirmed suspicions that he wasn't a clean-cut hometown boy. Their hot judgment ignited half-whispered phrases like a wave of gossip. When they finished dissecting my father, they speculated about a church member with a drinking problem that escalated as they spoke.

Now these two men and their wives sat on pews near us, one in front of us and one on the other side of Dad.

I'd always felt secure knowing my dad had a direct and vital connection to the Almighty. The rest of the world could fall apart, but my dad knew God, and God held the world.

But I drew no comfort from that connection now. I resented him for bringing reproach upon our family. Nick's quitting baseball was rooted in Dad. What awful sin had he committed, on top of his betrayal of the town, that kept him from the Holy Sacrament and repelled others? During my childhood, Dad had been victim to nothing. But now in his silence, powerless, he was a victim of disdain. My life hung in the balance.

The organ moaned. While others contemplated the Supreme Sacrifice, I agonized over my father's plight. My throat tightened as the plate of bread went down the row in front of us. If Dad received communion, everything would straighten itself out.

The man in the gray suit, stiff and pious, took the bread as it passed. I wondered if he'd asked forgiveness for his careless words earlier.

Mom received the plate and took a piece of bread. It came to Nick, then me. I passed the plate to Dad, my heart racing. As he took the plate, my breath quickened in hope. He hesitated—and passed it to the man in brown who eagerly took his portion.

A cloud passed. The stained glass brightened, but it

wasn't the light of God. It was the devil poking fun of me with false light and diffusing hopes. I squirmed on the hard, brown pew.

****

That afternoon, I braced myself and asked Dad why he didn't take communion.

"I don't want to eat or drink reproach upon myself."

"Rev. Perkins says that only happens if you're not sincere, or if you're sinning or holding a grudge."

Dad replied with silence.

****

At my next game, I watched for Nick down the road.

"Don't get your hopes up," Dad said from behind the team bench. "I don't think he's coming."

Jay Griffin stole second base four times and made two great defensive plays. I made two errors and got no hits.

On the way home, Dad said, "I know it's been rough for us lately, Tina."

"We hardly have any friends left."

He chuckled. "Be thankful the barber's still our friend so we can get haircuts. And the doctor."

"That's not funny."

"We have each other." Dad took my hand.

"Doesn't seem like we have Nick anymore." *Or you.*

He knew it, too. His silence told me. Nick wouldn't go fishing with Dad. He resented Dad and felt guilty at the same time. He found everything he needed at the park with Todd and Phil, in watching baseball on television, and following the newspapers on McLain's season, another good one. Dad felt replaced. I saw the hurt in his eyes.

But it was hard for me to blame Nick.

CHAPTER 28

"Folks are as pleased as a dog with two tails to wag," Dr. Kirby said. He and Roger Griffin sat in the front room with Dad. Jay and I played checkers while taking a breather from catching fireflies. "Phil Kepler runs a clean shop, that's for certain."

Roger nodded. "I've never seen the likes of it. Sakes alive, he's the getting-aroundest man I ever saw. His gumption plumb tuckers me out."

"He has a knack for running that park with all of its operations," Doc Kirby said. "And a knack for dealing with a slew of folks."

"A good delegator." Dad lit his pipe.

"It's a finely-tuned machine, that park," Roger said. "Every bit and grain as good as he promised. And busy to boot."

"I reckon he's got his 25,000 folks a day, fitting in comfortably as predicted," Doc added.

"That's over twenty times the population of Currie Hill," Dad said. "I've heard grumbling about overcrowded conditions, especially downtown."

"There's some rabble-rousing over all that, but Phil's knowing to ways of handling it," Dr. Kirby said. "No complaint is overlooked. He's got public relation people who do nothing but resolve folks' complaints all the livelong day."

"It still wonders me though," Roger said, "how in the Sam Hill he got everything up so fast—" he snapped his fingers— "in the swish of a cow's tail."

"He still has ties to all those companies up north," Dr. Kirby said.

Dad smirked. "As many connections as a dog has fleas."

Mom entered with a tray of glasses. She passed out iced tea and peanut brittle. "I wish he'd quit advertising. I can't abide all the crowds, folks coming in droves, packing the streets and shops."

"No wonder it takes me longer to get to the barbershop these days." Dad chortled. "Do you make house calls, Roger?"

"Ain't no time for that, Drew." Roger said. "I got customers lined up on my doorstep pretty near from sunup to sundown."

Dr. Kirby took a long swallow of tea. "Drew." He cleared his throat and adopted a serious tone. "We've heard tell you're going to be working with Phil."

What? I made a bad move. Jay double jumped my checkers and crowned his king.

Dad puffed on his pipe. "Interesting conjecture."

"As an architect?" Mom asked. "I thought they'd have it all designed by now."

Dad explained. "The diagrams you saw didn't account for every detail, Jennie. A work like that's never complete. They'll be adding and expanding for years." Dad waved his pipe toward the men. "The expansion occurs much the same way these gentlemen are expanding on the truth right now."

Mom rolled her eyes. "You'd think Phil would plumb give up on this Hamilton clan."

"I don't know what Phil says." Roger swirled his glass, ice clinking. "But there's rumors going 'round. A right smart of folks are buzzing about it, given your background and all."

"It's a grand idea, I'll tell you pointblank," Dr. Kirby said. "Would you consider it, Drew?"

Dad leaned forward. "Let me get this straight. Phil's said nothing about wanting me, but I'm supposed to up and apply for the job?"

"Sure, why not?" Roger chomped some peanut brittle.

Dad sat back, watching pipe smoke rise and curl. "Phil

and me working together, now that's a chancy thing. Whoever started that scuttlebutt should be taken to task."

"Is that a no?" Roger asked.

"It's about as far-fetched as Jennie riding sidesaddle on a sow."

Mom frowned. "If that's what it takes, I'm willing to try."

I looked straight at Dad. *Do it for her.*

Dad balked, then shook his head. "Look, there's plenty of folks willing to contribute to the success of that park. I'm not one of them. My architect days are over."

"Why so hasty to decline?" Roger asked.

"Truth be told, Roger, it's hard enough living here with that park swallowing up our town. Working there would be akin to tangling with a wild pig. Pure torture, plain and simple."

Dr. Kirby took another swig of tea, as if for courage, then set elbows on his knees. Hands circling his glass, he looked up intently over his spectacles at Dad. "Drew, perhaps it's a way to make amends. This park's in our community now, whether we like it or not. Since you had a hand in it from the get-go, you're given out to be the best one for making it work, so it pays off down the road."

"That's Phil's job. He's more than capable." Dad tapped the pipe on the couch. "He needs me no more than a hog cares for a holiday."

I could hardly concentrate on checkers. Jay made a triple jump and crowned another king.

"Then come back to town council," Roger said. "This town's wanting for good leadership, Drew. There's a hole where you once stood. Whatever your reasons for stepping down, there's more for coming back. What's passed is past. You've more than proven your loyalty to this town, that's for certain."

Mom spoke up. "I reckon you're in the minority with that line of thinking. Every which away, there's folks angry at

Drew for stepping foot in New York, folks angry that he bothered to come back, and folks angry that he never told them about the park before. That adds up to everybody feeling betrayed."

"Not everybody, Jennie," Roger said. "It takes a spell for things to settle down, but many want Drew back. Jim Drummond, for example. And Wally. Bob Hutchins." He listed a dozen men. "Simon and I, we consider you like kin. But we're asking you to consider this for the town's sake. A town that can benefit from your leadership."

"That's as crazy as all-outdoors," Dad said. "It's been almost a year since that park was been voted in and I can count on one hand the number of folks who traipsed out this way to give support. I don't fault them for not being able to confidence me. But I can't change their minds."

Roger seemed intent on studying his ice cubes. "It's awkward for them, see. It's a plumb hard pill for folks to swallow when they've trusted someone for a coon's age and come to find out he ain't who they thought he was."

Dad's voice rose as his face reddened. "If I'd failed there and came back with my heart still in New York, their feelings would be understandable. But I eventually despised my success. I wanted to return to what I had here. That's *different*." His last word hung in the air, claiming our attention until it dissipated.

Jay nudged me. My turn again.

"Of course," Dr. Kirby said. "But we're hoping you'll study on the situation for a spell, and consider working with Phil, or on town council. It'll help you ease back into town life."

"Phil and others are doing fine without me. The town will grow, as Phil promised, and you-uns will have no trouble fetching yourselves a lavish of good leaders."

The doctor took one last swallow of tea and set down the glass. He interlocked his fingers. "We reckon this would be a good move for you, to be involved again. I believe stepping out of active town council life did more damage to your name than finding out about your time in New York and your role in the park plans. You'll not consider this?"

Please say yes. Mom looked at him expectantly. Wouldn't he do it, for her sake, if for nothing else?

"Look, Simon, Roger, you all are setting a horse's leg instead of taking it out back and shooting it."

"Fiddlesticks!" Roger's arms swooped up, glass still in hand. Ice jiggled and tea splashed out. "This ain't beyond repair. It ain't fittin' to let life pass right on by you, forfeiting your influence, letting folks favor their wrong notions. I can't see why you don't jump at the chance to get back into town life again."

"There's not a whole lot worthwhile a man can do without a good reputation behind him," Dr. Kirby said. "Investing in the town will help rebuild yours."

"Like you did for twelve years," Roger said. "No need to stop now."

"I'm not indispensable," Dad said. "My influence is limited, and it's a choice they made—"

Doc cut in. "Folks were wary when you first moved back here, but once you got involved in community activities, they accepted you. It'll happen again."

"My first duty is to my family."

"Perhaps you owe it to your family then." Roger glanced at Mom. "It's a shame how folks stand off and look at your wife and kids and shake their heads and never know what to say to 'em. Maybe you can best be serving your family by working your way back into town."

I tilted my head toward Dad. *Please . . .*

Dad leaned forward. "I'm well aware of the treatment my family's getting. And it pains me more than it pains them since I feel responsible." His brow furrowed. "I know you speak to me as friends, for my own good. But there are other factors and you'll just have to take no for an answer."

What other factors? Jay jumped my two kings.

"Because you're so adamantly against the park?" Dr. Kirby asked.

Dad inhaled deeply and exhaled with an air of finality. "I've already committed myself to my life's goals. Neither working for Phil Kepler nor being town council chairman rank among them."

****

Someone pounded on our front door, startling me on a quiet evening after supper. Mom ran to answer it. Susan MacNeill stood there, tears streaming.

"Please, come, Miz Jennie. Mama's in a bad way. I don't know what to do."

Mom wasted no time following Susan out the door. "Tina, come along."

Dad and Nick were outside finishing chores.

"Where's your daddy?" Mom asked Susan as we walked.

"Don't know, ma'am."

I dreaded going, with Lucy ailing for weeks now. Besides, the satisfaction of doing good for others never outweighed my repulsion of the filthy house and sassy kids.

Poor, dear Lucy. I couldn't erase the image of a scowling, overbearing father who doomed his daughter to a life of shame because of one mistake.

At the MacNeills, Mom rushed to the back bedroom. I stood with Susan, tongue-tied. The acrid smell of urine overwhelmed me. The two-year-old toddled around with a soaked diaper.

"Tina," Mom called, "go fetch Dad. Have him call Dr. Kirby first. Run! Susan, fetch me a clean, wet cloth."

The MacNeills had no phone. I ran out, heart pounding, praying for Lucy.

At home Dad called the doctor and others to locate Barry, to no avail. Nick accompanied Dad and me to the

MacNeills.

Dad ran in to help Mom. Dr. Kirby raced in shortly. Some kids were in the bedroom, some drifted through the kitchen and parlor, crying, whining, or gazing vacantly.

Minutes later, Mom called all the children in. "Wait here," she told Nick and me.

My stomach churned. Nick stared at his feet.

Soon Mom returned and hugged me, tears streaming. "Lucy's gone. I'm staying here to help out. You-uns go home and get that pork stew out of the fridge and bring it over. These kids haven't eaten all day. Daddy'll stay here, too. After you bring the stew, go back home."

We left. Feeling numb, I could barely swallow. Even if Lucy was in a better place now, it wasn't fair. Barry was who-knows-where, as usual. She died the way she'd lived—without the loving support of her husband.

The image materialized, her face that night she told Mom about her first love. In that face was a long-lost youth, still clinging to a treasured memory of the only love she ever knew—ironically, the love that brought her a lifetime of grief. That same face bore the pain of rejection, the sting of hate and an unforgiving spirit—a legacy from her father. She didn't hate, but she lived with his hatred and the shame he'd willed to her in the form of Barry MacNeill. My mind couldn't conceive of it all back then, but my heart felt the wretchedness and grief of a destiny she'd been locked into. With mercy and forgiveness, her life would have been better.

As Nick walked silently, I imagined Lucy's loneliness. Hers was a life of Barry tracking in mud, toddlers whining, babies crawling, Jason's sassing. Dependent on neighbors and friends, she could lay no claim to the fruitfulness of her garden, take no pride in the cleanliness of her home. She relied on Mom's pork stews, Dad's and Bob Hutchins' fence-mending, Patsy Hutchins' cleaning skills. Furniture brought in from the barn, as good as new.

The barn! The silhouette of Ole Joe entering the barn

gripped me. What was the connection? Only one thing was certain. Ole Joe needed to know about Lucy.

We arrived home. I ladled stew into a smaller pot to take to Joe. I asked Nick to accompany me after taking stew next door.

Fifteen minutes later we headed to Joe's. I told Nick about seeing Joe walk into the MacNeills' barn at night, that he must know Lucy somehow and might be the one repairing her furniture. Nick was as shocked as I had been. "Only thing is," I said, "he ain't knowing to the fact that I seen him. I hope he don't get mad."

We arrived at dusk. When he opened the door, his smile lit. "Why, Mr. Nick and Miss Christina! A sight to behold. Is it the full moon already? That don't look like no zucchini."

"We brought you some pork stew," Nick said.

"You said you ain't the best cook in the world," I added. "But our Mom is."

"Well, ain't that a fine thing. Many thanks to you. Come sit a spell." We entered. "Does your mom know you be sharing stew with me?" Did he fear being found out?

"No, sir. But she's always giving food to neighbors so I took some of that." With no gift for words or timing, I swallowed hard. How would I gracefully tell him about Lucy?

He poured the stew into his own pot, washed ours out, and handed it back. He'd probably eat after we left. "Did you all come to work on your pictures?" He reached for the tool box.

"No, actually . . . well, no." I grasped for the right words. Nick's face seemed to say, *Don't look at me, this was your idea.*

"Well, then, you eat supper already? Sit down and let's have some stew."

Nick and I sat. "We already ate," I said. "We came to—"

"Y'all wanna hear another story?"

"No . . . we came 'cause . . . I have to tell you something . . . important . . ."

When he lit the lantern, his raised eyebrows came into view. "What is it, Tina?"

I fidgeted on the stool, my palms sweaty. "I reckon you need to know . . . not knowing how else you'd find out . . ."

He sat. "Child, you're painful to listen to. Just spit it out."

I took a deep breath and expelled words. "Miz Lucy MacNeill died tonight."

Joe's eyes widened, his mouth twitched. He leaned over, elbows on knees, face down, as silence stretched over a minute. Then he whispered. "Miz Lucy."

"I'm sorry."

"God rest her soul." At the wood stove, he picked up the coffeepot and poured a cup. "Y'all want a drink?"

We shook our heads.

He sat again, cup in hand. Darkness filled the windows. He cleared his throat. "How'd y'all figure I knew Miz Lucy?"

I glanced at Nick, as if the right words were printed on his forehead. "I saw you a couple times. From my window . . . at night . . . going into the MacNeills' barn."

Joe drank some coffee. "For five years I been keeping a promise to my brother." He sighed. "He was fifteen years younger than me. He met up with Miz Lucy 'bout twenty years ago. They had a special friendship, they did. He passed by her place whenever he had a chance. But nobody would've taken to the notion of them two being hitched up. You understand me now, don't you?"

We nodded.

"Robert, he was several years older than Miz Lucy, but it didn't matter to them. He saw her whenever he could. When she turned eighteen, Robert knew her daddy was wanting to marry her off. Some fella by the name of Simpson, I recollect. Sam Simpson. Y'all know the Simpsons?"

"He owns the ice cream parlor," Nick said. Sam, as responsible as a man could be, had married Marcia Wilcox and had five kids, two of them our teammates, Cue Ball and Eight Ball.

"Lucy and Sam were to be wed in the fall of '51. Robert, he knew he was gonna have to step out of the way altogether. But problems occurred." He stared at his coffee. "Miz Lucy found herself in the family way." He whistled. "See, Lucy's daddy found out about her and Robert. Bill Redmond was given out to be the worst bigot of all times. When he found out Lucy was going behind his back spending time with a colored man, he couldn't abide that." His voice cracked.

"Her daddy's hatred got the best of him. He was so ashamed of her that he broke it off with Sam Simpson and married her off to that MacNeill fella." An owl hooted. A branch snapped. "Didn't figure she deserved any better than that. He wanted her to live in the same shame she'd brought to him."

"That don't make sense," Nick said. 'Specially if no one else knew about it."

"Mercy was not a word he knew. He couldn't see fit to forgive. But Robert, see, he took the guilt on himself. He couldn't forgive himself after he seen what happened. He loved that girl, and he'd done her wrong. Now she bore the brunt of it."

Joe opened the window. A breeze blew in along with the triple chant of the whippoorwill. "After Lucy was married to MacNeill for two years, Robert noticed how rundown the place looked. He felt even worse. He vowed he'd help her in some way. One day he chanced to talk to her when no one was around. They made an arrangement. Whatever Lucy needed help with—furniture repairs, painting, tools and such—she'd put it in the barn and once a week Robert would drop by in the thick of night to fix it up for her. No one would know. Robert made me vow to continue the work if something ever happened to him. So when he died in an accident five years ago, I took up where he left off." The owl hooted again. Wind raked the branches and leaves.

"I only seen Miz Lucy a dozen or so times, when she'd venture to be up in the middle of the night and visit the barn. That's if Barry weren't home. She was a kind soul. If she had leftover cornbread or soup, she'd bring it out to me. Sometimes even a peach cobbler. She'd give me a quarter occasionally, though I refused at first. She'd thank me a million times and said whatever I wanted from the garden was mine for the taking, anytime." He winked.

I should have felt relief upon realizing we weren't stealing vegetables after all. But maybe my conscience was seared by then. All I could think of was Lucy and her sadness.

We arrived home shortly before Mom and Dad did. Barry had finally appeared in his usual drunken state. He seemed shocked about Lucy, and sat in the bedroom for an hour in a stupor. Dad called Rev. Perkins and the MacNeill and Redmond relatives. Mom fed the kids and put the little ones in bed. They stayed until Barry's sister arrived. Later, arrangements were made for Redmond relatives in Fenville to take the children for awhile.

Nick and I went with Mom and Dad to the funeral service at the church. We sang "Amazing Grace" and "It is Well with my Soul." In the back stood Ole Joe. A woman remarked on that man who lived alone on yonder mountain, seen in town periodically buying sugar and coffee beans.

PART V

Grandma Dorothy: Ginseng and Good Neighboring. "All bonds are fragile. They's only as strong as the tests they pass."

"We used to come up into these mountains to go 'sanging, down Nantahala way." Grandma Dorothy's knitting needles clicked busily. "My ma and I would hunt and tote it into town, selling it in exchange for calicos and ginghams."

"Then your ma sewed you a new dress," I said.

"Yes, we were in business as long as we got our hands on that 'sang. We had one spot nobody else knew about. But so did old Mr. Ratchet, a fine fellow to neighbor with. When he was took down with the flu, he still wouldn't reveal his secret place, 'cause the minute he was up and about he was gonna get himself some more. Darned if he was gonna find it all dug up by other greedy 'sang hunters. We thought he was doing right tolerable when he took a turn for the worse. He just up and died."

"Did he have a family?" Nick asked.

"His wife died years earlier, his kids were all grown up. They weren't knowing to where his patch was. I declare, there were never more folks in the woods than the day after Mr. Ratchet's funeral. They waited what they reckoned was a respectable amount of time, a whole twenty-four hours, mind you. Come what may, every one of 'em was aiming to be the first to find his patch. Whoever did would be plumb rich for certain the way the man had talked."

"Whoever found it was never gonna tell," I said.

"You can be mighty sure of that, little lady." Grandma's needles clicked faster. "One day Ma and I happened upon a right big heap of branches near a cove. We reckoned it was the perfect spot for an old still, but lo and behold, it was a huge patch of 'sang."

"Did you pick it?" Nick asked.

"Not yet, 'cause Ma says she wants to test something. She'd heard neighbors bragging about a new patch, a secret from all. So every day we checked and parts were gone. Meanwhile, Liza Duffey shows Chuck Hammill all the 'sang she got each morning, and Chuck laughed. He says, 'Is that all the better you can do?' He'd show her a pile, a mighty heap bigger than hers. Come next day, though, his pile looks measly next to hers. They kept outdoing each other. About that same time, they started complaining someone else was stealing their 'sang."

I offered a knowing smile. "Was that you and your ma taking it?"

Grandma's knitting stopped. She leaned forward as if imparting a big secret. "It surely was, but we three were the only ones knowing to that patch of Mr. Ratchet's." She resumed knitting, needles clicking. "Liza and Chuck complained about their predicament the better part of six weeks, threatening to trap them 'sang thieves, as if they owned the land themselves. Ma says to them, 'Did you-uns ever reckon you might be stealing from each other?' That did it. Liza and Chuck lit into each other something fierce, causing such a racket that Ma had to call Drake Cunningham from down the road apiece to break them up."

CHAPTER 29

I carried on with the same activities as last summer so things would feel normal. Weekly I visited Grandma Hamilton to bake or create apple-head or corn husk dolls. I helped Grandma Dorothy hook a braided rug she was making for my room. I picked out colors and scrap wool fabrics. Uncle Parker showed me how to shear her lambs.

Grandma demonstrated how to pluck a goose, claiming she once got a half bushel of feathers from one. The down grew back prettier than before. "I know you-uns are having a rough time." She handed me a feather. "Any time a soul's a-hurting, she's gonna grow even more beautiful, if she lets the Good Lord who's holding her do the plucking."

Old Lady Balch remained the best spinner of spooky tales. I'd wrap my arms around my knees to keep them from shaking, prickles skimming the back of my neck. But Nick and I made sure we were back by sunset. No moonless night ever caught us there, red pepper or no red pepper.

Rumor had it that some big black man showed up in town, stirring up trouble. The sheriff took him in for questioning and jailed him for a night. The next time we visited, Joe explained. "Went to buy me some coffee, but I wasn't stirring up no batch of trouble. A man'll call a crow a fox if he can get away with it."

That made me angrier at the townsfolk. Jay and Alex were the only kids worth seeing. Rex and Byron still faulted my father for no baseball in Currie Hill, taking all the zest out of a butterscotch sundae at the ice cream parlor.

I avoided Stan, since his next plan of attack was

murder.

The uncles still came for cards, as usual. Sometimes aunts and cousins tagged along, but laughter was strained through harmless small talk. Bonds once tight now stretched.

****

Todd and Nick sat at the dining room table like two businessmen, papers strewn all over. Phil Kepler kept them supplied with Xeroxed blueprints. Why other than for novelty's sake would Todd and Nick pore over papers all summer long?

I didn't want to lose Nick the way I was losing Dad. Dad didn't want to recover lost ground in town, which would have helped us all. If he wouldn't listen to the good sense of his well-meaning friends, he certainly wouldn't listen to me.

He didn't condemn Nick's working on the park, so we could join forces without guilt of disloyalty. Perhaps I had a chance winning back Nick.

I sat at the table. They didn't even look at me. They examined part of the Literary Heritage section, brainstorming designs for a food booth and puppet theater. I asked questions. Eventually they gave me eye contact and more than one-word answers. By evening's end, we were of one mind. Todd invited me to come over the next day with Nick. I hesitated--I had a game. But I gave a resounding yes.

The next morning, Nick and I were ready to leave. Someone knocked. I answered the door.

"You ready for the game, Tina?" Jay smiled wide and toothy, then frowned. "You ain't even dressed for it yet."

"I ain't going today, Jay." I couldn't look him in the eye.

"You're not feeling well?"

I couldn't lie, not to Jay. But I felt sick at that moment. "Just can't go, Jay. I promised Nick I'd help him with something important." There. So self-sacrificial.

Jay's face fell. He shuffled away.

Dad wouldn't let me quit baseball halfway through the season. I had to honor my commitment. Nick had quit at the beginning. That was different. I was used to that kind of reasoning.

I wanted to say, *Then how come you quit town council and the deaconry before your terms were up?* But I didn't dare.

After chores, when I didn't have a game, I'd accompany Nick and Todd to the park. I'd never had so much fun picking up litter. Sometimes we helped in a game booth with an adult. Other times Mr. Kepler let us dress up as Mother Goose characters and greet children as Jack and Jill, Little Bo Peep, Wee Willie Winkie, and others.

Dad asked if I wanted a vacation day from work to go fishing. But an afternoon sitting on the riverbank with him sounded long and tedious. I bit my lip when I refused his offer.

One evening we had chili dogs at Todd's. Afterward, Phil tossed us each a roll of Life Savers and humored us by examining our park sketches. "Not a bad idea. Mr. Flannery might even go for this." His usual commentary for affirming our efforts.

The doorbell rang. Phil answered the door. "Mr. Flannery, what a surprise! I didn't expect you so soon."

"Some appointments canceled so I thought I'd fly in a few days early." In stepped a man with gray hair that belied his youthful steps. They shook hands and exchanged pleasantries. Phil introduced him as his boss from New York City.

"Did you just arrive?" Phil asked.

"A few hours ago. I went straight to the park to have a look."

"What did you think? Did you have trouble stepping over everybody to get inside?"

"Impressive, Phil. You certainly know how to pull things together. It's a far cry from what I envisioned in January when I visited." Phil beamed. "I have a few concerns, though."

Phil escorted him to his office, the room we'd never been allowed in. The door shut us out, but thin walls invited us in.

Todd signaled us to keep quiet. "If Dad's in a bad mood tonight, I wanna know why."

Mr. Flannery fired questions about aspects of the park: design and layout, dates that sections opened, visitors, media and press, unopened areas, then figures and money.

"What are you driving at?" Phil said. "Are we out of money to finish this up? Are you dissatisfied with these plans?"

"The designs aren't consistent with the rest of the park. You've hired five different architects to design this same area and I see problems with each. I can't justify throwing money away like this, even if the park is raking it in. I want a designer who's both aesthetic and practical. Someone innovative and efficient. I have yet to see that combination in any of these sketches."

"Mr. Flannery, these are high quality. Look." Papers rustled as Phil pointed out finer features of several diagrams.

Mr. Flannery was not impressed and noted flaws.

"These are sure to be technological achievements when built to these specifications," Phil said. "What you deem a flaw is personal opinion. My head architect can make adjustments to suit your fancy."

"This is more than a matter of my idiosyncratic nature, Phil. These don't complement the original designs, which is crucial for a unified look."

Phil sounded exasperated. "Well then, do you have a recommendation?"

"Yes. I want you to get Drew Hamilton for this job."

"What?"

"Is that so incredible?"

"Drew hasn't worked as an architect in over twelve years. He's a farmer. He probably doesn't even remember the draftsman's alphabet."

"In my mind he's the only man for this job. He lives right here, doesn't he? I want you to hire him. He can head up the entire department. This is the last money I'll allot for this sort of thing. Make him an offer."

"Mr. Flannery, with all due respect, you don't know the man the way I do. He won't be bought. Money means nothing to him anymore."

"If you know him so well, Phil, you figure out how to get him."

"I've got several architects I'm considering. Let's look over their résumés and portfolios and you can give me some recommendations."

"I'm giving you one. I already gave you five chances. Five times you blew it. I'm not trusting your whim with any more designers. We know Hamilton's work and background. He's the only one I'll accept."

"Maybe you should speak to Drew yourself, sir."

"It's better that you do. You've worked together before."

"And if he refuses?"

"If you can procure him, it will be to your benefit. You have no option."

******

That night I asked Dad if he knew a Mr. Flannery. Dad said he was president of a New York engineering firm that once made amusement park rides, but had since expanded. I told Dad that he was at Mr. Kepler's house, but didn't mention why.

Dad attempted to entice me to go fishing but I declined, shutting out his hurt expression. I went through the motions of baseball but my heart wasn't in it, even for Jay's sake.

Nick and I still made trips to Coulder Pass, delivering muskmelons, cabbages, or rutabagas. Each time, we practiced using the hand tools. Joe introduced new ones. While Nick worked on a sailboat picture, I struggled with a cabin in the woods and botched three trees so far. Joe patiently guided, but wouldn't do the work for us. I cut myself only once.

Todd continued to buy Old Lady Balch's homegrown tobacco. Nick still insisted he wouldn't try anything but the manufactured stuff. So Todd chewed alone, no longer on the baseball diamond, but over the dining room table, when no parents were around.

CHAPTER 30

After supper, someone knocked. I opened the door to find Phil Kepler. My jaw dropped.

He had no Life Savers for me. Dad appeared and nodded stiffly. "Phil."

Phil stepped in, his starched white shirt brightening the room. I retreated to the sofa. Paprika jumped into my lap.

"What can I attribute this visit to?" Dad's taut voice adopted northern inflections.

"Drew, I'll get right to the point," Phil said as though only a day had lapsed rather than a year since they'd spoken. "I'd like to offer you a proposal."

Mom entered and stopped short upon seeing Phil. She gaped.

"Have a seat, Phil," Dad said. "Jennie, please bring iced tea."

I wondered if Dad wished he could whisk himself back to old times, to his friendship days with Phil. I read Mom's eyes. Surely iced tea was overdoing the hospitality.

Phil lowered himself into the old, stuffed chair as though it might collapse. I pretended to be entranced in my book, glancing up now and then.

"I'd like you to work for me, Drew. I need an architect, one of your caliber." He searched for a reaction on Dad's face. "There's one last section of the park we're trying to complete this year." He explained the tasks, how much time they required, and the pay.

Mom brought iced tea and sat.

Dad asked a few questions. I had the distinct feeling he

wanted to offer a hearty handshake, as if it would blow away all their differences and harsh words and restore their friendship. Instead, Dad's face tightened, his posture rigid. "Phil, you and I don't see eye to eye. In addition, I find it disturbing that twelve months ago you wanted to end my influence in this town for good, and now you ask me for help. Have you run out of options?"

"I wasn't the one who told the townspeople about your role in the park."

"No, you didn't have to. But if I'd let folks believe what you started out telling them, I wouldn't be any better off. So what's the difference?"

"I made my apologies already. I didn't come to grovel."

"I'm not asking you to."

Phil shifted and the chair creaked. He bit his lip, then displayed a cool smile as if it were preface to striking the bargain of his life. "Drew, my actions were wrong as far as it concerns you and your personal life. But I can make it up to you. I'll see that your reputation is restored."

"Have you tried already?" Mom's gift of bluntness brought a raised eyebrow from Phil, then silence. "I thought as much."

"Will you consider it?" Phil asked.

"No."

"I'll give you a week to think it over."

"No."

"Why not?"

"First of all, I no longer want to be an architect. Second, I'll always be philosophically opposed to the installment of that park here and all the changes it wrought. Third, I'm not interested in bargaining for my reputation. Fourth, we could never work together efficiently, for I don't believe that in all cases the good of the people is more important than the good of one. Fifth, this job has nothing to do with folks' welfare, so don't hold that out as bait."

Having used his ammunition, Phil was silent, then re-energized. "Name your price."

"You can't buy me, Phil."

Phil's eyes pierced Dad's. "You might as well know. Joseph Flannery wants you for this job. He was just here this weekend and requested you."

"The man's never met me. Put his mind at ease, Phil. There are hundreds of others on equal or better footing and not as rusty."

Phil looked my way, as if debating whether or not to say his next remark in my presence. "Drew . . ." He stopped open-mouthed then nodded toward the front door.

Dad followed Phil outside to the porch. I couldn't distinguish their words. After a few silent minutes, I went outside.

Sitting in the swing, Dad patted the seat next to him. I lay down and rested my head on his lap, welcoming the steady hum of evening, the crickets' rhythmical chirping. But I missed the stars, diluted in the pool of park light.

What had my father and Phil Kepler said on the porch? Dad's clammy, trembling hand stroked my forehead.

I had to break the silence. "What do you mean, the good of all the people not being more important than the good of one?"

The mountain dialect returned. "You recollect the parable of the lost sheep? The Good Shepherd left the ninety-nine sheep and went to fetch the stray one. There's another way to see it, too, putting me in mind of your mother." He ruffled my hair. The swing swayed back and forth.

"How's that?"

"Your mother wanted to be a grade school teacher, and would've been a powerful good one, too. She attended college, aiming to be a teacher when we started courting. Even if she'd finished school and started teaching, though, she would've given that up along about the time you and Nick were born. She reckoned it more important to be home as a mother of two than to be teacher to many."

"Hmm."

"Another example is when teachers punish the whole class for the sake of one student, when they don't know who the mischief-maker is. Maybe that's wrong in some cases, but sometimes God works that way. I mean, He allows others to be inconvenienced while He's trying to teach one person a lesson."

"I hate it when teachers do that. Miss Prinz does it and makes us all feel guilty whether we did something wrong or not."

He chuckled. "She's trying to get the culprit to confess."

"Nobody will, because then she'll embarrass them in front of everyone. That ain't right either."

"I reckon not. But sometimes shame works better than grace."

"How can that be?"

"It drives the point home even better, for those of us who are slow learners." Dad smirked. "Besides, Tina, unless we see how bad we are, we'll never know the grace of God."

Dad and his decisions were confusing enough, without all this talk about shame and grace. "What does that have to do with Mr. Kepler, and you not taking a job with him?"

"Just different ways of thinking. Two folks as different as he and I ain't gonna work long together before butting heads and locking horns."

Mom and Nick were silhouetted in the screen door.

Mom stepped out, followed by Nick. "What's behind this job offer?"

Dad ran fingers through his hair. I gave Mom my spot. Nick sat on the steps.

I circled the post and sat on the railing. "Mr. Flannery won't let Mr. Kepler hire anyone but you. Mr. Kepler might be in trouble if he can't get you." My father had to know this, at risk of punishment. Maybe he'd be inclined to tell us more.

And take the job.

"How do you know?" Dad said.

"Mr. Flannery said so himself at Mr. Kepler's house." I spoke as if giving a news report. "Says he's running out of money to hire just anybody and only wants you. Been through five other architects and didn't like any."

"How in the Sam Hill . . . ?" Mom murmured. "Does Mr. Kepler conduct his business in front of you?"

I wrestled with how to explain our eavesdropping and decided to not bear this alone. "Mr. Kepler was in his office but we heard him from the living room. Nick and Todd, too."

Nick's eyes blazed.

Mom's freckles darkened, visible even in the dim light. "You know better—"

Dad intercepted. "Is that all you heard?" Odd for him to prime us for information gleaned from an eavesdropping.

"Yes, sir," Nick and I said in unison.

Dad leaned forward, brow wrinkled. "Are you sure?" What was he afraid of us hearing?

"They said that was all, Drew."

"Jennie, this is important."

"I don't understand." Mom's voice grew pensive. "I hear everything you're telling folks, but what's the harm in working with Phil? It might help things get back to normal."

Dad stared at the darkness. "I can't ever work with Phil Kepler again."

"But, Drew," Mom said quietly, "we all have to forgive him and go on. What good is it to do otherwise? The damage is done but we've still got to live here, and face folks in town. Can't you just forgive him, take this job, and go on?" Tears rolled down her cheeks.

Dad's hand closed around Mom's. "Jennie, it's not what he's done to me. That ain't it. I deserved it. The problem is . . . what I did to him."

Dad got up and walked inside.

CHAPTER 31

On Saturday, July 20, the extended family gathered to watch Neil Armstrong take his first steps on the moon. The uncles and aunts cheered with us kids, but the grandparents shook their heads in disgust. For weeks, Grandma Hamilton claimed the whole thing was staged. "If folks go on the moon," she said, "all the cycles will be offset and the signs won't be rightly telling us when to plant our beans and corn and such."

By the time July 20 rolled around, she resigned herself to the facts. "Believe me, it's happening," she told anyone who would listen. "The cycles are already offset, have been for months. Look at this town, this family."

Somehow, sending rockets to the moon caused the big city lure and the park's invasion into town. Far be it from anyone to think our dishevelment was inherent to our family. The moon made a great scapegoat.

A few nights later, Todd, Nick, and I worked at our house on the park project, chattering like magpies.

After his fourth attempt at solving the dilemma of a congested restaurant courtyard, Todd smacked the sketch on the table. "Maybe your dad can help."

"Nah, he hates this park." Nick's voice had a bite.

Dad's face twitched as he read the newspaper. We discussed the problem another twenty minutes. Then he rose and headed toward the kitchen. He paused by our table and scrutinized Xeroxed copies from Phil.

"My dad made those," Todd said. "He tried to use our idea."

Dad smiled, squinted at the drawings, and sat. He made

marks and scratches. "This can't work efficiently. Try this instead." He explained the traffic flow in terms of the courtyard's layout and structure.

Todd's eyes grew wide. "Wow, thanks, Mr. Hamilton. This is great!"

"Thanks, Dad," Nick echoed, the most genuinely kind words he'd spoken in weeks.

Dad pelted us with park questions for an hour. He made sketches and labeled parts.

Todd lifted a diagram six inches from his face. "You make funny Ms and Ns."

"That's my trademark." Dad stood and tousled Todd's hair, then Nick's.

"Look who's talking." Nick pointed to Todd's drawings. "All your letters look funny."

"That's the draftsman's alphabet," Todd said. "My dad showed it to me."

****

At Griffin's barber shop, Dad, Nick, and I waited for haircuts. Roger informed Dad that business around town had increased so much that nobody could keep up. Tourists loved the area's genuine culture and handmade crafts, but to meet demands, shops would have to turn commercial. Bob Hutchins, Wally, and others would have to change their methods completely, turn down orders, or put people on a waiting list approaching a year long. Bob was considering closing his shop and moving out of town.

"But his family has owned that shop for generations," Dad said. "His lifeblood is here. He vowed he'd never move."

"Says he's fixing to move out for good," Roger said. "Doesn't want so much business, and can't stand the crowds." The Hutchins family lived above their shop.

After haircuts, Dad, Nick, and I strolled through the crowded town. He explained why everyone was upset about all the good business. "Time used to be their servant. Now it's their master and has them by the throat in a vice grip." It brought to mind lines at the bakery and shoe store. Nick and I peered inside familiar shop windows only to greet unfamiliar scenes.

We stopped at Bob Hutchins's carpentry shop. Still vivid was that day last year when Mr. Hutchins proudly toured me around, demonstrating his lathe. Just as vivid was the uncertainty with which he regarded us since.

The bell on the door jingled. Bob emerged from the back room.

"Good morning, Bob," Dad said. "I'd like to place an order."

Bob teetered between coming forward and staying put. He forced a laugh, his furry white hair bobbing. "You and a slew of fifty million others." He nodded across the room at folks admiring his chairs.

"This is more of a proposal," Dad said. Bob looked at him askew. "We've an old building on our farm, used to be part of the springhouse. I'm aiming to fix it up as my workshop, but I hear tell of rumblings that you might be needing a bigger place of your own. Since you don't have room to expand—"

"Expand? I'd rather shrink this business right now," Bob said in his sawdusty voice. "I'll soon be toting the wife and hightailing it out of this hog wild town."

"There's an old cabin 'round the corner from us in want of some hammering and painting. It's fittin' enough for a small family, a stone's throw from the old springhouse."

"I'm moving away. It's crazy as all-outdoors here. It's all settled with me and Patsy."

"The cabin sets on an acre. Along with the springhouse, I'd rent it out for, say forty dollars a month."

"What was that?" Bob's shoulders jerked.

"Forty dollars a month. If you need more room, the building could expand. Of course, this comes with one stipulation." Dad lowered his voice. "No factory potential. No commercial business transacted. Tourists, sure, if they chance to stumble by. But the home of a true craftsman it must remain. No compromising. And positively no advertising except by word of mouth. I'm telling you, nobody comes out that away. If tourists want your stuff they'll have to come get it, so as you can mainly serve the townsfolk. See, a man's gotta right to live in the town of his fathers, and nobody should give him cause to move."

Bob shuffled his feet. "Sounds plumb crazy. Patsy and me are already set on moving."

"All right, then, I'd order a wardrobe. Oak, four by seven feet, a rod on one side, shelves on the other. I'll pay you $650.00."

Bob's eyes bulged. "My price is $400.00."

For someone who always said we didn't have money to travel, Dad's insistence on the high increase baffled me.

"But I want custom-made detail and trim."

Bob thumbed through a notebook and perused a stack of papers. "I'd need a down payment of twenty percent. That's $130.00."

"I'll be back this afternoon after stopping by the bank. But I'll pay you in full. On one condition."

Bob asked what with raised brows.

"You make it on my premises, after helping me fix up cabinets for the springhouse."

"Bah." He waved us away. "You've got Ross and Eddie to help."

"I'd like some of your chairs."

"Look." Bob crossed his arms. "I already got a mighty heap of orders I'm tempted to cancel. You know extra money ain't no incentive. Besides, I don't make house calls."

My father grinned and gestured as if swatting flies. "Ah, yes, then forget the orders. Forget the chairs, the wardrobe, and fixing cabinets. How about it, though? An even exchange of $650.00 for moving your shop over to my place.

Sound fair?"

My dad was going crazy and I was embarrassed for him. Nick cringed, too, and slinked across the room.

"Why would you pay me for moving to your place? What's in it for you?"

"What's in it for me?" My father leaned over the counter. "Nothing at all, excusing the satisfaction of knowing that the Bob Hutchins family will not be chased away from this town but will live and work among us. That $650.00 will cover a heap of costs, the fixing up of the place, moving of machinery, and groceries for a week. In exchange, you could help me with woodworking repairs and putting up a new fence by the barn."

"Is this to ease your conscience?"

"I only need to know that I did all in my power to keep Bob Hutchins from leaving this town."

We left behind a flabbergasted man.

"Now that's a man sold on a great idea if I ever did see one," Dad said.

If the whole town thought my father was a washout, what difference did it make if he pulled a little buffoonery now and then?

Nick's mouth hung open. "Six hundred and fifty dollars! Wow! I didn't know we were so rich!"

"We're not," Dad said. "I'm borrowing this money from your college education fund. By the time you're in college I'll have it paid back."

CHAPTER 32

As days neared August, the heat was unrelenting. We woke every morning, drenched ourselves in cold water and by midmorning were drenched again in sweat.

Paprika and I romped through the woods, alternating between hide-and-seek and tag as the dog darted ahead and sniffed out berry bushes. The only clue of her whereabouts was the crackling sound of her body brushing against branches. Before I could grab her, she'd scamper off to find a new spot.

While I searched for her in the tenth round, a yelp sounded as though cut short by a yank on her collar. Out of the bushes stomped Stan Randall and Darrell Culver, Stan with a pellet gun and Paprika in hand.

Everything happened so quickly. I shouted at Stan to put her down. He did, with Darrell holding her collar. Stan shot at her within a three-foot range. Paprika jerked and yelped again, dissolving into whimpers. Stumbling, I couldn't get to her fast enough. Stan laughed and mentioned finally getting his revenge for everything--my hitting him and calling strikes, but also my dad's role in losing the sandlot and having no baseball in our town.

Fuming, I could barely see. Tears squeezed out, blinding me more. I tripped and fell flat on the ground.

Stan Randall whooped and sniggered. He cocked his pellet gun one more time, aimed, and shot. Paprika squealed. I screamed. Stan ran laughing into the woods with Darrell.

When I reached Paprika on my hands and knees, she blurred in my vision, a tangled mass of golden-rust fur streaked with blood. She lay in pain, whimpering. I picked her up and trudged to the field behind our house, wailing like a baby.

I called for my father. He sprinted over, took the dog into his strong farmer hands, and yelled to Ross at the machinery. Eddie bounded to my side and lifted me up like a rag doll while I bawled on his shoulder.

"Hush, the dog will be fine," he said.

In the house, Mom hugged me while Eddie spoke soothing words. Dad tended to Paprika's wounds. Ross called the vet.

Panting, I explained. Everything spilled out, every word Stan said. Ross ruffled my hair, fire in his eyes. Mom played nursemaid after the vet left. Dad gave me a big bear hug before heading back to the fields, but I felt no better. This cruelty was inexcusable. I would never forgive Stan.

That night, Dad called Mr. Randall and demanded amends. His dad sent money to pay the vet. But Stan offered no apology, did no penance.

Psalm One says the wicked are like chaff that the wind blows away. In the barnyard later, as I shook a handful of wheat kernels, chaff flew with the breeze while wheat settled in my hand. Envisioning Stan as those evil little chaff, I contemplated the unrighteous—Stan, that is. God's vengeance wasn't working fast enough to bring the wicked to ruin. He needed my help. God may have all the time in the world, but I didn't.

I found the spot where Nick and I buried the drunk chickens weeks prior. Wearing old garden gloves and holding my breath, I dug up the bag of chickens and stuffed them into another garbage bag, which I dropped into a big burlap bag and secured tightly. I had to dart away every thirty seconds to take in fresh air. I disposed of the gloves in the trash, then found an old box in the barn. I deposited the bag of chickens and sprayed the whole thing with my dove-lidded perfume bottle. I wrapped the box in birthday wrapping paper, and signed a card: To Stan from your Secret Admirer. That night in the dark, I delivered it to his doorstep and ran away.

****

One evening the uncles, aunts, and cousins came over. The uncles played cards. Electric fans only made the smell of sweat travel faster. Brian, Tommy, Melanie, Nick, and I stole to the creek to swim. By the time we reached home in the veil of dusk, we were slick with sweat again.

A sliver of August moon poked through wispy clouds. The poor guy stuck up there was surely thrown off balance due to Mr. Armstrong's supposed giant leap for mankind.

What did folks say happened on hot nights under a crescent of an old moon?

Mom, Aunt Elaine, Aunt Abby, and Aunt Sheila sat limply across the front room chairs and sofa, fanning themselves and drinking lemonade. At the table, men's backs glistened. The rule about shirts at the table had been abandoned along with the shirts.

The uncles laughed. No doubt each outburst pushed the mercury up another degree. I wanted to be naughty and tell them about Ross's and Dad's cheating secrets, but it would prove too strenuous in this heat. Instead, I slid down the kitchen doorway and sat astride the step, eyes on the moon, ears to the house.

The aunts left with the cousins, but the game went on forever. I squinted at the dazzling moon slipping in and out of clouds. Talk and laughter floated heavily, as though from down the road.

Soon the game broke up. Only Ross remained. Eventually, the buzz of conversation turned from dull static to clear words.

"I can't think of any good reason to turn him down," Ross said.

"I can't think of any good reason to accept," Dad replied.

"Well, I have a few." Ross spoke as a schoolteacher

talking down to a less-than-stellar pupil. "For one thing, it's good income. Money for the kids' college. Another thing, your brainpower could help a powerful lot of folks with your design knowhow. Plus, you and I could be in business together again at the sawmill. It's a fittin' change from backbreaking farming, and we could hire a few hands if needed. Another thing, it would get you back into the social swing instead of sitting out here on the farm."

"Ross, I gave Phil my answer. It's still no."

"Why? Just give me one good reason."

"Now my own brother demands a defense."

"That's right. I'm the only one who hasn't questioned you pointblank or judged you, even as I've been watching your family sink into despair before my very eyes. You can't tell me you've a higher reason to justify that. You couldn't have got yourself a better wife and kids if you'd ordered them straight from the Sears Catalog. But look at them! Townsfolk look on them with distant pity—"

"That's enough, Ross."

"I never infringed on your privacy before, never. But you ain't seeing what I'm seeing—"

"I'm very aware. And taking this job is no guarantee of folks changing their view of us. Besides, there are things you're not knowing to. And I'm already living the way I need to be."

"You mean like a hypocrite? I've never been a Bible-toting, Scripture-quoting, churchgoing man like yourself, but I know a thing or two about love from the Good Book, and I know the God who wrote it, and I know some things love *ain't*. And a good reputation is to be sought above riches—"

"Make your point, please," Dad said.

"Do you suffer from some sort of martyr complex? Are you earning jewels in your heavenly crown by carrying on like this? You could better your family's situation by just taking this job of Phil's. It's only short term. You'll give Phil the help he needs, which in turn ensures the park's success, which in turn helps everybody. Not to mention feeling like part of the town again and earning some extra money. Why reject that?"

"There's more than meets the eye here."

"Is pride gonna stand between you and your family?"

"The issue is not pride."

Ross jumped from his seat, knocking a glass to floor. It shattered. "Not pride?" he yelled. "Then what in the Sam Hill is it?"

I cringed. A bead of sweat dropped furiously from my chin onto my shirt. I'd never heard Ross yell at Dad.

Shadows flashed in the yellow light pouring through the screen door. Ross waved his arms as if an invisible heat monster stirred him. Perhaps the old moon's evil magic.

"Did Phil Kepler put you up to this?" Dad asked.

Ross stopped short. "Yes sir, he did. He asked me to talk you into accepting the job. Yeah, he's desperate, but he knows your skills. Yeah, he's been a fool about the way he handled you. But that ain't the point."

"I have no problem with you working for Phil. But I trusted it would never come down to a matter of sides, who's right and who's wrong, a matter of pitting yourself with Phil against me."

"Against you? I only want good for you. Do you think I'm telling you this for my own health and well-being? I've nothing to gain or lose either way, financially or socially. Folks know we ain't always of the same mind. I'm not the one that left for fifteen years. But I don't see your family getting a fair shake. That's the main issue here."

"Apparently, you don't know the issue at all, so this conversation needs to end."

"No!" Ross stamped across the room. "I've laid off too long as it is. I can't abide silence any longer. I'm not leaving till I've said everything I've needed to say."

I hardly dared breathe, as if by moving one muscle the angry demon loose in the air would descend and consume.

"I think you're too proud and stubborn to work under

Phil Kepler even if it would do your family a mite of good. You created this park, it was your baby. Even though you gave it up years ago, now it's his baby and you don't like that, do you? Phil is beholden to you, right? You should be in charge, as the employer, not the employee? Am I right?"

"You don't understand the situation."

"Well, I'll tell you something I do understand. When I see a little girl—" his voice cracked— "a little girl carrying home her little dog all full of blood and pellets, and she's a-crying at the downright cruelty—"

"That incident was a result of a long-standing feud."

"It's more than that. Makes me so mad I could wrestle a pig. Your wife is pitied for being your wife. Your boy can't play baseball because of your name. Didn't you hear Tina tell you what that dog terrorizer said? He—"

"I'm not taking any more blame for that park being voted in. I did everything humanly possible to stop it."

"But you *made* it! And folks'll never get over your past and your secrets as long as you sit out here and ignore them all. What are you proving by holding out?" Ross's voice reached fever pitch. "Do you want a medal? What is it you want?"

I clung to my legs pressed against my chest. I didn't want to hear one more word.

"I want you to leave," Dad said. "Right now."

Ross clomped to the door. "This ain't over, Drew. You've always been so community-minded. You were afraid of mobility and progress overshadowing community. Did it ever occur to you that you ain't got a community of your own no more?"

They left and Mom ran upstairs crying. Shaking, I stumbled outside to the hammock, blinded by tears. My chest tightened. I didn't want to ever go back inside.

CHAPTER 33

"What can you tell me about this?" Phil Kepler asked my dad in the front room.

In the kitchen next to Mom, I wiped a dish and cringed at Phil's sharp tone.

"That's a sketch I did for the kids one night," Dad replied with northern inflections.

"This piece of paper has cost me over a thousand dollars."

Dad chuckled. "That's what happens when you bring in competition. Buy your paper at the five and dime. It's cheaper."

"Don't joke with me, Drew. When I offer you a paying job to design this very thing, you flatly refuse me. Then, after I hire another architect, you conjure this."

"What's the problem?"

"I've gone through six architects in the past six months, because none could match the quality of this, which unbeknownst to me, Todd had in his possession for two weeks."

"What's your point?"

"Do I need to spell it out? If you were going to do this, why didn't you show me right away and save me time and money?"

"I had no intention of inconveniencing you. I was spending time with my kids."

"How much do you want for this sketch?"

"Nothing. You can keep it."

Phil's voice lowered. "Will you draw it up for me in detail?"

Dad laughed. "Is this your roundabout way of offering me a job? I answered that already."

"Will you reconsider?"

"Phil, why me? There are thousands of architects in the world. You've got an entire team of them."

"Because Joseph Flannery wants you, Drew. He wants you to head up my team of architects to assure consistency in design and style."

"He's given you an ultimatum?"

"He only wants *you*," Phil said through gritted teeth. No mention of his job possibly being in jeopardy.

"I see."

By refusing to work for him, did my dad want Phil to fail?

"Drew." Phil's tone dropped to reasonable. "We can work out pay and hours according to your liking. It would only be a few months, until the entire park is designed. No lifelong commitment. I need your help."

"Or else what?"

"Let's leave the *or elses* out of this. This is a fantastic opportunity."

"For you only."

Phil slammed his fist on the table with renewed vigor. "Unbelievable! There's only one reason you'd say no. Pure spite. Spite for me speaking out against you at the council meeting. Spite for bringing this park here in the first place, for taking on a project you once threw away. You're going to string me out again, aren't you? Once wasn't enough. You'll leave me high and dry like the first time. You're always proving you're the better one, first with your creation of the park, now with your disdain of it. It's not enough that you destroyed the plans years ago, when we both could've benefited—"

"Stop it!" my father yelled. "I was following my conscience, not trying to leave you high and dry. You take everything personally."

"Not without good reason."

Part of me wanted to run away. The other part wanted to whack Phil Kepler with my baseball bat. Unseen, I poked my head around the corner.

Phil's eyes hardened into a volcanic glare. "Nobody's ready for the whole truth, are they? But you have much more to lose this time than I do. I was merely the victim." He stepped closer to Dad. "Don't worry. Your secret's safe with me." He put the sketch in Dad's hand. "As long as you finish this drawing and five others I've got waiting for you. I'll get them to you first thing tomorrow morning."

Phil slithered away. Dad stood statue-like, ashen, paper in hand.

Mom whisked from the kitchen and went to him. "What's this all about?"

Dad sunk into the couch. "I can't talk about it."

Mom bit her lip, as if on the verge of breaking her vow to him.

****

The next Sunday, I thought of a strategy to use on my father. After church I said, "If I was old enough to take the Lord's supper, I wouldn't do it.

"Why not?" he asked.

"So as not to bring judgment upon myself," I replied the way the minister said it.

He didn't press me. I thought it would make him say why he hadn't been taking communion, but it didn't work.

That evening, after church and *Walt Disney's Wonderful World of Color*, he looked up from his reading. "Tina, did you say that about communion because I'm not taking it?"

I couldn't bring myself to put him on trial.

"I trust it's for sincere reasons and that you'll clear up the matter immediately."

Then why don't you? I surprised myself by bursting into tears. Unwittingly, I ran into his outstretched arms, into a tight embrace. He rubbed my back, nuzzling my hair with his chin. "Hush, baby, hush."

Beside him on the couch, Mom dropped her sewing. "Is this about Stan Randall? Granny sakes alive, Tina, you've got to learn how to forgive even your enemies. Your daddy and I had to forgive folks left and right, but it's the only way to go on."

I blurted through shaking sobs, "It ain't just Stan . . . I never . . . apologized to Todd."

"For what, honey?" Mom said.

"For hitting him," I mumbled into Dad's shirt. Dad's hands firmly pulled my head off his chest to meet my eyes. His voice wavered. "You hit Todd?"

I explained the whole thing, that Todd hadn't struck Nick out to be mean, but was feeling the same pressure as Nick to end the game. From the table, Nick verified each word with his nods.

Dad squeezed the breath out of me in a bear hug, not his usual method of preventing further wrongdoing. A tear trickled down my cheek. It wasn't my own. I'd never seen him cry before. "This is the fruit of my own sin," Dad murmured.

What sin? I couldn't tell if it was me trembling or him.

I pulled back, suddenly repulsed. Whatever he'd done, he'd dragged us down with him, an open target for folks' judgments. All for a sin he wouldn't reveal so that we could begin to understand and even forgive him. He seemed powerless, as defenseless as a mouse in the claws of the mighty eagle. My father used to be that eagle.

He held my wrists. "Don't leave in anger. Tina, look at me."

I stood still for Mom's sake.

"Tina, you used to be a rabble-rouser, back in first grade. Fist fights, lying, temper tantrums. One day you finally learned. But before then, you still needed me to love you. A lavish of it."

I bit my lip and looked at him askance, awaiting the punch line.

"Fact is, Tina. I need you and Nick and your mom the most right now."

He turned my wrists loose and I walked away, but I only got as far as the doorway.

"Wait," Dad said. "There's something I must tell you all, before you hear it from any other source."

I froze. Were we going to hear why he couldn't take communion? Would he reveal what Phil threatened him with?

"I need to talk to your mother first," he said. "Go up to your rooms."

Numb, I trudged upstairs. In my bedroom, Mom's weeping came through the floorboards.

When I returned downstairs a half hour later, Mom's eyes were red, cheeks tear-stained.

Dad rubbed his temples. "You need to know . . . about Sonia."

Gosh, what on earth did she have to do with anything?

Dad told us to sit. He leaned forward, head in hands, facing the floor. "When I worked with Phil on this park project in New York, we worked sixteen-hour days for months on end. This park was our life."

His fingers locked and unlocked. "I stayed at work more and more, got home later and later. Sonia gave up waiting for me at night. She was patient at first, but she needed me. I kept breaking my promises to her. Finally she gave up waiting for me altogether. One night I came home and she'd moved out. Packed her things and left. Left behind a note saying she wanted a divorce."

He glanced at us. I was spellbound. "I contacted her and promised to change. But I was married to my work, she said, always would be. She agreed to meet me for dinner weekly in a restaurant to talk things over. But all three times I was late, overtired, with only work on my mind. I wanted her back but wasn't ready to give her time and attention, until our project was done.

"She wanted to have children, raise a family, with a daddy who'd be home more often. I didn't want kids yet. I wanted my work and my pats on the back for all my efforts. Praise from my boss. She refused to meet anymore."

Dad wiped his sweaty brow, his demeanor reminiscent of the town council meeting that overturned our lives.

"She refused to see me until . . . one night three months after she'd moved out. I hadn't seen her for six weeks. She called and told me to come over, she needed my help right away. She sounded desperate."

Mom wiped her eyes. "Do you have to tell them?" Her voice twisted with anguish.

"They must hear it from me, Jennie. It's only a matter of time before Phil's ready to spill it all out." Dad's breathing slowed, each word carefully measured. "I drove to her place, but it was an hour away with the traffic. By the time I reached her it was too late. She was . . . dead. From an alcohol and aspirin overdose. She'd left a note. The phone call was her last attempt to reach out, to take back what she'd done . . ."

A tear rolled down Dad's cheek. Mom was pale. Nick stiffened. I numbed.

Dad's hands shook. "I had driven her to it. I never paid any mind to how much she was hurting inside, feeling neglected . . ."

"You can't blame yourself for her suicide," Mom said. "She made that choice."

"Don't sugar-coat it, Jennie," Dad snapped. "I failed miserably as a husband . . . and I never got the chance to know myself as the father of the baby she was carrying when she died. She was five months pregnant, her note said, and the autopsy, too. She never even told me."

He sat as if stuck. "Sonia's note said she was afraid I'd be angry about the pregnancy. She had no other family to turn to, only me."

The only sounds were Mom's sniffles and my heartbeat.

Dad sighed. "Phil was my best friend, the one who helped me get through it all. He'd always been there for me, so he didn't take it very well when I later stepped out of the project and left him empty-handed. He took it as a personal affront that I destroyed all our work. Lit a match to everything having to do with that park. It was my work mostly. But it was his springboard to success. He was fired after I left. But, unfortunately for me, I neglected to destroy one last set of blueprints and diagrams. He found those later with other models, took them to a different boss, and eventually brought them down here as originally planned."

He covered his face. "This is why I hate this park. I threw the best part of my life away to work on it. I threw away my wife and baby for this so-called achievement, for men's praise and approval. It's like keeping the chest and throwing out the treasure. I gave up everything I've come to hold dear. And now . . . I fear I'm losing it all again."

Mom's eyes reflected his pain, and her own, as he made her privy to knowledge he should've shared years ago. She went upstairs. We all had things to digest.

Back in my room, I lay on my bed. How could Dad talk so much about walking in the light when so much of his own life lurked on the dark side of the moon? Secrets that now revealed Mom, Nick, and me as the replacement family. We weren't enough in and of ourselves. We were my father's second chance at life.

Things done long ago in secret before I was born reached out to touch and mold my life now. I felt lost in an undercurrent of other people's whims, dreams, and mistakes.

All those times Dad tried to prod me to forgiveness of Stan, my mortal enemy, I never dreamed that my father himself craved forgiveness--from Mom, from the town. From Sonia and the unborn child.

For that moment, my fear of Stan's vindictiveness shrunk to flea-size. In a vacuum of many years' silence and in my mother's tear-filled eyes, I saw my father's hands full of things he'd stolen from us. It felt like my very life, my soul.

CHAPTER 34

I wanted Dad to succumb to Phil Kepler's threat of blackmail. Otherwise, Phil would divulge to the whole town about Sonia and the baby, another strike against us.

One afternoon, after an hour at Old Lady Balch's with Todd and Nick, Todd asked why we didn't go fishing with Dad anymore.

"Too busy," Nick said.

"Kinda boring," I added.

"Really?" Todd said. "He and I had a great time last week."

"Huh?" Nick and I chorused.

"Your dad and me went fishing together. He caught a bass but let me keep it. My dad and I cooked it up and ate the whole thing."

"You went fishing with our dad?" My jaw dropped.

Nick's face echoed my words, not without some jealousy either.

"Yeah, he said you-uns didn't want to fish lately, so he and I had a go of it."

We parted ways. Nick and I had to pick blueberries for Mom in the thicket beyond our field. After twenty minutes, I wiped my brow and glanced behind us at jeering voices. A half dozen kids stalked over: Darrell Culver, Ray Kamp, Tom Dempsey, Bart Chandler, Leonard Wheeler, and their inevitable leader, Stan Randall.

"What do you want?" Nick asked.

"We was just out carousing." Stan shook his head to peer through his bangs. "Reckoned we'd find you-uns here."

Nick set down his pail of berries and put hands on hips as if facing one person instead of six. He looked like he'd let nobody get by with another insult against our father.

"It's about time to thank Tina here for the lovely gift," Stan said.

"What gift?" Nick asked. I'd never told him about my retaliation.

"I'm talking about those tasty chicken legs Tina brought over the other night."

"Chicken legs?" Nick wrinkled his nose.

"Yeah, chicken legs. A dozen or so. Already good and dead so as all we had to do was stuff 'em in the pot and boil 'em. Mighty thoughtful of you, Miz Tina. Our family loves chicken." Stan licked his lips. "Um-hum. We just love chicken." Stan stepped closer, three feet from Nick. "The boys here and me, we all like chicken, and you know what kinda chicken we like best?"

"No." Nick stiffened.

"You!" Stan shrieked as his foot flew up and kicked the pail. It went flying and every berry spilled out, lost in tall grass.

Nick stood as if planted. "What do you want?"

"I'm collecting for everything your sister did to me." Stan named various verbal fights, two fisticuffs, the umpiring fiasco, and Paprika biting him.

"Tina ain't done nothing that wasn't in self-defense," Nick said, surely quaking. "Get out of here and leave us alone."

"Delivering dead chickens to our doorstep was self-defense?" Stan moved in, chin to forehead with Nick. Though sweating fiercely, Nick didn't flinch. "Come on, Hamilton, I'll let you have the first punch, *chicken*."

I stepped forward. "This is between you and me, not Nick."

"Well, the best way to make you pay for it is to take on your brother here. It's the gentlemanly thing to do."

They stepped in closer, encircling Nick and me. My

worst fear at that moment was that I'd survive whatever happened.

"We ain't never seen Nick here fight," Darrell said. "We're gonna initiate him into the world of men."

Without warning, Stan's hand met Nick's chin. Nick was sprawled on the ground. He jumped up, eyes flaring. Nick, the conscientious objector, lit into the kid. "Get back, Tina."

Stan and Nick rolled in the dirt while the other five cheered.

I couldn't watch Nick die, nor let his attempt at nobility rest on my conscience. I sneaked behind the boys with a huge branch and whopped three on the head at once.

Darrell, Ray, and Bart fell over. The other two jerked to their senses. Forgetting their code of gentlemanly conduct, Leonard and Dempsey prepared to pounce on me. I'd be a goner if they pulled the branch from my hand. They grasped and yanked. I held on. But the three prostrate boys scrambled up and grabbed my torso and legs. We crashed onto the ground and wrestled. Our yells filled the meadow.

Hatred whipped across my cheeks and pummeled my back. Their war whoops dazed me so much, I thought I was dreaming when the gunshot sliced the air. I was surely going to die.

Apparently, the boys on top of me thought they'd been shot, too. They all fell in a heap. Another shot exploded. Our screams died with its echo. Being face down in the dirt offered a peripheral view of boots in the grass.

"Well, well, well, you all figured to have yourselves a little tussle, did you? I bet y'all didn't figure on this!"

I lay dazed wishing the blurs before me were merely leftovers from last night's nightmare. The speaker's voice gradually gave recognition. I lifted my face from the dirt and grass, sunlight blinding, head pounding, blood dripping. Two booted feet walked as the butt of a gun nudged each boy in turn. Ole Joe.

"Now there's a fine white skin. I wouldn't mind having

it around. That there—" the gun pointed to Dempsey— "that's a mighty fine blue shirt. Looks a mite big for you, boy."

"Y-you can h-have it, sir," Dempsey said.

"Why would I want your shirt all dirtied up? Now, why y'all be wanting to pick a fight with these two, and a girl, no less. Fighting women's a shame. A low-down dirty rotten shame to anyone that ever wants to be a man." He leaned over until eye to eye with Darrell. "Y'all can only fight women with words. Even then it ain't a fair fight, because of what women do with those words. They twist 'em till you hardly recognize what you said."

Stan tried to stand. Joe told him to stay put, then let loose a flow of eloquent swear words that made one envy the skill. "I can be sassy as a jaybird, yes sir, surly as a bear. And I ain't for certain what I'll do with y'all if you ever pick a fight with these two again."

I hoped he wouldn't have them deliver vegetables to his cabin.

Joe leaned over Stan. "Don't ever be laying a hand on them again." More victim's advocate than our friend, he reloaded his double-barreled shotgun. The boys shook so much they looked like they were ardently nodding in agreement.

"Now scat!" Joe fired the gun once more.

I never saw six boys run so fast in all my life.

Joe turned to us. "If you-uns have any more trouble with them ruffians, just give me a holler." He disappeared into the thicket.

****

A week later, the boys blabbed all about it. They twisted the episode from their war games into a romper room frolic in which Joe roughed them all up for his own morbid delight. So when Joe appeared in town to buy coffee beans, he was arrested on the spot for loitering and disturbing the peace and was shipped to the jail in Marshall, the county seat. Thus, Nick and I weren't spared Stan's antics. Stan had the last laugh.

Surely all the previous gossip about Joe was make-believe, things that folks wished had happened so they'd have something to jaw about.

Nick and I confessed our friendship with Joe to Mom and Dad, minus the details of food deliveries, middle-of-the-night capers, and woodcarving. We asked Dad to help him.

My father went to Marshall to plead Joe's case but the officials wouldn't accept bail money. Ole Joe had to serve thirty days for "stirring up the peace, threatening innocent children, and loitering in town."

CHAPTER 35

The hot, magnetic August air seeped into my bedroom and stirred my brain. I felt like bubbles in a corked soda bottle, waiting for someone to open the lid so I could fizz out. I lay wide awake in bed, hands behind my head, awaiting Nick's signal. The house was finally quiet. Dad had stayed up later than usual, having run an errand. By now he'd consumed his corn flakes and turned off his reading lamp. Streaks of moonlight crisscrossed the dark valleys of my rumpled sheet, encaging me. The wind sucked deep, long breaths. The house seemed to constrict and expand with each one, gaining momentum for a brewing storm.

Nick's tap-tap on the wall jolted me out of bed. I stepped into the wrong overall leg twice before getting it right, ruffled the bed and packed clothes under the sheets next to Paprika, then slinked to his room.

Outside the window, subtle moonlight washed the night. Cattle were lowing at the Duncan farm. What frightened them? I withdrew from the window. "Nick, those cows . . ."

He nudged me. "Hurry up."

In the spirit of adventure, we'd considered climbing down a sheet ladder anchored to his bed, but figured we'd get caught. Instead, we tiptoed downstairs and out the back door.

The cows unsettled me. But I was yearning to do something defiant, something that showed Dad how angry I was at him, how unfair he'd been to Mom, to us.

Tonight, Nick was the risk-taker, no red pepper in his pocket. I was eager to find out why.

"Come on!" He grabbed my hand. We scooted off as a

warm gust of wind tried to knock us over. The full moon played hide-and-seek behind wispy ghosts of rainless clouds, and I dared not face its hypnotic glow.

"Does Todd know we're coming?" I asked.

"Yep."

Chances are Todd would be as restless as we were. It was our last week of summer vacation.

The wind blustered like a whirlwind with unpredictable starts and stops. When we stopped to catch our breath, I toppled onto the grass. We laughed hysterically, barely hearing our voices above the rumbling. Nick chased me, mimicking wildcat screams. Breathless, we halted again, echoing the wind's deep breathing. We swirled like fish at the mercy of an enormous tidal wave undercurrent.

In the neighbor's tobacco fields, wind gulped and left an empty silence. Laughing, Nick threw himself into cartwheel, then a somersault.

"Hush," I said. "What's that?"

He peered at me between tobacco plants and yanked off a leaf. "Nothing but a rooster crowing, Miss Fraidy Cat."

"Roosters don't crow at night unless it's bad luck. We should go back."

Nick laughed. "First the cows, now the roosters. A body might think you're superstitious." He trotted away. "Go back if you want, but you'll miss the surprise at Todd's."

We dashed across the meadow with its dips, as if running through the quaking stomach of a giant, the wind growling in hunger. Heat lightning flashed.

The Keplers' porch and living room lights were on, so Phil was probably up. We went to Todd's window. Nick rubbed the screen, tapped it, then knocked on the wood pane.

The window opened to reveal Todd who whispered his greetings.

"Get out here with that chaw," Nick said. "And fix your bed."

"What chaw?" I asked.

"Somebody gave my dad a can of chewing tobacco," Todd said. "You know—snuff. Not tobacco leaves, but the real manufactured stuff. Stuff the major leaguers chew."

"Is it any good?"

"Plan to find out tonight," Nick said. "You can, too, if you're not chicken."

"Go to the back door," Todd said. "Dad's due any minute. I don't want him driving up while I'm hanging out the window."

Todd joined us. We ran toward the woods as if playing Crack the Whip with the wind. Under an oak tree, we sprawled over the ground in delirious laughter. Todd opened the can of chaw and gave us each a piece, demonstrating proper technique. "Don't overdo it. And don't swallow anything."

The mysterious, howling wind proved to be the perfect accompaniment to such a deed.

Nick tried to look professional through his grimaces, but I didn't bother to fake liking it. Chewing chaw was worse than eating a mouthful of dirt.

Todd showed us how to spit. Nick tried, then me. "You got it, Tina!" Todd said.

Not exactly an accomplishment that warmed my heart.

A half hour later, I felt sick. I think Nick was, too, though he'd never admit it.

We plodded back. Another rooster crowed. Or had I imagined it?

We let ourselves in the back door since Phil hadn't come home yet. "Now what?" Nick said as if nothing could match our previous deed. He plopped on a chair, looking green. From shadows or tobacco I couldn't tell. I sank into the next chair.

"Can't you handle that chaw?" Todd said. "I thought you liked the manufactured stuff, Nick."

"I said that was the only stuff I'd chew."

Todd laughed. The phone rang. Todd answered it then reported that his dad would return in twenty minutes. His meeting ran late. "I've got to put this chaw back in his study."

"Does he chew, too?" I asked.

"Nah, he thinks it's disgusting."

We dragged ourselves up and followed Todd into the hall.

"Ah, the mystery room." Nick purposely quaked his voice. "We finally get to see it."

The room held a collection of papers, blueprints, books, and tools covering walls, tables, shelves, and desks. Nick and I surveyed the room, honing in on scale models of a restaurant courtyard, a theater, and a town square, as intricate as Jim Drummond's model railroad.

Nick's eyes widened. "Wow!"

Todd replaced the can of tobacco on the closet shelf.

"Did your dad make these?" Nick asked.

"Some, but so did your dad." He pointed to an artist's rendering of the theme park, the same one displayed at the town council meeting. The details mesmerized us. Todd removed a piece of tape from the bottom right corner, revealing the artist's name: Andrew Roderick Hamilton, a steady hand in all capital letters, with unique Ms and Ns.

For a moment I couldn't understand why folks resented my dad for creating something so beautiful.

Todd showed us more by Dad, an area from Turn-of-the-Century, and four scale models of other sections--all fascinating craftsmanship. Yet I couldn't help think of Sonia, dead Sonia and the baby. The price Dad paid for doing this work.

A car motored into the driveway. We ran out of the office and slammed the door. Nick and I dove under Todd's bed into a layer of dust. Todd went to greet his dad. Phil said he'd be in to say good night shortly. Todd returned and sat on his bed, Nick and I sandwiched between bedsprings and floor.

The house quieted. Perhaps when Mr. Kepler went to bed we'd make our exit.

Somebody knocked. We jumped. But it was too

muffled to be Todd's bedroom door. Another knock sounded--
at the front door. Company this time of night? Maybe it would
occupy Phil so Nick and I could escape through Todd's
window.

The front door opened. "Good evening, Phil." My
father's voice. Now we were in trouble. I thought he was in bed
when we left. Was he searching for us?

Papers rustled. "Here are your plans," Dad said.

Had my father succumbed to Phil's threat of
blackmail?

Phil shuffled through papers. "I can't believe this. You
haven't done a thing."

"No. And I don't plan to."

"So you're ready for the whole town to know about
your bastard child?" Phil snapped.

"Are you ready to ruin it forever between you and
Todd?"

"What are you talking about?"

"Can't you see?" Dad said. "You're exactly where I
was in New York thirteen years ago. This is why I lost Sonia,
why you lost Bonnie—"

"This has nothing whatsoever to do with that
situation."

"No?" Dad's voice rose. "You're going to throw away
Todd for the sake of this job, for the sake of one Joseph
Flannery who may just as easily write you off next week for
not remembering his favorite brand of beer."

Phil's voice sharpened. "My success with this park
does benefit Todd. You just want to see me fail again."

"No. That's all *you* see, whether you lose or win at this
job, just because you won't stand up to your boss and take the
consequences like a man."

"I've invested ten years in this job. I've no intention of
throwing that away."

"Ten years? That's as many as you've invested in
Todd—or is it?"

"What are you driving at?"

"I've gone fishing with that boy three times the past three weeks. That's more time than you've given him in a month. You can't measure success and failure only in business terms. We go back eighteen years together, Phil. I have your best interest at heart."

"Ha! If that were so, Todd wouldn't be here today. You have a vested interest in looking good, in having a clean slate."

"Phil, you don't really want to expose this. What will you gain? What will Todd gain? Some secrets are worth hiding. And I won't make it easier for you to keep your job and forfeit . . . your son."

Dad left but the words rung in my head. *Bastard child. Bastard child.* I didn't know what that meant, but it sounded terrible, surely something that would bring us more sighs, clicking tongues, and stares of pity.

Bastard child. How cruel the words sounded. I thought Dad had unloaded everything to us the other night. But there was more.

Bastard child. Maybe Nick knew what it meant. What had my father done?

All my thoughts and feelings lumped together in my stomach with the chaw. Nick said we'd better go. Where, I asked. Anywhere, he said.

Mr. Kepler came in to say good night. He turned off the light and left.

"Get out now!" Todd whispered. "I don't wanna get in trouble."

I scooted out from under the bed. "What's a bastard child?"

"I'll tell you later." Nick emerged, too, with an awkward glance at Todd. "Let's go."

"Going home?" Todd asked.

"No." Nick brushed dust off his arm. "I'm too mad."

"Say, you could go up to that old Negro's cabin, now

that he's in jail." Todd knew nothing of our friendship with him.

We could go home and get whipped--if discovered--or go home in the morning and get double whipped.

Nick wanted to hide out a day or two, and if I was smart I'd stay and not go tattle. He bore a hint of gleeful rebellion, as in the voice of a soldier who proudly disobeys orders.

I'd rather be grounded for a week with Nick than for an hour without him. I didn't even care about Mom worrying. After all, she never stood up to Dad and asked for the truth.

Silently we agreed on the double whipping. We couldn't go home yet.

No one would find us up the mountain. Ole Joe would understand.

CHAPTER 36

Dazed, I trampled up the mountain behind Nick, with no inclination to fear the wild dark. We arrived after the circle of a moon appeared again above the trees on a climb of its own. We let ourselves into Joe's cabin and latched the door. Nick offered me the dusty cot and took the floor with a flour sack pillow. We were wide awake.

Bastard child rolled around my head. "Nick, did you hear Mr. Kepler say . . ."

"Bastard child," Nick said without feeling. "It means Dad had a baby with somebody he wasn't married to. That's bad, Tina."

"When? Who?"

"How would I know?"

"You think Mom knows?"

"I doubt it."

"So . . . somewhere out there is a brother or a sister we don't even know?"

Nick fiddled with the lantern. "Yep."

An image of Lucy MacNeill popped into my head, Lucy and Robert, that little black baby, the shame and consequences of things that happen only in other people's families.

"Every time we learn something and get used to it, along comes something else. If he would've told everyone right from the get-go, none of this—" Nick made a broad sweep of his hand that encompassed two summers and a town-- "would have happened."

I shivered. Nick adjusted the lantern flame as shadows lumbered around the room. He slipped into an old plaid flannel shirt hanging on a hook. We played gin rummy with a tattered deck of cards. Then I scrounged in the cupboard for coffee while Nick played solitaire.

Containers wedged between vertical supports. Rusty, dusty tin cans stored odds and ends in cubbyholes. Three wooden crates were stacked in the corner. My coffee search became an excuse to rummage through crates and jars. Where was the box of Joe's carved pictures?

On the prowl, I moved the top crate to a stack of old newspapers. Tins cradled screws, bolts, nuts, and nails beside a jar of nuts, gathered as if Joe had been a squirrel storing for winter.

How could Nick tell red cards from black anymore? I adjusted the wick and unwrapped folded newspaper surrounding a bulky object. Inside was an eight-by-ten piece of wood, inlaid with intricate pieces, snugly fit together like a jigsaw puzzle—a picture of a barn and farmland with two cows, each section a different wood grain. My hand skimmed the smooth surface.

Nick slid his fingers over it. "Wow . . ." He touched the bottom right corner. "G. Fuller . . . That's Old Man Fuller, Tina," he whispered, as if acknowledging a sacred moment.

"I wonder where Joe got this."

Another crate revealed letters--chicken scratches and pot hooks of barely legible writing.

"Listen, Nick! 'March 1956, Dear Andrew, I can't use my machines as often now. Sometimes I fear I'll be gone before you get back. I know you're doing something important or you'd be here. I want you to have my tools and teach yourself to use them if I'm not here. Or find Joe Clemons, he can teach you things. I hope to see you soon. G. Fuller.'"

Nick studied the letter. "How'd Joe get this?"

As I read aloud a similar letter, Nick retrieved the box of tools that Joe'd been teaching us to use. He sat next to me, cross-legged, and withdrew a mallet and chisel. I picked up a knife and an awl. He stroked the mallet. "These must be Old Man Fuller's tools."

As if we might desecrate them, we returned the tools and letters to their respective boxes. Nick pushed the crate against the wall and propped up the marquetry.

The lantern sputtered, nearly out of kerosene. Nick extinguished the light.

Moonlight guided me to the cot. Through the window, a cloud passed over the moon. I pulled the sheet up. "What are you gonna say to Dad when we get back?"

"Don't know."

"What do you reckon Mom and Dad are doing?"

"Sending out the sheriff for us."

I shuddered. "Will he find us?"

"Nobody's gonna look for us here. We're safe. Besides, they might not know we're gone yet."

The wind stirred through loose boards, mocking us. Shadows disappeared, melded into one. As Uncle Eddie would say, it was as black as the Duke of Hell's riding boots. We could have been sitting in the middle of a prairie or a black hole in the sky. The only thing attaching me to that cabin was the twisted sheet in my hand. "Wonder if the sheriff can find us here."

"Maybe they're stalking up the mountain right now. To find the intruders in Joe's house."

"Will they be mad?"

"They'll give us as kindling to the blue jays on Fridays to stoke the fires—"

"Nick, stop it!"

"But they'll have to catch us first. We can climb down the ravine faster than they can."

The wind howled like a collision of four monstrous beasts at a busy intersection. How did Ole Joe sleep with such racket rocking his mountain? My voice quavered. "Mom'll be worried sick come morning."

"I know."

"If we don't go back, it'll cause a big commotion. What if they put us in jail?"

"Then we say howdy to Ole Joe. Tell him his place was looked after real fine."

"I'm serious."

"We ain't gonna go to jail. Geez, Tina, you're really something."

"We gotta go back tomorrow, first thing."

"That's easy for you to say. You haven't lost as much as I have."

My blood boiled. "What's that supposed to mean?"

"I lost baseball, pitching. My favorite thing in the world. I lost friends. Dad could've prevented it. And . . . he seems so far away. Like he's a big secret himself and wants it that way."

"We've both lost Dad." Whatever dangers lurked around the wild mountaintops, they were worth the risk. Dad had to realize how badly he'd wounded us.

Nick picked up a worn, thin blanket, barely enough to keep a bedbug warm. "We should get some sleep." He handed me the blanket. "We've got long days ahead of us scrounging around up here."

"Ole Joe will be out of jail in three weeks."

"We'll find us another place by then." Nick spread the flour sack on the floor.

The blanket did nothing for the chill creeping over me. I curled up, exhausted but far from sleep. The past week's events reverberated through my brain. Every loss, every tear, every dismal revelation. A gray horizon with no dawn. A dawn tainted with bleak possibilities as I pondered the bastard child.

The wind swooped and rekindled my anger. "How can you say you lost more than I have?"

"Tina, hush."

"You can't say that." My voice rose. "You don't—"

"Tina, shut up!" he whispered.

"No, you can't tell me—"

He jumped up, flung himself on the bed, and covered my mouth. "I hear something outside. Hush."

We stiffened on the bed, a tangle of arms and legs, his hand still over my mouth. He got up and looked out the window. Wind wound around the cabin, hissing and whirling down the mountain. Between its gasps I strained to hear. Something scuffled in the stones just yards from the cabin.

I mouthed the word, "Bear?"

Nick pulled me off the cot and pushed me down next to him. "No. Human," he whispered as if it were the worst species we could encounter.

The scuffling grew closer. My heart raced. I buried my face in my knees, ostrich-like, wishing myself invisible.

Someone tested the latch. Tapping jarred me. Another tap followed. A circle of light appeared at the window by the door, but didn't reveal us.

The flashlight went off. More footsteps. Nick nudged me. No way could we fit under the short cot, the space lined with canned goods. We slinked to the opposite wall. The light shone where we'd crouched earlier.

Glass shattered on the floor boards. Nick grabbed my arm. We jumped up and rushed to the door. Nick fumbled with the latch.

Someone was climbing through the window behind us.

In desperation, I shoved Nick's arm and grabbed the latch. Somebody was inside, steps away.

The flashlight went on again, blinding me. The latch went up. I pulled open the door, wanting to be sucked out and whisked down the mountain. Instead, the wind lashed in. A man grabbed my arm. Fingers coiled around me. Nick and I were stuck in the same deadening grip. We kicked and flailed and screamed.

"Hold on, now." A voice burrowed through my shrieks. "We were all wondering what bear to tear apart in order to find you-uns."

It was Uncle Ross. I collapsed into him, panting.

Nick jerked away. "What're you doing, scaring us to death like that?"

"Now who's scaring who?" Uncle Ross said. "All Currie Hill and the entire Ross and Hamilton clans are a-wondering what bear ate you both. What in the Sam Hill are you doing in this godforsaken place? If I weren't so relieved to find you I'd take to paddling you over my knee." He let go of us and yelled down the mountainside, "I found 'em! Up at the cabin!"

"Why didn't you call out?" I asked. "We thought it was something dangerous."

"You wouldn't have answered me. Reckon I had to give you a big scare first."

"How'd you find us?" Nick asked.

"Look, young man, I'll be asking the questions here. You better be glad I found you before danger did. I'm so mad I can't spit straight. Let's go."

We resisted his nudge.

"Nobody's gonna wallop you. They'll be too happy to see you."

We didn't budge. If we went back now, the family would breath a collective sigh of relief, then everything would go on as if the last six hours never happened. As if there were no bastard child. "But how'd you find us here?" I asked.

"Your ma suggested it. Said you-uns were friends with Ole Joe Clemons. Now I ain't staking out with you, and I sure as heck ain't going back without you. Move along."

Still we remained.

Ross closed the door and sat on an upside-down bucket. "All right then." He softened his tone. "How come you left and didn't come home last night?"

More scuffling outside was swallowed by a hooting owl and rustling leaves.

"Our father's a bad person," Nick said.

Ross shook his head. "That ain't for you to say. Your

pa's one of the most godly men I know."

We blurted out everything. What we knew about Sonia. The dead baby. What we'd heard at Todd's. The bastard child. I examined Ross's face to see if it registered guilty or not guilty on Dad's account.

Ross seemed to digest our words. "You sure about all this? An illegitimate baby?" We nodded. "Just how long was this jury of two gonna stay here? Till you reached a verdict on your daddy?"

We shrugged.

He sighed. "I know nothing about this baby. Or Sonia and that baby either. But I know one thing for certain."

My stomach was queasy. What else would we find out about our father tonight?

"I don't know all your daddy did, but it was a long time ago, before he figured out a few things. And here's the truth. Only God can forgive and forget. Folks don't forget. They can't. God can remove our sins farther than east from west, but we can't even move 'em to the back doorstep. The only reason your daddy never 'fessed up is 'cause he figured no one would forgive him. Ain't that right, now?" My eyes blurred with tears. "Your daddy loves you, powerful much. And I'm guessing what he needs right now is forgiveness."

The latch went up, pricking my frayed nerves. My heart thumped. Whether man or beast, I didn't care. I already felt as though I'd been torn limb from limb.

The door opened. There stood my father.

CHAPTER 37

Uninvited tears stung my cheeks. I didn't want to see him.

Dad shined his flashlight on us. "Go on down, Ross. Tell Jennie the kids are fine and feisty as ever. We'll be back after a spell." Ross left and Dad took his place on the upturned bucket. Nick and I sat on the cot. I wadded Joe's blanket in my lap for solace. Next to me, Dad's flashlight cast eerie shadows across the room.

I wanted to run down the mountain away from Dad. But a grief like mine wouldn't disappear into the surrounding silence. It would only expand.

Dad's face was haggard, probably from a battle of years locked up inside, finally overtaking him. "I heard everything you just told Ross."

Now I wanted to bury my face in his shirt, feel the smooth cotton and smell the field hay.

"I never wanted to tell you-uns about this. But I see you need to know." He took a deep breath. "There are things you don't plan in your life, things that under scrutiny of daylight you'd run from, because the end is trouble. But when you're hurting, and you're not thinking past tomorrow in the middle of a cold, dark night, you forget to put a hedge around yourself. You're sucked into whatever helps you through the moment, the salve that only goes skin deep."

Maybe he was drawing out one last moment before our lives would be changed again—forever.

"What, Dad?" Nick's voice was as wispy as a shaking leaf.

"I'm beholden to Phil Kepler. I owe him a debt I can

275

never repay. 'Cause of something I stole years ago."

I was trembling and worn out from trying not to.

"Shortly after I lost Sonia and the baby, I depended on Phil and his wife Bonnie for help and comfort. They were true friends, always there for me. But one night I went to Phil's and only Bonnie was there. I was at wit's end. She was the shoulder I cried on. One thing led to another . . ."

I covered my face with the blanket, its stench assailing me no worse than my father's words. I wanted to cry out *stop*.

"You've suffered too long from my silence. And you need to know . . . about the baby."

I stared at my father in horror.

Nick's voice cracked. "Who is that baby?"

"You see that baby almost every day."

I was locked in the moment, trapped.

"They'd been unable to have kids of their own. Phil thought it was a miracle baby, and Bonnie didn't tell him otherwise. She knew it was mine, a baby she wanted to keep, thinking it would help her marriage, then later left behind as a bad mistake."

We stared at him.

"Another one of my bad mistakes. Not just that night, but leaving that child behind, as if I had no responsibility for bringing him into the world. But I do believe he's in very good hands. He's wanted and loved."

"Does Todd know about this?" Nick asked.

"No, but Phil's ready to tell the whole town . . . if I don't work for him."

Nick glowered. "Why does Mr. Kepler want anything to do with you or your work after what you've done to him?"

"I reckon he made peace with it shortly after Bonnie told him, when Todd was still a baby. Five years later she left both of them. When Phil first came to North Carolina, he had it out with me, but we shook hands and agreed to keep quiet about Todd. We believed that was the best arrangement for everybody. Phil realized that Todd was the only child he'd ever have."

So many threads ran through this knotted mess, I couldn't discern which one to acknowledge first. "Does Mom know?"

"Yes, I just told her."

Nick shook off his limpness and stiffened. As he shifted on the cot, jagged shadows jiggled on the wall. "Is there anything else we're gonna be hearing about you?"

"No, you've heard everything. I never wanted you to know these things. I wanted to spare you the pain of my mistakes. With Phil living in this town I've had to stare my sins in the face every day. My heart has ached enough."

And mine's only starting to.

"I need you to understand. I made these mistakes before I married your mother. For some reason God allowed me to follow paths of destruction in order to whet my appetite for truth and grace." Dad's pain-stricken eyes pierced mine. "But I reckoned it best to live alone with my mistakes."

"It can't be better hiding the truth than telling it," Nick said.

Our accusations hung upon my father's form with ease, a perfect fit. He'd received the blows. His posture bent with them.

"I'm sorry, Nick, Tina. I'm terribly sorry. This is why I can't take communion. It goes beyond bad feelings toward Phil. I know God forgives, but covering up for my past takes more gumption than I have."

"That's why you should've told us before!" Nick shouted. The flashlight sparked a dizzying display of shadow and light. "You should've told the town earlier about designing the park."

"It's not that easy, Nick. Folks wouldn't have understood. Some still don't."

"Maybe Todd should know the whole truth," I said.

Dad grimaced. "It'll tear him apart."

"Saying nothing will tear all of us apart," Nick

retorted.

"You sure Mr. Kepler's gonna tell everybody about it if you don't work for him?" I asked.

"Yes, but he'd be hurting himself and Todd as well. Puts me in a quandary."

As I leaned against the wall, the cot creaked. The flashlight rolled off, its light spinning the cabin's shadows into a whirling mass.

Dad picked up the flashlight. He surveyed the cabin, each corner and cobweb getting its turn in the spotlight. "What is that?" The pool of light revealed a wooden rectangle poking out from the shadows, next to the crate of tools and letters we'd rummaged through earlier.

Nick picked up the wooden piece and handed it to Dad, in exchange for the flashlight. Nick honed in on the picture.

Dad held the marquetry of Old Man Fuller as if it were fine glass. His fingers wandered over the surface of oak, chestnut, pine, and hickory pieces and came to rest on the name: G. Fuller. "I thought all of his work was destroyed in the fire." He looked up. "What do you know about this?"

Nick pulled out the box of tools and pushed it over. Dad picked up each tool as if handling priceless jewels. He turned them over, one by one. Nick retrieved the box of letters.

It seemed like I was watching Dad in a dream. To speak would have made him vanish and the moment disappear forever, sucked into that black hole where dreams fade into morning and are forgotten. But this scene I'd never forget.

Trembling, Dad read the letter Nick and I read earlier, voice wavering. Tears pooled in his eyes. His fingertips roamed the wooden picture--the barn, fence, and cows. "Nick . . . Tina."

Nick leaned toward him. I sat next to Dad on the floor, my hand on his leg.

"I was with Gerald Fuller when he made this. I watched him cut and lay every piece." He paused. "With every measurement and cut, I marveled at his craftsmanship, his eye for detail, his love for beauty. All these things he wanted to pass on to someone who would treasure them . . . and keep them alive." Dad's eyes brimmed again. His voice cracked. "But I was too late."

The grief of his words pierced my heart, his heartache swallowing me.

Nick handed me the woodwork I'd been making. "Maybe it's not too late."

Nick picked a knife from the toolbox--the box Joe said belonged to a friend of his.

Our eyes locked in a moment of understanding. This was Joe's plan all along.

I fished out an awl and screwed a fork-shaped point into it. Slowly, I pressed the tip into a chunk of hickory that vaguely resembled a cloud. Nick peeled shavings from his sailboat picture. In between scrapes, I glanced at Dad. He gazed at our handiwork.

My father's warm, damp hand covered mine. His arm encircled me. I collapsed into him and buried my face in his shirt. I inhaled the smells I loved, the dirt and field hay. My father.

In spite of the broken promise, Old Man Fuller had reached over the years and left part of himself with Dad. With all of us.

****

Dad escorted Nick and me down the mountainside. We arrived home at five o'clock in the morning. Five vehicles lined the roadside, including a sheriff car. Weeping, Mom popped out of the house and embraced us. We were passed from one aunt and uncle to another and smothered with hugs. After people left, Uncle Ross gestured to the front door. "Nick, Tina, there's someone waiting here to see you-uns."

Dad took my hand and led me inside, Nick following. I tracked the front room's light like a moth, squinting, as if walking from one dream into another.

In Dad's favorite chair sat Ole Joe.

Nick and I stopped dead in our tracks. Nick gawked. "What in the Sam Hill—"

"It's who, not what," Ross said. "And Sam Hill has nothing to do with it."

"I believe you three know each other," Dad said. "A handshake would be right proper."

Ole Joe extended his hand and I shook it. "Why, Nick and Tina. Powerful good to see y'all again."

My greeting was not so eloquent. "How'd you get here?"

Two worlds had crossed like arrows aiming for the same target, swift and sure.

Dad explained. "I finally convinced the Madison County Jail authorities to let me bail out Mr. Clemons, so he's free till his court date. Couldn't pick him up till late last evening, when the phone call came after bedtime. He slept at Ross's last night, until he heard Ross and me bumbling like bees in a tar tub about you-uns missing. He'll be Ross's guest a few nights before he returns home."

"You're a mite familiar with that place, I reckon," Mom said.

Nick was still wearing Joe's old shirt. Would Joe be angry we were at his cabin?

Joe grinned as if he'd been treated like a king, was enjoying it, and wasn't aiming to move from that chair for another week.

"Your ma and I been talking about Ole Man Fuller," Joe said. "He lived near my neck of the woods. His stories could make the blue jays forget it was Friday."

"You knew him?" Nick glanced at me.

"Sure did. Ran across each other many a time. Why, the last time I saw him I helped him with his well. He was right grateful and gave me one of them wood pictures right off his wall. That's a month before that fire took most everything.

Anyhow, I wanna give it to your daddy on account of the fact Ole Man Fuller would want him to have it." Joe scooted forward. "Fact is, I got another gift for your daddy."

I squeezed my father's hand for assurance. "He knows."

Joe's face lit up. "Well, don't that beat all." Joe stood and faced Dad. "I could only save his hand tools during the fire, Mr. Hamilton, and letters he'd written to you in his house, but never sent. I took a few before other folks came up the mountain and cleaned everything out. I'm the only one he had a chance to teach his skills to. And he asked me to teach them to Drew Hamilton, if I ever met him. Well, I done better than that."

Dad grasped Joe's hand. His voice quaked, just above a whisper. "Thank you, Mr. Clemons. Thank you."

Nick and I went to our rooms. In a trance, I picked up the wooden baseball player. Hours earlier, I might have heaved it across the room just to watch it smash and splinter into a million pieces. Its delicate details representing hours of tedious work, fashioned by my father's hands, mocked me. His hands were those of a destroyer.

Thoughts cluttered my head: how my father forfeited his first family, wrecked his best friend's family, and risked his current family for the sake of covering up mistakes of the first two. I felt myself being sucked into a tunnel of shame, a tunnel of darkness with no light at the end. Dad had pulled us down this tunnel. We were no different from Lucy and Robert, from all the Lucys and Roberts in the world. Lucy, the unforgiven one, forever covered in shame.

Why was it easier to overlook the sins of others than to consider forgiving Dad? Would I always have a heart full of sympathy for Lucy MacNeill, but none for my father?

Yet something kept me from hurling that wooden creation. My grip loosened before I fell upon the bed in total exhaustion.

CHAPTER 38

Ole Joe stayed with Ross for three strange but delightful days. He repaid us in the only way he could: bouquets of wildflowers for Mom, rocks scrubbed till they shined for Nick, and a small woodcarving for me. He guided us through our own carved pictures, until they were ready to set on the mantle next to the one from Old Man Fuller. Uncle Ross replaced the broken window in Joe's cabin. After Joe returned home, I asked my mother to help me make him a quilt, despite my aversion to sewing. I couldn't bear to think of him on cold winter nights with that rag of a blanket.

Welcoming a new sibling should be like sitting in a boat and we all move over to make room but keep floating down the river without losing balance. But this felt like Todd shot up through the bottom. Dad navigated his life by protecting his secrets, and the rest of us trailed in the wake of his decisions.

My father's failure was Mom's Camelot in reverse. The man she loved fiercely had broken some sacred code of integrity long ago in secret. Now it shattered her world. Camelot was over.

Some nights from my bed, I overheard Mom and Dad argue, their voices winding upstairs. I guess that's what honesty does. Maybe that's why some secrets are never brought to light. You can live your whole life with an untold secret, but after five minutes of knowing one, you fall apart.

For a while I dared ask no questions. But one plagued me enough to summon my courage. I asked Mom if she regretted not knowing about Dad's past sooner.

She sighed and reminisced about their courtship, their first twelve years of marriage, their work together in the garden, their enjoyment in Nick and me through all the stages of childhood, oblivious to the past. Thinking aloud, she asked how things would be different if she or the town had known more. Had Dad cheated her or done her a favor? Had he deprived them from the bond that comes from open hearts? Had she been naive or wise in allowing his privacy?

So she replied in words of Dad's. "There are no *what ifs* in a God-centered universe. The way it happened is best."

****

On Friday night, four weeks after our night in Joe's cabin, I lay in my bed pondering everything. Last year, at age ten, I regularly searched for the man in the moon—the one who'd burned his brush pile on Sunday—and thought my world would never change. But now, a year later, I looked instead for signs of an orbiter and an American flag, and wondered what else would change as the years unrolled before me.

I resigned myself to the fact that we'd never be the same. I'd only begun to understand that growth comes not only from facing pain, but from digging where it hurts to probe— until all that is hidden comes to light and overturns our world.

In the moon's gentle glow, I fingered the baseball player woodcarving, its intricate artistry a testimony of even Stronger Hands than those that sculpted this wood. Dad was evidence of a life that allowed grace to shape it into something far better.

It seemed like ages since Dad told me stories on the riverbank of logging and hunting, ages since I'd allowed him to. Their sweetness had all but disappeared in view of other realities. But in the storyteller was a man, perhaps now a mere teller of tales, but later a man, my father, whom I could begin to know again. Maybe. If I wanted to.

For inside my heart a swamp of anger loomed, with a

stench worse than any garbage heap at the MacNeill house. I didn't wonder anymore how Lucy MacNeill's father could hate so much, and that frightened me. I, too, was capable of being lost in that swamp, sinking into bitterness, sucked into resentment, far from the light of God.

But I didn't want to live in that swamp. It might take years to sort out all my feelings, but I instinctively knew the right thing to do.

I rolled out of bed and stumbled over my sneakers on my way to the door. I slipped into untied shoes and stepped into the hallway. A ribbon of light under Nick's door beckoned me.

"Nick!" I whispered to the door, then peeked in. Several baseball cards lay scattered on the floor near the wastebasket, the missed target. I picked them up. "What in the Sam Hill are you doing? These are Denny McLains!"

"I ain't never having another hero again."

"But he just had another great season, 24-11. Nine shutouts, Most Outstanding Pitcher. He wasn't a fluke after all." I waved the cards. "What more do you want? Thirty games every year?"

Nick scowled. "Having a hero, I get mighty letdown sooner or later. Better to get rid of 'em altogether."

"Alex would give good money for these McLains. Granny sakes alive, Nick, you ought to have your addlepated head examined."

Nick hurled a handful of cards to the floor. "Man, Tina, you don't get it. I'm not talking about thirty-game winners."

Taken aback by his tone and the jumble of Tigers and Yankees strewn on the rug, I sat on his bed. "I'm sorry, Nick. What's wrong?"

"People, that's what wrong. Ain't no one to depend on." He brushed a tear. "He's still so far away."

Our father was traveling an uphill road we couldn't imagine: surviving mistakes with humility, standing with courage, and walking in the right direction with gracious resolve.

Yet all that time his hand extended our way.

I swallowed hard. "I been thinking, Nick. Something Uncle Ross said last summer. When he was a kid, nobody believed him when he made a change for the better."

Nick stared at me with brotherly disregard. "Yeah, so what?"

"I been studying on that. Maybe it's not the falling down that matters. It's the getting back up." I bit my lip. "Maybe it's not the mistakes you make, but what you do after you make 'em."

I picked up the McLains, set them on the dresser, and left. Paprika nuzzled my ankles and followed me downstairs. I went outside through the back door. The kitchen's yellow light spilled onto the yard, overlapping the moon's white glow. The moon drew my gaze like a magnet. Nothing looked different up there. Yet now I knew not to trust appearances.

I traipsed to the shed, tripping on my laces. Aided by kitchen light, I rummaged through tools, rakes, and shovels. Finally, behind a ladder and tangle of ropes, I found my father's fishing pole. And mine, abandoned in a back corner, untouched for weeks.

I pulled Dad's out, but my line stuck. With a yank, I jerked around and came face to face with Nick.

"What are you doing out here?"

I held out the poles like two scepters. "Getting ready for the day." I headed toward the house.

"Wait!" Nick poked around in the shed and retrieved his own fishing pole. We went inside and upstairs with our cumbersome load.

We propped the fishing poles against the wall by Dad's and Mom's bedroom door.

There would be light yet. Dad had promised that.

Back in bed, I began to find that light. Under the moon's gaze, I imagined the joy on my father's face in the morning when, with fishing pole in hand, I would tell him our plans for the day.

Author Note

Dear Reader,

Thank you for choosing to read *All That Is Hidden*. I am honored.

This story grew from a month of teacher aiding in the mountain schools of western North Carolina. The teacher aide, however, had the most lessons to learn.

The people I met there created meaningful lives by a route much different from those seeking the prosperity of "The American Dream." Even with humble surroundings, meager possessions, and simple goals, these people enjoyed rich lives, and missed out on nothing.

Moved by this experience, I wrote an award-winning story upon returning home. It was published in the college magazine. Even after I tucked it away, memories of the people and their Appalachian hills stayed with me through the years, beckoning me to revisit their towns and hollows, daring me to dig deeper into their lives.

After years of researching and writing, *All That Is Hidden* was born.

If this story touched your heart in some way, it has served its purpose.

Blessings,

Laura DeNooyer

Want to help?

If you enjoyed this book, please leave a review on Amazon: https://www.amazon.com/-/e/B07SYCMHRH

In a Book Group?

I'd be thrilled to visit your book group as a guest author, either in person or via Zoom. Contact me through my website: https://lauradenooyer-author.com. Check out my Book Group web page for additional information.

Interested in authors and their books?

If you'd like to follow my Standout Stories blog for book reviews and author interviews or receive my newsletter, sign up on my website https://lauradenooyer-author.com.

Contact Me

I would love to hear from you! Contact me at https://lauradenooyer-author.com/contact/.

ACKNOWLEDGMENTS

I am a turtle on a fence post. If you see a turtle on a fence post, you know it had help getting there.

Besides spending a month in the Mars Hill, NC area during college, I took another trip later to get the lay of the land. A book of southern Appalachian dialect and idioms came in handy. So did the 1968 and 1969 *Farmer's Almanac*. Multiple *Foxfire* Books by Eliot Wigginton proved invaluable for understanding the people, traditions, and lifestyles of the area, relaying details of spinning, weaving, cooking, planting, crafts, beliefs, superstitions, and much more.

I'm very grateful for the help, support, and encouragement of so many people who made the creation of this book possible:

•The folks of Buncombe, Madison, and Yancey Counties in North Carolina who inspired this story by extending hospitality to twenty-two Calvin College students in 1978: Richard Dillingham and others of Mars Hill College; Richard Chase, the resident storyteller who captivated us with his Jack tales and Grandfather tales; the local blacksmith, the carpenter, and many other people (names unknown to me) who gladly shared time and talents.

•Dr. Steve Eberly of Western Carolina University, for vital help and encouragement as my literary consultant, for checking the accuracy of geographical, historical, and cultural details to aid in capturing the Appalachian spirit.

•Barbara Eberly and Rose Ann Watson, for valuable help with proofreading, for excellent advice and generous amounts of time.

•Karen Peterson, literary agent David Morgan, and John DeSimone (A-1 Editing Service) for professional critiques and story development.

My writers' group was priceless. Many thanks to Cathy Blaski-Liptack, Elizabeth Martorell, Jan Rozek, Karen Dahlman, Rita Trickel, Mary Sather, Alice Winkler, Steve Lawry, Myron Ratkowski, Maynard McKillen, Tom Meyer, and Mary Tompsett, Jim Krivitz, Jill Arena, Andrea Siverling, and Carol Logan.

Numerous friends made it possible to complete this project: Benny and Becky Lane, Laverne Dietzel, Dyan Barbeau, Dr. and Mrs. Clarence Omans, Mari Paffenroth, Jill Steinke, and Norma VanDorf. Thanks to my parents, Don and Ann DeNooyer, for letting me tag along with them to North Carolina, and to my sister Carol Garcia, who's always rooting for me.

I'm much obliged to my great-uncle Harry Robinson, for his woodworking labors and artistry--the inspiration for part of this story.

A special thanks goes to my husband, Tim, for enduring the never-ending writing process and helping me nourish the dream.

Book Group Discussion Questions
for *All That Is Hidden*

1. How would you define progress and family/community values? Is what Dad said true? "Cities and big business and enterprises can only be base and depraved, despite their good intentions." How are "progress" and family values at odds? Are they mutually exclusive? In what ways might progress impede family values and community, and in what ways might it help?

2. Folks said, "Those who took on city-ways and failed belonged to neither them (city-folk) nor to us (mountain folk)." Is it ever possible to have the best of two worlds? Do we belong to either one world or none at all? What about living in one world for a time and moving to a different one later?

3. Is Mom's character weak or strong? She says to Tina, "When you love someone deeply, and he loves you, you don't have to make him prove it to you by making him do something he doesn't wanna do. That really doesn't prove love anyway." Is that always true? How does that apply to her situation with Drew? Was she being wise or naive in marrying a man with a silent past? Should she have insisted on knowing more?

4. Is Dad's character strong or weak? Was Drew wise for keeping silent, or was he being selfish? Was he being a "martyr" of sorts or a coward? In what ways was he dealing with his past throughout the story, and--in retrospect--what hints are there of his secret?

5. Why did the townsfolk change their speech when speaking with Phil, other northerners, and tourists? How do we do that in ways not as noticeable as speech?

6. Childhood ambivalence: as a child, how did Tina deal with

her attitudes--both loyalty and anger--toward Dad, and in observing adult conflict in general? Is there any clue as to what conclusions and attitudes she has come to as an adult? What recourse does a child have when parents are hurting her in some way and won't listen, change, or make amends? Consider Tina's tactics of "getting even" with her father and trying to get his attention (getting the chickens drunk, refusing to go fishing, running away). Was there anything else she could have done?

7. Ole Joe says, "Folks only rule your life if you let them root in your heart." Is Joe referring to people taking root or to their cruel behavior taking root? Respond to both meanings and the difference between them. Discuss Joe's remedy for dealing with conflict: "Some people have peace in the middle of the storm but I like to come in out of the rain myself." Is this wisdom or cowardliness? Consider this in light of Joe's role in the story.

8. Dad says, "I don't believe that in all cases the good of the people is more important tan the good of one." In what situations might it be more important to consider the good of one over the good of many? How does that apply to Dr. Kirby's statement, "There isn't a whole lot worthwhile a man can do without a reputation behind him." Does that apply to one's own personal effectiveness or does it apply to the number of people one can influence?

9. Ross says, "Only God can forgive and forget . . . God can remove our sins farther than the east from west, but we can't even move them to the back doorstep." What does it mean to "forget"? Is forgiving synonymous with forgetting? How important is it to forget? Upon what basis do we determine who is "deserving" of forgiveness and who's not? Is it harder to forgive family members than others? Why or why not?

10. Dad says, "Shame drives the point home even better, for

those of us who are slow learners." In what situations might shame work better? When might grace work better? Does shame come from within or without? Is shame possibly a "wake-up" call to danger, or grace in disguise?

11. How did Old Man Fuller keep his promise to teach Drew his craft, despite Drew's failure to return before Old Man Fuller died?

12. What was Lucy MacNeill's role in Tina's life? What was Stan Randall's role? What do each of them represent?

13. Was Ross right or wrong when confronting Dad, challenging him to take the park job? What is ironic about this confrontation? Were Dad's reasons and motivation for not taking the park job clear and justifiable at the end? In other words, was Drew's attempt to keep Phil from making the same mistake of wrong priorities that Drew had made thirteen years earlier his only way of finally taking responsibility for Todd?

14. Things are not always what they appear to be--even on the moon: Ole Joe as comrade vs. enemy, Denny McLain's "fluke" season, Dad and his past, the man in moon vs. a flag and orbiter on the moon. When have you trusted appearances and regretted it later? How do you decide when to give the benefit of the doubt?

15. How does the moon function as a symbol throughout the story? Consider Dad's secrets as well as the folklore references to the moon versus the 1960s space race.

16. What is the significance of the old family stories incorporated throughout, at the beginnings of Part I, II, III, IV, and V? How do they correspond to the unfolding of events? (Old Man Fuller, Giants and Moonshine, Vittles and Courting, Bear Dogs and Mercy, Ginseng and Good Neighboring)

About the Author

Laura DeNooyer thrives on creativity and encouraging it in others by spotlighting creatives of all kinds on her blog, Journey To Imagination. She features authors and their books on her Standout Stories blog. A Calvin College graduate, Laura taught middle school and high school writing and art for nine years in Milwaukee. For the past eighteen years, she has taught writing to home schooled students. Between those two jobs, she and her husband raised four children as she penned her first novel, *All That Is Hidden*. An award-winning author of heart-warming historical and contemporary fiction, she is a member of American Christian Fiction Writers. When not writing, you'll find her reading, walking, drinking tea with friends, or taking a road trip.

Visit Standout Stories here:
http://lauradenooyer-author.com

Visit Journey to Imagination here:
http://lauradenooyer.com

Fifteen Minutes with Mr. Baum
~ Laura DeNooyer ~

A whimsical and poignant novel
rooted in a girl's childhood friendship
with *The Wizard of Oz* Author, L. Frank Baum,
set in Macatawa Park, Michigan

Most fairy tales have happy endings, but is it too late for this one?

Once upon a time, there lived a girl who didn't know she was a princess, or that three dragons pursued her . . .

Sought by dragons of a different kind.

In 1980 after college graduation, during the summer of her private rebellion, Carrie Kruisselbrink takes a job with the disgruntled town recluse, Mrs. Charlotte Rose Gordon, to help clear her husband's name of a 1918 crime. But Carrie never expects to encounter her own fears, elusive dreams, and soul-searching.

As Mrs. Gordon unfolds the story of her oppressive childhood and delightful friendship with *The Wonderful Wizard of Oz* author, L. Frank Baum, Carrie and Mrs. Gordon find common ground in battling their respective dragons. In this modern day fairy tale that weaves through 1980 and the early 1900s, Mr. Baum's influence impacts their own personal quests on a hero's journey neither anticipates.

Praise for Fifteen Minutes with Mr. Baum

"L. Frank Baum comes to life in the pages of *Fifteen Minutes with Mr. Baum*. So do Janie, his young protege, and Carrie, who falls under his spell eighty years later. I'm glad I got to know all three. They are people worth knowing."
-- Anita Klumpers, author of *Button-holed*, *Winter Watch*, and *Hounded*.

"As Mrs. Gordon slowly opens the curtains of her turn-of-the-20th-century childhood, L. Frank Baum leaps off the pages with all the technicolor wonder of his *Wizard of Oz*. And nobody is left unchanged. Thought-provoking and entertaining, this book will have you celebrating the whimsical, pondering the spiritual, and never looking at a plate of vegetables the same way again." -- Elizabeth Daghfal, columnist and blogger

"A great read from the first page to the last, offering a rich set of relatable characters we can root for, a strong sense of history--spanning decades--and a beautiful sense of place."
-- Rita Trickel

"One woman is plagued by self-doubt as she faces her future. The other is haunted by bitterness and regret as she unfolds her past. Baum's invitation to joy and imagination throws out a lifeline to them both as they navigate troubled waters and family dynamics." -- Alice den Hollander

"Laura DeNooyer's *Fifteen Minutes with Mr. Baum* is an engrossing novel of revisiting, recollection, repentance, and redemption. This is a satisfying read with an ending that leaves the reader smiling and wishing she could continue on the journey with them." -- Sue Brinkmann

Fifteen Minutes with Mr. Baum

Part I -- Leaving Home

Once upon a time, there lived a girl who didn't know she was a princess, or that three dragons pursued her . . .

Chapter One
Carrie: May 28, 1980

Two weeks after college graduation, Carrie Kruisselbrink stormed from her house like a prairie gale. Mom handed her an overnight bag, but Carrie left with an overstuffed suitcase.

She wasn't going back.

The storm started brewing in childhood, but this particular morning, the temperature spiked when she emptied the dishwasher. Feeling like Cinderella. Endless chores, but never the palace ball. Her mother chose that moment to pounce.

She thrust a paper under Carrie's chin. Skimming the list of elementary teacher positions, Carrie resisted the urge to rip it into a hundred ragged pieces and cast it to the wind.

She trudged upstairs to her bedroom and closed the door. Even with Bland Mushroom-Beige walls that her mother refused to let her paint yellow, this room brought respite.

But not for long. The room shrunk and the headboard rattled as Mother barged in. She scanned the whirlwind view. Gusting at ninety miles per hour, she tidied Carrie's desk. "Most teachers have contracts already."

Good. "Please leave my desk alone."

In the updraft, Mother rearranged pens. "When will you mail more resumes?"

Never. Carrie winced, thoughts spiraling. "Later." How could she admit she failed Philosophy of Education? She'd be disinherited. Though she'd walked at graduation, she had no diploma, no teaching certificate, and could no longer pretend she cared. Because she didn't plan on retaking the failed class. Ever.

Carrie fanned her face and opened the bedroom window. Three thousand square feet in this house, yet claustrophobia suffocated like pre-storm humidity.

Her mother slammed the window shut. "Your sister had three teaching offers by graduation. What's your plan?"

Carrie inhaled, drawing strength from the VanGogh sunflower print that sufficed for cheer. She swung open the closet door. Plan B, in effect: *Take charge of my own life. Now.* "I'm going to Oma and Opa's." Two hours northwest on Lake Michigan should be far enough away.

"Fine." Mother left and returned with an overnight bag. "Here. Don't forget resumes, envelopes, and postage."

Keep your stupid bag. Carrie plopped her huge suitcase on the bed. She tossed in shirts and shorts. Home decorator magazines. Sundresses and sandals. Colored pencils and doodle-filled sketch pads. A pile of books from Children's Lit class: *Mary Poppins*, *A Wrinkle in Time*, several Chronicles of Narnia.

"Why all the kids' books?" Mother asked.

"I like them." Angry retorts galloped through her like gathering winds, but she bit her lip. Like usual. She tucked *The Princess and Curdie* in sideways.

"What about your date with Brian on Saturday?"

"I'll call him." According to her parents, dating Brian was her crowning achievement. Her only achievement. They'd dated six years, now anticipating a summer packed with fancy restaurants and Brian's baseball games. With Brian, she might finally get to the palace ball.

Then the deluge. "When are you going to do something worthwhile? For two weeks you've moped around, read silly books, cluttered my kitchen baking cookies . . ." Words whirled and lashed, twisting into a column of anger.

Blinking away burning tears, Carrie rummaged through the bookshelf. "Where's *The Tasha Tudor Book of Fairy Tales*?"

"It's falling apart. It's in the garbage downstairs."

Panic surged like a thunderclap in a squall. Carrie dashed down the steps and dug through trash. She retrieved it-- ripped binding, pages dangling, egg yolk dripping, coffee grounds stuck. In a torrent of tears, she wrapped it in a clean garbage bag and whisked upstairs to her bulging suitcase. Now topped with a stack of resumes.

Carrie scattered the papers and replaced them with bagged book remains.

Mother rolled her eyes. "Figures you'd value dilapidated fairytales over anything practical." She stalked off.

****

Wolcott, Population 945, the sign announced.

Carrie longed for safety--a place where Oma's heart spilled into Dutch phrases and Opa's smile proved genuine.

Ginger-haired Oma greeted Carrie with a hug on the porch. Stepping from the garage, all sweat and axle grease, Opa grinned, then picked up her suitcase with a huff. "How long you plan on staying, Carrie Bell?"

Carrie plopped onto the porch swing. "I'll never measure up to their expectations."

Oma sat beside her. "They're just excited for you to follow the family footsteps into your first elementary classroom. We're proud of you, *liefje*. College diploma and all."

Carrie grimaced and blew her nose. "Any job openings here in Wolcott?"

"Burger Flipper hires in summer," Opa said.

"Ed, that's ridiculous." Oma swatted the air. "Arlene would throw a fit."

"Maybe that's exactly what I want." Carrie sniffed.

"Isn't Brian popping the question soon?" Opa asked.

Oma nudged her. "This move might prompt him to buy that ring."

Marrying Brian would swoop her away from her parents for good. Up to Petoskey.

"Regardless," Opa said, "you're welcome here, Carrie Bell."

After lunch, Carrie walked McKinley Street, a stroll through yesteryear: Victorian homes with turrets, wrap-around porches, gingerbread trim, and perfectly placed pansies as dainty as ruffles on a lady's dress. But the disastrous year of midnight studies, research papers, and student teaching still trailed her.

A dark green house with white shutters and plum-striped awnings sported a chest-high picket fence. An invitation rather than a boundary, the fence drew her to view the yard's secrets.

Four triangles of spring blooms surrounded a winding brick pathway punctuated by a green bench. Why were similar colors clumped together rather than interspersed? Lilac bushes hovered over purple pansies and early irises. Yellow daffodils and primroses cheered in unison. Rosebushes huddled with fading tulips. Blue splashed over violets and late hyacinths.

"I need help."

Carrie jumped at the unexpected sharp voice.

An old woman rocked in the porch's stark shadows. Wearing a large-brimmed hat, sunglasses, and baggy dress, the figure seemed disembodied. "Please water the sunflower seedlings along the fence."

Odd to stop a stranger. Carrie stepped through the gate. Was she arthritic? "Such a lovely garden."

"True. I'd expect nothing less." The woman nodded. "The watering can's full."

Carrie picked up the can and spilled. "You weren't kidding."

"I never kid." She drew out never like pulling yarn

from a skein.

Something about this lady teased Carrie's memory. Wincing under the woman's stare, she watered. "Sunflowers are my favorite, the epitome of summer."

The woman recited:

> *"'Ah, Sunflower, weary of time,*
> *Who countest the steps of the sun;*
> *Seeking after that sweet golden clime,*
> *Where the traveller's journal done;*
> *Where the youth pined away with desire,*
> *And the pale virgin shrouded in snow,*
> *Arise from their graves, and aspire*
> *Where my Sunflower wishes to go!'"*

Amazing! "William Blake."

"You know something that matters. Did Mr. Blake inspire your love of sunflowers?"

"No." Carrie squinted toward the sun. "No matter where the sun or how weak the light, the sunflower faces it."

"Mature sunflowers always face east," the lady snapped. "But in this poem, a girl rooted to the ground is scorned, doomed to face the sun, forever from reach. No optimism here."

Carrie tensed. If she wanted criticism, she'd have stayed in Barrowdale. Speed-water the plants and leave. "Maybe it's about being trapped on earth while yearning for the divine."

"Hardly. Preoccupation with the divine interferes with one's true, worthwhile aspirations."

What's this lady's problem? Anger at God? "Or it's a slighted lover."

"Or any unfulfilled desire. Surely you've heard William Blake was well acquainted with fairies who lived in fields near his cottage. Muses for his poetry and art."

"No . . ."

"Alas, logic and reason kills them." She quoted:

> *"The good are attracted by men's perceptions,*
> *And think not for themselves;*
> *Til experience teaches them to catch*
> *And to cage fairies and elves.'"*

"The end of imagination," Carrie murmured.

"Since fairies are associated with flowers, he said each flower whimpers when it's picked. The loss hovers like a cloud of incense."

"I love how he envisioned it."

"Do you now? That's admirable." The woman straightened. "Especially considering what happened to my flowers in 1969. Remember, Miss Caroline?"

How'd she know her name? "Should I know you?"

"Kids these days. Off to college and--poof! The old are forgotten." She flung her hand as if tossing weeds. "Come here." She hobbled into the house as Carrie climbed two daunting porch steps. The woman returned, shaking a sheet of paper.

Carrie read the childish handwriting: "'I, Caroline Kruisselbrink, age eleven, being of sound mind, do solemnly swear to never kick, hit, bat, or roll a ball into Mrs. Gordon's flowerbed, or step foot onto said sacred place, ever again for as long as I live, so help me God. June 1969.' Oh, my . . ." Carrie looked up as the woman removed her sunglasses.

Mrs. Charlotte Rose Gordon. Nothing like her beautiful name, except for the thorns. Images washed over her: Carrie and Jodi kicking to each other down the sidewalk, the ball rolling into the garden, flattening tulips, then old Mrs. Gordon, who'd always been old, shouting from the house. The fence appeared a week later.

That mishap almost brought their childhoods to a screeching halt, if not for the advocacy of Carrie's grandparents. Carrie deemed Mrs. Gordon a witch of the

Hansel and Gretel variety, the darling Victorian home of stained glass and gingerbread trim like candy, enticing them. The house was even cotton candy pink back then. Carrie never walked that block again. In town only three times yearly, she soon forgot its location.

Here, eleven years later, sat a hunched shadow of the woman who'd stomped around the garden, smacking their ball with a broom. "Mrs. Gordon." Carrie smoothed her rattling voice. "Good to see you."

"Is it now?" Mrs. Gordon slipped sunglasses back on, peering at Carrie over the top.

"I'm sorry for the trouble I caused." Under Mrs. Gordon's gaze, Carrie shrunk to age six.

"I'd appreciate compensation."

"We bought new bulbs."

"Finish reading."

Carrie clutched the paper. "'P.S. If I fail to keep this oath, I'll make it up to Mrs. Gordon as she sees fit.'"

The woman pointed to Carrie's feet. "You've failed your vow miserably. Today, you stood in my garden, once again indebted."

"You invited me."

"No such stipulations in this contract."

"I was eleven when I wrote that."

"No statute of limitations, either."

Carrie flicked the paper. "I can't believe you saved this all these years. It was within reach, like you expected me any moment."

"I heard about graduation and figured you'd visit your grandparents soon."

Had she perched on the porch for two weeks watching? Crazy lady. "Shall I plant more perennials? Read poetry?"

Belying her witching powers, she patted the wicker settee. "Come."

Carrie gingerly stepped up, the creak in each step like a squeal of derision. She sat.

Mrs. Gordon removed her sunglasses. Bags under her eyes stood out where a map of wrinkles long ago settled in. "You'll help me clear my husband's name, God rest his soul."

"How?"

"In 1918, he was doomed to prison for a crime he didn't commit. Fortunately and unfortunately, he died of cancer before his trial."

"I don't see how to help." And why'd it matter now?

"I need a scribe, good at research. You just graduated, so perfect timing. My eyes aren't what they used to be."

Oh, yes, they are. Just as beady as before. "Mrs. Gordon, I'm applying for summer jobs. And teaching jobs this fall." How'd that lie spill out?

"That's autumn. I'm offering a job now, saving you from a summer of fast food." With one tongue cluck, she relegated all fast food to the abyss.

"I accidentally trample your flowers, then owe you my summer years later?"

"You're a feisty one."

Carrie crossed her arms. "I'm the feisty one?"

"I'll pay you what you're worth."

Carrie shifted forward. "What am I worth to you, Mrs. Gordon?"

"What you don't realize--" her eyes bore into Carrie's--"is what I'm worth to you."

"Meaning what?"

"Never mind that. It's money that concerns you college kids." The woman sighed, as if the old days were nothing but cherub children, apple pies, and sunflowers. "I'll pay $250.00 every Friday if I'm satisfied with your efforts."

"How will you measure that?"

The woman resumed rocking. "One criterion you already meet. Spunk. Plenty of it. You don't roll over when you meet an obstacle."

That obstacle being Mrs. Gordon? She'd surely change her mind if she saw Carrie's usual demeanor at home.

"Miss Caroline, you're in the right place at the right time."

"That's debatable."

"See? You have spunk. Like me. The only reason the Broderick Resort and Tearoom was so successful."

"You ran the tearoom by the lake? Before the Brindlewood Cafe?"

"I take full credit. For what it used to be."

No wonder the woman disdained the notion of fast food.

"Finish watering. Come at nine tomorrow with notebook and pen."

"I never said yes to this venture."

Mrs. Gordon slipped her sunglasses back on, eyes disappearing. "But you cannot say no." Not a command. She spoke as if it were destiny.

****

Coming soon: *Fifteen Minutes with Mr. Baum*